ALSO BY MICHAEL TALBOT

To the Ends of the Earth

A WILFUL WOMAN

MICHAEL TALBOT

A WILFUL WOMAN

ALFRED A. KNOPF

New York   1989

THIS IS A BORZOI BOOK
PUBLISHED BY ALFRED A. KNOPF, INC.

Copyright © 1988 by Michael Talbot
All rights reserved under International and Pan-American Copyright Conventions.
Published in the United States by Alfred A. Knopf, Inc., New York,
and simultaneously in Canada by Random House of Canada Limited, Toronto.
Distributed by Random House, Inc., New York.

Library of Congress Cataloging-in-Publication Data
Talbot, Michael [date]
A wilful woman.
I. Title.
PR9619.3.T257W55   1988   823   88-45316
ISBN 0-394-55296-2

Manufactured in the United States of America
First Edition

For my friends and colleagues
at the Department of Special Collections,
Boston University

A WILFUL WOMAN

1

"By God, we've done it! New South Wales is ours! Allow me to be the first to congratulate you, sir."

"Thank you, Mr. Ball." A shorter, darker, older man stepped from the foremast shrouds and returned the salute. Arthur Phillip replaced his tricorn hat and turned away, hiding any further show of emotion.

HMS *Supply*'s commander took a telescope from the binnacle locker and joined his commodore at the weather rail. "Well, we've certainly caught the Indians unaware!" Ball laughed, squinting against the sun's glitter over water as naked black shapes ran between the low surf and the drab scrub, some trying to launch a bark canoe, others to escape by land.

"It was always my intention that I should," Phillip replied. "Were they not so agitated it might have indicated that M. de La Pérouse had already claimed Botany Bay and turned the local kings against us. In the event, surprise gives me the upper hand. I intend keeping it that way: there'll be problems enough controlling those items," the commodore added, nodding forward as a bosun's rope kept the men moving, their bare feet slapping scrubbed planks, "once ashore and off the leash."

"Oh, our marines will keep them in hand, sir."

Phillip said nothing. He envied the young man's assurance. His own had been sorely tried these past eight months, flogging a ragtag convoy of troops and convict laborers halfway around the globe. Then, six months after leaving home waters and a week after putting out from Table Bay, he had struck his pennant aboard the lumbering frigate HMS *Sirius* and transferred his command to the more nimble brig.

Alone now, except for the convict transport *Alexander*, Arthur Phillip had battled gales, ice floes and blizzards to outpace a French squadron which was also racing time to reach the east coast of New Holland.

Eventually, less than an hour ago, *Supply* had made her landfall. She had completed the longest outward voyage ever undertaken by the Royal Navy. Phillip had clambered aloft to the foretop as the brig ghosted between two low headlands. His options were now as narrow as the neck of water between them. He would either come down in disgrace, if La Pérouse's flotilla was at anchor, or he would descend in triumph if the French were not.

The British commodore had triumphed.

Against all odds, Arthur Phillip had confirmed London's right to the Pacific before Paris could claim the South Seas. Sixteen thousand miles of pain, and hunger, and mutiny and thirst had won a new world for Britain after the loss of her American colonies. And yet, in all his lonely life, Phillip had never been more alone than he was at the summit of his naval career.

A year and a half's sailing time lay between even his simplest question and getting a reply as he braced himself to shape, to rule, to defend a colony which was still only five sheets of paper inside his despatch box. A colony whose unwilling, unwanted citizens were also under lock and key in their floating cages, somewhere astern of *Supply*.

Not that another man's answers would have been of much value to him: there were hardly any precedents in history for what now had to be done. Thieves and whores, cheats and murderers were going to be reduced to thrift, and industry, and sobriety while they hewed the wood and cut the stone and raised the first British outpost south of the equator.

The governor-designate of New South Wales wiped his hat's sweat-band, tucked the handkerchief up a sleeve and tilted the brim against a subtropical sun. "Sway out the gig, Mr. Ball."

"Aye aye, sir!"

"Accompany me on the tour of inspection."

A bosun's whistle shrilled again, feet slapped again, men cursed again as Phillip crouched below into the brig's great cabin where his sea chest and belongings had been lashed under tarpaulin. He dragged out a long, wooden case and laid it on the chart table. The catches snapped open. He took out one of two fowling pieces and rubbed a rag over the mutton fat which had protected its steel, then reached for the brass powder flask to check that it was also dry and serviceable since last being used, on his Hampshire farm.

Phillip had tightened the lock-flints between their leather pads by the time *Supply*'s commander climbed down the companion ladder and bent under the door frame. "Ready, aye ready, sir."

"You may take that," the older man indicated his second gun. "A brace of duck will challenge the cook to attempt something other than boiled salt horse, tonight."

"I'd be damn' glad if he would."

Phillip tapped his bullet pouch. "But load only one barrel with bird shot. Reserve the other for a heavier charge."

"I've already ordered the boat's crew to draw muskets and five rounds apiece," Ball replied. "That ought to be enough, surely?"

"Perhaps." Phillip shrugged off his coat and rolled the shirt-sleeves underneath. "However, in such novel surroundings as we now find ourselves, one must never tempt Providence. Not that I anticipate immediate ill will from the indigenes," he went on, slipping a spare flint into his waistcoat pocket, "but treachery tends to strike when it's least expected, as James Cook learned in similar circumstances only a few years ago."

"Yes, sir."

"I must therefore balance natural prudence against my duty to respond to the local inhabitants' friendly overtures," Phillip continued.

"Yes, sir."

"Which, I trust, will not be long forthcoming," Ball's superior officer went on, and on. "However, the instant my commission is proclaimed, British law will apply to everyone, without exception. Crime will be punished and even the poorest Indian's property will be as secure as if it were ours," he concluded, reaching for the powder flask.

Supply's commander followed him on deck and down into the gig. He also tilted his hat against the noonday sun as Phillip loosened his cravat, surveying the anchorage while naked shoulders bent over the oars and water rolled under the transom. " 'The Lord God took the man and put him in the garden of Eden, to dress and keep it. . . .' " He smiled, briefly. "A strange feeling, is it not, Mr. Ball? We are about to set foot upon a land where there are no yesterdays to impede our progress, only an endless succession of tomorrows drawing us forward. Speaking personally, I find that a rather exhilarating prospect: anything is likely, nothing is impossible—"

"Sir?"

Phillip nodded. He enjoyed the familiar sound of his own voice. It was often his only company as a commodore over two warships and nine merchantmen. "During the recent war I had the honor to command HMS *Europe*. There were many occasions, in the Gulf of Campeche, when I wondered to myself if those early dons ever anticipated that— behind the coastal ranges of Mexico—lay cities the equal of any they'd left behind in Spain? Perhaps their first impressions were of only a few naked Indians squabbling around a canoe?" He glanced at Ball. "Such being the case, who can tell what wonders we shall soon behold on some high mountain? Or upon the banks of a river greater, even, than the Hudson or St. Lawrence?"

"Naked or not, I'd say our savages are hellbent on making trouble for us now!" The younger man gripped his gun and turned to the coxswain. "Helm a'port!"

The gig swung away from the beach and followed the shoreline at a safe distance as several dozen Indians loped along the sand, shouting, shaking spears, warning the strangers to be gone.

Phillip snapped his spyglass shut. "Mr. Ball? After crossing three oceans it is our plain duty to cross the last ten yards of water. Kindly direct that we turn inshore again."

"Aye aye. Sir."

The commodore checked his priming powder and flints, hitched the gun on its leather sling and got ready to be lifted onto dry land as the gig beached near another of the natives' canoes. The barelegged sailors were still carrying Ball as Phillip advanced up the beach, holding a small mirror, flicking its dazzle from side to side.

"Warra? Warra?" The Indians halted, then started backing away from this sorcerer with the power to hold a splinter of burning sun. *"Warra-warra-warra!"*

Phillip laid his gift on the ground, then politely stepped aside while one of the savages edged forward, prodding at the trinket with his spear. *"Guwai dununju . . . ?"* He bent suspiciously and—*"Wujun!"*—saw a staring black face trapped inside the white magician's thing!

Ball halted beside his commanding officer, gun cocked, trigger finger poised. Phillip pointed as the ochre-daubed shapes grabbed the mirror from hand to hand. "Don't you notice something odd about them?"

"Odd?"

"Their complete lack of feathers." Phillip frowned. "The ones I saw in the Americas generally had feathers sprouting from every point of the compass. Ours don't. Why?"

"Damned if I know!" *Supply*'s commander was backing away, upwind, away from these Indians' rank, doggy smell.

"Perhaps it's only the inland tribes who use feathers here?" Phillip continued, stroking his chin. "That was the case in Mexico, I'm told. Primitives on the coast, civilization beyond the mountains. An interesting paradox."

Ball was more concerned by the haloes of green flies which shimmered around each one of these primitives' heads, or crawled over the fishbones thrust through nostrils thick with bubbles of snot. "If you ask me," he coughed, "our Indians could use some civilization now! Starting with a decent handkerchief apiece!"

"An excellent idea," Phillip agreed. "I'll have some trade cloth torn into small squares. They can be distributed when next we meet."

The Indians had lost interest in the sorcerer's shiny toy. They held their own breaths and peered closer at these ghostmen with the stink of death on shabby blue serge and mildewed white flannel, sour and un-washed after weeks of bitter sailing from the Cape of Good Hope.

The late Stone Age was facing early Industrial Man across a gap of forty centuries and neither side was quite sure which steps to take next.

Uncertainties and time for idle speculation had never been any part of a royal marine's life aboard the transport *Alexander*. The sergeant rapped out his orders and the corporals packed troops over the side, head to tail, into a waiting cutter: sitting to attention; muskets clenched between their knees; scarlet tunics buttoned hard under the chin; knapsacks and cross-belts stiff with pipe clay. Waiting. And waiting.

Gaunt faces lined the rail above them: some of the government men and women were penned aboard the barque, lagged to penal servitude at Botany Bay for the terms of their natural lives. "Poor sods," one mur-mured, chasing an itch under the wreck of a shirt. He trapped it and squashed something between his thumbnails, then glanced at a taller neighbor, also idling, watching the guards wait and wait in the little cutter. "That's what comes of joining the marines, Ben. We 'ad it tons better in the infantry, but even that can be a regular bastard at times. Buggered if I know 'ow I stuck it for seven years. . . ."

"Well, I reckon you're best off not 'aving no more to do with suchlike things," the younger lag replied with a solemn nod.

"You're not wrong," Joe Cribb agreed, wiping the dead louse across his breeches. "Still, times were different Over There, in Americky. For instance, if it'd been me kicking arse'oles ashore, the lobsters would be there by now and the job 'alfway done. But what can you expect?" Cribb went on, fair-mindedly. "If one army bloke is worth ten marines, and one ranger is worth ten bootfaces, where does that put me? About one 'undred times better than that shitwit sergeant, Fitch," he concluded with an expressive shrug. "That's why they won't see me for dust once I'm ready to move. . . ."

"What?" Ben Thorpe inched closer to the dark, whippet-thin lag.

"We're bolting." Cribb's mouth was a barely moving slit. "We're off, like a bride's skirt, for Chinaland."

"*Uh?*"

"Chinaland. It's up the road from 'ere. I'll 'ave a word with 'er ladyship, later. She'd probably like to pop along," Cribb added, eyes tracking a strikingly attractive woman on the poop deck as she tucked up a strand of coppery hair which the breeze had teased from under her kerchief. "I bet she's read Bulldog's maps: she'll know where's where and what's what. . . ."

Thorpe was also watching the government women's leader go below, to supervise the shipmaster's midday meal. "I reckon Mrs. B. knows what's what, all right!"

"Watch that mouth." Cribb turned cool. "Mrs. Brandon's never been nobody's mollisher."

"Er, right, Joe."

"She's different from the rest. She's special."

"I only—"

Cribb ignored his friend's mumbled apology. "There's a lot only alive now because of what that lady done for us, Over There."

"I didn't mean nothing."

"Lucky you didn't. I'd 'ave snouted any other sod."

"Your trouble is you can't never take a joke." Thorpe stared at his toes.

"That a fact? Well, that joke of yours is about as funny as the Bottommy Town frogshit Leafy's been selling us." Cribb was kneading his fists, glaring ashore at the sand, at the scrub, at the hostile silence. "The cheating, lousy, lying mongrel. So where's that river of fire? And the 'New Jerusalem' Reb Mordechai was supposed to've promised us once we got 'ere?" The lag shut up.

Footsteps closed from behind. Duncan Sinclair halted, a rope cob tucked under his belt, sleeves rolled, ready for action. "Mr. Cribb!"

The lag faced *Alexander*'s shipmaster. "Captain?"

The elderly Scot jabbed a thumb forward at another of his cargo, now crouched behind the pig pen, weeping. "What's up with Mr. Levi . . . ?"

"Why ask me?"

Sinclair considered the question. "I'm asking because you two were as thick as oaten brose after leaving London River. Now, for some reason, Mr. Levi is piping his eye. . . ."

Cribb shrugged again. Lag against lag was the right and proper thing, at times. But lag helping free was wrong, all the time. That was pimping. Peaching. Betraying Us against Them. "Rum cove, Leafy," Cribb replied. "Up one day, down the next. I suppose 'e must be crying because 'e's so 'appy we got to Bottommy at last."

The Bulldog almost smiled at the exceptionally privileged lag. "Happy, Mr. Cribb? All the keening I've heard between Senegal and the Sugar Isles and I thought the niggers were only complaining about their rations, but you say they were happy? I must remember that in future. However," he went on, "yarning like this won't earn the baby a new bonnet. Collar half a dozen of your men and get them ashore on the double: I want firewood, I want fresh water."

"Right." Cribb turned on his heel. "Ben! Sly! Croak! Maggot! Nob! You too, Ratbag!"

They stepped from the listless crowd of onlookers and followed their leader over the side. Cribb made himself comfortable on the cutter's midthwart. He ignored Sergeant Fitch, in the stern sheets, as the transport's crewmen bent to their oars.

The cutter grounded a few yards from the water's edge. Fitch tucked his rattan cane under one arm. "Landing party! Number!"

"One!"

"Two!"

"Three?"

"Four!"

"Five."

"Six. . . ."

"Odd numbers will advance to port! Even numbers to starboard! Port and starboard, advance!"

The marines scrambled over the sides, muskets gripped overhead, wading ashore to seize the beach. Cribb winked at Ben Thorpe as the lightened cutter floated closer to dry land. *Alexander*'s men stowed their oars, heaved empty barrels onto the beach and dragged their boat the rest of the way.

Cribb sauntered after them, the last off and—"shittt!"—toppled, clutching at Thorpe for support. After a year aboard the barque it was firm ground which was now out of control, pitching and yawing, over and around them. The lags flopped like turtles on the hot sand, wobbling upright, cursing as they fell over again. And again.

The crewmen gradually lost interest and stopped jeering. Cribb helped Thorpe to his feet. The marines were now patrolling a picket line, warning off the Indians as an empty barrel was rolled to the nearby spring. It was time for wary coves to start looking busy.

"Sod!" Cribb hissed to his friend. "Buggerlugs got there first!"

Alexander's second mate had been the quickest off the mark. He was now lounging comfortably in the shade of a tree. He opened his clasp knife and whittled a fat brown curl of stick tobacco as the marines' sergeant strolled over to join him. The petty officer rubbed baccy between his palms. "Like a puff?"

"Ta." Fitch slackened his tunic collar.

The sailor chipped sparks inside his tinderbox and breathed on the shredded rope. The marine leaned closer, sucking heat into the bowl of his pipe, then settled back to watch the next barrel being manhandled up the beach. "Bloody 'ot." Fitch trickled smoke at the shade.

The sailor nodded and drew on his clay cutty. "But they still reckon it's January, back 'Ome."

"January?"

"That's what they reckon."

"Bloody 'ell. . . ." Fitch whiffed more smoke. "You remember when we poked this lot aboard?" He aimed his pipe stem at a pair of lagged items who were now manfully dragging a dead branch into some other shade before going to work on its twigs, snapping them one by one. "That would've been about this time last year, wouldn't it?"

"I suppose it was. Cold enough to freeze a fish's bum." The petty officer hawked and gobbed at the memory. "D'you remember that old crawler the 'ulks couldn't use for no more work?" the mate asked. "Not surprising, with only one pin. Even Bulldog reckoned 'e was too knack-ered, so I 'ad to shove 'im down the plank again. What a bleedin' laugh that was . . . !"

Fitch was also grinning as he relived a bleak day on the Thames when the prison hulk *Retribution* jettisoned its derelicts and hard cases for transportation to the ends of the earth, to New South Wales.

"Trouble was, the screws reckoned 'e was now off their rations and kicked 'im back for another go," the merchant seaman went on. "We'd still be there, playing push and shove, if the silly old fart 'adn't jumped for it. I mean, stands to reason, clinked with all that chain and stuff, 'e just 'ad to go through the ice." The mate glanced down from a tuft of summery cloud. "A blind man could've seen there was no 'ope of bolting, even if Crawler 'ad got a couple of pins to run with. Right?"

"Right."

"Still, you mark my words, there's some fly coves among them."

" 'Orseshit!" Fitch blew smoke. "Useless lot o' shaggers."

"So what about Bulldog's little flea?" the mate queried innocently. "The one 'e treats like a regular ge'man since getting the rest to man the pumps? During that storm off Demon's Land?"

Fitch sniffed and spat. "Cribb's nothing special."

"No?" the petty officer went on, slyly needling the redcoat. "I'd 'ave reckoned being a sergeant, or something, was special enough."

" 'E never 'eld proper rank!" Sergeant Fitch had risen to the bait. " 'E was what they called Temp'ry. Chrissakes, I should know! I was Over There. Nearly got took at Yorktown, where the Yankee Doodlers got the Green Devils, so that's why I know 'e was never a proper soldier. Besides, if 'e really was their sar'nt major, my cock's a fried egg!"

"Where's the salt and pepper?" *Alexander*'s mate grinned back, paring another curl of tobacco.

"Hn."

"Any'ow, what's green devils got to do with the price of onions?" the sailor went on, rubbing more flake.

Fitch eyed the man's baccy pouch and hoped there'd be enough for a refill. "Well, they called themselves 'Rangers' but we reckoned they was King George's bad bargains. I mean, they was all sorts. Tories, Doodler turncoats, stuff from every regiment you ever 'eard of, and some you'd not. That's why they didn't wear proper, regulation scarlet," the redcoat sergeant went on with another contemptuous sniff. "They only got green jackets, to 'ide among the trees. And fight dirty."

"Uh huh." The mate had refilled his pipe. As an afterthought he offered the remaining crumbs of tobacco to the other man, then rolled another gob and hit a large red ant as it scurried down the tree trunk. He peered closer. " 'Ere! Looks like some others got this place before us. What's it say?"

Fitch also squinted at the smooth gray bark where someone had once knifed a few uneven letters. "Dunno." He scratched himself. "Looks like a ship's name. HMS *Endeavour*? 1770?"

"Poor sods."

"Yeah." Fitch was about to lean against the eighteen-year-old inscription when he straightened again. "Marine Asky! I've just about 'ad a gutsful of you today! Guard that fuckin' front or else them Indians will stick you full of arrows and good riddance!"

The sergeant eased into the shade again and picked up the conversation. "But you mark *my* words, Jack Thomas, there's a powerful lot more behind what we're a-doing of now than most blokes reckon, and that's a fact."

"Get lost."

Fitch dipped a knowing wink. "There's gold. There's di'monds."

"Bollocks."

"Bible oath!" Fitch insisted, getting much closer and dropping his voice. "There's gold and di'monds in this New 'Olland place. I mean, if there wasn't, what the 'ell 'ave we been sent for?"

Alexander's mate blinked uncertainly. "Search me."

"Well, then!" Fitch tapped his pipe stem on the other man's chest. "Just before we got to Africky, a chum of mine on *Sirius* was inspecting the guard when Mr. Rose begun one of them fights with Sparrow Legs—" the pipe stem aimed at Phillip, now strolling along the beach with *Supply*'s commander—"and 'e told me, in Capetown, as what they were shouting about was gold and di'monds. So there."

Thomas scratched his neck. "First time I ever 'eard anything about it—"

"Of course!" Fitch replied. "It's a secret. I mean, if the Frogs 'ad known there was gold and di'monds they'd 'ave sent their navy to give us lip as we sailed in. Stands to reason."

The other man pulled a face. "That's as may be, but I still reckon this Bottommy Bay's the arse end o' nowhere. I tell you, just as soon as we've chucked off the cargo it's Chinaland for me, then 'Ome. You can shove all them di'monds, I'll take my chances with the Chinees." He reamed his pipe bowl with the point of his knife. "You know what tea costs in Canton? And what they can flog it for in London? It's money for old rope once a bloke slips in a few boxes on private account. Another good run and I'll be set for life."

"Is that a fact?" Fitch's pipe jabbed harder. "Well, after just two or three years out 'ere, digging for gold, I'm going to be—" He stopped short. "Uh oh, 'ere comes trouble." The sergeant of marines stowed his pipe, straightened his collar and marched into the sun again. "Stan' fast the guard!"

The six redcoats jerked to attention, facing their fronts, bayonets leveled at the distant Indians as the two naval officers walked closer, fowling pieces crooked over their arms. Phillip touched his hat brim. "Carry on, sar'nt."

"Sah!"

The two bluejacket officers strolled past and halted by the spring where peaty water was being scooped into a leather funnel to fill a keg. Ball reached for the ladle. He took a sip, shuddered, handed the rest of the water to his commodore to try. "It tastes even worse than it looks, sir."

Phillip sampled a mouthful, slowly. "Appearances can be deceptive, Mr. Ball. I'd have said this was a most refreshing change after the bilge we've subsisted upon these past several months. Indeed, Mr. Cook was at pains to point out how therapeutic the waters are at Botany Bay."

"Yes, sir." Ball watched a pelican circle above the seine net which *Supply*'s crew were hauling for supper.

Phillip returned the ladle to the nearest seaman, knee deep among reeds and sedges, then looked around at the thickets of nameless undergrowth. "Not much chance of bagging any duck here. However, if we follow the trickle inland we could find a larger swamp where there might be a chance of getting something for dinner."

Ball was personally of the opinion that they'd have an even better chance of being riddled with Indian spears, from an ambush. "Perhaps we ought to come back at first light tomorrow, sir? Birds seem to prefer feeding along seashores in the morning, don't they?"

Phillip considered the suggestion. "A good point. Besides, although the natives seem docile enough at the moment, one must never put temptation in their way. Moreover," Phillip went on in the schoolmaster tone which so irritated the younger man, "I do not doubt that messengers are speeding the news of our arrival to their kings. I must be ready to greet them, whether or not they come in peace. We shall return aboard, immediately."

2

SUPPLY'S GIG embarked the two officers and rowed back to the brig. Phillip saluted the quarterdeck and inspected progress aboard. The men were being kept busy with port routines now, sewing, patching, scrubbing, polishing. The devil finds work for idle hands to do. There would be no idle hands aboard HMS Supply until the bosun piped them forward to the galley for their rations of "smiggins"—rice boiled in beef water—then aft again to stand the night watches.

Phillip led the way below and tossed his gun on the cot's blankets, then squeezed behind the chart table and sat down, silhouetted by the westering sun in the stern windows. He reached for the thin cord which ran through hooks in the roof timbers and gave it a hard tug. "So concludes our first reconnaissance, Mr. Ball, and thus far certain factors appear to be in our favor." There was a tap at the door and Phillip's manservant peered around it. "Ah, Bryant. Serve the main course."

"Aye aye, sir. Um. Wine, ge'men?"

Phillip waited for Ball to answer: his own private cellar was still aboard HMS Sirius, wherever she might be, somewhere between the South Indian Ocean and the Pacific. Supply's commander had no option but to nod. "Yes."

Bryant returned from the pantry, drew the cork and poured two measures of claret before going forward again to see how the officers' grilled fish was coming along. Phillip raised his glass to his host. "Long life and honor." He sipped. "Now, where was I?"

"We were about to settle New Holland?"

"Eventually, yes, but first we must consider this bay's meager assets. That spring, for example," Phillip went on, "I doubt if it'll ever produce more than one hundred gallons an hour. Of course, we could dredge it deeper and build up the sides with timber but the water would remain of very dubious quality, not that we can ever say as much in front of the men. Such being the case," he went on, "what'll be our position when—or if—there are another nine vessels to replenish and revictual?"

"Rather uncomfortable."

"Quite." Phillip swirled his glass. "Now, assuming that some of our convoy have survived the transit from Africa and catch up with us, this anchorage and its hinterland will then have to maintain a permanent settlement of—what?—about a thousand men and women, none of whom were too fastidious or sound in limb when last I inspected them." He looked up from the wine. "That spring simply won't do: we'll need to cast further afield for alternative supplies of water before I'm satisfied with Botany Bay."

"But surely, sir, Mr. Cook said—?"

Phillip's finger silenced the younger man. "With respect to his gallant memory, when *Endeavour* spent a pleasant week here botanizing, back in 'seventy or 'seventy-one, the government had not directed her to empty London's cess bucket upon such unpromising soil, thereafter to cultivate fruits and vegetables, flax and timber, for our convoys of Chinamen. Mr. Cook was bound to see this location from a more sanguine viewpoint than I, just as his melancholy experience with the Hawaiian Indians indicates that he was not invariably right in other matters concerning the South Seas."

Ball hesitated. "But you saw them today, sir? They run from the flash of a mirror. Heaven only knows what they'd do if ever we gave them a volley of musket fire, or touched off an eighteen pounder. Leap away from their shadows, most likely!"

His attempt at humor was misplaced but Phillip was saved from having to reprimand him as Bryant ducked into the cabin again. The servant put a wicker basket on the table and searched under the straw wadding for a couple of pewter plates, an earthenware crock and a four-ounce tile of ration bread apiece for the two officers.

"That'll be all."

"Aye aye, sir."

The commodore waited until the door had shut, then reached into his coat pocket for his personal cutlery, scraped a thumbnail between the fork's prongs and took off the casserole lid. The ship's cook had excelled himself, for once. The mullet was hardly burned and a pint of dried beans had been boiled to mush with cheese rind to make a tasty garnish. Ball took his share of the meal and began enjoying it in silence.

Phillip rapped his bread on the edge of the table and brushed away the weevil dust before spooning fish juice over the biscuit to soften its flinty crust. He reached for his glass again. "So, you are of the opinion that, because today's Indians would run for their lives if we clapped our hands, tomorrow's will be so obliging?"

"Well, in a manner of speaking, yes, I suppose I am," Ball replied warily. "Why not?"

Phillip reached across to his cot and felt under its damp hay bolster for a book. He caught most of the pages as they fell out of their binding and shook open his spectacles. "Sir Joseph Banks loaned me some volumes from the Royal Society's library: they're the sum total of everything we'll know about New Holland until my journals are published." He unstuck a few leaves. "This one, for example, was written by M. Pierre Purry, a Swiss gentleman of good repute who once owned an indigo plantation on Sumatra—so he had plenty of practical experience managing Indians."

Phillip shifted himself, getting the light at a better angle before moving his finger along what was, in fact, little more than a prospectus offering shares in risky ventures to an unknown land. " 'Who knows what there is in New Holland and whether that country does not, perhaps, contain richer mines of gold and silver than did Peru or Mexico? Therefore, the first thing we must do is disembark five or six hundred men, all well chosen, to spy out the country. I'll admit that fewer might do and that Christopher Columbus had not nearly so many when he set out to discover the Americas, however, there is always the danger that we deceive ourselves if we imagine that the inhabitants of New Holland have no more courage than the Aztecs or Incas. Why, for example, should the New Dutchmen not have fortified towns as well? And if we have had the use of gunpowder since two or three hundred years, why should not these people have invented other machines of war yet more terrifying than bombards and cannon . . . ?' "

Phillip snapped the book shut. He laid it aside with his spectacles. "You notice the reference to fortified cities? And the likelihood that at least some of the Indians could have gunpowder?"

"Of course, sir, but surely it's far too early for anyone to be certain one way or the other?"

"Mr. Ball, my experience of the world has proved that it is never too early to take precautions. Therefore, assuming *Lady Penrhyn* hasn't gone down with the rest, I shall direct Lieutenant Dawes to put his engineers to work the moment she arrives. Meanwhile, you and I can begin searching for a suitable fortress site."

Ball emptied his glass and emptied the rest of his bottle into it before his commanding officer could reach for a third refill. "Didn't our Swiss indigo planter mention gold and silver, sir?"

Phillip grimaced. "Who doesn't? Major Ross used to harp on about nothing else. El Dorado this, El Dorado that! There wasn't a damned thing I could do to shut him up." The commodore checked his tongue: this wine was potent. It was reviving memories of many blazing arguments with his commandant of marines aboard HMS *Sirius,* plodding down the Atlantic to southern Africa, the same man who—unless he had been providentially drowned in a gale off Van Diemen's Land—would be Phillip's lieutenant governor in New South Wales.

Fourteen years in the Royal Navy, since enlisting as a ten-year-old boy, had taught Ball the virtues of silence with senior officers.

He said nothing while Phillip finished gnawing the corner off his ration biscuit and glanced across the table again. "Like many another I could name, Ross fails to grasp the significance of this expedition to the Antipodes—" The commodore wiped his chin dry. "To the great majority in London I suppose we seem little more than scatterbrained public benefactors, scavenging the gutters of the capital before transporting its unwanted riffraff to distant parts." Phillip licked his fingers clean.

"From its point of view, Cabinet is content to let the world believe the absurd stories we've put into circulation. If not, if our enemies in Carlton House and the Commons were also privy to the real figures for this enterprise, it would be concluded that His Majesty's government had either taken leave of its senses or fallen prey to a most untypical philanthropy. Because, whatever it is we're doing in New Holland, it is most certainly *not* the conveyance of derelict felons for their reformation and the safety of our property, back Home."

"No, sir?"

"No, sir." Phillip had reached inside his waistcoat pocket. He took out a toothpick case. "Now, concerning your original question about gold, etcetera, the only riches we'll ever need to garner at Botany Bay are still one thousand leagues north, in the warehouses of Canton, awaiting the arrival of *Alexander* and any other survivors of Captain Sinclair's convoy. Then, God and the French permitting, next year those tea chests will pay their duty at London to underwrite our latest war with Paris."

Ball leaned forward. It had always seemed improbable to him that lagging a few hundred criminals off the map would be more than a splash from a puddle when taken from the army of broken soldiers and civilian thieves who now robbed and killed for a living along London's alleys. "Then we're not to be a convict colony?"

Phillip shook his head. "We are to be a colony with convicts: there's a world of difference. *Apropos* the French and their warmongering, I'm quite aware how much my officers wish they'd never volunteered for duty in a garrison as remote as New Holland. You could now be blockading the enemy's ports and I can't say I'd blame anyone for wishing to be in the Atlantic or Med' rather than the South Seas, putting aside prize money for old age and infirmity as I did when we took Havana back in 'sixty-two."

Phillip wiped his toothpick across his cuff. "However, at the risk of appearing repetitious, things are rarely what they seem to be in matters of statecraft. For while the hopes of the world at large are focused upon our government and its actions to counter the French, Mr. Pitt's hopes rest upon us and our actions here."

"I'm afraid I've lost the connection, sir."

"It's really very simple, Mr. Ball. Victory in Europe will be the outcome of trade with India and the Celestial Empire." Phillip flexed the slip of ivory between his fingers. "We lose one, we lose all. Don't look so surprised, nations live as much by prize money and plunder as the rest of us, only in their case it's called taxation and revenue. The excise taken from the China and India Customs is our nation's collateral which secures loans in centers as far apart as St. Petersburg and Frankfurt. And those bankers' drafts are the invisible levers which lend such amazing power to our army and navy. . . ."

Ball smiled uncertainly. "But what in Heaven's name has this Godforsaken blot on the map got to do with, well, trumping the Frogs?"

"Everything." Phillip sheathed the toothpick and slipped it back inside his waistcoat. "The French crown has spent a considerable fortune, which they can ill afford with bread rioters and a surly populace to placate, funding the Dutch to revive that alliance which cost us so dearly in the American colonies. Put another way, the doors of the Cape and Malacca Straits have been slammed shut against our eastern convoys, so where else can our Chinamen turn for fresh vegetables and water, new spars and rigging?"

" 'Pon my word, sir, I don't know."

"Few do, Mr. Ball, and yet those same merchant vessels must somehow continue encircling the globe with our trade or all else is lost." Phillip reached for the bell's string again. "So now you're privy to Mr. Pitt's design when he directed me to be here, alone in the Pacific, rather than remain there with everyone else in the Mediterranean and Atlantic.

"Like yourself, I know where I'd rather be, but liking or not liking an order is no part of our calling as king's officers." He tugged the string.

"We must go whither we're sent and, once there, strive to make the best of what's available. In this present case we've been despatched to New Holland and our task is to be ready to refresh our ships which double the Cape of Good Hope for Van Diemen's Land, thence north to the Formosa Passage and Canton." The commodore stopped. "Ah, Bryant. Serve the coffee." He glanced across the chart table. "Will you join me, Mr. Ball?"

"No, thank you, sir," the younger man replied, standing to stoop between the roof beams. "If you'll excuse me, I'd better make my rounds."

"Of course. The strictest attention to duty is also expected in our profession."

3

PHILLIP WAITED until his servant had warmed a pannikin over the spirit lamp in the officers' pantry and strained it through a piece of rag into a cup. The cabin door clicked shut. The lonely man behind it was alone for the first time since dawn, free to drop his public mask, free to permit himself one heartfelt grin of relief at the setting sun. By God, he had done it! Jakob Phillip's boy *had* beaten Admiral Count de La Pérouse, Knight of St. Louis, *grand seigneur*, lord high everything!

The grin mellowed as Phillip awarded himself a spoonful of sugar to sweeten the coffee's scorched bitterness. After making sail in a frigate which had been sinking even before the British coast fell below the horizon, and finishing the race eight months later in a brig which any sizeable man o' war could have swung inboard as a pinnace, he, Arthur Phillip, had won the greatest prize of all—an empire. And enough of the British expeditionary force, *Supply* and *Alexander,* had struggled through with him to secure James Cook's claim to Botany Bay and the western Pacific.

Every Frenchman in the South Seas could now make landfall on *La Nouvelle Hollande* and the British governor, himself, would snap his fingers under their haughty noses. Instead of raising the golden lilies of France, the *messieurs* would have to swallow their pride while they fired salutes for the red, white and blue flag of New Holland.

Others might still believe the publicly stated purpose of French scientific discovery, but Phillip knew otherwise. His strongbox, stowed a few inches away from the chart table, held a digest of despatches from Lord Dorset—Britain's ambassador at the Court of Versailles—especially the one which began: "Number XXIV has reliably informed me that M. de La Pérouse will shortly depart from Brest, and that sixty *prisonniers d'état* from La Bicêtre were, last Monday night, conveyed under guard and with the strictest secrecy aboard his flagship *L'Astrolabe*.

"Given that M. de La Pérouse will not only be investigating the capacity of the Fur Islands to supply *La Compagnie des Indes* with pelts for the China trade but will also be evaluating the timbers of New Zealand and Botany Bay to provide that company's vessels with spars, etc., it is the opinion of XXIV that these prisoners will be set ashore at the most favored location to establish a logwood camp.

"This opinion has been endorsed by Admiral De Suffren who is confident that his ships can, with little additional difficulty, extend their patrols from Port Louis, Mauritius, to protect any such French presence in the South Pacific Ocean. VII confirms that one and a quarter million *louis d'or* have been transferred to the Ministry of Marine's account to ensure that M. de La Pérouse's force lacks for nothing to achieve the covert purpose of this voyage. . . ."

But Phillip not only knew the French hidden agenda, he also knew the French much better than most Royal Navy officers. At the most desperate juncture of the recent war—when Britain battled alone against the combined powers of Holland, France, Spain and the American rebels—Commander Arthur Phillip had been given leave to take a rest cure beside Lake Léman, a mile or so from the Franco-Swiss border.

Five weeks later, on the hills around Toulon's dockyards and arsenals, a bespectacled Herr Doktor Anton Mahler had begun collecting beetles for his students back in Frankfurt-am-Main. Four months later, in the Admiralty's Charts & Surveys Office, Captain Arthur Phillip transcribed the information in his botanical notebooks to complete a detailed analysis of the enemy's Mediterranean fleet. And now, only this morning, Commodore Arthur Phillip had won again.

The smile faded. The French frigates could have been at anchor, waiting as *Supply* shortened sail into Botany Bay. The only alternative then to an honorable and quick death by his own hand would have been to face a stacked court martial after hauling back to England with his lost tribes of cheats, whores and burglars.

The men of power at Home would have enjoyed destroying a half-Jewish upstart in their well-bred world of privilege and ease. As the prime minister's protégé and Farmer George's plenipotentiary in the Pacific, Arthur Phillip could count on no friends at Carlton House where

Pitt's—and his—parliamentary enemies were paying court to the soon and future king, George, Prince of Wales. The British commodore had no doubts that, had today gone against him and he had chosen to live until his verdict had been handed down, the politicians' masters would have executed him as readily as they had sacrificed Admiral the Honorable John Byng after he failed to take Minorca, back in 'fifty-six.

The coffee was no longer sweet.

Phillip had been a seventeen-year-old seaman when his commander-in-chief was led before a firing squad on the quarterdeck of HMS *Monarch*. Thirty years had eased the memory of much else but nothing would ever erase that black noon when the royal marines' muskets muttered across Spithead. More than any other single event in his life, Admiral Byng's death had taught Arthur Phillip that skill, and courage, and devotion to duty were never enough: the prudent man had to build constantly his connections among Britain's kingmakers, the nation's invisible rulers, the Interest.

He pushed the cup away and reached for his journal, took a fresh quill from the sheaf in his writing case and began shaping the feather while his mind shaped a safe, neutral account of today's work for London.

Like every serving officer of the Crown he had to keep a strict record of the government's time and money entrusted to him, ready for a committee of scrutiny upon his return to England. Without exception all such journals were written with future careers in mind. Parliament's most distant proconsul was no exception to the iron law of self-interest.

Phillip chipped a spark into his tinderbox, lit the sealing wax candle and hardened his quill's nib over the flame. He checked the previous day's entry in his journal before dipping ink and continuing down the page. "18th Jan'y 1788. Fair weather. NE breezes. Thermometer 75°, barometer 30.21 and steady. Being come to our destination at last, and without sighting any other occupation of Botany Bay, proceeded directly ashore. Several Indians approached and were rewarded with gifts, etcetera. General mortality, nil. Sick, nine."

That chore done, the governor-designate of New South Wales was free to rally his allies around Westminster. He took out a fresh sheet of paper and smoothed it on the chart table. It hardly mattered that his letter could not reach its address until *Alexander* completed her voyage around the world from Canton, sometime next year; for the moment it was enough to be conversing in imagination with someone far removed from this brooding, alien landscape.

Phillip absentmindedly dipped ink. The first news of today's victory ought to have gone to his wife if only she'd given as much attention to their marriage as he believed he had before their final separation. Or to his own son if only Charlotte had given way on that point, as well. Instead, he would have to be satisfied with the younger son of his closest friend and neighbor in Hampshire, Mr. Secretary Rose, the master of Britain's Treasury Office and William Pitt's chief tactician in the chambers of power.

George Rose had been delighted when his wife, the former Miss Theodora Drummond of the Sugar Isles, agreed that the half-pay naval officer and adjoining farmer should be their second boy's godfather. Phillip had gladly accepted the honor and the young lad had grown up with an attentive, kindly uncle whose property bordered Rose's larger estates at Lyndhurst.

Phillip swished the quill from side to side, trying to compose the right greeting. Baby Billy? Young Bill? Neither would do any more: the boy had outgrown them as he'd outgrown his first breeches. The next time they shook hands it would probably be as Mr. William Rose, a gentleman scholar at one of those Oxford colleges, studying to take his place in the world of affairs, like his father before him.

The ink had dried. Phillip swore under his breath, dipped the nib again and got ready to dot and cross his letters with the grim precision his father had drilled into every one of his students, hunched over their slates in the lodging house which the foreign schoolmaster had shared with so many other lost men. Phillip grimaced. Respect, wealth, a place in the sun had been that refugee's quest, as well. Perhaps, for Jakob Philipp, the climb from a ragpicker's cellar on Frankfurt's *Judengasse* to a garret above London's Bread Street had been as steep a climb in the world as it had been for his only surviving child to reach the viceroyalty of that world's largest, least-known colony. Perhaps.

London had been Reb Jakob's New Jerusalem and England his Promised Land, flowing in milk and honey, where he'd eked out a living by translating correspondence for tradesmen while trying to thrash song, dance, deportment and grammar into their sullen children. There had once been an eccentric clergyman who'd bought lessons in Hebrew so that he could try reading his Scriptures in the original, but such paying pupils had been very rare in the slums around Billingsgate fish market.

Phillip disciplined himself—the past exists only insofar as it serves the present, just as the present only matters while it secures the future—and set to work. "Headquarters, Botany Bay, the eighteenth day of January, 1788. My dear William. Three things only were lacking to complete my satisfaction today. One was the approval of your esteemed father; the next was the presence of your respected mother; and the last, but not least, was your company as we first set foot upon the soil of New Holland.

"Dr. Gulliver's account of his travels in the South Seas, which you so generously presented to me when last we met, are a pallid reflection of the many wonders we should have beheld. So, shut your eyes and try imagining an almost cloudless summer day not three weeks after Christmas. However, instead of snowflakes, birds similar to ibis, pelicans, spoonbills and parakeets wing past without the least concern as we row ashore.

"Behind us extend two low headlands—one named by Sir Joseph Banks for himself, the other for his assistant, Dr. Solander, when they passed this way on their great voyage of exploration around the globe—and, between the capes, is a narrow strait which has all the appearance of a human wrist on the chart if we imagine this bay of botanical wonders to be a clenched fist, aimed at the shore, its thumb and little finger extended some distance into the trees."

Phillip considered rewriting this awkward paragraph: there were too many commas. Reb Jakob would have demanded further clarification and more full stops. The governor-designate sighed, reached for another sheet and numbered it. "These digits appear to be the mouths of creeks which flow from a greater river inland. Between them, corresponding with the 'knuckles,' is a beach of golden sand lapped by ripples of the most amazing clarity."

Phillip stopped again. He could not afford to appear ridiculous when a post office spy eventually opened this packet of letters to sniff out treason while hunting for titbits of gossip to sell around London's coffeehouses. But young William would understand, as would the parents to whom the boy must show his letter first. George and Dora would also understand, just as they'd understood and stood by Arthur Phillip when Lotte's moods drove away his other friends.

Phillip returned to a happier present, to the brighter future. "Our Indians bear no resemblance to Dr. Gulliver's manikins with their tiny cities and the midget fleet which he towed into battle for them. Indeed, I doubt if our grown-up Lilliputians would recognize either class of item! Far from being small, they are of moderate height with sooty black features which, so far as one may judge (it being impossible to see their skin's true hue behind the accumulation of grime), are not without some good points. Some are quite handsome, with intelligent eyes and well-shaped ears, tho' with rather spindly legs.

"There is, however, one curious detail shared by the New Hollanders. Every man, for such only we saw today, has a front tooth missing as if it had been deliberately broken out. They also wear a fishbone stuck through the nose, doubtless to their great discomfort. I can only surmise these things are badges by which they might be recognized in battle by their kings, for not one man had so much as a stitch of uniform upon him, or even a single feather such as Indians elsewhere adorn themselves with."

Phillip checked himself again. Not only would the post office censor be searching his words for hidden meanings, so would Theodora Rose as she read this letter over her husband's shoulder. He must clarify the picture for her. "Appearing thus *au naturel* they exhibited not the least immodesty nor did they anything which might have offended our sensibilities. English, of course, they have not yet learned to speak. However, I remain confident that, given sufficient patience and understanding, the indigenes will seek to establish cordial relations with us.

"Tomorrow I shall proceed ashore with the officers of my staff and begin our explorations in earnest. In due course I shall inform you of our further discoveries. Until which time I desire to remain, as ever, yr. affectionate godfather, Arthur Phillip, Captain General & Governor of New South Wales."

He sanded the ink dry. Legally speaking he wasn't yet entitled to use a viceroy's style and rank—those would come only after his commission had been declared to the assembled garrison by the judge advocate general—but after today's work he felt that he'd earned the right to stretch a point in his own favor.

Phillip's smile died as he got ready to share his innermost thoughts with young William's father. He rang for Bryant and, while the servant fetched more coffee and a candle for the cabin's lantern, began sifting his private correspondence from the older Rose. The worm of worry was gnawing at Phillip's earlier good humor.

The most recent despatch from George contained none of his normally veiled warnings from Westminster's bearpit. Enciphered midway through the previous year and addressed to the Admiralty's agent in Rio de Janeiro to await the British convoy, Mr. Secretary Rose had been frank to the point of personal risk when he spoke of the European crisis and its likely effects on the Botany Bay expeditionary force—.

Phillip looked up and impatiently gestured for Bryant to leave the tin pannikin where it was, to be quick about lighting the lantern, to get out. He waited for the cabin door to swing shut, then returned to fretting over last year's news from Europe and its impact on the Pacific. A hopeless task. At this distance from the center of power he might have been playing whist, blindfolded, unable to read his own hand, unable to see the cards being dealt against him.

The Peace of Paris, sealed barely five years earlier, had only paid out the side bets on the American war: nothing of substance had been altered on the main table where the great nations cut and bid for worldwide stakes. That treaty had been a peace only in name, a truce before two exhausted wrestlers grappled again for the decisive throw. Phillip could only guess what must have happened in the past several months. The French would have ordered a fleet and a garrison to occupy the mouth of the Rhine, crushing Britain's trade and foreign credit, squeezing the wealth of the nation of shopkeepers into the empty pockets of *la grande nation*. And at home the dull, plodding Farmer George would have been declared insane, at last, leaving a penniless empire in the flabby hands of a perpetually bankrupt prince regent.

Phillip's lean, Levantine face was impassive as he tilted the pannikin over his empty cup, spooned out a grain of burned barley and sipped the tepid, bitter drink. Despite all his encouraging words to young Ball earlier this evening, he knew that the prospects for Britain's most recently conceived colony were bleak. New South Wales could be aborted at any moment, especially once the French began flattering the Indian kings with cheap gifts and baubles. Or the little colony might linger into a sickly infancy before being cut short by orders from its stepparents in London. Phillip was no stranger to the realities of political power. Instead of the planned resupply by a second fleet of transports, outward bound for China, the next British vessels to anchor on Botany Bay could as easily be carrying orders for its governor's recall in disgrace.

But, as he had already noted today, appearances are deceptive. Several selves crowded behind the painfully acquired mask of an English country gentleman. One was inflexibly Continental, prone to brood over every imagined slight to his honor, swift to give blow for blow. And there were often glimpses of another self, aflame with the half-breed's ambition and determination to excel among the established and comfortably born. Because, although he lacked family connection and influence, never once had he lacked courage.

Arthur Phillip had learned that in adversity is opportunity as he fought his way up life's crowded ladder, from lodging house to Poor Boys' School at Greenwich, from ordinary seaman to lieutenant, from golden epaulettes to a viceroy's commission. And now that he was within reach of the top he was not about to lose his grip or his nerve.

He crouched, smoothing another sheet of paper: his inquisitors on the board of enquiry would discover that, although he and Rose were out of power—displaced by the prince regent's cronies—they were by no means powerless. The quill began a furious scratching. "My dear George. New South Wales is ours. God Save the King.

"M. de La Pérouse (whom the many prophets of doom hoped would be here before me, since his flotilla had such a head start in the South Seas) has yet to materialize and, for aught I care, may even now be contemplating his folly upon some tropical reef, surrounded by the wreckage of French hopes. For my part I shall hasten to implement our plans, declaring His Majesty's government *de jure* as well as *de facto* in New Holland and its adjacent territories.

"After enduring the severest gales imaginable, my advance squadron— being HMS *Supply* with the merchantman *Alexander* in attendance—cast anchor and I went ashore at eleven before noon to begin an inventory of our domain.

"It is still too early to pass comment upon Sir Joseph's observations of this land but it appears we have sufficient water and building material to raise a modest defense for our present numbers. If, however, others of our expedition have survived the transit from southern Africa, I shall be forced to reconsider our position and act in the best interests of our nation as I then perceive them to be."

Phillip trimmed the candle wick and went back to work, frowning through his spectacle lenses. "I cannot yet say if *Sirius* and her convoy were as fortunate as we to survive off Van Dieman's Land, but I fear that her poor state of repair (which had manifested itself in every possible degree before we began the last stage of our voyage from the Cape) will not have proved equal to the severity of the passage. Such being the case, I am sadly resigned to her loss from His Majesty's service."

Phillip rested for a moment and flexed his aching fingers. It was harder to resign himself to the loss of the frigate's captain, John Hunter. During their months together, sharing the same cramped mess table between Portsmouth and the Cape, the isolated commodore had grown to value, to trust, to like the elderly Scot. Without Hunter's sober common sense the aloof and often touchy Phillip could have been provoked into disastrous words and actions—especially when forced to deal with that other Scot, his commandant of marines and lieutenant governor, Robert Ross.

Phillip gritted his teeth. There, at least, was one member of *Sirius*'s complement who would never be missed. Where John Hunter had been cultivated, Ross was not. And where the former had always been open to discussion, the latter remained as stubbornly blinkered as an army mule. And while the Royal Navy officer had never been immoderate in his cups, the redcoat major had often proved himself to be a drunken boor. It had been one of Arthur Phillip's greatest misfortunes that his deputy distinguished himself at the relief of Gibraltar, back in 'eighty-one, since when Robert Ross of the Royal Marines had been favored by Admiral M'Lord Howe of the Navy Office.

Phillip swore quietly and returned to putting the best face on a bad case for his own patron, at the Treasury, barely one hundred yards across Whitehall. "I shall set *Alexander*'s draft of laborers to work, clearing and leveling the site for a stockade near the watering point. We have sufficient ordnance aboard *Supply* to give a good account of ourselves if, by any mishap, another power disputes our right to be here. I also judge our reduced number of guards to be still strong enough to maintain discipline in the colony until further relief is sent out.

"Thus, despite the probable loss of much of our impedimenta, I am able to report that Britain's status as the paramount power in the South Seas has been set upon firm foundations. I am equally confident that you will continue frustrating any moves, in Cabinet, to withdraw this garrison upon the grounds of economic or political expediency. Such a course of action, were it carried through, would be fatal to our nation's grand design in the Orient. However, I know you are more than aware of this, already.

"The hour grows late and I shall continue this despatch as news comes to hand. I desire to remain, as ever, yr. loyal friend, Arthur Phillip."

4

"I SAID, good morning, Mr. Levi!"

The defiant lag crossed his arms. "What you want now?"

"A civil answer would make a fine start to the day," Kitty Brandon replied. "Tch! You disappoint me. I fail to see how a gentleman with all your advantages in life could now be traipsing around with a face as long as a gravedigger's shovel—"

"Out the way!"

"You *dare* to speak to me like that?" Mrs. Katharine Brandon had been a force to be reckoned with on the English stage: she still had formidable presence. Levi backed off as she stepped forward. "I am extremely vexed with you! Since arriving at our destination I have noted a marked change in your attitude to our friends!"

"Friends, she says!" Levi's fingers splayed like spider legs and clutched at his ragged shirt, then flew apart. "Name one!"

"There's Mr. Cribb. And—"

"He spit on me, I spit on him, there! Feh!"

"So I've noticed." Kitty Brandon's tone was, if possible, even more chilly. "When I questioned Mr. Thorpe he told me that you'd struck Mr. Cribb—"

"He start!"

"And then cursed everyone within earshot—"

"Because they calling me Jew *zhlub!*" Levi's hands clawed at his shirt again. "Because they say what I tell about Bottommy Town is all lies—!"

"Enough!" She raised her hand. "Mr. Thorpe has told me all I need to hear. Great Heavens, are you the first man in the world to repeat a story only to find later that it was false?"

"But—!"

"Enough, I said! There's no time to waste by raking over yesterday's ashes when tomorrow threatens to burn every one of us to the ground. You will therefore make up with Mr. Cribb at the earliest possible opportunity."

"Never! That bootface soldierman tell me—!"

"Devil a damn I care what he told you!" She softened her voice. "Mr. Levi? I've always regarded you as a man of the most uncommon sense." Her cat green eyes crinkled at the corners. "You stand far above the common ruck of our companions in disgrace." She smiled for him alone. "During all our weary months at sea it was a delight to observe how you and Mr. Cribb shared and shared alike. It pleased me because, if a foreign gentleman such as yourself and an original such as he can dine from the same bowl without too many upsets, there's got to be some hope for the rest of us: it's a knack which we of the theatrical profession must learn from our earliest days if we are to survive, let alone thrive upon the public's fickle fancy. Or upon this madhouse of summer-in-winter," she added as more unchained men climbed into *Alexander*'s cutter to begin another day's work ashore.

One of the lags turned behind a sentry's back and forked a pair of fingers at the pig pen. Levi's jaw clenched. He jerked forward. Kitty Brandon's hand flattened against his chest. "Control yourself!"

"You see what he do?"

"You'll be seeing blue stars unless you start paying attention to *me!*" She crossed her arms. "I took you for a man of judgment and experience: I'd better not be mistaken. Such pride as yours has been the ruin of many another who thought he was fated to ride through the world, perched atop Fortune's wheel without once falling underneath. It is, I might add, a singularly masculine vanity."

"No!"

"Yes. Because we ladies, by contrast, have to endure discomforts which not even you could begin to imagine," she went on in a level voice. "Such a dame school prepares us to work for future gain, to take every moment as it comes and be damned glad for any trifling crumb of comfort in Lord Luck's pocket. For which reason I'm now telling you to swallow that pride because, unless you do make up your quarrel with Mr. Cribb, pride may be the only thing left to swallow once we get ashore—"

"*Shveig!*" Levi tried shoving past. "In Warsawa I don't need no Cribb! In Bokhara I eat good without no bloody fusilman soldier!" He pounded his forehead with bunched fingertips. "I got *yiddisher kop!* Nothing else in London save me when you all going to make me hang! But I got brains—!"

"By God, I wouldn't be so sure of that!" Kitty Brandon snapped back, stepping sideways, cutting off his escape. Levi halted as she raised her finger and her voice. "We are not in London! We are not in Arseover! Nor are we in Dublin, Boston Town or any of those other pest holes where I performed in the Colonies! We're nowhere, do you hear me? We're at nothing more than a name on an otherwise blank sheet of paper in Captain Sinclair's chart bag and the quicker you get that into your thick skull, the better for both of us! Because I don't give a tuppenny damn for you, Mr. Levi. Nor do I even care for Mr. Cribb. Or for any other man who considers himself a born lord of creation. But, by God, I cherish myself and those poor, witless molls who look up to me for help and protection!" The finger swung, pointing astern to where six or seven government women were spinning marline for *Alexander*'s sailmaker.

"What that got to do with it?"

She ignored the question. "Therefore, it is precisely because Mr. Cribb was a bootfaced soldier, as you so elegantly express it, that we need him."

Levi tilted his chin. "I seen plenty soldiers. In Berlin I seen hundreds—hep, hep, hep!—and not one with the brains of my little toe."

Kitty Brandon tilted her chin. "I have also seen soldiers. Almost four thousand of them. And it would have brought tears of pride to the eyes on the back of a copper penny to see them die. Starving and naked we might've been, on our march from Canada. But every man was a lion, that day at Saratoga—"

"Phui! With bare hands I croak bigger bugger here!" Levi's foot stamped on *Alexander*'s deck. "Alone!"

"Which is another brave event I remember well," Kitty Brandon agreed, quietly. "A sweeter mill I'll never see as the day you put up your maulers to thrash the living breath from that pug. However, you didn't do it alone—"

"I did!"

"Be silent. Mr. Cribb and Mr. Thorpe were your seconds."

"Was nothing!"

"I'd say it was everything," she contradicted him. "Anyone can face anything, with allies fighting beside him. But it takes a rare courage to attack one against twenty, to rip the gun from another's grip and hold off a pack of animals from a broached keg of grog. Which, as you will clearly recall, is what that 'bootface' did on this very same deck not two weeks ago. . . ."

"Hn!"

"Because such a man as Sergeant Major Cribb happens most infrequently. Few will ever know what he had to do to win that rank—"

"Kill!"

"Of course. I have no doubt there's as much blood on his hands as yours, Mr. Levi, but such is the way of the world," she agreed. "However, Joe Cribb achieved the highest possible rank a person of his birth can reach in the king's service, and he did it leading the only unbeatable troops we had in the American colonies—Colonel Tarleton's Rangers. God alone knows how he did it. It'd be worth a hundred guineas just to hear him tell. But, as you know, he says very little about his years Over There. Sufficient to say that he came back Home and is with us now, which is why I'm urging you to extend the cordial right hand of comradeship again. Please?"

Levi's mouth tightened. "No."

"Why?"

"Because I don't need no bugger like him to save me in Newgate. Is same here."

Kitty Brandon's face also tightened. "I see. We are determined to be stubborn. Very well, I shall have to tell you about Winchester Castle. A filthy stone box which I shared with many another unfortunate while certain grand gentlemen of London debated whether or not to hang *me*—"

"All this I hear! I see Dr. Balmain now, let me go!"

"Not until I've finished, you don't!" She sidestepped again, blocking his path. "One of my companions in distress was a young country girl, Betty Lloyd by name. Being alone and far from her family she did what many another has done before, fall on her back for the first pair of breeches which unbuttoned and told her she was pretty—"

"Dr. Balmain want me—!"

"A few months later she was no longer so trim or slim and the same fine gentleman was now flattering some other hapless dell," Kitty Brandon went on in a flat, controlled voice. "At which point Betty again did what many another has had to do, no longer being fit to churn butter from dawn to dusk, she stole a length of cloth to make little clothes. When the shopkeeper looked through his window she tried to put back the piece of linen, but a felony had been committed, and the draper was determined that his noble English justice take its course with that common little Welsh thief."

Levi looked uneasy. "Why she not going to see anybody? When she getting fat?"

"I doubt there was an obliging Mr. Leafy Levi with his half-crown packets of 'stomach powder,' " Kitty Brandon replied without emotion. "I do know that she'd tried jumping off stools and sitting in the river but she was still stuck with her problem when we befriended each other in the condemned cell. Of course, England's law in its mercy had not passed judgment of death upon an unborn child, merely upon its wicked mother. So Betty copped a belly plea until her time was ripe."

Levi wiped his face. "Please—"

Kitty Brandon ignored him. "I delivered the child and a finer boy you never saw, but so strong was her affection for the little mite she wouldn't let go of him, even when they came to take her out to the marketplace to be killed—"

"Please!"

"Rather than rip the baby in half, our jailer allowed her to keep it at her breast while she went aboard the cart with those others to be hanged that morning—"

"Please!"

"I am told she was still screaming when it was her turn to have a rope knotted round her neck. Then they whipped the horse. The cart pulled away. And, finally, she dropped the reason for her downfall."

Levi had clapped both hands to his ears. Kitty Brandon looked puzzled. "What? Does my tale shock you, sir? Heavens! Such incidents are commonplace. Evidently you have yet to learn there are chains stronger than iron links, but perhaps you've been taught to call them skirts or petticoats? However—unlike certain men I could name—we ladies have learned that all the sulking in the world won't strike them from our legs, therefore Dame Experience has schooled us to cope by other means."

She tapped her own forehead. " 'Brains' did you say, Mr. Levi? No! *We* have to supply those while you, in general, provide the brawn. Which is fair exchange because brains, such as you boast of, are weak things indeed without another's muscle and backbone. Whereas brawn, without brain, is nothing more than a bowl of cold pig's jelly—if you get my meaning. For which reason neither your famous wits nor mine will ever amount to a pinch of snuff without a Mr. Cribb to keep the rest at a respectful distance from ourselves and my Betty Lloyds!"

She stepped sideways. "Sure, he can be headstrong and difficult, but aren't those the very qualities which made the rebels flee for their lives whenever they saw his troops riding to serve another dish of 'Tarleton's revenge'? And is that not the very man we're going to need in the days and weeks and months—God help us—years ahead? Which is but another fair exchange. Because without us to support him, Mr. Cribb will never be more than a brave knuckleman. But without those knuckles I'll be lucky to stay even as I am, and it's damned certain you'll remain an outsider, without connection, not worth a brass farthing!"

Kitty Brandon unfolded her arms. "Think well about it. Good day, Mr. Levi."

5

" 'MORNING, SIR." Bryant heeled the cabin door shut. "Weather glass looks a bit down but there's still enough blue up there to make britches for a Dutchman." He set the pannikin of warm shaving water on the chart table and pulled the stern windows' canvas blinds.

Phillip muffled a yawn. "Coffee."

"Aye aye, sir. When you've done with the tin, like."

His master remembered: this was *Supply*. The refinements of life, like coffee pots, were stowed aboard *Sirius*, most likely with crabs and shrimps scuttling around them. He motioned for Bryant to go, then dropped his legs over the side of the cot to open the skylight and wedge his pocket mirror on the poop deck's rim.

Phillip splashed water at his face and began brushing a lather while he looked aloft at the red St. George's cross of his commodore's pennant, but not even that could lift his spirits this morning. The wind had backed southeasterly during the night, there could be dirty weather from that quarter before long. He must remind Ball to warp the brig farther offshore: this anchorage would catch the full force of a stiff blow and there was not a fathom to spare under *Supply*'s keel.

Phillip grimaced at himself in the mirror, snapped the razor shut and rang for Bryant to take away the pannikin while he dressed for breakfast.

He was still finishing a ration of beef and biscuit when Ball clattered down the companion ladder. "Enter."

"Lookout reports sails bearing east by south three quarters south!" the brig's commander announced, hat under arm.

"Hell!" Phillip caught his head on a roof beam as he jerked upright. "The French!" He led the way on deck, buckling his sword, and snatched a telescope from the binnacle. "Damn! Damn, damn!" He tugged the dry brass tubes and got the focus. He wiped their eyepiece with his sleeve and tried again. There was no mistake, though, the barques *Scarborough* and *Friendship* were leading his main force under shortened sail. Bowsprits nodding, the battered British merchantmen were limping in column astern between the two capes. One by one his convoy was plodding to a halt, *Prince of Wales* and *Lady Penrhyn, Charlotte* and *Borrowdale, Fishburn* and *Golden Grove,* and HMS *Sirius* bringing up the rearguard.

"Thank God. . . ."

The expeditionary force had kept together and kept going across an almost unknown ocean, but not without heavy cost. Every vessel now had jury-rigged spars and patched canvas aloft; every one had spurts of water slicking her scuppers from the pumps below. But every one had survived the Antarctic's gales to make landfall on a six-hundred-yard gap in an otherwise uncharted coastline.

John Hunter had plotted their track from Africa with little more than a quadrant, a defective chronometer and a lifetime's experience of the sea. It was the masterwork of a master navigator.

Phillip steadied his voice. "Make to *Sirius:* well done."

"Aye aye, sir." Ball faced his sailing master. "Make to *Sirius:* well done!"

"Aye aye, sir!"

The bosun's whistle shrilled, calling up the gunner to prime *Supply*'s six-pounder while the yeoman of signals knotted his flags from the code book. The clusters of Indians fell silent as a stick of colored bunting spilled into the wind, then howled as the blank charge spat smoke and rolled a thunderclap.

Ball had more urgent problems. His telescope groped into focus around the convoy's flagship. *Sirius* was lowering her gig. More pipes shrilled across the bay as the frigate's commanding officer went over the side, blue coat tails flapping. Close behind, almost tramping on his fingertips, was the marine battalion's commandant. The two elderly men sat to attention in the stern. Hunter nodded at his coxswain. "Give way, Evans."

The redcoat's temper was not so controlled. The French had failed to occupy Botany Bay. Ross would not be winning his colonelcy after destroying the enemy in battle. His disappointment was understandable.

Blood-drenched beaches had always been lucky places for Robert Ross. Thirty years ago, while shells plowed overhead from British battleships, the Royal Marines had waded ashore through storms of French bullets to start rolling the enemy from Canada. He'd won his first wound at Louisburg and, with it, his first rung up the steep and painful ladder from crofter's lad to king's officer.

Ross stared at the barren scrubland. Ross glared at its offensive silence. Ross glowered at the red and white pennant on *Supply*'s peak. Not only had the shoebox of a brig survived, so had Phillip or else his colors would have been struck, his body pitched over the side, and Ross would now be governor of New South Wales. Instead, with every creak of the gig's rowlocks, his hopes of glory were fading and, unless Phillip obliged by catching blackwater fever or dengue, there would be no triumphant return Home for Robert Ross, first nabob of the South Seas.

The gig's coxswain trimmed alongside *Supply*. Hunter almost missed his footing on the tumblehome's thick mat of green weed, then led the way aloft as Ball came to attention, hat off. "Welcome aboard, sir."

"Thank you." Hunter saluted the quarterdeck and turned to study the empty horizon beyond Cape Banks as Ross puffed through the entry port, breeches stiff with pipe clay, a tarnished silver gorget plate chained across his grubby linen cravat.

The marines off *Supply* and *Alexander* had been paraded as a single unit for their commanding officer's inspection. Ross fingered the nearest man's brass buttons. "Name!"

"Marine Asky, sah!"

"You're a disgrace to the corps!"

"Sah!"

"Seven days' pack drill, sergeant!"

"Sah!"

Ross had resumed control over another squad of the two hundred men who would answer directly to him, not Phillip, in the months, the years ahead. Satisfied, he marched aft with Hunter and Ball to where the governor designate was waiting to receive them. Hats were again doffed in salute—a silvery pigtail blowing in the wind under Hunter's tricorne, a gray horsehair wig like iron wire jutting from under Ross's—then replaced.

Phillip nodded impartially at both of his senior officers. "Shall we retire below to refresh ourselves?" He turned. "Mr. Ball. That sky's unsettled. Be so kind as to run out a kedge and warp a further cable's length offshore."

"Aye aye, sir."

Phillip beckoned for Bryant to follow him into the cabin with another of Ball's clarets. The cork squeaked and the servant poured out three measures of wine, carefully leaving a mouthful for himself in the bottle: with any luck it would still be there when he cleared away, later.

The door clicked shut. Phillip raised his glass to Hunter. "Thank you. It will be my especial pleasure to see that your achievement is recognized in my despatches to the lords commissioner of the Admiralty."

"Sir."

Phillip glanced at Ross. "And thank you, too, major."

The three officers drank in silence.

Phillip had never known Hunter to be so cool. Something was evidently troubling him. Something more than their disagreement when the convoy mustered off Cape Town and its commodore had insisted in going ahead to reach Botany Bay first. Ross, by contrast, had always been a pebble in life's shoe. It was not hard to imagine the reason for his black humor: there were no Frenchmen to slaughter. But it was less easy to fathom the tension between the two Scots because, until the Cape, Hunter and Ross had seemed to get along tolerably well.

Phillip made himself comfortable on the edge of the chart table. He motioned for the other two men to make themselves easy on whatever they could find in this cluttered cupboard of a cabin, but both preferred to stand. "Very well, gentlemen, you may speak freely. Are there any matters which you'd like to bring to my attention before making the formal reports which I'll expect in due course?"

Silence.

"I see. Are we not fortunate to have traveled so many eventful miles and still be in total agreement with one another. Perhaps some minor points of difference will emerge as we proceed," Phillip observed drily. "However, those can wait. Of far greater importance to me is the immediate future of this colony. There is much to be done before His Majesty's authority can be established in due form. We shall maintain an appearance of unity in front of the men, at all times. Mutinous and dirty they may be, but they'll be looking up to us for direction and example under very trying circumstances."

Hunter nodded. "Sir."

Ross still looked as if he had bitten on a bad tooth. "As you say. Sir."

"Precisely. It will be as I say." Phillip glanced from side to side at the other two men. "I'm giving everyone fair warning: the powers entrusted to me by His Majesty's commission are considerable. I shall have no hesitation in breaking any man whom I judge to be endangering the colony's well-being."

"Sir."

Ross stopped gnawing the inside of his cheek. "Aye."

Phillip straightened from the table. "My flag will transfer to *Sirius* where I shall chair a conference after dinner tonight: you will both kindly attend. I shall also require your company commanders, Mr. Ross: captains Shea, Tench and Campbell. Captain Collins will be present as my judge advocate general and Mr. King will be my flag lieutenant." He glanced at Hunter again. "Can you think of anyone else we ought to consult at this point?"

Sirius's commander considered the question. "Might it not be an opportunity for the Reverend Mr. Johnson to be included? As a mark of courtesy to the civilian element?"

Phillip shook his head. "The longer I can delay his sermonizing, the better." He reached for his hat and checked that his pockets were stocked with pieces of trade cloth. "Very well, accompany me ashore while I resume my tour of inspection: we must at least give the appearance of working in harness. Oh, major? Be so kind as to ask your sergeant for a couple of men. The Indians were meek enough yesterday but who can tell what orders their kings have given them overnight?"

Ross clicked his heels and Phillip gestured for him to go ahead through the door, then touched Hunter's arm to slow him a couple of paces. "What the hell's happening, John?"

"Later, sir," Hunter replied, just as quietly.

6

SUPPLY'S GIG took all three officers and, with a tight squeeze, the two marines in full battle order. Phillip made sure that Hunter sat between him and his deputy as the crew bent to their oars, stroking toward the less thickly wooded south shore and what appeared to be a river mouth.

"I propose making a short, waterborne reconnaissance inland," Phillip announced, determined to maintain a public show of official unity. "Thereafter I shall retrace our route to check the accuracy of Mr. Cook's observations from that small hillock, over there."

Hunter followed his commodore's pointing finger. "Sir."

"Hn!"

Phillip ignored Ross and smiled brightly. "Indeed, if only half of what has been written about New Holland is true, we're exceedingly fortunate to be here. As I remarked to Mr. Ball only yesterday, this Botany Bay could well become a second Garden of Eden with such an abundance of timber, food and water. Why, I'd wager that, with sufficient application of effort, we shall soon be—"

"Heating iron for the Mohawks!" Ross was tugging a service pistol from his belt.

A dozen or so naked women were harvesting oysters from a thicket of mangrove roots. The Indians' heads flicked up. They had heard the shout from the rowing boat, they could see the oar blades advancing like black crab legs, they dropped their loads on the mud and floundered for cover.

"I'd have thought such items singularly ill equipped to do us much harm, major. . . ."

"And I tell you it's a bloody trap!" Ross had finished priming his pistol. "Chief Pontiac's murdering heathen tried the same trick at Fort Detroit!"

Phillip let his finger trail in the water. He looked back at Hunter. "Your experience of the American colonies was rather more constructive, captain. Did I not hear that your charts of the St. Lawrence are the standard by which others' are measured? Such being the case, how do you now rate our chances of finding a similar watercourse?"

"I can't say, sir. It's far too early for anyone to hazard a guess. But to judge from the fallen trees which've been washed downstream, and from the height of the debris over there," he pointed at a mass of bark and dead branches snagged in the crown of a living tree, "I'd say there were considerable floods hereabouts—"

"And I tell you it's a death trap!" Ross insisted as the gig's bowman began fending off submerged logs with his boat-hook. "Stay on this course and we'll be stuck full of arrows like pin cushions!"

Phillip had learned to ignore his deputy's opinions. "An interesting observation, Mr. Hunter, but would such flooding rule out a larger, more navigable river system somewhere between us and the coastal ranges?"

"Only time will tell," the other man replied, shielding his eyes and watching a pair of white spoonbills lift off between the boat and a rampart of swampy undergrowth. "God alone knows what could be lying in wait for us even around the next bend—"

"I told you so! Sitting targets! Now we're for it!" The gig had scraped to a halt on a sunken tree.

Phillip took his finger from the water and tasted it again. "Still very salty. I'd say this tidal influence extended inland for quite a distance, wouldn't you, Mr. Hunter?"

Sirius's commander scooped up a mouthful and spat it out. "Agreed."

"In which case there'll be an ebb," Phillip concluded. "Let us defer further explorations until we can be certain of the local tides: it would never do to find ourselves stranded here by low water." He nodded at the coxswain as the bowman strained to shift them ahead. "Go about."

"Aye aye, sir!"

The bowman's naked back dripped with sweat. He grunted, shoving harder on the boat-hook. The oarsmen heaved together, digging great whorls of water with their blades. The gig inched astern and Ross lapsed into an angry silence as they began stroking downstream again, past the abandoned mangrove swamp, out onto the open waters of Botany Bay. A hail of Indian arrows had yet to cut down the governor and his successor had yet to fight the notable rearguard action which would bring everyone else to safety.

"Starboard."

The helm came up. The bowman coiled his mooring line, crouched and jumped over the side. The rest of the crew tossed their oars, stowing them along the thwarts, and clambered into the water to drag the gig ashore. They linked arms and lifted the officers onto the beach. The two marines were last off, marching through the shallows, boots splashing, muskets shouldered, halting in front of their battalion commander.

"Fix bayonets! Right face! Follow me—!"

Phillip removed his hat and fanned himself as the three redcoats advanced in skirmishing order toward a grove of dark green bushes and some taller, misshapen trees with rags of silvery bark fluttering from their trunks. With any luck an Indian war party was lying in ambush. Their stone clubs and hatchets would perform a useful service for the colony. Ross could win some minor fame as a lesser Captain Cook, the first man to be killed and eaten in New Holland, and John Hunter could step into his vacant shoes as the next lieutenant governor. Everyone would gain. Phillip cocked his head to one side, waiting for Ross to tramp from sight.

Disappointed, he turned to check that the crewmen had mounted a guard around the gig, then looked at Hunter as the other man unbuttoned his waistcoat and loosened his neckcloth. "Well, John, our lobsters ought to give us fair warning if there's trouble in the offing. Let us allow them to beat a pathway up that hill while you tell me what the devil's been happening since last we met."

"It will prove a bitter draught, sir, one best swallowed whole. I'll be brief." Hunter fell into step with his commodore as they began pacing up the beach. "Major Ross put me under arrest—"

"He *what?*"

"Confined me. Within minutes of you crossing to *Supply*, back there off Africa, he came down to my cabin and informed me that as lieutenant governor he would assume command of the colony when you failed to reach New Holland." Hunter raised his hand to silence the other man. "With respect, I said this would be a bitter draught. Please allow me to get it down before I also choke."

"Proceed."

"I then informed Major Ross that, contrary to his belief, if you were to fall at your post, His Majesty's dormant commission would appoint me to be your successor in New South Wales. Whereupon he told me that he had two hundred men under arms and that they guarded the magazines and strong points aboard every vessel in our convoy. He then called a sentry and instructed him to be particularly vigilant who entered and who left *Sirius*'s great cabin: his intention was plain.

"Since when, until this very morning in fact, he has conducted himself as if he were captain general of El Dorado," Hunter went on in the same, plain, Edinburgh burr. "For instance, Campbell has been promised one thousand acres and fifty laborers to clear them—'slaves' is the preferred expression—and Mr. Dawes is to become a justice of the peace once he's built the fortress from which Major Ross intends to emulate Major Clive's conquest of Bengal."

Phillip's face was like dark granite. "I wondered what he might try. Continue."

Hunter had worked for more than a year with this energetic, emotional man: they understood each other's moods. "I know how you feel, sir. I've spent many of the last forty-odd days considering this sad state of affairs. After all," he added, "if the brig had gone down, and if *Sirius* had been the first to reach Botany, I'd now be having to assert my authority over a battalion of troops whose commanding officer would be countermanding my every order."

"Damned impudence!"

The two men had almost reached the tree line. Hunter slowed. "You may recall an occasion when we spoke about Major Ross as our convoy was outward bound from the Canaries? If so, you'd remember that I said, when the world regards him it sees only a threadbare old redcoat, an officer whose main qualification for this challenging task is M'Lord Howe's belief that our military ought to have some post of honor in a colony which they may soon be defending against enemies internal as well as external."

Sirius's commander stopped in the shade and removed his blue serge tunic, slinging it across one shoulder. "However, you may also recall we spoke of that Major Ross he himself admires in the mirror, after his Sunday shave. That reflection is never splotched with strong liquor, nor is it ever soured by envy for the promotions which pass to other, better-connected English officers. In his imagination he is always manly and masterful, as befits the future Lord Ross of New Holland. . . ."

"That's absurd!"

"Perhaps, but it's what he believes," Hunter replied quietly. "I respectfully urge that our best course of action is to avoid doing anything which causes him to lose that face. As I also remarked when we left Teneriffe, every man needs his dreams and, if another pricks the bubble of vanity before it bursts of its own accord, a mere nuisance may become a sworn enemy for life in less time than it takes to puff out a candle."

"A mere nuisance?" Phillip hunched his shoulders. "The man usurps my authority, he puts my deputy under a form of arrest, he continually stirs up mischief among my officers, and he's still only a nuisance? What the hell does he have to do to become dangerous?"

"Nothing. That will be up to you."

"Uh?"

Hunter looked the other man in the face. "You can respond exactly as prescribed by fleet regulations and order Captain Campbell to put his battalion commander under restraint, pending general court martial. However, the moment you do that the colony will be split asunder, before hardly one of us has set foot ashore. God knows there's little love lost between bluejacket and redcoat so I doubt if Campbell's company would dare obey your orders: he's a very Roman disciplinarian."

"And mad."

"All the more reason to 'gae canny,' " Hunter replied, glancing up at the sky to read the time. "By sundown we could both be listening to the sentries changing over outside the great cabin while the new captain general continues planning his war against the local Incas and their wretched diamond mines. And who'll dispute his right to act as he pleases? Two hundred bayonets are a compelling argument in any language and he does hold the lieutenant governor's commission, so it'd be years—if ever—before London sorted out the legal arguments *pro et contra*. In the meantime, you'll be utterly ruined because, as I'm sure you know, our Major Ross has sound connections with M'Lord Howe's interest."

"I'm unlikely to forget."

"I thought not, but the fact has to be mentioned." The two men had begun moving again. "Now, as I read our problem, Ross has the upper hand, whether or not he cares to exercise it. He can march back this instant and order his pair of bootfaces to shoot us dead on the spot, and they'd obey him. However, with every passing hour he'll lose that advantage as the routines of foreign service are established—and his troops pitch their tents ashore under the guns of our frigate." *Sirius's* captain could have been discussing tomorrow's weather.

"There's also a second factor in our favor: between the battalion commander giving an order and his sergeants implementing it is the necessary agreement of his company captains." Hunter wondered how his own commanding officer was taking this mild lecture. "The senior, Jimmy Campbell, has never been the same since *Galatea* blew up around him. He'll mindlessly obey Ross even if ordered to march his men backward off a cliff—"

"A pity he doesn't try," Phillip commented, pushing through some twiggy undergrowth.

"Then there's Captain Shea," Hunter went on. "Undoubtedly an Irish gentleman of great personal charm and gallantry but it's only a matter of time before that cough gets the better of him. In an open rift between yourself and Major Ross, John Shea must side with legitimate authority—yours—or else his pension will be forfeit and his widow left destitute. Which leaves the residue of power with captains Tench and Collins."

"Go on."

"Well, in my opinion, young David Collins is our strongest card to play at the moment. His father—the General Collins—commands the Plymouth Division and so the son is free to snap his fingers at whatever Ross may think. He's also your judge advocate with all the financial advantages which come with that post. It's therefore reasonable to assume that he'll interpret the law to favor his own interests."

"Go on."

"Which brings us to Mr. Tench," Hunter concluded. "As a member of the Welsh border gentry he's clearly destined for advancement. Like Jack Shea he knows which side his biscuit's buttered upon and can be trusted to act accordingly." *Sirius's* captain ducked a springy branch and straightened again, dusting soot off his waistcoat from the burned bark. "Were I in your place—which I might've been—I would now be making it my task to isolate both Ross and Jimmy Campbell by cultivating Tench and Shea."

"That must be why we're called the United Kingdom."

"Sir?"

"Nothing." Phillip fell silent for several plodding paces, hands clasped behind his back. "You've evidently given much thought to this matter."

"I've had every incentive," Hunter replied. "I could easily have been in your shoes. It would've been an unenviable promotion."

"Ross should've been put out to pasture years ago." Phillip's shoulders were still hunched as he trudged up the sandy track. "He's got to be mad wanting to be governor of anywhere, especially a colony which is hardly more than a line of latitude and two coordinates."

"Sir?"

Phillip slapped flies from his face. "The resounding titles which our Mr. Ross so craves are only given to conceal the painful horns of a dilemma. You see, John, as ruler of New South Wales I am simultaneously the most and the least. Every other person, yourself included, can look up to me for an indication of favor and progress. My nod says you're following the right course, my frown means that you'd better mend your ways: a subordinate's life has its compensations. But once we've reached the top of the greasy pole, to whom can we then look for approval?"

"God?"

"Not so, my friend." The governor was unbuttoning his own waistcoat as the day warmed up. "A lifetime's experience has shown me that the Almighty has greater concerns than Arthur Phillip. In New Holland, as elsewhere, God helps those who help themselves, just as it'll be 'God help' those who don't help themselves first. Which means that, more than any other item of equipment, I really need a crystal ball. I need one to peer behind certain doors in Whitehall and I certainly need one to eavesdrop whenever His Royal Highness, George, Prince of Wales, is receiving homage from his political toads and moral toadies. Instead, I've been given a quarter of a million pounds' worth of ordnance and stores by a government which is most likely to be out of power, in order to complete a task which is anathema to the empire's present masters. Also an unenviable promotion. However, to return to your original point, you feel that Ross could now be planning some kind of *coup d'état?*"

"Yes."

"Then I'm afraid we must agree to disagree," Phillip replied, pausing again to fan himself with his hat. "I've also spent a disproportionate time pondering my deputy's strange ways and, although I can imagine him leading many things, I can't picture him at the head of a mutiny or insurrection. So to do would be a denial of everything he's lived and fought to achieve."

"But—"

"One moment, John, I'm not finished. You see, there's one important factor which is so obvious we tend to overlook it: Ross is intensely proud of being an officer of marines, though Heaven only knows why. Ambition may've soured him but he remains a creature of routine: if a given action isn't in Regulations then it can't be done. It's the eternal tug o' war between redcoat and bluejacket, as well you know. Doubtless he leads boarding parties with great dash but he'd be useless on the quarterdeck where we're expected to think before we act. In a nutshell, Ross will always obey a superior officer's commands: I happen to be that superior."

Hunter shook his head. "With respect, sir, you're way off mark. I've already been put under arrest once."

"Correct. But at the time our gallant major thought he was next in line to assume power. Now he's not, although it does sound as if he's still having a spot of bother. . . ."

The two naval officers quickened their stride and reached the crest of the hill where a sizeable clearing ran from side to side. At one end stood the two marines, muskets leveled from the hip, bayonets aimed down the glade. At the other end was a village of bark shelters, a large midden of oyster shells and about twenty Indians shaking their spears at the uninvited strangers. Ross stood at the head of his troops. He might be outnumbered six to one but he had never once retreated and he was not about to start now. Sword drawn, boots stamping grit, he was putting himself through the Regimental Drill Manual before leading an attack.

Phillip paused, wondering whose side to cheer on, but the Indians might not understand a friendly shout from him and would probably continue their massacre after dealing with Ross.

"Get out the way!"

Phillip quickened his pace. He reached the middle ground and raised his hat to the Indians before arranging a square of calico on the ground, a string of colored beads and one of the mirrors.

An Indian edged forward as Phillip rejoined Hunter at the side of the clearing, but a much older, more grizzled man cuffed the young warrior aside and strode forward. *"Djirabali! Garindji wingala nai!"* he commanded, rattling his sheaf of spears at the blue and red ghostmen.

Phillip raised his right hand in greeting and tapped his chest. "I, friend!" Then, for lack of anything else to say, added, *"Soy amigo! Freund! Ami!"*

Graybeard was not convinced. Muttering, he selected a spear, flexed his arm, took aim. The whipstick slim shaft lofted over and down, shattering the mirror, splitting the cloth.

"Squad will prepare to give fire!" Ross yelled.

Phillip stepped onto the middle ground again.

"Prime—!"

The governor faced his marines and began walking up to their leveled muskets.

"I said, get out the way!" Ross's sword was up, ready to execute the order to shoot.

Phillip halted in front of the muzzles, touching his hat brim. "Thank you, major. That could've been rather unpleasant if you hadn't been here to support me."

"Sir! I—!"

"And did you notice the way he handled that spear?"

"Sir! I consider—"

"Heavens. I'd wager a shilling that old fellow could hit it at fifty yards. We'd better keep him in mind as we continue our explorations."

"Sir! I consider your action to be highly imprudent! I—"

"You're absolutely right." Phillip gave a crisp nod. "However, it's His Majesty's desire that we be patient with the natives. We mustn't expect too much from them until they've had an opportunity to learn our language and customs. Besides," he added with a shrug, "was it worth expending powder and shot to warn off such a sorry lot?" Phillip gripped his lieutenant governor's elbow. "I've seen quite enough of this place for the moment. Let us return to the boat and continue along the coast for a short while: who knows what things of real value we might not discover?"

Ross hesitated, then sheathed his sword and ordered his troops to take the rearguard while the three officers led the way downhill, followed at a safe distance by the triumphant Graybeard's war party. The gig's crew stopped yarning and began looking busy as the reconnaissance came back through the tree line. Phillip, Hunter and Ross were carried aboard. The two marines marched through the shallows and clambered over the side, sitting to attention while the oarsmen began stroking toward Cape Solander and what seemed to be another, more peaceable group of Indians, throwing fish from a canoe.

"Be careful not to swamp their craft," Phillip warned his coxswain. They beached a few yards away and, this time, there were no interfering elders to spoil the occasion as Phillip laid out more gifts on the ground.

"Boolah! Boolah!" The squares of calico, the hawk bells, the small mirrors were ripped from hand to hand, sniffed, tasted, chewed, felt, shaken. "Yari? Yari?"

Phillip smiled. "You see what I meant, gentlemen? There was no need for us to be severe with them."

Hunter said nothing. Ross was unlacing a shabby leather purse to take out a coin. He shoved it under the nearest Indian's nose. Then, to prove

that Phillip was not the only linguist, he said *"Voo! Wo ist le oro? Geld!"*
After a lifetime fighting alongside German allies while they killed
Frenchmen, Spaniards and Yankee rebels, Robert Ross was also a man of
the world.

The Indian snatched this ghostman's dull golden disc and peered into
it, hoping to see another funny face moving on the tiny yellow mirror,
but all he could find there was George III's pudgy profile, which refused
to make him laugh no matter how hard it was banged or twisted. The
Indian lost interest. The half-guinea plopped on the beach. Ross lunged,
trying to dodge scuffing black feet before the coin was lost forever. He
scrambled around on hands and knees, sifting the dirt with his fingers.
"Bloody hell!

7

BOTANY BAY was changing, was being changed. There would be no going
back to the friendly silences of yesterday for Graybeard, crouched among
his trees, watching as the smelly demons took away firewood and water,
or rowed messages between the transports and men o' war where ham-
mers banged and cobs slashed, driving more imps aloft with smoky pots
of tar to daub the cables, the ropes, the lines.

The luckier crewmen had been ordered to wade into the shallows and
drag seine nets for their officers' dinners. And then their petty officers'.
And then their own. Splashing like urchins in a London puddle, after
summer rain, they untangled strange fish from the mesh—a sort of sea
perch, a kind of flat ray, and something like a mullet.

Nor were the marines idle. Outlying guards had been posted, pacing
off their beats in the heat of the sun, unable to stop the occasional Indian
from strolling down to bring light relief to the other men toiling on the
beachhead. A bit of rag had been knotted to a length of fishing line as a
lure and left on the sand. Whenever an Indian bent to snatch it up, the
string was twitched and the savage generally lost his balance.

A platoon of troops was taking a break in the shade while they
munched their rations. A curious Indian had been tossed a pork bone as
his reward for standing still while the ghostmen draped him in a fatigue
uniform of blue and white striped shoddy. He was also laughing as they
fell around him, hooting at the ridiculous figure he cut in baggy smock
and breeches. The corporal then tried poking a dram of rum down the

young man's throat, but he stopped laughing and tried to spit out the fiery spirit.

New Holland was proving to be contrary in other ways, too. Sailors from the transports had been sent ashore with their sheath knives to cut fodder for the officers' sheep, the colony's cattle, the governor's horses. But what had seemed lush and inviting through a telescope was proving to be coarse and skimpy as the seamen turned farmer to bind up sheaves of greenstuff.

Not only were this land's grasses a sham, so were its trees and shrubs. None of them were the guavas and bananas and custard apples and bread-fruit which other ships' companies had harvested in the South Seas. But perhaps they would make useful timber, instead.

A saw pit was dug by six marines on punishment patrol while another pair of defaulters bounced dull axe blades off an ironbark. The two men cursed monotonously as they chipped a way through the trunk, then swore viciously as it toppled across the pit, splintering into flying sapwood and corky rot.

Sirius's boat rowed the governor ashore for his afternoon inspection. He returned the beachmaster's salute. "Everything in order, Mr. Tench?"

"Sir."

"Splendid. Keep up the good work. You too, Mr. Dawes," Phillip added, with another nod for a younger officer of marines.

He began his stroll, northward along the beach, away from the confusion of the watering point. It felt good to be alone again with his thoughts. Now, tonight's agenda—

"Captain Phillips!"

"Damn." Phillip halted and faced the scrub where the convoy's chaplain, Richard Johnson, was picnicking in the shade with his wife, Mary.

The civilian got to his feet, brushed crumbs off his lap and hurried down the beach. "Captain Phillips. May we have a few words?"

"Of course, Mr. Johnstone."

"Er, *Johnson*. No 't', if you please."

"Rather like Phillip without an 's'?"

"I suppose it must be, yes."

"It is," the older man agreed, pleasantly enough. "Now, what else may I do for you?"

The clergyman began frowning with concentration. "God's hand is manifest in the workings of our enterprise."

"Splendid, pray ask Him to keep up the good—"

"As witness of which, every one of our boats has arrived safely," the young cleric went on. "Therefore, it seems to me, we ought now to join together, soldiers and sailors alike, to render thanks unto the Almighty for His many blessings."

"Now?"

"Yes. We have arrived."

"I had noticed," Phillip agreed, drily. "Very well, put your proposal on paper and send it over to *Sirius*."

"But—?"

"Good day, Mr. Johnson. My compliments to your lady wife."

The chaplain watched the governor stride away, along the beach. He turned and paced back to where Mary waited in the shade.

"Well? What did he say?"

"It's not what he said, it's the way he said it," Johnson replied. "I am to make an official submission and send it to *Sirius*, for approval."

"But couldn't he have told you now?"

"Of course he could." The chaplain sat down and tugged at a stem of razor grass. He winced and began sucking his finger. "I think I should have another word with him, later."

"Yes, I think you should," his wife agreed. "It is quite evident to me that Captain Phillips is not showing the respect we might normally receive. I'm hardly surprised that Major Ross and other notables are in such disagreement with him."

"But I thought you favored our governor? Especially after he'd complimented you upon your zeal for matters horticultural at Rio de Janeiro—?"

"*That* was before he had us put out of our quarters so that a horse might be accommodated at the Cape of Good Hope!"

"Of course—" her husband was unlikely to forget—"but other officials were equally discomfited—"

"*You* are not just another official," Mary Johnson snapped. "I won't allow anyone to treat us as if we were of little account. You are absolutely right to insist upon a service of thanksgiving. Everyone must be seen to acknowledge God and your authority as a minister ordained—"

"I realize that," the chaplain interrupted. "However, I am equally aware of my anomalous position in the circumstances we now find ourselves. Remember, I am neither of the military faction nor the naval interest. Indeed, you and I are practically the only normal citizens. As such it will be wiser if we strive for impartiality, neither favoring Captain Phillip nor Major Ross in their squabbles, at least until we can see more clearly who is going to prevail here."

"But—!"

Richard Johnson began to frown again. "You will cease meddling in matters which do not directly concern us."

"They most certainly do concern us!" Mary might have vowed to love, honor and obey this man when her father gave her away early the previous year, but there are exceptions to every rule. "My dowry was not given so that we might live like gypsies, in a parish of murderers!"

Richard Johnson kept his eyes shut for several seconds. He opened them again. "Mary? You knew perfectly well that I had been called to tend a mission field, and that conditions were bound to be less comfortable than we were accustomed to in England—"

"But nobody told me it would be like this!" The young woman swung her fist at the empty sea, the occupied beach, the silent bush. "This place is so—is so hateful!"

Her husband reached out, gently bringing her hands together again. "My dear, nobody told anyone it would be like this. How could they? Hardly anybody has been here before us."

"B-but it's all so unfair!" Mary's wrists trembled in his grip. "You were a scholar! A gentleman! You could have asked Mr. Wilberforce to obtain a country living for us! We could have had our own orchard, and a garden, and neighbors. . . ."

Richard brushed her cheek before letting her chin rest on his finger. "And now we have none of those things, not even a rectory?" He shook his head and smiled at her. "Dearest, I realize it has not been easy for you aboard the ship, but now we're ashore again and it won't be long before things return to normal. I promise."

She sniffed, trying hard to smile back. "I—I'm sorry. But it is all so unfair. Captain Phillips treating you like that. He's probably envious because he never went to Cambridge."

"Neither has anyone else, but I sense no more than the usual polite indifference from our officers."

"That's why it's so unfair. Everything feels so wrong."

He held out his left hand for her to grasp as they got to their feet. "If it is any consolation, I imagine there are many others who secretly share our feelings about Botany Bay. Come. Let's continue searching for a place to build our home."

Mary Johnson fell into step with her husband. "I'm sorry." She looked down at the coarse yellow sand. "It's just that it's not what I expected. I shall try harder to like this place." She looked up again. "I promise."

The chaplain had slung his knapsack over one shoulder, the leather water bottle over the other; he was squeezing the leather strap into his cut finger to staunch the ooze of blood. "My dear, it's not this place we shall have to try harder to like, but most of its inhabitants."

Mary Johnson did not reply.

She had slowed to a stop and was shading her eyes against the sun. The governor was no longer hurrying along the beach. He had also stopped. He was speaking with someone. Someone female. Someone with rich, coppery braids. Someone with a confident tilt of the chin, even when being addressed by a member of the Quality.

"What is it?"

"The Brandon woman."

Richard Johnson shielded his eyes. "Where?"

His wife's face tightened. The governor appeared to be conversing with the convicted murderess who, since leaving Africa, had shared a straw bag with the chaplain's lady under *Alexander*'s chart table. "Mr. Phillips seems to prefer her company!"

Johnson glanced sideways. "I doubt that."

"You don't know her the way I do!"

"I should hope not." Johnson lowered his hand. "But no matter what she has done in the past, she is still a member of my congregation. If ever she chose to speak with me about something which troubled her—as, most likely, she is now doing with Captain Phillip—I do hope you would not think I preferred her company to yours?"

"Of course not."

The young couple resumed their walk to the spring where the duty officer, Tench, was dictating orders to his deputy. The two men glanced up from Dawes's field notebook as the civilians strolled closer. The only free English lady below the equator was bound to arouse interest, particularly as months of the same bugle calls, the same duties, the same punishments yawned into years of colonial service relieved only by cards, drink and gossip.

Tench made a *galant* heel click. "Your servant, ma'am."

She quickly tidied her hair and smiled back.

Richard Johnson made a curt nod. "Fine weather we're having, is it not?"

"It most certainly is," Tench agreed, saluting the husband as well.

The chaplain folded his arms. "I've been speaking with the governor. He's also of the opinion that we ought to have a service of thanksgiving, once I've given him the details. Look, when will it be convenient for you to assemble your soldiers?"

"That could be rather tricky at the moment," Tench replied. "God knows it's hard enough putting them back into their traces after idling for so long aboard ship. Allow them to stop work now and we'd have the devil's own job starting the wheels rolling again. What do you say, Dawes?"

"I think such a service would be an excellent idea, sir," the younger man replied. "The Lord has extended His protection over us since we left Home: it's our plain duty to return thanks for His blessings."

Tench noted Mary Johnson's reaction to this unexpected support for her husband's opinions. He glanced back at the engineer officer. "Of course, but you know how things are for us? Do this, do that, do everything else at the same time?" He took Dawes's notebook and flicked through its pages. "See what I mean? Nothing. Just Corporal Perkins's awkward squad and the defaulters. We can't spare anyone else."

Dawes peered over his company commander's shoulder. "What about Corporal Drury's sappers? It shouldn't have taken them this long to dig a latrine pit, surely?"

"I wouldn't bet on it," Tench replied. "They know I've got them bracketed to go aboard *Fishburn* for our tentage once they've finished bogging. As for the rest of our numbers—here and here—you'll need them to relieve the outlying pickets." He looked back at the puzzled clergyman. "How would a dozen do? Would that be enough for the right thing?"

"No, certainly not, everyone has to be present."

Tench pulled a long face. "Then there's not a hope in hell. Look, why don't you have a quiet word with the major? Explain the problem to him. He'll put it on the agenda for tonight's meeting and you'll get an answer *toot sweet.*"

"I'm not going."

Tench sensed rather than heard Mary's sniff. He smiled. "I don't blame you, padre. I'd have declined if I'd been given the chance. These meeting things just drag on, getting nowhere, you'll be better off in bed." Much better off.

"Yes."

"Speaking of which, have you pitched your tent yet?"

"We're still making our choice."

Tench smiled at Mary Johnson. "Then may I suggest you try over there, before too many others lay claims to it?" He pointed at a spot about ninety yards to the left of the spring, where the ground rose and the trees stood farther apart around a natural clearing. "It's quite well sheltered from the elements, and the view, particularly to the south, is almost like England," he added, still pointing. " 'The spacious firmament on high, with all the blue ethereal sky, and spangled heavens, a shining frame . . . .' "

Richard Johnson blinked. "Did you just compose that for your book?"

"Alas, no," Tench replied modestly. "Mr. Addison's genius far exceeds my humble talent with the pen."

"I'm sure that's not so, captain," Mary Johnson interrupted. "I anticipate with the keenest pleasure hearing more when you can spare us the time. Why, when you read your description of Teneriffe—at the Cape—it was as if I were seeing that island's quaint vistas for the very first time. . . ."

"You are too generous, ma'am."

"No, she's not," her husband contradicted. "You really do have the gift of words." Tench was also astute with words. He had contrived to sell an account of the voyage to New South Wales even before leaving London. Debrett, publisher to the peerage in Piccadilly, had paid handsomely for the privilege: another example of family connection favoring this dashing officer of marines, Johnson supposed.

He folded his arms tighter. "I have been asked to collect my sermons. Peabody & Chapman of Paternoster Row have indicated their interest in printing them once we return from the Antipodes."

Tench inclined his head. "Could they have done less? When a scholar of your standing chooses to garner the soul's harvest, his fame is assured, his laurels forever green. Indeed, if I may be so bold, it is I who look forward with anticipation to many future occasions when you will invite me to share your thoughts." Tench was feeling inside his pocket for the silver repeater which had measured his steady advance from an ensign's commission in the American colonies.

He thumbed the watch lid to read the time. "We'd better do visiting rounds now, Dawes, then I'll hand over and get myself ready for this evening's powwow." He faced the civilians and clicked his heels. "Your servant, sir. Your servant, ma'am. . . ."

Mary Johnson led her husband toward the small, secluded knoll about ninety yards to the left of the spring.

Tench glanced back at Dawes. " 'Know then thyself, presume not God to scan; the proper study of mankind is—'?" He cocked an eyebrow and pocketed the timepiece with a discreet flourish. "Woman."

Something which Phillip had been doing since pausing to observe one of the government's at her work with a laundry basket. "You there!" He aimed his walking cane. "What do they call you?"

She straightened, composed and erect. "Mrs. Katharine Brandon. How may I be of service to Your Excellency?"

Phillip was knocked aback. This item's speech was utterly unlike the guttersnipe yowl of his other female convicts, although it did have the hint of an accent which he could not quite place. He leaned on his cane. "What's the name of your vessel?"

"The barque *Alexander*, Captain Duncan Sinclair commanding."
Phillip frowned. "For what offense were you transported?"
"Murder."
Phillip stiffened. "Did you say 'Brandon'?"
"Yes." She smiled. "I'm that one."
"Good God!"

The governor remembered now. Fortunes had been made by London's pamphlet writers after this self-assured young actress killed Sir James Hardwicke during a lovers' tiff, in a playhouse, about two years ago. In a world of perfectly regulated justice she would have swung immediately after her crime of passion, but she did not.

Phillip also remembered that, when he and Mr. Secretary Ross met for the last time, George had been still furious at the Interest's meddling in *l'affaire* Brandon. Because, instead of stretching a rope, this brazen Irish beauty had lied, cheated and blackmailed her way off the gallows' cart in a bravura display of influence mongering.

The governor had removed his hat to wipe the sweatband. "So how do you find your new home?" He gestured at the wilderness.

"Quite interesting and warm," she replied with another lingering smile. "It suggests to me that, no matter how deep the snow in winter, it will never be as bitter as the Colonies. Such being the case, I'm confident we'll manage once the parts have been learned and we've rearranged the scenery to our satisfaction."

"I'm damn' glad someone thinks it possible." Phillip had forgotten which pocket held his handkerchief. He found the piece of solid cambric and mopped his hat. "So, what were you doing in the Americas?"

"I campaigned with General Burgoyne."

"I see." Phillip put away his handkerchief. "Well, I won't pretend that our situation in New Holland will always be to our taste, but I am also confident we shall succeed in due course." He replaced his hat. "Good day to you, ma'am."

8

KITTY BRANDON straightened from her curtsey and watched the governor resume his walk along the beach. The shadows were starting to lengthen, it was time to return home and supervise dinner. She took up her workbasket, gathered Sinclair's shirts off the bush where they'd been drying and walked back to catch *Alexander*'s boat.

The government women's leader was not halfway to the embarkation point when she noticed two government men dragging a dead branch into a comfortable spot of shelter. They had settled on their haunches and were arranging twigs in heavy-looking bundles when Kitty Brandon halted behind them. "Good afternoon, Mr. Cribb. Good afternoon, Mr. Thorpe. You're both very busy."

"Yes, ma'am." Cribb stood and faced her. "Bulldog's special orders: 'e wants lots of firewood."

"And I'm sure you're just the men to provide it—eventually." She hitched the workbasket on her hip and looked around at the other fatigue parties blundering about the beach. "With the exception of your two selves, I doubt if there's another who could tell me the difference between his arse and his nose. Did you ever see a more disgraceful muddle?"

"Only Yorktown."

She grimaced. "Then I'm glad my part in the production was paid up before they dropped the curtain on that last act."

"So'm I." Cribb shuffled his toes in the hot sand, hunting for the right words. "You was special, Over There." He bunched his fists as the compliment blurted out, awkwardly. "Bulldog's looking after you all right? You're all right? I mean, if there's anything you want done special, I'm the cove to fix it, right?"

Her green eyes crinkled at their corners. "Why, thank you kindly, Mr. Cribb. Indeed, now that you raise the matter there is one small thing which bothers me more than it ought. . . ."

"Right-o!"

"It's Mr. Levi."

"Uh? I'll bash 'is—!"

Her finger silenced him. "On the contrary, Mr. Levi and I remain on the most cordial terms. It is you and he who seem to be violently at odds and yet, until so recently, you were the closest of friends."

"I never said that!"

"No, I did." She was no longer smiling. "I trust that I am not mistaken in my opinion of your character. . . ."

Cribb shifted his weight to the other leg. "Leafy told me Bottommy was going to be all right with gold palaces and things. And I told the other blokes. And now they're blaming me. And I'm the mug who could've bolted, easy, back there in Rio, but Leafy kept saying Bottommy was going to be better." Cribb's arm swung. "So look at it! There's bugger all!"

"It would seem Mr. Levi was wrong," Kitty Brandon observed. "What difference does that make? Heavens, if we fell out with everyone who'd repeated a story, only to find later that it was false, we'd still be living up a tree like those poor creatures." She pointed as a sentry challenged some stray Indians: his musket thumped smoke, spraying bird shot at black ankles.

"But—!"

"But nothing. I expect to hear shortly that you and he have been reconciled and are in the state of harmony which you both pursued for so many difficult months aboard our ship."

"Not bloody likely, I won't!"

"You *dare* disagree with me?"

Cribb backed off. "Well, it's like this, 'im and me sort of—"

"Enough!" She raised her finger. "I simply refuse to believe that, if you extended the cordial right hand, you and he would not become as close as this again." The finger crossed with its neighbor. "Consider it well."

Alexander's second mate touched his hat brim to the captain's woman as she came down to the landing, then heaved out the load of firewood which had just been put aboard the gig, making room for her. Thorpe scratched himself and watched the boat pull away. He turned to look at Cribb again. "She's not wrong about you being in a regular shitty with Abe. And I reckon she's right. Abe's a good mate, Abe is."

Cribb itched to take out his anger on this stolid peasant, but Thorpe stood half as tall again as his leader and it would have been easier to punch over a brick wall. Besides, the plodding Saxon ox could explode with terrible rage when goaded too hard.

The smaller man unclenched his fists. He turned and strode off to find somewhere to be alone, but that was not easy with detachments of men from eleven ships chopping, sawing, digging, looking busy. Like a squad of marines from *Prince of Wales* who were finishing a latrine pit for their officers.

Cribb was about to swing away in another direction when the sappers' corporal looked up. Both men took second looks. Cribb slowed uncertainly. "That you, Ted Drury?"

"Shit."

"Strewth, it is! What the buggery are *you* doing 'ere?"

The redcoat corporal was also laughing. He advanced, stuck out his hand and gripped hard. "What a bleedin' turn up! I never reckoned I'd see a fly cove like you get lagged!"

"I'm just passing through," Cribb winked. He peered into the pit and then back at Drury. "Still at the same old game, eh? Still digging 'oles? I reckon that last one could've been a bit deeper. . . ."

"So could all of 'em, Over There."

"Blood oath."

The other troops had taken the chance to down tools and begin a quick smoke break. Cribb wrinkled his nose as the four men shared a pipe of West Indian *modongo*, the acrid baccy sold to soldiers at tuppence a stick. "Still stinks like rotten dog guts, Ted. You'd better chuck the lads some good stuff." The lag palmed a nugget of the lighter, officers' issue tobacco which was currency aboard *Alexander*, after dark. " 'Ere, why don't we join 'em for a puff? I've got plenty."

"You're on!" Drury checked that nobody in higher authority was nearby, then dropped out of sight with his guest. He crouched low and made himself comfortable. "Listen in, you lot," the corporal commanded, taking the pipe and shredding the quality tobacco with his clasp knife, "this 'ere ge'man is Sar'nt Major Cribb. One of us, Over There."

"Fucking 'ell. . . ."

"That's all right, son." Cribb winked at the youngest private. "Plenty of water's gone under London Bridge since Ted and me done a job together. These days the name's Joe." He stuck out a hand. They gripped, thumbs crossed.

Drury had loaded his pipe. He struck tinder and passed it by seniority. Cribb's cheeks puckered. The marine corporal scratched his chin and counted off the years. "That would've been when we done for Black Bess, wouldn't it?"

Cribb's eyes shut.

"Who's she, corp'?" the youngest private asked, scheming a way to stretch this work break by spinning yarns from a war which had ended before he took the king's shilling and enlisted.

"She was an it." Drury trickled smoke and passed the pipe to the next in line. "I'd reckon she was the biggest mortar gun them Frogs ever used on us."

" 'Ow big?" the youngster prompted.

"Big enough to chuck a bomb as big as a sack o' spuds, that's 'ow big," Drury replied, taking the bait. "You'd see the bastard things going up and up and up till they'd sort of 'ang there in the sky. Then they'd start coming down again, getting bigger and bigger and bigger and there was bugger all we could do about it."

"Except keep digging," Cribb added, eyelids squeezed tight, tensed for the silent crash.

"You're not wrong." Drury rolled a gob and spat along the trench. "Still, you and me fixed the bitch."

" 'Ow, corp'?"

Drury wedged his feet on the other side of the empty latrine. "Well, it all begun once the Rebels *really* started shelling us. . . ."

Cribb's eyelids squeezed tighter, trying to hold back memory.

The remnants of Britain's army in America were dug in around the small port of Yorktown, fighting to win time until the Royal Navy could bring up reinforcements. But the only warships now on Chesapeake Bay were bringing up more Frenchmen and munitions for the enemy. The ranger companies had eaten their horses and were now serving in the trenches as snipers, harassing General Washington's pioneers as they dug saps toward the British lines.

Cribb could still hear the relentless clink of picks and shovels between salvos from the American positions. Very soon the enemy's grenadiers would be crouching along the third parallel. The Royal Artillery's field pieces were no longer keeping them back. Every time a British battery opened fire, the French siege mortar belched flame, lofting another eighteen-inch bomb into Yorktown.

"Things wasn't looking too good," Drury said. "Then the boss—not Mr. Dawes, 'e'd already copped that one on the face—sent for yours truly. Big Brass 'ad ordered the sappers to spike the mortar gun, *toot sweet,* so guess who got the short straw." Drury studied his pipe bowl. "Still, lucky for us, this gent's blokes said they'd come out with us." He looked back at the silent lag.

Cribb was not listening.

Mist was crawling off the Atlantic.

Dawn was close. A whitewashed patch was daubed on the back of his ragged green jacket. His men were going to follow it, over the top, into the darkness. No muskets or pistols were going on this raid—in such weather they were bound to misfire—just Indian hatchets, and weighted sticks, and a sergeant's dirk with brass knuckles, for himself.

Frightened.

Face tilted. Waiting for the red flare to soar past as the whistle shrilled and he was first away, covering Drury's laden marines with their demolition charges, throwing ladders over the enemy's trenches, scrambling across, coshing, stabbing, hacking a track for the French gunpit. Hammering an iron spike into the mortar's touchhole. Tossing satchels of gunpowder through the bomb locker's door—!

"And that's 'ow we done it," Drury concluded quietly.

Nobody spoke.

The pipe made another round before Cribb could open his eyes again. "Been a bloody long time, Ted."

"My oath."

"Now we're on other sides. Funny."

Drury scowled. "What other sides?"

"You're a guard. A screw. A trap." Cribb flicked a second nugget of tobacco at the other veteran. "If I bolted, you'd 'ave to drop me cold."

"Sod off!"

"If only I could, mate, if only I could." Cribb straightened, resting his elbows on the rim of the hole for a moment before climbing out. "Still, thanks for the chinwag. Keep in touch."

9

"COME IN!" Phillip commanded, dipping his quill to end another day's journal entry.

Bryant peered around the door. "Er, begging leave, sir, but would you like us to get the doings ready? It's getting dark."

"So I observe." Phillip squinted at the page and ruled off. He sprinkled sand, then glanced up. "Well? What're you waiting for?"

"Aye aye. Sir."

Bryant held the door open and helped the other officers' steward drag the surgeon's table into the great cabin, six feet of oak board with leather straps which could be braced across the chart table if *Sirius*'s cockpit flooded in battle and the casualty station had to be shifted aloft. The stewards heaved the operating table over, clean side up, and laid for dinner. Bryant checked the wine bottles which had been cooling all day down the iron bores of the cabin guns, wrapped in felt cartridge bags, while the other servant fetched a second lantern.

"Will that be all, sir?"

"Until the gentlemen have assembled, yes."

Phillip stood by the stern windows, hands behind back, and looked over his anchorage. Other lights were blinking across the bay's lazy, subtropical swell, from the marines' watchfires set at exact intervals along the beachhead. A bugler was sounding the plangent, descending chords of "Sundown" and the quarter guard's drums were beating the routines of service around his battalion. He'd been right in his assessment of Ross. Now, if only the Indians would oblige—

He turned. "Come in, damn you! Oh, sorry, John."

"All officers have assembled and now await your further commands, sir."

"And how's you-know-who?"

"Rather like he's thrown away half a guinea," Hunter replied. "Notwithstanding which, he's put on his best bib and tucker to honor the occasion."

"I'm flattered."

"Perhaps it's a token of respect?"

"Perhaps." Phillip squeezed past the dinner table, stepping across to the narrow cupboard which would carry his pickled body back to England if he should die overseas and have asked not to be tipped over the side. He pulled open the coffin's vertical lid and shook out his blue frock coat with its two broad gold stripes of a commodore sewn around the collar. He crouched to get another look at his reflection in the stern windows. "How's that?"

"A credit to the service, sir."

Phillip checked that his queue ribbon was neatly tied on the nape of his neck and straightened his cravat. "You may lead them in now. And bestir Bryant."

"Aye aye, sir."

The officers of marines marched in step behind their battalion commander, turned as one man and stood to attention, hats under arms. Lieutenant King took up his position beside Hunter to represent the Royal Navy. The commodore acknowledged their bows. "Thank you, gentlemen. Let lack of formality be our rule this evening as we address ourselves to the present and future state of the colony."

Ross faced his staff, heel-toe-thump. "At ease!"

They unclipped their swords and handed them to the stewards. Phillip nodded at Bryant. "The glasses." He waited until the corks had been drawn from six bottles which stood in rope rings to stop them toppling over whenever *Sirius* snubbed her cables. "Claret, anyone? I can vouch for its pedigree," Phillip added, noting Tench's grimace at Collins. "Mr. Pitt was at especial pains to see that a few dozen were sent out to mark such occasions as these." He noted Collins's response to that and swirled the garnet red wine as the other officers were served. "I give you our first toast of the evening: His Majesty."

"God bless him."

"Aye!"

Phillip waited until Ross's company commanders had made themselves comfortable on the stools and ammunition trunks which were the cabin's only moveable furniture. "And now it is my very pleasant duty to congratulate you personally," he went on. "The fact that we have reached our destination intact, and on time, is cause for the greatest satisfaction. That we have done so at all is due to the manner in which sailor and soldier hauled together under your inspired leadership, major." Phillip raised his glass a second time.

"Of course, we have both been fortunate in the caliber of those chosen to serve with us in this, the empire's most challenging post of honor. That a man of your distinction and service should be here," Phillip raised his glass to Campbell's vacant tic, "is surely evidence of the regard with which His Majesty's government views our endeavor?"

The commodore smiled at the next officer in line. "And I well recall the conversation I enjoyed with your father, the General Collins, when we last met, at Court. It was also his opinion that the opportunities of the Sugar Islands would soon be eclipsed by those of the South Seas.

"And what more could anyone say about your achievements, Mr. Shea?" Phillip had to pause until the pale, sweaty face had finished coughing. "Your gallantry is too well known for any further comment from me. I can only add that, when the day comes for the French to combine with Indian allies here, I shall rest easy knowing that John Shea's company stands to arms.

"As indeed will be the case when your men go into action, Mr. Tench." Phillip raised his glass again. "Your conduct when *Triton* engaged superior numbers, and subsequently during your imprisonment by the Rebels, points to those qualities of valor and fortitude which must ensure your continued advancement in New South Wales."

The governor hesitated. "However, when all is said and done, our individual achievements are but the first few paces on a hard day's march. There will be obstacles. The Indians could be so classed, of course. Who knows what their kings are planning for our discomfort? And the French are another potential threat to our peace if they finally arrive to claim New Holland. But both are of less weight, at the moment, than that third unknown which must be kept constantly in mind. I refer, of course, to our cargoes. . . ."

There was a stir of interest and even Ross began paying attention as Phillip went on. "Incredible though it may seem, we know hardly anything about those items who've been sent to work for us. It is exasperating to think that such objects could've been brought halfway around the globe, at considerable public expense, only to find that their papers are still in some contractor's pigeonhole, but such is the case."

Phillip waited for Shea to finish using a bit of rag and slump against the coffin-cupboard to recover his breath. "Nobody can tell me why our laborers were convicted, for how long they are sentenced to penal servitude, and what skills—if any—they bring." He shook his head. "Clearly they will be confused when eventually we allow them ashore. We'll have to be patient until they've accustomed themselves to the novelty of these surroundings and have recovered their spirits which, I don't doubt, are low after the rigors of our journey. Happily for us, Nature has placed all mankind under the governance of two excellent schoolmasters, Dr. Pain and Dr. Pleasure. It will be for them to indicate the paths our laborers choose to tread and I can assure you that the stubborn will soon find themselves in the former's classroom!"

Tench sighed gently and shut his eyes as the older man developed this lecture. "However, for every 'stick' we must provide there must be a corresponding 'carrot' so that the more willing donkeys are encouraged to continue along the right path. For example, when my commission is proclaimed, I wish it to be marked by a half-day's respite for all and an extra measure of grog for the troops: kindly note that, Mr. Collins."

"Very good, sir."

"But as I was saying, long before we reach that point in our program we shall have had to cope with any amount of stupid misbehavior." The governor shrugged. "It'll be unavoidable. Few if any of our laborers can have strayed more than a street or two from the sties into which they were littered. Their experience of the wider world, such as we take for granted, will be nil. Therefore, in addition to everything else, we shall be expected to do their thinking as well. Such is the nature of the beast. They will try our tolerance but we shall have to persevere until they've learned their lesson, regardless of which schoolmaster birches them."

Phillip turned to his flag lieutenant. "Mr. King? Instruct the merchantmen to submit detailed lists of names and alleged skills before their cargoes are discharged into government service."

"Aye aye, sir."

"The shipmasters will also note on their manifests which items can be trusted and which are the natural troublemakers," Phillip continued. "I shall also require the names and descriptions of their informers with an account of what we owe them for services during our voyage: it is of the utmost importance that our networks of spies be kept intact and functioning as the settlement establishes itself." The governor frowned at his staff officers. "Never forget, like loose fire, mutiny is best stamped out before it can reach surrounding combustibles. . . ."

Phillip rested his knuckles on the table. "Stupid and unwilling our laborers most certainly are, but never underestimate their capacity for violence. If anyone should doubt that, cast your minds back a mere six or seven years to certain events in the capital." His fists clenched. "More than a few of Gordon's rioters must've been swept off the streets and carted out of the kingdom aboard our enterprise: if the rabble could burn all London to the ground, God alone knows what they'll be capable of here!"

There were murmurs of agreement as he went on. "Happily the

powers entrusted to me are sufficient and I shall have no hesitation in using them to the utmost severity of the law. Because we must be under no illusions, gentlemen, our cargoes are not only dirty and disaffected, they are also extremely dangerous. Popular opinion would have us believe that they've been sent away to contemplate their misbegotten lives and, perhaps, reform themselves. Nothing could be further from the truth. They've been sent here to work! And if any fail to grasp that simple rule of conduct let them tremble, for the rope and lash are but a pen's stroke away on my desk!"

"Bravo! That's the spirit!"

"Thank you, Mr. Campbell." Phillip checked his agenda and looked up again. "Those are the necessary first steps. Without organized labor we'll never be able to commence the systematic cultivation of foodstuffs or build the storehouse to safeguard them. Our commissary's supplies are finite—even without the usual spoilage, spillage and theft—so that of every hundred rations we land at least fifteen will be unfit for swine to eat.

"It's no exaggeration to say that, until our first harvest is under lock and key, we'll resemble a vessel whose leaks exceed her power to pump out water. Speaking of which, that spring may have been adequate for *Endeavour* but it'll never do for a permanent garrison of our size. I've also noted a lack of quarry stone for Mr. Dawes's sappers to build magazines, bastions and a deep-water jetty. Therefore I intend surveying that other anchorage sighted by Mr. Cook, then we can decide which offers the best choice of sites." There were surprised looks as the governor went on. "I'll only be away for a few days during which time my deputy can practice his duties: I've itemized his guidelines which we can discuss over dinner." Phillip was reaching for the bell cord. He gave it a sharp tug. Bryant popped his head around the cabin door. "You may serve now."

10

DINNER WAS about to be served aboard *Alexander* as the overhead trapdoor slammed, the padlock clacked shut, and the prisoners' buckets were unhooked from their ropes. The hold's aristocrats took their time sorting the biggest lumps of grub.

Cribb gave a contented burp and licked his wooden bowl clean. "Bene tucker."

Thorpe gnawed the ham bone he'd won in his ladle of skilly. Feeding was too serious for talking.

Earlier, as the shore workers were counted aboard, Cribb had palmed a twist of army tobacco into the cook's apron pocket: now there were also two spoons of slush—the tasty scum off the officers' boiled beef—to garnish the extra bread, captured in a quick run of hazard dice with a sentry while *Alexander*'s mate yarned to Sergeant Fitch.

Cribb began grating his own, premium quality tobacco with a rusty nail, then tipped the shreds into a small fold of paper—almost the last of his *Exhortations to Chastity,* an uplifting tract schemed from the convoy's chaplain, back in Cape Town—and rolled himself a slim smoke. He licked both ends, leaned over the pale candle flame, and eased back on the plank next to Thorpe's home shelf. "Bene day, too. . . ."

Light, bright, open spaces belonged to the free: night and shadow were a prisoner's private property. All around the foetid hold, busy as dung beetles, men were making trade, gambling, stealing, swindling, lying, punching, weeping, laughing. Life had returned to normal for the unfree and they were their own masters until the bugler warned them that tomorrow's sun was coming up.

Their sentry could be trusted. For the past quarter of an hour Marine Richard Asky's musket had been propped against the main ladder while he enjoyed the perks of obedience—a woman, from the smaller cage forward of the main hold—giggling among the tiers of casked stores.

Cribb's face glowed as he sucked smoke. "Dirty Dick's making a regular feast tonight."

"Lucky sod. I wouldn't mind another go at some muffin and jam," Thorpe mumbled round his bone. "I reckon that'd be just right after a good feed."

"Depends who's buttering it," Cribb cautioned the younger man, fair-mindedly.

"Well, my dad reckoned all cats are black in the dark, and I—"

"So's dogs. They're not much in my line, either."

"And I—"

"I mean, the likes of 'er is all right for the likes of Dick Asky," Cribb went on, "because the army don't give a cove much chance to get better. But once 'e's free to pick and choose, 'e ought to be more choosy."

"And I reckon—!"

"Because there's more to living than stuffing your guts or wiping your whisker splitter up some mort's skirt," Cribb cautioned, sensibly. "Stands to reason, if you're going to make something of yourself, you've got to 'ave style, you've got to be picky and know what you want, or else you won't get it. Now, take me for instance—"

"Hn!"

"All right, don't. Take 'er ladyship then. You seen the way she chatted with Sparrow Legs today?" Cribb asked. "Chin up, back like a ramrod, eye to eye?" The lag clicked his tongue with admiration. "That was always 'er style, Over There. She 'ad generals, and colonels, and sirs, and suchlike, twisting round 'er little finger. . . ."

"Still 'as," Thorpe grumbled. "Bulldog's a lucky bugger."

"O' course! She's got style. That's why we get on so good," Cribb replied. The smoke glowed inside his cupped hand, then faded again. "And I reckon we're going to do even better in Chinaland. . . ."

"Ur?"

"You're coming too," Cribb was quick to add.

But Thorpe was not so quickly reassured. "Um. Where's Chinaland?"

"Don't you ever listen?" Cribb controlled his impatience. "It's just up the road, we'll be there in two ticks once I've got the trotters fixed."

"Trotters? I not seen no 'orse in years and years!"

"That don't mean you won't be seeing one soon, though." The older, more experienced man was accustomed to his friend's slower wits in matters of importance. "While you was 'elping Buggerlugs shift that other barrel of water, I 'ad a chinwag with some blokes cutting fodder for something. And they told me there's 'orses out there on the other boats. I mean, it stands to reason, there's got to be dragoons or rangers to scout the Frogs while our lobsters get dug in," Cribb went on, patiently trying to educate Thorpe in the ways of a world far beyond East Anglian beet fields and rows of turnips. "So, soon as them prancers 'ave been got ashore, I'm snaffling 'alf a dozen. Then me and 'er ladyship, and you, can leather them for Chinaland and 'Ome. . . ."

Thorpe was deeply troubled. "Um? Joe? I'm not sure if—"

"Shut up." Cribb was in no humor for gloomy warnings, not when he could already hear the brisk clatter of hooves and feel the wind in his face. "Stop being such a worry guts. You just leave everything to me."

11

"AND YOU can strike that fal-lal, Mr. Bradley!" Ross pointed at the commodore's pennant snapping in the early morning breeze.

The officer of the watch looked uncomfortable.

"Strike it!"

"Sir."

Ross continued pacing *Sirius*'s quarterdeck, listening to the halliard blocks' squeal and chatter as they lowered Phillip's pride. He halted, planting both fists on the starboard rail, watching a pair of gaff-rigged cutters beating out to sea under a streaky red sky. Now he was the acting governor of New South Wales and about half the adjacent Pacific Ocean: it felt good, very good, and the weatherglass was unsettled. Within the next few hours a squall would probably overset Phillip's open boat and only the sharks would know or care what happened next.

"Mr. Bradley!"

"Sir?"

"Sway out the gig! Full honors!"

The port watch assembled on deck to repeat the ceremonial which had just despatched Phillip. Ross didn't care, he knew his dues, and he took his time going over the side.

Hunter watched through the stern windows, finishing a breakfast of cold fish pie as *Sirius*'s gig pulled away. He licked his fingers and climbed the companion ladder to the deck house. "Good morning, Mr. Bradley."

"Good morning, sir."

"I notice our pennant has been struck."

"Er, yes. Mr. Ross's orders."

"Quite proper. Our acting governor must be alert to such points of etiquette. By so doing he frees the rest of us to potter along with the day's business."

"Sir?"

Hunter wiped the eyepiece of his telescope. "My compliments to the master gunner: exercise all crews and cartridge handlers." The flagship's commander focused the glass around a short line of redcoats on the beach as Ross began his tour of inspection. "We can never be too prudent. One never knows when one might not have to heat iron for the Indians. Or the French. Or whatnot."

"Aye aye, sir!"

Ross was also concerned about camp security. His subaltern of the guard was getting a lecture on the need to stay alert against surprise attack from the Indians.

"There don't seem to be so many hanging around, sir."

"Then all the more reason to prepare for trouble, Mr. Dawes! They're sneaks. Only yesterday forenoon they stole a guinea from me, in broad daylight!"

"Sir."

"Dismiss." Ross continued marching up the beach to the nearest bivouac fire. Ten blanket rolls and knapsacks had been laid out, nine men and one boy motionless behind them. Ross returned the corporal's salute and inspected the kits, especially the tenth. He looked at the young face above it. "You stood your full turn of guard duty?"

The lad stared dead ahead. "Sir!"

"And the orderly officer read out that the penalty for falling asleep, while a sentinel, is execution by firing squad?"

"Sir!"

"Take leave of Corporal McPhee: it's time to continue your lessons."

The gentleman volunteer obeyed with skill and precision: pigtail greased and floured, scarlet tunic and breeches cut down from a much larger, much older uniform. John Ross was a credit to his father. Another year's campaign service and he'd be eligible for an ensign's commission.

Some might have thought the boy a trifle young to be shouldering the duties as well as the epaulettes of an officer at twelve years of age, but his battalion commander knew better: the sooner he started, the sooner he could draw pay and win seniority. Meanwhile he could mark time as an *aide de camp* to the future governor while adding another few inches of height. Then, once his father returned Home from the conquest of New Holland, the young veteran would be ripe for further preferment. And a suitable marriage.

Robert Ross clipped the boy with his rattan. "Shoulders back, stomach in, head up! Never forget who you are, what you are, where you are!"

"Sir!"

The major was a model drill instructor: heels crunching, fist punching back, front, back, sword gripped at his side, shaming the navy's men as they loped around the beach, half-naked, humping loads of wood and water. "What a shambles! But while you-know-who's laying down the law we'll not get any better!"

The young lad was not expected to comment. These lonely monologues were an essential part of his training in the profession of arms.

Ross had shaded his eyes, was looking out to see beyond Cape Banks. "This weather could turn. When it does, our luck turns with it." He almost smiled at the serious little face strutting beside him. "It would've done your heart good if you'd been at the conference last night. I didn't beat about the bush. I told you-know-who to his face that we'd been ordered to occupy Botany Bay, not some other flyspeck on the map. But does our fine English gentleman ever listen to advice? Not him! He's still determined to chase moonbeams up the coast because 'this location does not entirely suit my needs.' No discipline. None. Never had any. But he's supposed to be a king's officer. Hn! Can you imagine what his precious navy would be like without us to give it some backbone?"

John Ross could. During his four years of service with the colors he had seen that His Majesty's men o' war were, almost without exception, floating jails crammed with resentful, rebellious inmates. Recruited by hunger or the press gang, allowed fourpence a day in worthless paymasters' receipts, Jack Tar detested Tommy Lobsterback even more than he despised the Frogs. Frenchmen were usually a distant danger on his horizons, but the volunteer redcoats were a permanent wall around him, guarding a ship's strong points, protecting her officers against their crews. Without the threat of the bosun's lash and the promise of a royal marine firing squad, it was doubtful if one unit in ten of the Royal Navy would ever put to sea.

"Pipsqueak old woman," Ross continued with gloomy relish. " 'Commodore'? That's like calling him a brigadier general. Not that I'd exchange my rank for his because to be an officer in the corps is to follow the highest possible calling."

"Sir."

"And never forget, we look after our own. That's why Mr. Campbell's still on the strength," Ross said, halting to watch his senior subordinate taking over from C Company. "Poor old devil. Should've been put out to graze years ago. But what he'd get for his commission wouldn't keep body and soul together more than a twelvemonth. And being wounded in the head like that isn't going to make him a welcome poor relation at another's dining table." The battalion commander hesitated. "At least, the way things are, I can keep an eye on him. Come."

For the next twenty-four hours Campbell's men would be protecting their officers against Indians, sailors and prowling lags. But their duties were not being made any easier by the fact that it was midsummer in New Holland but midwinter north of the equator, in Britain, where regulations stated that greatcoats, gloves and mufflers should be worn until the first day of May. Buttoned tight, muskets shouldered, Campbell's troops could have been guarding the snowy ramparts of Quebec.

"Good morning, Jimmy."

"Sah!"

"I've just been telling the boy a few things about our work. He's shaping up, but one of the hardest lessons to drum into anyone's head is to know when enough's enough," Ross added as his comrade fell into step. "Regulations must be obeyed or else we'd be no better than that heap of dung," he pointed at a work gang of government men, foul and hairy. "However, never forget that such rules are as much for our guidance as others' obedience."

"Aye?"

"Aye, so you'd better get those bloody coats stowed away."

"But it's January!"

"And hot." Ross halted and, almost gently, loosened Campbell's garrison cloak. "There. Better?"

The troops certainly felt better as they resumed their duties, stripped down to red serge tunics, thick gray flannel breeches and black spatterdash gaiters, white crossbelts laden with twenty rounds of ball cartridge, an eighteen-inch bayonet and a short slasher for close combat.

"I've also been telling the boy about last night," Ross went on, continuing his tour of inspection. "It beats me where London could've dredged up such a nincompoop as you-know-who. You saw him buttering Collins and Tench? Wheedling himself into old Collins's good books back Home, I wouldn't wonder. You knew Arthur was a major general now? But even as an ensign he knew how to better himself. Married the right sort. But it's an ill wind that blows no good. Our spindle-shanked Sparrow Legs has yet to realize that his precious judge advocate is half Frazer!"

Campbell's vacant stare cleared for a moment. "Not Frazer o' Aird?"

"By a collateral line, I'm told. Kindred of the fourth degree to the Master o' Lovat, no less." Ross felt like a cat at the pantry cream jug. "Although his mother's people now hold a tidy estate over in Ireland, they're our sort of people, you may be sure. Mark my words, once we're forced to do you-know-what, our senior legal officer will know where his loyalties lie—"

"Aye!" Campbell laughed, shaking his head.

"And in due course I'll be able to say as much about the other one he hobnobs with, young Tench," Ross went on. "There's good land in the family, I'm told. Which only leaves us with the big Bog Hopper to pull into line and we'll have done the trick."

"Shea's the one!"

"True, not that he counts for aught," Ross cautioned. "Couldn't stand the war. No connections worth a damn, either. But he won't last, then we'll be free to auction his place." The battalion commander's boots crunched across wet shell grit and seaweed. "You knew, of course, that M'Lord Pitsligo is kin to young Kellow's mother? She's a Forbes, from Aberdeen. Her money bought our paymastership. I consider a quick captaincy to be quite in order, don't you?"

But Campbell's attention had wandered again. Then he suddenly jabbed his friend in the ribs and pointed at some Indians who were sauntering down to their beach, ignoring the sentries as the sun and temperature rose. Graybeard saw a plump mullet steaming inside a camp kettle. He reached for it and—

"Bloody hell! The loons don't even know boiling water." Ross shook his head as the elder bounded away on one leg, flapping the scalded fingers. "I can see we're going to have to smarten them up before recruiting labor for the plantations."

"Aye?"

"Aye. Now, where's young Tench hiding himself?" The major of marines glared around his beach. "Got his nose stuck in some book where he hopes we won't find him, I'll wager!"

12

ROSS WOULD have lost that bet. The battalion's junior captain was, in fact, taking his ease on a grassy knoll some distance from the spring while he dictated last night's events for Dawes to copy into their report book. "The quarter guard's tent was clean and in good repair. Each relief, both going on and coming off sentry, was duly inspected and found fit, alert at his post and acquainted with his orders. I therefore have the honor to remain, sir, your most obedient servant, Watkin Tench, Captain."

He stifled a yawn and leaned back in the shade. "Thank God that's over. You know, Dawes, time was when the only paper a soldier needed was that which wrapped our cartridges. Now, I swear we need the damned stuff to ask permission every time we wish to blow our noses. 'If all the world were paper, and all the seas were ink, and all the trees were bread and cheese, what would Ross do for drink?' "

Dawes glanced up from his notebook. "Shall I add that postscript?"

"Don't tempt me! I doubt if our beloved major would be in any shape to appreciate a joke." Tench clicked his tongue. "You should've seen him at last night's confab', like Jack Horner in a corner, hardly said a thing all evening except 'bloody hell!' It's a mercy for the rest of us that we're not promoted upon our speed when uncorking bottles or else Reckless Robert would now be the corps' commandant general and we'd be suffering for it."

"Poor old devil."

Tench arched an eyebrow and pulled a stem of grass to nibble. "Poor? Of course. Old? Naturally. Devil? Yes. But a poor old devil in the usual sense of the phrase? Never."

Dawes was shaking his head. "You're wrong. If only for simple Christian charity one must strive to be merciful and tolerant."

"I beg your pardon?"

"We must pity any fellow human who has never understood that his own worst rival resides within himself," Dawes continued, putting away his pencil and shutting the report book. "In my opinion, Tench, if only our commander had learned to moderate his behavior, he might've won those honors he craves. But, as it is, the years have not been kind to him and we ought to make allowance for the fact."

"You're miles off target!" his friend laughed. "The only allowance he needs is the same as any other man: five hundred pounds per annum and five hundred acres freehold to spend them upon. Allow me that much before I die and I'll not envy a king in his castle. Still, better luck next time." Tench shut his eyes and relaxed against the nearest tree trunk. "I almost bagged two thousand a year, in Jamaica, then the confounded girl got yellow fever a week before dearest papa was due to transfer the dowry. I still miss her, though, it was such a pretty little property."

Dawes was frowning. "But have you not considered God might've had some other purpose? It's possible, you know. I've often felt His guiding hand, especially in moments of loss," he added, unconsciously rubbing a crust of scar tissue where the shell splinter had ripped open his left cheek from nose to ear. "We should not be resentful, but welcome them, as marks of Grace."

Tench opened one eye. "And I'll lay half a crown you're about to tell me it's the Almighty's plan we should be suffering loss upon this Antipodean abomination of desolation. Yes?"

"Yes."

"Keep the money. Pop it in the poor box next time you're passing a church."

Dawes was not offended with the other man: theirs was an attraction of opposites. "I should in any case. But speaking of the previous matter, yes, I think I do feel a certain call to be here in the South Seas."

" 'Call'? Why . . . ?"

The young engineer officer chose his words with care. "The Pacific is so vast. There must be many lands with pagan peoples awaiting the Gospel's light. Perhaps I shall be permitted to become their friend and teacher?"

"*Teacher?*" Tench sat up straight. "My dear comrade, I do hope this sun hasn't addled your brains so early in our stay. Be careful, this is no longer fair England where 'in somer seson, softe is the sonne.' " He smiled. "But seriously now, nobody in his right mind could want to be a chalkstick when, by judicious use of rank, he might win a choice parcel of land . . . ?"

"I might." Dawes riffled the notebook's pages. "I might be of more service as a pedagogue than I am as a soldier." He glanced up. "It must be so if it gives me more happiness to hear one classroom of infants chanting their catechism than it would to see all the parade grounds on earth, filled with grown men, obeying my commands." The book snapped shut. "Peace has her victories no less than war."

Tench smiled with gentle bewilderment. "Look, I know there's a new spirit of evangelical whatsisname, and that some of us are evidently catching it, but I do hope you'll learn to moderate such novel opinions whenever Bellicose Bob is within earshot. Speaking for myself, and strictly *entre nous,* I heard quite enough of my father's efforts to thrash knowledge into the breech end of pupils who were incapable of absorbing it through the normal organs of sight and hearing. . . ."

Dawes blinked. "I thought your father was a—?"

"Squire of middling property?" Tench concluded with a slight grimace. "Well, I suppose that's the impression I've allowed some to cultivate, without straying too far across the border of truth. However, the sober fact of the matter is that I was born and bred above just such a schoolroom as the one you've so fondly described: I know the din chastised—as well as catechized—infants can raise. Believe me, the humble village flaybum's world is rarely one where 'gladly wolde he lerne, and gladly teche.' "

"But—"

"Please, allow me to finish," Tench insisted with a smile. "Had not Sir Wynne Williams been a sort of uncle, on my mother's side of the family, I'd now almost certainly be downstairs trying to teach ungrateful little imps how to reckon up to twenty without using their toes, how to sign their beastly names without blotting every second letter, and how to conduct themselves like gentlemen without tripping flat on their snotty little noses." Tench parodied a *galant* bow from the waist. "Believe me, given the choice between such a drudge of an existence, or enjoying the life we'll soon be shaping for ourselves in this colony, I know which one I'd seize with both hands."

Dawes went back to riffling his notebook's pages. "So you think there really could be gold here?"

"Why not?" Tench stood upright to brush his breeches and clip the sword scabbard to his belt. "The streets of New Spain were said to be paved with the stuff for the dons, why not New Holland's for us? Restless Ross is determined that a host of gilded 'Inkers' await our pleasure, so, like it or not, I expect we'll soon be building a road through the forests of El Dorado. At the end of such a journey I'd say there had better be gold!"

Tench scratched his shaven scalp and replaced the gray wig, using a mirror glued inside the crown of his hat to give a rakish tilt over one eye. Satisfied with the effect, he turned, wishing it were as easy to adjust to this brooding landscape of sun and shadow, so unlike the dappled mists of an English wood—

"*Djirabali!*"

"Good God!"

"*Baribun maninadji nai! Garindji wingala nai!*"

Tench's sword was at the high guard, his right foot planted forward, left wrist balancing for the counterthrust.

Graybeard stood with four other elders on the edge of the hillock, one hand dangling, the other gripping his sheaf of spears. Very, very slowly he raised the scalded fingers to point what seemed to be an old bone or stick. "*Djnumbala. Daringadu.*"

Dawes recovered first. Hat under arm, he walked across the clearing and bowed. "Good morning. My name is William." He tapped his own chest. "Wil-liam." Then he pointed at the skeletal pattern of yellow and white ochre stripes between the Indian's chin and groin. "What is your name?"

"*Garindji wingala nai!*"

Dawes nodded. "Please excuse my ignorance but I do not yet understand your tongue. However, I shall try and learn it. Meanwhile, here is a lesson in English: My name is William." He tapped his red tunic again. "William."

The bone quivered. "*Djnumbala! Daringadu!*"

Tench leaned on his unsheathed sword. He coughed politely. "Mr. Schoolmaster, sir? Far be it from me to interrupt anyone's first lesson in English, but perhaps he's telling us that his name is Ringadoo?"

Dawes considered the suggestion. He smiled again at the native. "*Numb balar, Ringadoo?*"

"*Wujun!*" Graybeard shook his bone and glared at the two ghostmen. The four elders were getting restive in the shadows behind him. He stamped his feet. "*Daringadu-u-u!*"

"Thank you. And my name is William. I trust that we'll have further opportunities to speak with each other."

Tench sheathed his sword as the five Indians turned to stalk away, Graybeard bringing up the rear. "And thank you, 'Wil-liam,' that should make an entertaining paragraph once I've smoothed off the corners. Speaking of which, I'd suggest we get back to lines before Reproachful Robert serves us with the rough edge of his tongue."

But, for once, Tench had misjudged his commanding officer. Ross was continuing his son's education, exhorting him to grasp every chance which fortune might throw their way as two other officers—Collins and Kellow—strolled closer, conversing with a third man.

"Ah, Mr. Collins! There you are." Ross folded his arms. "I was only speaking about your gallant father not five minutes ago. I have always regarded his personal favor with considerable gratitude. A sound man. We served together at Louisburg, you know?"

"Yes. I know."

"And now his son's my judge advocate general." Ross beamed. "You are to be commended, young man. Not even old Arthur had been made a 'general' at your age, though he was ever a sound 'judge' of men and a fearless 'advocate' of discipline. Continue to follow his lead and you'll not go far wrong under my command."

"Thank you. Sir."

Ross's sunny mood extended to the other officer. "And how are we today, Mr. Kellow?"

"In fine fettle, sir," the battalion paymaster replied with a brisk heel click. "May I have the pleasure of presenting Mr. Charles Nash?"

"Delighted, I'm sure!" Ross hastened to accept the hand which the third man was offering him. "This is indeed an unexpected honor!"

That was not strictly true. With less than fourteen hundred persons in the colony, free and lagged, sailors and marines, it would not have been much longer before the lieutenant governor met the one man who had enjoyed a style of living which penniless officers could only dream about. And yet here he was, strolling along the beach at Botany Bay as if it were Pall Mall or St. James in London.

"Buck" Nash could have been dead.

The laws which hanged five-shilling thieves also applied to the abductors of heiresses. However, the delicate question of *ravissement de garde* was raised before the case came to trial and the girl's uncle was made to see that an admission of carnal knowledge—before a jury of twelve good men and true—would have made her "used goods" on the highly competitive London marriage market. The capital charge had been dropped. Instead, a plea of *nolle prosequi* had been entered in exchange for a pledge of silence and four years' banishment under a writ of *exsilium est patriae privatio*.

Charles Nash had conducted his own defense, brilliantly.

"I trust Lieutenant Kellow's attending to you, sir?" Ross enquired.

"I could not be in better company," Nash replied with a charming smile.

"I'm delighted to hear it." Ross bobbed his chin. "Now, don't forget, if there's anything we can do to be of service, don't be backward in coming forward, as they say!"

"You can depend upon that, major," Nash chuckled, sharing his good humor with the other officers. "However, I see that you are very busy, I must not be allowed to detain you any further. Your servant, sir."

Ross nudged his son as the three younger men resumed their walk. "That's the way they do it," he whispered. "That's the way the Quality get ahead."

John Ross was not the only one being nagged this morning. Richard Johnson had taken a late breakfast in the shade of some bushes overlooking the bay. The colony's chaplain was now jotting notes in the margin of a book while his wife jiggled her watercolor brush around an enamel mug, waiting for the solid blue sea to dry on her sketchpad.

A gang of government laborers shuffled across the foreground. One of the shabby, nondescript items slowed, peering back at the civilian couple.

Mary looked at her husband. "Richard? I do trust, when you are appointed a justice of the peace, that you will never allow false sentiment to cloud your judgment of what is right."

"Mm." Johnson underscored a sentence.

"The lower orders appear to be more numerous than upon the boat," she continued, picking through her paint box to find a matching green for Botany Bay's sparse vegetation. "They go everywhere. Without restraint."

"Mm?"

Mary Johnson steadied her hand to color one of the spindly local trees, turning it into a robust English oak as she improved its appearance on paper. "It is plain to me that the proper divisions between class and class will have to be clearly defined from the very outset. Or else they'll get above themselves. They could even become insubordinate. It would be like the time they burned—they burned Papa's shop." The young woman's voice tended to rise sharply whenever her throat tightened.

Her husband had put his pencil aside. "My dear, you're quite safe. I'm quite sure Major Ross has everything under control."

She tried returning his smile. "Of course. I'm sorry. But so many of the convict class have been allowed to take liberties. They'll have to be curbed again, once ashore, among us."

One convict in particular would have to be put in her place: the concubine who ruled *Alexander* from the main cabin where she cohabited with the ship's master, Duncan Sinclair.

Mary Johnson was trying hard to put her own confused emotions in their place, as well. But it was not easy. The chaplain's lady had not taken kindly to the slightly older woman's air of inborn strength and authority. Even at the worst moments of their transit from Africa, when the barque was running before an icy gale under bare poles, the convicted murderess had continued to display complete contempt for risk and danger and the rules of conduct. Indeed, "Mrs." Brandon had made no secret of her pleasure whenever she went on deck, wrapped in one of the captain's cloaks. And never once had an officer rebuked her impudence. If anything, they had become even more servile and obsequious.

The bright green had dried on Mary Johnson's brush. She ignored it. "Richard? Have you spoken to anyone else about the service of thanksgiving?"

"No. Not yet."

"I really think you ought. I think it should be done without further delay. It would not only establish our standing in society but would also be an opportunity to proclaim the benefits of due subordination to God's command. Unless that's done, it will become increasingly difficult to maintain the correct divisions between master and man."

"Hm."

"You will try, won't you?"

Richard Johnson nodded. "Yes. Of course. I have been giving the matter some thought." He was tapping his pencil end over end on the open book. "It occurs to me that our acting governor might approve that which Captain Phillip is somewhat reluctant to grant—"

"You think so?"

"We're about to find out." Her husband had stood. "Major! Major Ross!"

"Bloody hell."

The colony's first gold hunt halted. Six men with shovels, and another pair with a sieve, were about to embark for Cape Solander where they would dig sand until sundown or until the lost half-guinea had been restored to its rightful owner.

The chaplain joined them. "May I have a few words with you, major?"

Ross considered the request. "Be quick."

Johnson frowned with concentration. "God's hand is manifest in our enterprise, as witness of which every one of our boats has arrived safely. It seems to me that we now ought to join together, soldiers and sailors alike, to render thanksgiving to the Almighty for His many blessings."

"Now?"

"Yes, now."

"I don't suppose you've already asked a certain other person . . . ?"

"Actually, I have. The question was raised with Captain Phillip."

"Who turned you down flat."

"Certainly not. It is pending a written, formal request. However, that would be unnecessary when a single word—from you—could achieve the same result."

His first day of governorship was coming laden with gifts for Ross. And yet, despite this further opportunity to undermine his rival, Ross was a man of strong moral convictions. He remained a staunch son of the Reform Kirk with no time for English mummery and High Church clergy. "No."

Johnson stood his ground. "I think you should reconsider that, major."

"Reconsider, eh . . . ?"

The chaplain hesitated. He looked along the beach where claws of surf were reaching up, stroking the golden sand. "Captain Phillip believes this is a second Garden of Eden. I can only agree with him insofar as Satan's power is as evident here as it was in the first."

"Oh, aye?"

Johnson looked back. "I've seen what we have aboard *Alexander*. Our colonists seem to revel in their depravity and lewdness. It is my profound hope that a service of thanksgiving, conducted properly, will awaken at least some to their moral peril."

"How?"

"Surely that's obvious?" the chaplain replied. "Due subordination to God's command is the very weft and woof of an ordered and orderly population. Without the strands of faith to bind together our endeavors, the whole cloth of society will be torn asunder, with no one sure who is man and who is master." The chaplain's frown hardened. "I tell you plainly, without the Gospel's discipline to curb their baser impulses, our lowest class will soon be beyond restraint." He shrugged. "If that were ever to happen, the consequences would be incalculable."

Ross could not fault this opinion of his convoy's living cargo and appeals to tighter discipline were always bound to strike a sympathetic chord. "Very well. Permission granted. Parade them next Lord's Day. Take Romans, chapter thirteen, verse two for your text. 'Whosoever therefore resisteth the power, resisteth the ordinance of God: and they that resist shall receive to themselves damnation.' "

"But—"

"Dismiss." Ross turned, sword gripped, heels together. "Squad! By the left! Qui-i-ick march!"

13

"WELL, HELLO, Kate. No bouquets, please!"

Kitty Brandon straightened. She turned, a knife in one fist, an assortment of plants in the other. "Well. Hello, Charley."

Nash had shaken off his two hangers-on and was now free to seek his own company. "I was wondering when we'd meet again. A small world, is it not?" He smiled. "Me. You. And all that," he grimaced at the wilderness.

"I'd hardly say it was small," she replied. "More likely a world brimming with surprises: yesterday the barnyard rooster, today a feather duster."

"So, if the bouquet's not for me, who is the lucky fellow, Kate?"

"A friend. He can't yet come ashore to look for his own herbs and simples."

"A friend?" Nash sighed quietly. "But then you always were lucky, I suppose. Just look how you wriggled out of that Hardwicke business. A lesser woman would've landed in the cart, no doubt at all. But, with friends, we were able to pull the right strings for you."

" 'We'?"

Nash was puzzled by her response. "Surely you don't think that Dicky Sheridan and that old fumbler, Burgoyne, managed it all by themselves?"

"Of course not," she replied. "The Interest looks after its own. But I'd say that the two honorable gentlemen you've just named did have a keen personal interest in my continued health—if not happiness."

"So whom do you think they consulted?" Nash asked. "It was a foregone conclusion they'd eventually have to come to me for a few pointers which, of course, I freely gave—"

"How provident." Kitty Brandon was also smiling. "A full dress rehearsal for your own dazzling performance, in court, when there was every hope you'd be necked for stealing an heiress."

"Touché!"

"So I'd say we're quits, wouldn't you, Charley?"

The gentleman was not paying attention. He had taken the woman's knife and was trimming a small nosegay of blue flowers from a nearby shrub.

Charles Foveaux Nash had suffered three sharp setbacks in as many years. The first had been after his guardian had left him almost two hundred thousand pounds in East India Stock, freeing him of any further need to drudge at the law. The second blow struck when he left the Inner Temple, moving westward to be nearer Carlton House, where he blazed through every penny in eleven glorious months with the prince of Wales. The third misfortune nearly leveled him after his elopement with the Earl of Denbigh's niece in the mistaken belief that her wealth would become her husband's.

A man as skilled in the law should have been more wary. Miss Elizabeth Beaumont only had the use of eight thousand pounds a year from a contingent legacy. It was an imperfect usufruct which her uncle's

displeasure immediately canceled. At which point the vengeful young
lady claimed abduction, a squalid scene ensued, and Buck Nash was lucky
to leave England with his neck intact.

He straightened, tucking the flowers in a buttonhole of his linen shirt.
"There."

Kitty Brandon retrieved her knife. "You always were more concerned
with the appearance of things."

"Of course, one might as well be out of the world as out of the
fashion."

The convicted woman surveyed Botany Bay for several moments, then
looked back at the confident, affable Nash. "I'd say we've lost on both
counts."

"Only for a brief while, then it's Home again."

She shook her head. "I got Life, which is one hell of an improvement
on the alternative, but it's still a devilish long way to travel just to make
a new home."

"It need not be," Nash replied. "Like yourself, Kate, I'd rather be
savoring the many pleasures of Covent Garden than enduring our officers' eager attention. However, when I depart upon the next convoy,
why shouldn't you be found a snug corner in my luggage . . . ?"

Kitty Brandon returned smile for smile. "That's uncommon civil of
you. Why, I've often been called a baggage, but this has to be the first
time I've ever been luggage!"

"You see? You're utterly wasted here!" Nash laughed as well. "Please, I
insist, no more arguments. Without further ado I shall become your most
devoted Orpheus, braving all to return you from this Underworld to
reconquer the hearts of the metropolis!"

She clapped prettily. "I wish I hadn't heard that line before, you did
it so well. But surely you know me better? I have also proved that flattery
can get one anywhere—if not everything—and that nothing succeeds like
excess."

Nash bowed with humble admiration.

Richard Sheridan's illegitimate half-sister combined the lilting charm
of her brother with an indefinable something from her mother—the
young dowager Countess Brandon—with whom old Thomas Sheridan
had shared an interest in Dublin's Smock Lane Theater. "Kate, you're
adorable. . . ."

"And I'm head over heels in love with you, Charles!"

"No, believe me, I'm quite serious," Nash hastened to assure her.
"I must've attended every one of Dicky's opening nights. Whenever
you were billed to appear, the Theatre Royal became a second home as

well as second heaven. Who will ever forget your response, as Lucy in *The Rivals,* when your mistress told you: 'My smelling-bottle, you simpleton!' "

Kitty Brandon's eyes twinkled like icicles. "I hope you also approved of my exit, at the end of Act One, after Mrs. Malaprop presented me with another letter to Sir Lucius O'Trigger . . . ?"

She clicked her fingers, refreshing her memory. " 'Let girls in my station be as fond as they please of appearing expert, and knowing in their trusts; commend me to a mask of *silliness* and a pair of sharp eyes for my own interest under it! Let me see to what account I have turned my *simplicity* lately—' at which point, you recall, I opened the ledger—'For abetting Miss Lydia Languish in a design of running away with an ensign!—in money, sundry times, twelve pounds twelve! . . . From the said ensign, within this last month, six guineas and a half—about a quarter's pay! Item, from Mrs. Malaprop, for betraying the young couple to her—when I found matters were likely to be discovered—two guineas!' "

"*Bravissimo.*" Nash saluted her undoubted talent and beauty.

"But, alas, all that is behind us now," she went on in a more subdued voice. "Let's lay our cards on the table, fairly and squarely, and decide what's to be done to make this second home rather less hellish. What's it you really want, apart from that which you'll never get even if you were the last man left alive on earth . . . ?"

Nash did not answer directly. Instead, he gestured at a gang of lags, gathering more firewood for one of the transports. "The vulgar speak of sending coals to Newcastle: England sends savages to the South Seas." He glanced sideways, hoping to see a smile at his witty play on words.

Kitty Brandon frowned. "Yes?"

Nash stopped smiling. "Can't you see that we are misfits here? Can't you understand that we shall become even more so as time goes by? I'm a gentleman, you're a woman of some polish, and both of us are surrounded by that class of animal," he nodded along the crowded beach. "I can't say what effect they have on each other, but by God they frighten me! You remember the events of 'eighty, of course?"

"Vaguely. I was in the Colonies. There was a war on, as you may recall."

"There was also war on the streets of London," Nash replied curtly, "and I was trapped in the very thick of it. I tell you that I saw things, I smelled things, I felt things you would never believe possible."

"True. I have led a very sheltered life."

Nash shrugged. "I experienced the rabble for what it really is, a plague of black lice, spewing from every alley and sewer to suck the blood from our world, hating us even as they fed off us."

"Hm, the profession might have missed something after all," Kitty Brandon mused aloud. "You've the gift. My devoted brother could take a few hints on the balance of a telling phrase."

Nash was not paying attention. The old sweetness of life had gone up in smoke that torrid summer and what fell down again were the gray cinders of a new order between master and man. "They should've been herded into the Thames and drowned."

"Charley, let's get on with present problems, shall we? Particularly as they apply to the future. . . ."

"I am." He pointed at the nearest lag. "Those items are today's problem, and tomorrow's, and every other day we are confined here. Don't forget, I've had eight whole months aboard that damned boat, observing a miniature version of what this 'colony' will soon become. You and I must stand together—"

"Because 'divided we fall'? Hardly an original solution," she replied. "So, what do you propose that we now do to prevent the bully boys from muddying your fine clothes?"

"I've already begun." Nash was brisk. "The officers will be no problem. Their major almost kissed my hand—"

"Good, at least Ross knows that much anatomy," Kitty Brandon observed.

"Therefore we can count on the protection of his men if we encounter any trouble from the rabble—"

" 'If'? Tch! Moments ago you were promising me fisticuffs, now you're starting to throw cold water on the fight. What is this?"

"A serious proposal, so listen carefully because I am not in the habit of repeating myself." Nash frowned. "As I said before, I've had eight months in which to note the habits and customs of our future citizens on the *Prince of Wales*. Now, as you probably don't realize yet, there are about fifty women and roughly the same number of troops aboard the boat—"

"Princely wails indeed!"

Nash disdained comment. "Even so, with every man satisfied, it is often dangerous. Captain Mason—with whom I traveled as a passenger, of course—has approved certain measures which, *pour force majeure,* have turned his command into a floating brothel."

" 'On the good ship *Venus,* hell's teeth you should've seen us. . . .' "

"Pay attention." Nash disapproved of such impudent, gutter humor. "If those things can happen under ideal circumstances, what will it be like when the rest also want that of which there is not enough to go around already? There are only about two hundred of your sisters in distress, Kate, and almost twelve hundred men of all categories. Now, what does that suggest?"

"Let me think. Give me time. Trouble . . . ?"

"That's pitching it short!"

"So what act of philanthropy do you now have in mind?"

"This. You will add your dozen women to my fifty and we shall reserve them exclusively for the soldiers. While we look after them, their officers will look after us, and the rest can go hang so far as I'm concerned."

"You have missed your vocation, Charley. You should be running a bagnio in Vigo Street."

He nodded. "Actually, I did own a couple. I won them from old Nat Fields at the Pineapple Tree Club—"

"Who won back three, with interest? Tch! I must've seen him and 'Cock' Shaw play that game a dozen times." Kitty Brandon was not impressed. "Something tells me you're still out of your depth at Bottommy Bay. Look, I'll cut you a deal, fair and square. Put your lot with mine and I'll look after the shop for both of us." She held out her hand. "Shake . . . ?"

"*You?*"

"Why not? In affairs of this nature it is best if one lady protects the others' interests. After all, they are our priceless assets, particularly when we have to oversee them overseas, as it were."

" 'Ladies'?" The gentleman began to smile. "Kate, believe me, they're common drabs. I've just endured eight months—"

"Mr. Nash, I have endured rather more than eight months and I am telling you that rain will fall upwards before I let one of my young Betties fall into the clutches of a whoremaster like you."

"What?"

"My offer stands. I shall look after your *Prince* girls and see they look after you. But if you so much as lay a single finger on any one of my young ladies aboard *Alexander,* I shall not hesitate to take the necessary steps."

Nash was having great difficulty controlling his face. "I always knew you were a wilful woman, but never did I think you were mad—!"

"So now you know differently." Kitty Brandon was gathering up the rest of the herbs for Levi's experiments. "Take care. Keep your side of the hedge and I'll keep mine. But if you are ever tempted to come poaching for more game, watch out for mantraps."

14

PHILLIP'S PENNANT broke at the masthead and *Sirius*'s gun punched smoke across the bay. The commodore returned his officers' salutes. "Thank you, gentlemen. Mr. Hunter? A few moments of your time, if you please."

"Aye aye, sir." He followed down the companion ladder and shut the door as Phillip tossed a blanket roll at the cot, then turned, slackening his cravat. "Superb, John, that Port Jackson is absolutely superb!"

"But I thought we were going up to Broken Bay, the one on Jimmy Cook's chart?"

"We've no need." Phillip reached for the bell cord and summoned his servant. "Ah, Bryant. Coffee for two. And how's the hen been performing?"

"Got an egg yesterday, sir."

"Boil it."

"Aye aye, sir."

Phillip looked back at his senior captain. "Anyhow, as I was saying, just on the off chance of there being something of note, I took a cursory look into Port Jackson before continuing up the coast. Not that it seemed particularly inviting, nothing more than a gap in the cliffs, which is why Cook must've pinned a name on it but otherwise left well alone." Phillip was making himself comfortable at the chart table, legs outstretched, hands behind neck.

"But the moment I passed between the headlands I knew we were at the mouth of the very river system you and I were seeking. Not that I've seen much evidence of native gondolas, or temples, or gardens," he went on, "but they'll have built their towns further upstream where the river is more easily forded, probably like London to the Thames. But for the moment it's enough that we've a better harbor than I dared imagine. I'd wager every penny I own the entire Royal Navy could ride at anchor in perfect safety."

"I'm much relieved to hear it."

"So am I!" Phillip was buoyant again after months of worry and doubt. "As Gibraltar is to the empire in the Med', so is Port Jackson to the Pacific. I tell you, we could build ten, twenty fleets from the stands of timber which come right down to the shoreline! And there must be at least a dozen coves, all with fresh water, the best of which I've honored with the name of M'Lord Sydney."

"Let's hope he's still able to repay the compliment with some practical help," Hunter cautioned.

Phillip chose to ignore the warning. After a break from the fret and fume of his little colony he didn't need to be reminded of the greater world's larger problems. "Be that as it may, until there's news to the contrary we'll have to assume our faction still holds the upper hand in the vipers' nest. Speaking of which," Phillip was sitting forward, "what's my deputy been doing while my back was turned . . . ?"

"Overseeing the construction of Fort Ross."

" 'Fort Ross,' eh? Doesn't believe in wasting time."

"Neither do I," Hunter replied. "Our gun crews have been exercised."

"A sensible precaution," the other man agreed. "I've also been giving some thought to our defense against the defenders." He reached for his writing case and took out a fresh sheet of paper. "Let's make a start by blowing away the cloudy ramparts of Fort Ross: that'll save us from having to blow them up, later." He dipped his quill and began a list of orders for the marines' commanding officer, ashore.

"I think you could be about to be saved that task," Hunter said, looking through the stern windows. "There's a boat hauling our way. Unless I'm mistaken it's carrying the individual in question: would you prefer me to leave?"

"No." Phillip continued writing. "If we're to contain our gallant major's thirst for glory we had better coordinate our actions. Have you spoken with Tench, yet?"

"Briefly."

"And . . . ?"

"I believe he's amenable to reason, sir."

"Good." Phillip was about to add something else but the marines' boat was bumping alongside the flagship. A pipe sounded. Ross tramped across the deck. Down the ladder. Into the cabin, hat and sword gathered under one arm. His heels clicked.

"Ah, good afternoon, major. Please be seated. Permit me to congratulate you upon the discharge of your duties as lieutenant governor: I'm sure it augurs well for our colony's future." Phillip flexed his pen and tossed it aside. "So what do you have to report?"

"Your orders have been carried out as per directions. Sir."

"Splendid. I was confident they would be. Well, I am also the bearer of good news. I'm sure you'll be delighted to know that we're moving to broader, greener pastures. We sail from Botany Bay on tomorrow's tide."

The officer of marines remained as impassive as the frigate's figure-head. "Why?"

Phillip was finding it more difficult to hold his smile in place. "Because, in my opinion, Botany Bay is unsuited to our task: you must've heard me discussing these very points at dinner the other night? Port Jackson, I've discovered, is eminently satisfactory in every way. I propose exchanging one location for the other."

"And which were we ordered to occupy . . . ?"

"Well, as it happens, Botany was the designated destination—"

"Then a lawful command is being disobeyed."

Phillip's swarthy face had lost its color. "By God. You have the effrontery to sit there—"

Ross got to his feet.

"I will not be spoken to like this!" Phillip's fist hit the table. "You'll—!"

"Leave?"

"Yes! No! Sit down and stop acting the fool!"

Ross obeyed with ponderous dignity and arranged the frayed cuffs of his working tunic. "If anyone is playing the fool, as you so term it, that person is not I. Sir."

Hunter coughed. "Tomorrow's ebb, did you not say?"

"Yes."

"Then I'd better prepare to break moorings. And our military will also need advance notice before demounting their bivouac." *Sirius*'s captain leaned forward, touching the paper under Phillip's clenched fist.

The governor had been given time to recover. "Since you're determined to be so punctilious in your pursuit of orders, major, there's the next installment!" He skimmed the paper at his deputy.

Ross ignored it. "My men aren't going to like this. Sir."

"Like this?" Phillip was shaking now. "They'll damned well do as they're told!"

"Only if I tell them, first."

"What?"

Ross almost smiled. "We're not sailors. We took the king's shilling of our own free will, not because the impressment service bought us from bawdy house keepers while we were drunk."

"By God—!"

"Only another royal marine can tell him what he will, or will not do. Sir."

"You're my deputy! You'll obey my orders!"

Ross ignored the naval officer. He turned and glanced at the door. "Marine Wiggins!"

It flew open. The sentry slapped his musket sling. "Sah!"

"What is the first duty of a sentinel?"

"To see that only those pass having first advanced, been recognized and have given the countersign of the day. Sah!"

"And if they don't . . . ?"

"To raise the alarm. Sah!"

"And if called upon to step aside by superior force . . . ?"

"A sentinel will remain at his post until properly relieved. Or is killed. Sah!"

"Dismiss."

"Sah!"

Ross turned as the door snapped shut again. "Now let's call in one of your men. Sir."

Phillip said nothing.

Ross took his time. "Doubtless Mr. Hunter has told you that I put him under restraint off Africa? He was mistaken. I was merely demonstrating the loyalty and devotion to duty of *my* men. Without whom neither of you would necessarily awaken in the morning. Sir."

"Have you quite finished? Major."

"For the moment." Ross folded the sheet of instructions without reading them, clicked his heels and strolled from the cabin.

Hunter was ready to follow. "I'd better away to my duties as well, sir." He passed the commodore's servant coming in with a tray, but he had not reached the deck before Phillip hurled the plate at Bryant, who ran away to abuse the cook for botching his master's egg. The cook had a sharpening steel in one fist. The steward reeled from the galley, clutching one side of his head.

Tempers were no better ashore. By sundown the sawpit's planks had been dug up and the trenches of Fort Ross filled in. Only Graybeard and his people had any reason to celebrate as they watched the last of the evil-smelling ghostmen march down to the water's edge with their tents, their cooking pots, their shovels, their wheelbarrows.

"*Djnumbala daringadu-u-u!*" The chieftain raised his head in triumph as summer dusk settled across the land. He had defeated the sorcerers.

15

"THERE'S NO DOUBT, sir!" Ball was soaked with spray after being rowed across from *Supply*. "They are the *Boussole* and *Astrolabe*, all right—!"

"Damn!" Phillip strode over to the lee rail. "Damn, damn, damn!" He sighted again on the notch of horizon between capes Solander and Banks. The telescope's disc framed two French men o' war, their topgallant sails set aback, tacking against an offshore wind, unable to follow the more nimble *Supply* into Botany Bay.

Until moments ago there had still been a hope that the two interlopers were Dutchmen blown off course to the Spice Islands, or Spaniards from Manila, or privateers cruising the South Seas. Instead, an avalanche of worry was starting to creak and rumble above Phillip's head.

The French admiral, out there, had also been commissioned by a great power to annex this remote anchorage. If the British convoy had been delayed by only a few dozen hours on its transit from the Cape, their positions would have been reversed. Phillip could have been standing off while La Pérouse sent out a boat to display the French colors. "Mr. Hunter!"

"Sir!"

"My flag to *Supply!* I sail for Port Jackson immediately. *Sirius* will cover the rearguard. Mr. King! Attend me. Speed is now of the utmost importance!"

"With respect, sir, I must counsel you against such a course of action," Hunter interrupted quietly. "The weather glass is falling. It would be highly imprudent—!"

"There is no further time to lose, Mr. Hunter. That damned Frenchman has Cook's observations, too! If he can't make landfall at Botany then he's bound to proceed north to Port Jackson before me!" Phillip whipped round. "Mr. Ball! Prepare to cast off! Mr. Bradley! Make to all: embark stores, break mooring, stand out to sea!"

"Aye aye, sir!"

"Bloody hell." Ross stood in the shelter of the deckhouse, wrapped in his cloak. He glanced at Campbell. "And that's our captain general? At the first sight of a Frog, he runs! But at least our hands are clean, Jimmy. I've kept all his orders, in writing, ready to present to the court of enquiry after we've done you-know-what. . . ."

Campbell grinned with a happy tic and watched the confusion which Phillip's spoken commands were spreading like fire aboard the other vessels.

The tiny brig was first away through the bay's steep chop, jib sheets flying, main course and spanker set as she plowed for the open sea. Behind her, *Sirius*'s gun barked orders at the melee of transports as sailors heaved up, hauled down, cursed and swore; as lines and ropes thrummed in the rising wind; as canvas boomed and bellied from the yards; as the convoy began fighting its way piecemeal from Botany, chivied along by the flagship's signals.

"Governor of New Holland? Heaven help us when the Inkers attack!" Ross told his deputy. "The man's not only a fool, he's a coward to boot. Now, here's what I'd be—" Ross stopped. "Holy Jesus!"

Prince of Wales was bearing down on *Friendship*, spray surging as the smaller barque clawed to windward, but the gap was closing faster than her wheel could be spun over. Twenty yards. Ten. Seven. Five. Three, two, none—! The *Prince* rammed her, shearing the jib-boom, collapsing her new mainsail in a welter of falling tackle while, down below in the cages, the cargoes howled and wept as timber hulls crunched, and rolled, and ground together.

"A splendid sight, you'll agree." Phillip beckoned King to the windward rail and pointed at the passing shoreline.

"Yes, sir."

The rest of the British expeditionary force, which had covered sixteen thousand miles without mishap, was now trying to sink itself by hurrying over the last eleven or twelve. But neither officer could see their orders being carried out as Cape Banks fell astern, nor could they see the French squadron now that *La Boussole* and *L'Astrolabe* had faded into the offshore murk.

King squinted into his telescope. The ocean behind him was a gray waste under low curtains of cloud but, as often happens, fingers of sunlight were beckoning over the land, touching the forest and a distant range of mountains. Much closer, as *Supply* chinned and butted her way northward, curl upon curl of surf rolled onshore, smashing, bursting, tossing white spray up the pale yellow sandstone cliffs.

"And it's all ours, Pip. . . ."

King said nothing. The bosun's cob was speeding men to the braces as *Supply* readied herself to tack for a break in the rocks.

"Ready about!" Ball commanded through his speaking trumpet.

"About ship, there!" the bosun called.

"About ship it is!" the helmsman replied, spoking his wheel arm over arm, eyes slit, watching the wind pennant.

"Let go and haul!"

"Haul there, haul!"

Supply's yards heaved over, laying her on course for the entrance to Port Jackson. Far astern, *Alexander* was breaking through a gauzy shower of rain, leading the rest of the convoy after their commodore. The brig continued around the southern promontory: a full storm could have been blowing on the Pacific but, within moments of coming back on course almost parallel with her one up the coast, she would have been snug and safe behind a natural breakwater.

Sheltered by the high, sandstone escarpment, *Supply* was feeling her way under shortened sail between virgin stands of timber indented by coves and calm beaches.

"It's even better than Gibraltar," Phillip said with quiet satisfaction, once more in control of himself and the situation. "It'll take us only a few days to fell those trees, there and there, and float a boom against the French." His fingers swung as *Supply* bore past a low reef—shaped rather like a sow with a litter of piglets in tow—and continued altering course inland, along the watery track of afternoon.

"By the ma-ark, fifteen!" The lead-line men were forward on the chains, chanting their soundings for the shipmaster to note in his pilot book.

"Deep eleven."

"By the ma-ark, seventeen!"

The shores of the river mouth were inching together. A fitful sunlight gilded the haze which drifted across from some Indian campfires, among the trees. A bark canoe scurried for shelter, rocking on the brig's wake as she closed her last mile into Sydney Cove.

"Helm!" Ball commanded through his trumpet.

"Helm it is!" The ironbound wheel began winding the brig to port, her sheets pounding aback, her blunt bows framed by a roughly U-shaped cove sheltered on both sides by rocky ridges and the timbered valley of a freshwater brook.

"Let go!"

"Let go, there!"

"Letting go!" The bosun's mallet swung, the shackle pin snapped open, the anchor dropped and *Supply* rocked to a stop as five fathoms of cable snaked through her hawse hole. A pipe shrilled and the men doubled away to clew up canvas and stow slack lines. The voyage from Portsmouth had ended. Now the work of settlement could begin.

Phillip rubbed his hands together. He turned. "Mr. Ball? My compliments to your marines: despatch a color party ashore. And that spar we spoke of? Have it swayed over the side. You have the picks and shovels? Splendid. Then let us waste no further time!"

The commodore settled himself among the ropes, tools and weapons of the longboat as marines became *matelots* and leaned into their sweeps, towing the spar back to Sydney Cove's easternmost point. They beached the boat and became soldiers again, trampling through the scrub, muskets slung over one shoulder, the length of Baltic fir bumping across the other, following their officers.

"This will do." Phillip halted, shading his eyes and watching *Alexander* pick her way into view, down Port Jackson.

"Right-o, me lucky lads." The corporal jabbed his thumb at a pocket of soil among the rocks. "Shift it."

The marines peeled off their tunics and became a fatigue squad of pioneers, shovels chucking out black dirt, oyster shells, fishbones and knobs of charred wood, deepening the hole for the spar to be stepped and braced by ropes tied to nearby bushes.

A loop of line had been run through a block at the head of the spar and *Supply*'s union flag bent on. The marines buttoned their uniforms, dusted off their hands and shouldered their weapons, three ranks of three men apiece, a color party now.

"Would you do us the honor, Mr. Ball?"

"Thank you, sir." The youngest of the three naval officers moved forward and waited for Phillip's nod. He tugged the line and the British colors spilled onto the breeze overhead.

"Number one rank! Prime! Cock! Fire!"

The muskets crashed. A flock of lorikeets screeched into the trees. The second rank of redcoats advanced.

"Cock! Fire!"

The third rank marched forward.

"Fire!"

Phillip replaced his hat. The empire had just extended her frontiers by one and a half million square miles, though almost a billion acres of what or where still had to be decided as the commodore reached inside his coat pocket and took out a rather dented spirit flask. He unscrewed the silver cap, which also served as a small cup, and poured himself a good measure of cognac. "His Britannic Majesty, George the Third!"

Then it was King's turn to flick back a dram. And then Ball's.

"Thank you, gentlemen." Phillip slipped the flask into his pocket again. "Once *Sirius* rejoins us I'll transfer my pennant. There'll be a conference aboard her tonight. You will both attend."

Sunset burned like a furnace above the trees. Phillip stood at the salt-rimed stern windows of his flagship, watching the last merchantmen straggle into Sydney Cove. Only *Friendship* was not yet present: there had been some carelessness with her rigging and she was sheltering in one of the outer coves: no doubt she would complete the last three or four miles tomorrow morning. Meanwhile, the colony's senior officers were being assembled. Hunter would soon be down to—

"Enter!"

The frigate's captain stepped past the rigid sentry. "Whenever you're ready, sir."

"Thank you, John. All present and correct?"

"Mr. Shea begs leave to absent himself."

"Sick again?"

"I'm afraid so."

"Damn. Oh well, I suppose we must proceed without his support." The governor designate was making himself comfortable behind the surgeons' operating table—cold refreshments would be served after the conference—and prepared to receive his officers as they stooped into the cabin and faced him across the pool of lantern light. Ross and Campbell finished a whispered conversation.

Phillip reached for his spectacles and smoothed the parchment arranged in front of him. " 'We, reposing especial trust and confidence in your loyalty, courage and experience in military affairs do, by these presents, constitute and appoint you to be Governor and Captain General of our territory called New South Wales and of all the country inland to the westward as far as the one hundred and thirty-fifth degree of longitude, reckoned from the meridian of Greenwich, including all islands adjacent in the Pacific Ocean, and of all towns, garrisons, castles, forts and other military works which are now, or may hereafter, be erected upon the said territory.' "

He paused to emphasize what was about to follow. " 'You are therefore to carefully and diligently discharge the duty of Governor in and over our said territory by performing all manner of things thereunto belonging. Furthermore, we do hereby strictly charge and command all our officers and soldiers who shall be employed within our said territory and all others whom it may concern, to obey you in every particular as our Governor thereof, according to the rules and disciplines of war, and of such orders as we shall send you under our signet or sign manual.

" 'Given at our Court of St. James, the twelfth day of October 1786, in the twenty-sixth year of our reign. By His Majesty's command. Thos. Townshend, Viscount Sydney.' "

Phillip let the commission roll itself shut. It would have to be read to everyone, free and government labor, when the colony was formally proclaimed, but what mattered most was its effect on these few men tonight.

Ross and Campbell were whispering again as Phillip removed his spectacles. "So now we understand each other, gentlemen. But what do those fine words mean, stripped to their bare essentials? They mean work. From me. From you. From those chattels who've been drafted to labor for us. And let no one be under any delusion, there'll be no time for idle daydreaming or imaginary complaints. Any man I discover forming cabals or fomenting unrest will be punished with the utmost rigor of law."

Ross stopped whispering.

"Remember, in my capacity as captain general, I shall sign court martial warrants. Disobedience will be mutiny, and mutiny means death. Make that known to everyone under your command."

There was a subdued shuffling of feet and Campbell stopped twisting a loose thread on his uniform.

"Our work begins at first light tomorrow. You will have your written instructions before leaving this evening, so I shall be brief now. Mr. Dawes? I wish for a detailed survey of the cove and its surrounds: pay especial attention to the availability of quarry stone and brickmaking clay."

"Sir."

Phillip trapped his deputy's wandering attention. "Mr. Ross? You will disembark your men upon the west bank."

"First I'd better look at the east—"

"It's already been taken."

"By who?"

"Me."

"Why?"

"Government House."

Phillip had chosen well. A governor's mansion on the east bank was his reward for being first into the cove and first in the colony. Now, not only would he be getting the sea breezes before they scoured odors and infections from the main body of the encampment, the higher, better-drained site was also two cables' length from Ross's future headquarters. Under the circumstances it was the best anyone could hope for.

"Mr. King?" Phillip clicked his fingers. "I shall need those muster rolls of government property—what skills it claims to have, what its names are, what work we can make it deliver—and I'll need them without delay."

"Aye aye, sir."

16

"ENTER!" Phillip looked up from his journal. "Yes? What is it, what is it?"

"Um. Mr. King's boat's approaching, sir." The brown paper and vinegar poultice on the side of Bryant's head not only made him hard of hearing, it also made him more anxious than ever to please his master. "More coffee, sir?"

"Yes, yes."

Sirius's gig bumped alongside. Phillip could hear footsteps coming down the companion ladder. Bryant squeezed aside as the commodore's flag lieutenant walked past, shirt-sleeves rolled, waistcoat unbuttoned. "Good morning, sir."

" 'Morning." Phillip took off his spectacles and rubbed them with a piece of wash leather. "So how're we going?"

"Much better than I imagined possible," King replied, accepting the nodded invitation to be seated. He opened his despatch bag, took out a wad of papers and spread them across the table in six heaps—one for each convict transport. "These are the manifests you asked for, with their names and the alleged terms of penal servitude." King shrugged. "Human nature being what it is, our merchant masters have doubtless fitted the facts to suit themselves, but at least they put on a show of cooperation with authority."

"I was going to ask about that." Phillip glanced at the topmost sheets. "How on earth did you bestir them to action in so short a while?"

"Simple. I told them quite bluntly that, unless I'd a complete tally of government property in their charge—especially the lagged items—there'd be no impression of the colony's seal on their invoices when they set sail for China: I allowed them to imagine the scene if they returned to London having just lost a small fortune."

"I'll wager that gave them food for thought!" Phillip was leaning back, warming his shoulders in the sun which poured through the cabin's open skylight. "It's not often one has the pleasure of putting one over men like Duncan Sinclair. His damned *Alexander* has been a constant headache, right from the start—"

"She might still be." King reached for one of the papers. "Contrary as ever, our Captain S. actually wishes to pay hard cash to retain the services of a woman he's been traveling with."

"Government property, of course?"

"Of course," King agreed. "First he tried bribing me. Then he tried bluster. Then he pretended to give way. However, I wouldn't put it past him to try some other tack as the time draws near for him to weigh anchor."

"Like trying to smuggle her off?" Phillip asked.

"I'd say it's a distinct possibility," King agreed. "He wants to take her to Canton, told me so himself. They're very thick together."

"Evidently. You put him in his place?"

"Of course." King pushed the paper away. "She'll be tallied ashore with the other dozen or so women aboard that floating pesthouse. Or else no seal, no money."

"Correct." Phillip steepled his fingertips. "We must keep that sort of thing in mind, especially when the convoy gets ready for its onward passage to China. I'll require every vessel to be fumigated with brimstone. We must smoke out the trollops they'll try hiding aboard.

"The trouble is, until we've proper barracks, I fear they're going to prove more trouble than they're worth. What we really need is a house of correction, something like the Bridewell, where they can be kept segregated and employed. Too many have been allowed to take liberties aboard the transports: Sinclair's slut is a case in point." Phillip hunched forward, elbows on the table. "Did you know there are rumors that some of our gentlemen are actually encouraging these liaisons?"

"Really, sir?" King managed to sound startled, although the only surprise for him was that the Old Man still regarded these rumors as rumors.

Among the expedition's junior officers it was an open secret that George Johnstone—a lieutenant of marines aboard *Lady Penrhyn*—was protecting Esther Abrahams and her infant daughter. And there were several others for whom eight months at sea, cooped up in boxes no larger than a couple of English cottages, had blurred the natural barriers of class because, in a floating township where adult males outnumbered the rest by six to one, it would have been incredible had not the younger and prettier women bettered themselves. Under the circumstances, even the ugliest old firecracker off the streets of London had to be sitting on a gold mine, King knew, although Annie "Tongs" Inett—a cheerfully unrepentant pickpocket from Worcester—was more to his taste.

"It's such a messy business," Phillip went on. "Unless we watch our step there could be squally weather from that quarter. However, I'll use these lists to remove temptation." He indicated the heaps of paper. "That done, the sturdiest males can be put into gangs and set ashore to build shelters. Then we'll unload the females directly into their camp where they can start washing and mending; that ought to do the trick."

King was saved from having to comment as Bryant tapped nervously at the cabin door. "Um, coffee's ready, sir."

"Don't bother me now!" Phillip glanced at his flag lieutenant again. "Kindly accompany me. I intend seeing how Miller's overseeing the disembarkation of his stores."

Until yesterday this body of water had been without a name and without a purpose but all that was being changed, Phillip thought as he settled into the gig and looked around during the haul ashore. Now, nearby, *Friendship*'s carpenters were swaying on their planks over the bows, hammering spikes into the replacement jib-boom. Aboard other vessels men were sawing, chiseling, splitting lumber; boiling tar, pounding oakum, spinning fresh rope; hauling up bales of tents and boxes of tools from the holds; emptying slop buckets over the lee rails; easing themselves at the heads.

"I consider it of the utmost importance that we institute a proper system of rationing to control the insolent and lazy," Phillip continued. "Those who show the proper spirit of subordination will be fed and clothed: those who don't, won't. That'll bring 'em to their senses."

King was saved from having to comment on this Utopian ideal, too, as the gig stroked through a drifting mat of rotten straw, the convicts' bedding from *Charlotte*, last changed at Cape Town and now dumped over the side for the tide to flush away.

"Should that fail, I suppose we can always count on those as an alternative means of persuasion. . . ." Phillip was shading his eyes as a company of marines high-stepped through the shallows. They formed fours at the water's edge, turned right and marched away to the tucker-tuck-tuck of a drum. Their noncommissioned officers were not inclined to persuade anyone today, or any other day. Canes prodding bellies, slashing buttocks, they were assembling gangs of prisoners, herding them toward the tree line where fires had already been lit to dry the redcoats' equipment and steam the lice from their uniforms. The lags were put straight to work clearing ground for their guards' tents, fetching firewood, filling water buckets and chucking lumps of rock at stray Indians who got too close.

"Hardly the most striking specimens, are they?" King observed, halting beside Phillip while they looked around at the smoky confusion.

"Two weeks from now you'll be astonished at the difference," Phillip replied. "Ah, there's Dawes. The very man I need to see. Carry on."

"Aye aye, sir."

Phillip strode up the beach to where the young officer of engineers was running a surveyor's chain between small red pennants. "Everything proceeding according to plan?"

Dawes slung his satchel of instruments and wearily straightened. "Sir."

"Splendid. Stand easy, stand easy. Now, concerning the storehouse, I think you'd better build a couple. There's no point putting all our eggs in the same basket: two will halve the risk of an accidental fire devastating us.

"I'm also concerned about our defenses against the Frenchmen. We ought to have at least one battery of guns covering our approaches, over there, with supporting magazines. We'll also need permanent barracks for the garrison.

"And don't overlook the actual settlement. I shall require a main street which is appropriate for a capital city, with ample space reserved for law courts, treasury buildings, churches and so on."

The governor was not the only one shaping a vision splendid; his deputy had fixed the battalion's headquarters where it would command a full view of the parade ground. It was of no concern to Ross that undergrowth still covered the only flat area for several hundred yards in any direction, or that a storm had once toppled a huge ironbark which would have to be sawn up and burned before even a platoon of troops could march past their commander's marquee. The government's labor force could handle that.

But first they would have to be taught the meaning of work and that was going to be a slow and painful process, Ross realized, watching a gang of pasty-faced Londoners trampling over heaps of tent cloth, picking up bits of rope at random, getting in each other's way. He swung the flat of his sword blade at the nearest item as it stumbled past.

"Ow! What's up, guv?"

"Use the bloody mallet to drive those pegs or I'll use your bloody head!"

"Wha'?"

Ross turned away in disgust and left his sergeant major to apply the necessary correctives with a rattan cane while two grinning marines stretched the convict's arms around a nearby tree trunk.

But it was not only the labor which was trying the major's patience, or the persistent flies, or even the heat. There was the choice of name for this imagined Gibraltar. Fort Ross had a forthright, manly ring to it, something which Phillip's namby-pamby Sydney most certainly did not have. The marines' commandant had been proven right when the lags promptly corrupted the name to Sinny. Now, not four and twenty hours ashore, even his own officers were starting to refer to their new home as Sinful Cove.

Robert Ross had nourished many grudges during his long years of service to the Crown, and by no means had all been self-inflicted. Until recently, until the epic siege of that other—the real Gibraltar—poverty and lack of connection had dogged his career. Now, just as he was starting to get ahead as a lieutenant governor of somewhere, the promotion was turning sour. Because, even if Phillip believed that by reading a two-year-old document all their troubles would vanish, Ross did not.

Bitter experience had taught him that an officer's commission can bring more problems than it solves. Ross knew that, while he maintained a tight rein, he commanded a battalion of reasonably steady troops, but there were also the equivalent of three battalions of the law's convicted slaves to be broken into harness. The volunteers were outnumbered by conscripts. Fully three-quarters of the colony's strength was everything which Ross despised. It was civilian, it was English. Only the fragile membrane of regimental pride and discipline could save his men from being contaminated by the very objects they were supposed to be guarding.

"Sar'nt major!"

"Sah!"

"There's going to be trouble unless we keep the lads busy. Get that bloody parade ground cleared and leveled."

The pioneer company was disembarked and marched to the head of the beach. In front of them stood the trees, many rising a sheer eighty or ninety feet into the hard blue sky. Everything about them was wrong. Their bark was wrong: flaky, fluttering in tattered gray strips. Their leaves were wrong: dagger-shaped and brittle. The trees of New Holland were not the trees of Home. They were alien. They were hostile. They were in the way.

"Right-o, me lucky lads. . . ."

The first pioneer axe swung, biting out a chip of pink bark. The second blow knocked away an orange slice of sapwood. The third landed with an arm-jarring jolt, snapping the handle clean in half, leaving the axe head stuck fast in the solid brown trunk.

Others were having no better luck reshaping the landscape. The forge bellows were already snorting as the blacksmith tried straightening bent crowbars, curled shovel blades, blunt billhooks. It was plain that the contractors—private businessmen who'd underbid each other in London to equip a public enterprise in the Pacific—had shipped out their cheapest trade goods after invoicing the Treasury for fair quality and full measure. The difference was their profit and palm grease for the ordnance department's clerks.

"Never gets no better, sir." The storekeeper was standing with Phillip under a tarpaulin awning, waiting for another load to be dragged ashore. "Just the same in Americky. Never could tell what we'd find next. Regular lucky dip, Over There. 'Ere too, I'll bet."

The governor said nothing. There was nothing anyone could say which would make a scrap of difference to the tub of green rot just broached by the cooks. The smelly mold may once have been oatmeal, but the date— 1786—branded on its end staves, was clearly a fake. Until last year the "8" had either been a "7" or even a "6" until a contractor's chisel reworked the figure.

During the past decade or two this barrel of decaying filth had been traded, discounted, bought, stolen, gambled, lost, found again and rolled from warehouse to warehouse until the deal was struck which got rid of it forever as convict fodder in the South Seas. Andrew Miller was right, things never did get any better, nor would they until a dozen contractors had been stood against the Victualing Office wall and shot by firing squad. But the men of power around Westminster would never allow an action so direct and healthy, Phillip also knew.

Military contracts were a standing invitation to coin money. Fortunes had been made by the suppliers of embalmed mule, fermenting bran and maggoty pease which had masqueraded as pork, flour and soup for the king's army in America. And during his own years of service at sea Phillip had often been expected to feed his crews with barrels of pebbles, old paper, rags and bakehouse sweepings. This oatmeal had at least been edible, once.

"Very well," he told the storekeeper. "Recover what you can and consign the rest to the pig swill."

Miller scratched a rather red nose. "O' course I'll do my best, sir, but it won't be that easy all the time."

"We're not here because it was thought New South Wales would be easy any of the time," Phillip replied. "Remember, what can't be cured must be endured."

"Yes, sir."

That problem solved, Phillip turned to go, then stopped. He frowned. A gang of lags was plodding nearer, laden with firkins and hogsheads, barrels and tubs for the colony's supply dump. One item stood out from the remainder—and not only because of the trifling load he held under one arm—but also because of the shoes and stockings, the white cotton shirt and the straw hat such as gentlemen of leisure wore for excursions into the country.

Phillip aimed his walking stick. "You there! What the devil are you doing?"

The straw hat came off and was held flat to the chest. "Charles Nash. Your Excellency's most humble servant."

"Damned right you're my servant." The governor was unusually gruff. "I know who you are, it's what you are now which concerns me."

"Between ourselves, I'm not sure either," Nash replied in a civil voice. "Nominally I'm helping Lieutenant Kellow to maintain his accounts but there's little call for pay at the moment, so I thought I'd volunteer my services to Miller here." He nodded affably in the storeman's direction.

"And what about those?" Phillip's stick was aiming at the lags grouped behind Nash. "They're hardly the sort I'd associate with Carlton House unless somebody like you had slipped them through the back door."

Nash smiled politely at the older man. "My experience of His Royal Highness is that he's equally at home in any company. But as for these chaps, they're my response to a request for more help to get things on shore. Of course, if Your Excellency objects to my trifling contribution I'll be quite happy to stand aside. . . ."

Phillip said nothing. Even at the best of times there would have been muddle and confusion while troops and equipment were sorted out on the beachhead, but these were not the best of times and this was certainly not the best of places. The Ordnance Office had forgotten to send out taskmasters for New South Wales's work force. Now, fully half the number under his authority did not know where they were, did not know what they were doing, did not know where to go next.

The governor glanced at his storekeeper. "Very well, this—ah—gentleman can continue running errands, and you'll let me know how he copes with having to work for a living." Phillip looked back at the younger man. "There are no heiresses to be stolen here, Mr. Nash. You will find that hunger has scant respect for birth, high or low. Proceed with your duties."

17

" 'URRY UP, f'Chrissakes!" *Alexander*'s mate yelled from the stern of her longboat as another load of male convicts fumbled under the seats for their belongings.

The petty officer was under pressure. Duncan Sinclair had fulfilled his contract to bring a cargo of laborers to New Holland and now his orders were to make haste for the last leg of his voyage to Canton. But first the cages had to be knocked down, foul ballast shoveled over the side, an entire vessel freshened with tarwash. And before any of those could begin the male lags had to finish the officers' shore quarters, and the marines', and the women's, and their own.

"Get a bleedin' move on, you lot!"

Cribb took his time stepping over the gunwale into the water, then waded ashore, quite steady on his feet. Most others were not. They'd not been ashore at Botany Bay. Freed from the weight of their fetters, the latest batch of lags was flopping about on the hot sand while earlier arrivals whistled, jeered and clapped.

Cribb stepped over one of the floundering shapes and tightened his belt, a strip of canvas twisted round a fistful of copper coins and about thirty ounces of tobacco, the working capital from managing *Alexander*'s barbershop.

Thorpe, his lather boy, hitched an equally plump bank roll. "Now then, Joe, where's Chinaland?"

"There." Cribb pointed beyond a campfire which was crackling out of control toward a makeshift hospital.

"Before we go I reckon we should 'elp Abe," Thorpe announced, pointing to where *Alexander*'s surgeon and his convict assistant were flogging back flames with blankets. Levi ran inside the tent to drag another off the sick and dying.

Cribb had more important decisions to make. He got his bearings then, suddenly, grinned and shouldered his bundle—a square of sailcloth and a stiff blanket tied round a sailor's jacket, a wooden bowl, the barber's razor—and began sauntering toward a dejected mare which had been tethered to a tree.

"But what about Abe?" Thorpe was uneasy. "We can't just leave 'im without saying so!"

Cribb said nothing. He began stroking the mount's ears and whispering spells. Then he crouched, a gypsy horse coper appraising the mare's knees and pasterns. "This *kushtigai*'s an officer's prancer; she's got barb blood: I snaffled one like 'er for myself, when we done old Jefferson's palace, Over There." He straightened, winking at the worried farm boy. "She'll fly like a bloody cannonball once she's proper shod—"

" 'Ere! What's that you're doing with that there 'orse?"

Cribb jerked round. A sort of sailor was scurrying toward them, water slopping over the rim of a wooden bucket, one side of his head swathed with rag and brown paper.

"You can't touch that!" Bryant snorted to a halt. An underling, he was always glad when there were others below him to bully and browbeat. "That's the governor's 'orse!"

Cribb sniffed manfully but he couldn't stop a tear sliding down his cheek. "S-sorry, sir, we didn't mean no 'arm, really we didn't. . . ."

"I should think not! That's the governor's 'orse! I'm the only one allowed to do anything with it! Don't you let me catch you near it again! Now, bugger off before I call the guard!"

Cribb wiped another tear and obeyed, then winked at Thorpe and squared his shoulders again as they marched past the sentries which Campbell had posted against Indians and Frenchmen.

The first batch of lags rounded up by the marines had proved to be useless as tent-raisers: they had now been demoted to scrub clearing while a fatigue party of redcoats manhandled bundles of canvas onto the razed patches of dirt.

"Your blokes look like they could use a bit of an 'and with that job," Cribb said, halting beside the senior private.

"What if they do? What's that to you?"

"Nothing. But we might be able to 'elp. The name's Cribb, fusileer, Seventh Regiment o' Foot. You can call me Phoss."

"I can call you any fucking thing I like." The private scratched his crotch and peered at the lagged item. "So what's your bellyache now?"

"That lot." Cribb jabbed a thumb at the other government men, wandering around, getting nowhere. "I'd rather join the king's service, again. At least a cove knows what's what and who wants it done. 'Ere, give us those ropes while your blokes get the poles steady. Chrissakes, soldier, move!" Cribb turned. "Ben! Grab 'old and get ready to pull on the count of three!"

"Er—?"

"On the double!"

"Um. All right. I suppose."

The mottled gray and green canvas wedge wobbled upright and steadied itself in the light breeze while the fatigue party hammered down its
pegs, but not too hard. There was no point in ripping out the rope
grommets. Like much other equipment sent to New South Wales this
tent had last seen service in the Americas, after which it had been rolled
damp and shipped back to England, then stored until being transported
through equatorial heat to the South Seas.

"That's the ticket!" Cribb gave Thorpe another encouraging wink.
"Now, the fly sheet!"

Thorpe stuck his fingers through one of the gray splotches. He shifted
sideways to a stretch of white canvas and began worrying in case someone
blamed him for the rip.

"One, two, hup—!"

Cribb dusted his hands and joined the marines as they trudged along
to raise the next tent. And the next. And the next. The senior private
joined him as its fly sheet flicked over the ridge pole and was laced down
to the count of three. "What did you say you 'andle was . . . ?"

Cribb adjusted the guy rope and made sure its cleat was exactly in line
with the others. "Phoss."

"That's a funny one."

"Not if you're inside any place I've just torched," Cribb replied,
squinting along the line of tents. "It's short for phosphorus, the stuff I
used to burn down shops with."

"That why they clinked you?" the marine asked, reaching inside his
fatigue overalls for a stumpy clay pipe and a small bit of *modongo*. Cribb
palmed an inch of his own tobacco. "Do yourself a favor, it's me
birthday, I've got tons more on the boat."

The guard fondled the sweet golden leaf before flaking it into his pipe
bowl, then checked there were no officers on the prowl and crouched
behind the tent to chip a spark into his tinderbox. "So that's what you
done after you got out?" He puffed smoke up his sleeve to hide the
evidence. "Torch shops and such . . . ?"

"Paid good and it beats going 'ungry." Cribb finished briefing a
moody Thorpe to stand watch while he squatted on the small patch of
shade.

"I was cleverer," the guard replied between contented puffs of smoke.
"I made lance-corporal in Americky. They asked me to stay on with the
colors when we got back 'Ome. Best day's work I ever done when they
pulled my name from the 'at. Another twelve years and I'll be in the draw
for two bob a week, for life!" He savored more smoke and every soldier's
dream of finding a silver florin in his pocket, every week, if he survived

to become a ticket in the regimental paymaster's lottery. "You ever get sent Over There . . . ?"

Cribb hung his head, then glanced up uncertainly. "You must've seen tons o' battles?"

"I was at Savannah."

Cribb was suitably impressed. "And the guv'nor?" He nodded to where Ross had last been sighted. "Was 'e there, too?"

" 'E was every-fucking-where," the marine grimaced. "A regular shitfire. Trouble is, when there's nothing to do, it's desperate 'ard keeping 'im 'appy."

"One o' that sort? Still, 'e ought to be glad once we get stuck into the Frogs. When do you reckon that'll be . . . ?"

"Soon." The guard puffed more smoke. "You seen that fleet o' three deckers waiting for us as we stood out from Bottommy? I did. You mark my words"— he prodded the lag's chest with a sticky pipe stem—" 'alf the Frog navy's going to give us what for. . . ."

"Then it's a good job we've got the cavalry," Cribb observed, glancing over one shoulder, checking that the governor's man was doing the right thing by the tethered mare. "Where's the dragoon lines . . . ?"

"What dragoons?"

Cribb blinked. "Shit, you'll need Rangers in this sort o' country!"

"Hn. We got us. Three companies o' boots and some little guns. That's it."

"You've got to be joking!"

"Some joke."

"But—?"

"Twig!" Thorpe hissed.

Cribb was on his feet. "Just you leave 'em to me, sir!" He turned, snapping his fingers for Thorpe to follow, and marched past Ross.

"What's that item been doing here . . . ?"

"Tenting. Sah!"

"That makes a change." Ross stroked his chin. "Very well, keep them moving."

"Sah!"

Cribb slowed once he was out of sight and searched around for a comfortable length of fallen wood to carry over one shoulder while a baffled Thorpe steadied the other end. They were now officially employed.

"I don't see why we need this," Thorpe grumbled from the rear. "None of them other coves 'ave got none."

"None of them 'ave got much between the ears, either," Cribb replied, continuing his inspection of the campsite. "Another couple of days and

Windbag's going to be kicking arse'oles. There's gun pits to be dug, and trenches, and bomb shelters, and magazines, and I'll bet all London to a brick I know who's going to be doing it."

"Who?"

"Not me." Cribb had altered course and was walking toward a field kitchen where gangs of lags were jostling around, hoping to get fed.

Andrew Miller had been glad to let Nash volunteer for this chore. The acting assistant paymaster and storekeeper nodded, the cook began ladling rations of pea skilly thickened with oatmeal, the first convict to get a share up-ended his bowl and drank it dry. His face puckered; he vomited. The second lag kept his meal down even less time. Nash wasn't wasting any of the colony's moldy rations while they could be used to balance the food put aside for himself, for his followers, for the cooks, for the armed sentries who were bashing the lags into line.

Cribb slipped behind one of the jeering crowd. "Sly."

"Wha's up?"

"Get Croak, Maggot and Plug."

"Why?"

"Because I say so! And because we can whip our fangs into beef, and ammo' cheese, and brown tommy biscuit. . . ."

"Sounds like another dose o' Red Jooz and gold palaces to me," Sly grunted.

"I tell you it's fixed!"

The guard was waiting as his small gang of picked lags trudged nearer, each one carrying a piece of firewood. The redcoat dipped a wink at Cribb, then pitched his voice loud enough for his commanding officer to hear. "Listen in! If I catch any o' yous not working, I'll kick 'is balls around 'is ears, and that's a promise!"

"Charming," Sly murmured to Plug.

"You 'eard the gent'?" Cribb faced his squad. "Sly? You and Mag' over there. Croak and Plug, over 'ere. Ben? Stick close."

"Where's the grub?" Sly leaned on the bit of stick which was his contribution to the marines' fuel heap.

"First we got to work."

"Go pull yourself." The stick fell over as Sly straightened, glancing at Plug, the enforcer in Cribb's family aboard *Alexander*. "More Red Jooz. Next thing the little fart'll be promising us—"

Cribb's fist struck low, folding the other man around his gut.

Sly writhed on the dust, rolling a shiv from one armpit, slashing Cribb's hocks to cut their tendons—!

Cribb's heels came down together on Sly's staring face. The former street-chieftain dropped into a fighting crouch, thumb pressed flat along the dropped knife's bare steel. "Come on, come on. . . ."

Plug backed off, dragging his unconscious mate with him. The family had now dwindled down to Thorpe, the contract strangler Croak, and Maggot the freelance graverobber. Cribb's reputation as a leader had taken eight months to build up below decks, but less than eight seconds to start crumbling once Levi's dream of a New Jerusalem in New Holland had turned into a nightmare of heat, scrub, insects.

"Right-o, let's go."

By midafternoon a small village of tents and officers' marquees had been raised beside the future parade ground. Cribb, meanwhile, had stayed close to the marines' cooks, keeping their fires stoked, carrying their buckets of water, sharing a few flakes of baccy, introducing himself to the right people in the right way. All of which meant that, by the time Maggot, Croak and Thorpe had finished their work, each man had earned a chunk of pickled meat, half a bag of broken biscuit and the right to scrape out the troops' boiler.

Cribb had managed to sustain his followers' loyalty for a short while longer.

Charles Nash had honed his wits on the more fashionable streets of London. The rations he had saved by issuing moldy oatmeal to the lags were now being divided among the cooks, the selected marines, the chosen convicts. Their master kept back nothing for himself. "Until tomorrow, then."

Nash left his followers to pig in and strolled uphill to the officers' lines where Collins and Kellow were sharing quarters until something more suitable, more permanent, could be built for the judge advocate general. "Good day, gentlemen. May I join you?"

"Of course, though I'm afraid our furniture still leaves much to be desired," B Company's second-in-command said, turning over an empty bucket.

"You're wrong." Nash smiled back at Kellow and made himself easy on the improvised seat. "I'd rather know comradeship under these conditions than have to endure what passes for 'friendship' in the gilded opulence of a palace." The former drinking companion of the prince of Wales made an expressive shrug.

"Good God, why?" Collins laughed. "A palace is not without its attractions, you know. The only gilded opulence we enjoy in the king's service is the lace around our collars, and that tends to tarnish over time."

"You undervalue yourselves." Nash waited for Kellow to finish filling three glasses with negus—*agoardente*, water, nutmeg and sugar—the only ingredients which made it possible for a refined palate to drink the raw Brazilian rum. "There was even a time when I hoped to follow the profession of arms, myself. But the war stopped too soon. Thanks." He accepted the glass and raised it in salute. " 'Long life and honor.' That is what we say, is it not?"

"Yes. And occasionally some of us even manage to enjoy both," Kellow replied.

"In Sinful Cove . . . ?"

Collins made a wry smile. "I doubt it. The items are here to suffer, and we're here on sufferance, that's the only difference."

"I'd say it was a considerable difference!" Nash disagreed. "By my reckoning we've at least three-to-one against, on the field, which are deuced steep odds when you examine the handicap against us."

"Handicap?"

"Yes." Nash glanced back at the younger Kellow. "While Miller was called away for something I volunteered to help feed the Great Un-washed. There was a bit of a scene. I was damn' glad to have some of your chaps on hand to beat them back into line. Here's to military discipline!" Nash raised his glass again, saluting the Royal Marines.

"That at least we may always count upon," the judge advocate agreed. "The first item to cause trouble is going to find his tripes unraveling on the point of a bayonet."

"True. But can we claim as much for the other lot, our brave lads in blue?" Nash wondered aloud, putting his glass down. "I had a word with Phillip today, the governor, His Excellency. Seemed a bit off-color for some reason, even if he does evidently have a dab of the tar brush in him. Is he always so rude?"

"He's never had much to do with us, has he?" Kellow glanced at Collins. "You've probably been more in his company than most, David. What's he like behind closed doors?"

The judge advocate sipped his negus and weighed the question for several moments. "Difficult to say. Bit of a stickler for detail, I do know that. Doesn't suffer fools gladly. Tends to keep to himself. But all in all he seems reasonable enough—for navy."

"But isn't even that open to doubt?" Nash persisted. "Didn't I hear that he was just a farmer or something?"

Kellow was quick to nod. "That's what I've heard. According to my sources he's spent more time off the active list, or away in foreign parts, than actually fighting. That's probably another reason why The Boss can't stomach him at any price."

"Do you mean that Major Ross and Phillip disagree?"

"Disagree! My God, they've been at each other's throats since before we embarked!"

"I find that very difficult to understand." Nash shook his head. "From my limited experience of Major Ross—we spoke briefly the other day— he struck me as being an eminently sensible, practical person with both feet on the ground. Indeed, I'd go so far as to say that he's the kind of man I'd be proud to shake by the hand, anytime."

"I don't wish to imply otherwise." Kellow hastened to correct a wrong impression.

"I never imagined you did." Nash smiled back. "But all this talk of bluejacket and redcoat means absolutely nothing to me. I am merely a civilian gentleman of town and country, which puts me in the best position to tell a man for what he is, not what he seems to be. Isn't that so, Collins?"

The judge advocate general frowned. "Ye-es, but there're times when Battling Bob doesn't know when to cease fire. . . ."

Nash also frowned. "I don't follow?"

Collins shrugged. "Ross is magnificent facing an enemy, but when there are none he tends to go out and find 'em. Mark you," he added, "I'm not saying he doesn't have reason. By now there must be a hatful of metal inside his wounds, and I do know there's a handful of offspring farmed out as poor relations, so be on your guard. There are days when it's best to say 'Yes, sir!' no matter the question."

"That boy isn't his only one then?"

"Heavens, no, just the first to go out to work."

"Work?" Nash made a comic grimace, put down his empty glass and stood. "I'd better get back to mine before it gets too dark." He lifted the door flap, hesitated a moment, then turned again. "Look, it's going to be some time before my things are unpacked from the *Prince,* but when they are would you care to come over for dinner one night?" He shrugged modestly. "Because of the peculiar circumstances of my 'offense' I was entitled to bring along a few crates of personal belongings and I can assure you they don't *all* contain bedding and crockery. . . ."

The other two men shared his laughter.

The officers had brought their own marquees and mess furniture; the government had issued its troops with tents which ranged from poor to terrible; now the seven-hundred-odd convicts were to get their accommodation, sixty-nine pounds' worth of old sailcloth bought from Portsmouth dockyard just before the convoy left home waters. Andrew Miller and Nash finished rummaging through the bales of rag, recovering those pieces large enough to rig a shelter over the commissary office. The rest were tossed in a heap on the beach and left.

"What a balls up. . . ." Cribb stood well back with Thorpe and watched others punch and kick to get at the choicest bits, their only shelter until they could build sheds for themselves. "Couldn't organize a piss-up in a pot 'ouse."

Thorpe nodded. Not only had he fed better than most today, Cribb had traded a large sheet of almost new canvas from *Alexander*'s sailmaker. An old campaigner, he'd also marked a large tree, partially eaten away by termites, then hollowed when a bushfire seared past.

Another couple of lags had also noticed and claimed the shelter first.

Cribb grabbed one tenant's feet and threw him outdoors while Thorpe slammed a knee into the other's head as he crawled upright. The two screaming men ripped back, fists flailing. Cribb blocked a swung punch and coshed his man cold while Thorpe kicked the other's cods.

"Not bad, not bad." The new landlord peered around inside the tree. "Better fix the *benda*."

Cribb's sheet of canvas was pegged over two forked branches and ridge pole, gypsy style, making a weather-break at the low doorway.

"Yes, I think this'll do."

18

PHILLIP TRIED reviewing the day's progress while he finished a solitary dinner in the great cabin, but there was little good news for his journal.

The second Fort Ross was becoming a rip-gut barricade of shattered timber and branches, behind which the colony's lieutenant governor had withdrawn for the night, and the first gangs of convict labor sent ashore today had proved to be even more useless than feared. After a year on the transports—waiting in London, then Portsmouth, then en route to New South Wales—many were poxed, or tubercular, or ruptured, or palsied, or otherwise unfit for hard work. And the healthy minority were, without exception, work-shy, pilfering schemers.

Alexander's surgeon had been amputating a set of toes when the governor inspected the makeshift hospital tent. The item strapped to the table had struck a foot with his mattock while being shown how to clear ground, though whether it was just clumsiness or the equally probable malingering had yet to be decided. In either event one hundred lashes wouldn't replace his toes and another idle mouth had been added to the already long list of those who drew two-thirds rations without lifting a finger in return.

Phillip crumbled more biscuit into the pallid, lukewarm slop of his fish soup. Only the Indians had yet to become a problem: if anything they seemed to be withdrawing into the trees. Their kings were probably planning some mischief and the British governor was more worried than he cared to admit.

The marines' fire would be wasted against spears hurled from ambush with Graybeard's accuracy and range, Phillip knew that much. At more than thirty yards, there was little point in the average British soldier aiming his firelock: only the bayonet decided modern battles and Phillip doubted if Graybeard's warriors would allow any surviving redcoat to get that close before melting away to strike from another flank. It was a dispiriting prospect to face. Even if the Indian kings' main armies were no better equipped than these naked savages on the coast, exploration inland—by land—was going to be a long hard slog until dragoons could be raised to carry war into the enemy's camp.

Phillip shoved away the empty bowl. He had once taught himself to read Spanish by copying a secondhand edition of Bernal's *Relato de las Indias,* an account of Cortez's campaigns written by one of the *conquistadores* who had fought their way across the mountains of Mexico to seize the Aztec empire. Phillip had learned more than another language. He had learned that—even with breastplates, and iron helmets, and cavalry, and wheeled guns—the captain general of New Spain had nearly been defeated by Indians with wooden swords and stone clubs. Two and a half centuries later, the captain general of New Holland was facing an even less certain future with nothing more than three companies of light infantry, five saddle mounts and four small brass cannon.

There was a timid rap on the door. Bryant poked his bandaged head around the side. "Coffee now, sir? And cheese?"

"Yes."

The governor waited until the door had shut again, then stood and leaned against the stern window, watching the sunset's embers. The Indians were out there in the besieging forest, but closer to hand the threats were becoming more insistent. Someone, somewhere in the convict lines, was having an argument. Voices were being raised. Yells. Sudden silence.

Phillip turned his back on the colony. He had more urgent problems to grapple with, like putting food into thirteen hundred mouths once the existing stores were eaten up. He waited until Bryant had served dessert and reached for something to read while he ate. *The Compleat Husband-man & Almanack Anno 1764* was nearest on his small bookshelf. He riffled its dog-eared pages with their penciled sums and notes in the margins.

This volume had grown old in his service, since coming ashore to marry and, he had hoped, live happily ever after on his new estate in Hampshire. Strictly speaking it had been Charlotte who had bought the small farm from the sixteen thousand pounds in West India Stock left by her first husband, but it had been the ambitious young Lieutenant Phillip who had taken up the decrepit acreage and whipped the fields into shape again. *The Compleat Husbandman* had been his log and pilot book combined, never far from his pocket or saddlebag as ditches were dug, hedge withies plashed, dung spread, bulls put over heifers and account books kept with the ruthless arithmetic of a man o' war's quarterdeck.

At first the Lyndhurst property had stopped swallowing money. Then it had begun to balance expenditure with income. And, finally, just before Charlotte had taken up residence at Bath and he had gone back to sea as a captain in the queen of Portugal's navy, the modest country estate had posted a profit as its mutton and tallow, wool and hay, beeswax and honey, cheese and dried apples won markets at Winchester.

Phillip had stopped flicking pages. The evidence was there, inked across the flyleaf, proving to the world that he had confounded those who said it could never be done—and that he would never do it. The Vernalls, Blackacres and Glasshayes fields had returned a net profit of £531.17.6½d for the year 1773/4. The heavily underscored figures were proof that he, Arthur Phillip, Esquire, had entered the middle rank of the English gentry, an unencumbered freeholder worth five hundred pounds a year. Later victories, at sea and on land, had never given him such a keen pleasure as that one year's farm receipts.

He was not smiling as he tasted the tepid coffee and opened the almanac at this morning's bookmark, a slip of paper on which he had adjusted the British calendar for agriculture below the equator. Assuming his figures were correct, a European September's work should begin in March at Sydney Cove, about one month from now.

" 'So far as there can ever be a beginning to farmwork it is in this month that the husbandman must gird himself for the labours to come,' " Phillip read, squinting as he followed his finger along the printed line. " 'The fields have all lain at fallow since last harvest and now ripe manures must again be carted to the strips whereon will be sown the winter oats before snows do bind the soil fast. Let also the husbandman make good heed of the magpies he counts overhead. If more than five such birds wing to the right on the eve of Michaelmas quarter-day, it will surely be a fierce wet Christmastide and the seed will never shoot thereafter but will lay rotten in the ground. But if less than five magpies go past his left shoulder, winter's icy breath will—' "

The governor let his book fall shut. Carting dung and counting birds had eventually earned him a living in Hampshire but he was seriously questioning their value in the South Pacific: like much else he could name, they were wrong. But what alternatives were there? Where could be even begin anew? At a pinch he could confiscate the Indians' granaries, when he found them, but that would be a stopgap measure against famine unless the colony learned to feed itself in the meantime.

He was weary of his own company. He reached for the bell cord. His servant peered round the door. "My compliments to Mr. Hunter and Mr. King. Ask them to kindly step aft. And bring more coffee."

"Aye aye, sir."

The governor had tidied away the day's work by the time the other two men entered the cabin. "Make yourselves comfortable, gentlemen." He gestured at the folding stools which his manservant had taken down from the wall nets. "You may pour now, Bryant."

Phillip waited until the man had gone back to the pantry and shut the door, then joined his colleagues at the stern, seating himself on the broad ledge to enjoy a cool night breeze through one of the open windows. He stirred his cup and craned his neck to look up at the motionless Clouds of Magellan, ablaze with star fire and unfamiliar constellations. "He was right. . . ."

"Sir?"

"Lyndhurst's vicar, Harry Tancred," Phillip replied, looking down at Hunter again. "Just before I left home he insisted in telling me that, once in the Antipodes, I'd be standing upside down. It caused him no end of bother. Yet, oddly enough, he's being proved right, for all the wrong reasons. Because, with every passing hour, I do feel more and more as if I've been stood on my head in a world where 'hot' means cold and 'stop' means go."

"I know the feeling, sir."

"I thought you might, John." The governor was peering aloft again at the vault of stars. "Still, old Orion seems to've adjusted quite well. See? He's also standing on his head. There's his belt and sword, where his ankles ought to be, while his shoulders—Bellatrix and Betelgeuse—are now his knees. A strange world, to be sure. However, only young Dawes is being paid to stargaze, the rest of us have rather more down-to-earth

·tasks." Phillip looked inside the cabin. "How's your crop of problems, John?"

"Thriving." The elderly Scot swirled his coffee and drank it.

"I'd noticed we're still taking water."

Sirius's commander could also hear the rhythmic whunk-a-chunk of pump rods vibrating the frigate's timbers. "As soon as may be I'll lay her ashore and broom the bottom with fire, then Chippy can caulk her seams. It's the most we can do without a dockyard and the very least we need to stay seaworthy."

"But let's say we engage the French . . . ?"

"Our first broadside ought to save the *messieurs* a job," Hunter replied without emotion.

Phillip said nothing. The twenty-four-pounders' recoil would probably rip out their eyebolts and smash the gun carriages straight through the opposite walls. If HMS *Sirius* did sink herself in battle she would not be the first man o' war to do so in the history of the Royal Navy. The frigate was a fighting machine in name alone. In truth she was the former victualler *Berwick* which had been burned to the waterline, salvaged, then cobbled together from dockyard oddments: some of her timbers had been to war in Queen Anne's reign, almost a century earlier.

Phillip glanced at his flag lieutenant's round, young face. "What about you, then?"

"Actually, I'm getting my shore legs," King replied with a smile. "Just after leaving you this morning I saw one of those large, jumping rats which Mr. Cook noted in his journal."

"How fortunate someone's having a good time," Phillip observed stiffly. He picked up the farm almanac again. "Campbell may be able to pretend that it's winter by trying to enforce greatcoat regulations, but the rest of us must endeavor to face facts no matter how confusing they appear."

He opened *The Compleat Husbandman* at random. " 'Now is come the season of frosts when straw and hay must be down put in lane mires frequented by cattle, the better to get their manure. Soot and ashes must also be spread in mossy places. And now should the tasker be busy in his barn, threshing all manner of grains, but let him not lay up any store for the granary yet lest the corn prove musty in damp weather. And let the husbandman take heed of the thornberry which, if the leaves curl up—' "

The book slapped shut.

"That's it in a nutshell," Phillip concluded. "Until the day we encounter frosty lanes and cattle dung, granaries and thornberries in New

South Wales, I don't think we'll get much further help from this rather incomplete husbandman—"

He replaced the almanac on its shelf.

"In plain terms we're all starting from scratch when it comes to feeding ourselves by our own unaided efforts. Because nothing can hide the fact that, even if every one of Miller's barrels and tubs are filled with food in good condition, we'll be facing starvation within two years, or about seven hundred days." Phillip checked a sheet of paper on the table.

He leaned back again. "However, if we go directly onto half-rations we ought to survive, with considerable belt-tightening, for another year or so. All of which is based on the pious hope that our contractors haven't been up to their usual tricks with faked invoices."

The governor was unsure how much he dared admit to anyone else in the colony. "I see our position as being like that of castaways in a leaky boat: no matter how hard we bail the water will gain on us and we must tire. In what is another example of this land's inverted logic, our ration scale is that water, the less we have the deeper we sink and the sooner we lose heart."

Hunter frowned. "But surely the resupply fleet has been promised no later than eighteen months from now?"

" 'Promised'?" Phillip looked up from his folded hands. "Did not the contractors promise that our rations would be quite different from the usual filthy junk they sell to the public account? And do you know what Miller showed me today?"

"I can guess."

"Quite. But let's assume that everything is amazingly transformed at Westminster," Phillip continued in the same withdrawn voice. "Let's pretend that our political masters are gentlemen, and that opposing gentlemen—also of the highest honor and probity—have not bumped them from the Treasury benches in Parliament to get their snouts into the pig trough of patronage, we are still no nearer to resupply.

"The last I heard we were about to go to war in Europe over that Dutch business. The moment that happened I can assure you New South Wales slipped from the middle of the priority list to the very bottom. And even if a convoy were assembled to relieve us, you and I know what hazards would lie ahead even without the French and Dutch privateers attacking it for prizes."

Phillip hesitated. "Not to put too fine a point on the case, we're at the wrong end of the longest supply route I've ever heard of. We're at the far ends of the earth and I'm nearly at my wits' end." The attempted joke failed. "I'll wager any sum you care to name that the next vessel we see from England will be a despatch boat ordering our recall, in which case we'll also need provisions on hand for the return journey."

Hunter broke the silence. "What's to be done?"

"Just two things, John. We keep a tight grip on our reserves of food and work like hell to feed ourselves. Nothing else matters."

"That should create some interesting situations," King said. "The items I enumerated for those muster lists were hardly the most promising farm workers."

"So I've noticed." Phillip turned over another sheet of paper. He ticked down the columns of names and trades from one of the transports. " 'Wig maker.' 'Catgut spinner.' 'Sturdy beggar.' 'Cinder sifter.' 'Pure hunter'—?" The governor glanced up. "What the devil's that?"

King made an eloquent shrug. "If my memory serves me right that one used to push a wheelbarrow through the streets of Bristol, collecting dog turds for sale to the tanneries."

"Oh. I see. A useful accomplishment." Phillip tossed the paper aside. "Dammit, I need cowherds, not vinegar caskers! I need plowboys, not eel sellers! Above all I need simple, industrious, obedient souls who won't chop off their toes the moment someone puts a sharp tool into their idle hands!" He looked at the other two men. "At this moment I would gladly pay ten thousand guineas to anyone who could prove to me that he knew what to sow, where to sow it, and when to reap a harvest. And he'd be a bargain at twice the price."

"Your money's safe," Hunter replied. "We're stuck with what we have. So what're we going to do with it?"

Phillip took up his penciled memorandum again. "You're going to leave *Sirius* and her many problems to Mr. Master Keltie. Instead, you're going to take the longboat, a sounding line, a bearing compass and a drawing board and you are going to discover that river which will be our safe, swift highway into the interior. You will observe stands of timber for shipwright's work, flat plains for farmland, and fast streams for the mills which will grind our wheat. You will also note the Indians' customs and attempt to create a favorable impression while assessing their worth as field workers and the location of their barns, etcetera."

"Aye aye, sir."

"I am also concerned by the apparent lack of numbers," Phillip continued. "There were so many at Botany. But here, only a few miles away, I've seen only the odd few trying to pilfer and pry. They could be planning something. Take along sufficient powder and shot." The governor looked back at King. "Meanwhile, you're going to take Norfolk Island."

"Sir?"

"As soon as practicable you will embark stores and labor to assume possession for the Crown."

King whistled quietly. "But that's well over a thousand miles away—"

"It's also abeam our shipping route to Canton," Phillip said. "If M. de La Pérouse decides to copy our example and abandon Botany Bay it would be logical for him to lay claim to Norfolk. In which case we'd have a nest of corsairs at our back door, as the Isle de Réunion is to Bombay."

Hunter was shaking his head. "Is it likely the Frogs would ever want to garrison such a remote spot? After all, they're at war, at the ends of the earth, and very likely at their wits' end, too."

"Correct." Phillip ticked another item off his list. "Nobody can be sure of their movements or intentions. But while there's a risk that Pérouse also has orders to take Norfolk Island I must do everything in my power to frustrate him. There are two other, closer enemies—fire and pestilence. It'll be useless sowing fields of wheat if fire gets among them when they're tinder dry and ready for harvest. One moment's stupidity could lead to the blaze which would cost us a year's work, and, very possibly, our lives. A daughter settlement on Norfolk is our first line of defense against devastation. As for an outbreak of fever, we've hardly arrived and one can already smell the change." He glanced at King again. "You're going to be damned glad to be a thousand miles away."

King already felt the tingle of authority as he planned lists of equipment and convicts, starting with Annie Inett's name.

"But what about the French threat?" Hunter persisted.

Phillip put away his memoranda. "That's my responsibility. I'm paying a courtesy call on our guests at Botany, as governor of the British colony they've chosen to visit. M. de La Pérouse also has plenipotentiary status. Britain's position as the paramount power in these waters will be recognized."

19

"MORE PUDDING, Mr. Johnson?" Kitty Brandon enquired, smiling across the lantern light. "Cook was prodigal with today's flour ration: I shall have to speak with him about it."

"Thank you, no. I've had ample sufficiency."

So had Duncan Sinclair but that still did not stop him stabbing the slab of suet duff and hoisting it back to his own plate at the head of the table. "I'll not see good food go a-begging!" He scratched his collar of whiskers with the fork prongs and frowned severely at his passenger. "It is quite evident you have much to learn, young man. The belly is ever a troublesome neighbor. Unless you quieten it now, by tomorrow it'll be grumbling again."

He slapped the fork down. " 'They shall be burnt with hunger, and devoured with burning heat, and with bitter destruction. I will also send the teeth of beasts upon them, with the poison of snakes from the dust!' " *Alexander*'s Calvinist master was proud of his ability to hurl these Biblical thunderbolts at the English clergyman's head.

Johnson smiled indulgently. " 'Serpents of the dust,' captain. 'With the poison of serpents *of* the dust.' Deuteronomy, chapter thirty-two, verse twenty-four, I believe?"

"Aye. But——"

"My turn," Johnson reminded him, rather enjoying these nightly jousts over the dinner table. " 'Therefore if thine enemy hunger, feed him: if he thirst, give him drink: for in so doing thou shalt heap coals of fire on his head.' "

Sinclair gobbled up the last of the pudding and licked his knife clean. "Paul the Apostle to the Romans, chapter twelve, verse twenty."

"Well done! Now, reflect a moment——"

"I've not finished." Sinclair settled back in the captain's chair under the inverted compass which hung from the rafters so that the shipmaster could check on his helmsmen above decks. "The feeding and watering of friends or enemies ceases the moment that hunger of which you spoke begins to nip *your* belly. Once there's short commons on the table, it's every man for himself."

"I disagree." Johnson was shaking his head. "St. Paul said nothing about first feeding oneself. Therefore, it is our Christian duty to——"

"Wrong!" Sinclair sprang his trap. "Second Timothy, chapter two, verse six!" He girded up his loins for a hearty, hairsplitting dispute on points of doctrine. " 'The husbandman that laboureth must be first partaker of the fruits'!"

Three years at Cambridge University had taught Johnson many ways to cope with agile, untutored minds which only regarded Holy Scripture as an anvil upon which they could hammer their crude lumps of knowledge. "My dear Captain Sinclair, you disappoint me. This is not the first time we have analyzed the fallacies of contextual illogic, is it? And yet here you are again, still trying to draw a valid inference from two invalid premises."

Forty years at sea had taught Duncan Sinclair the difference between theory and practice. "Have you ever starved?"

Johnson was thrown back on the defensive. "Not exactly, but it often seemed as if starvation would soon be our companion whenever we dined in hall at 'Varsity."

Sinclair leaned forward. "Hunger and belly cramps are the constant companions of all who go down to the sea in ships and make their business upon great waters." The compass bowl creaked in its dry brass gimbal rings as *Alexander* swung at her moorings. "St. Paul was also a seafarer, wherefore he wrote that only those who work shall eat." The master mariner watched the young cleric's face. "Now, why do you think he chose to make that point . . . ?"

Johnson shrugged. "So much depends upon our context, does it not?"

Sinclair ignored the diversionary tactic. "The good apostle learned his lessons in the school of personal experience, a course of study which I would commend to all who seek to dress a pennyworth of knowledge with a shilling's worth of words. 'And when he had thus spoken, he took bread, and gave thanks to God in the presence of them all, and when he had broken it, he began to eat.' Acts of the Apostles, chapter twenty-seven, verse thirty-five."

"Captain, really!"

Sinclair silenced him with a look. "Like many another of our brethren on the oceans, shipwreck taught Paul that, when there's but a single piece of bread and two empty mouths, food must go into the worker's, not the one who's unwilling or unable to haul his weight. Because when the strong grow weak from hunger what hope is there for the already feeble? Where's next year's plenty when the sower cannot cast this year's seed because there is naught to sustain him through the hard day's labor?"

Johnson rapped the cabin table. "God will provide. Scripture says—!"

"What do you say, ma'am?" Sinclair glanced down the bare wooden planks. The chaplain's wife prepared to defend her husband's principles, but the master had looked past her, to the murderess for moral support.

Kitty Brandon considered the question. "I'd say there'll always be diners and dinners. And given any choice I know which I'd prefer to be."

"Meaning?" Mary Johnson's voice was charged with meaning.

"I'd have thought that I, of all people, spoke plainly enough?" Kitty Brandon replied. "However, since you insist upon more simple words, let's say that in the simple world it's simply eat or get eaten, and that only a simpleton graces another's plate when, with a little forethought, he or she can be sharpening the knife and fork instead."

"Don't be absurd!"

Mary Johnson was too slow. The slightly older woman had reached out and patted her wrist before it could be snatched away. "There, there, we understand. It must be a terrible strain now that you can no longer observe the vulgar pressing their noses against the window of your father's shop in Cheapside. Sadly, for those on the other side of the glass, Our Father which art in Heaven has decreed that life is only enjoyed by those of His children who remain 'swifter than eagles, stronger than lions.' Second Samuel, chapter one, verse twenty-three or -four, I believe."

"That is a double blasphemy!"

"Does it make me doubly wrong?" Kitty Brandon asked, smiling up the table.

Sinclair was relishing every blow of tonight's verbal brawl between his woman and the parson's lightweight. He laughed and shook his head. "Now dish her with Proverbs sixteen—!"

Richard Johnson's cheeks flushed. "Sir! I object to the tone of that remark!"

Kitty Brandon allowed her smile to embrace him as well. "I'm sorry, padre, I don't appear to be explaining myself very clearly tonight. Allow me to rephrase myself by returning for a moment to Captain Sinclair's original statement."

"Yes?"

"You recall that he spoke of bread going to the strong rather than the weak in times of hunger?"

"Yes?"

Mary Johnson's fists were clenched out of sight in her lap as the other woman continued to speak.

"Surely it's a natural rule of conduct?"

"Explain yourself."

Kitty Brandon shrugged and swirled the drink in her glass. "During the advance from Montreal to Ticonderoga all camp followers drew only two-thirds of a man's ration. It seemed perfectly logical to reserve the beef and biscuit for those who had to work most and walk farthest. After all, we ladies only had to carry a musket and pack whenever a man was sick or wounded. Nor were we expected to toil behind a bogged artillery piece—though often enough we'd hitch up our petticoats and throw our shoulders to the wheel—but since our needs were less, so were our feeds."

"I fail to see the connection," Richard Johnson announced.

"You will." Kitty Brandon was no longer smiling. "I'll wager all London to a China orange there will soon be twelve ounces of salt horse on your dinner plate and eight on your wife's—"

Mary Johnson had taken enough. "I'll have you know that we are here of our own free will! We have our own provisions and shall partake of what we like, when we like and how we like!"

The convicted woman nodded. "I was going to mention those later, but since you've raised the matter we might as well deal with it now. Watch out for the storekeeper's thumb, it'll weigh a ton as he tosses your ration on the scales, but of course you must've learned about short weight behind your father's shop counter."

"My father is a freeman of the City of London! He is a liveryman of the Grocers' Company!"

"*Really?* I can't imagine anyone ever being livid while he can make free with a city, peddling sugar and spice and all things nice," Kitty Brandon replied. "But don't let my remarks disturb you, it's only envy which makes me say such wicked truths. Heavens, had I been so fortunately placed, devil a raisin or fig would have been safe." She smiled admiringly at the other woman's taut face. "I bet you a five-shilling crown to a halo that your fingers were often your mouth's best friends."

"That's a lie!"

"I've just won a halo." Kitty Brandon glanced up the table as Sinclair rocked back with laughter in his chair. "I've never owned such an unusual item before, Duncan. Do you think it would fit if I took in a few tucks? Or should Mr. Johnson keep it in safe custody, haloes being more in his line of trade, until I've learned the latest fashion?"

"You—!"

Mary Johnson was having little luck this evening. There was a thump on the door and *Alexander*'s first mate ducked into the cabin. "You wanted on deck, *kaptijn!*"

"Aye aye, Mr. Olsen."

"Captain?" Kitty Brandon enquired as Sinclair clambered to his feet. "While you're out, be so kind as to ask Miss Dundas to report to me."

The door banged shut and the Johnsons were left alone with the government woman. The silence lengthened and still she made no attempt to leave the cabin while the fare-paying passengers retired for the night. Instead, she slowly rolled a tumbler of watered brandy between both palms. "Who's for a game of forfeits? Or shall we divert ourselves by trying to guess what's on each other's minds?"

Richard Johnson brushed the questions aside. "We've heard quite enough."

"On the contrary, we've hardly begun. I'm betting you a halo to a crown that your lady wife wishes I were dead after that remark about her girlish pilfering in your father-in-law's shop."

"Enough, I say!"

Kitty Brandon sighed and shook her head. "I've lost. The look on her face tells me how my wager's gone. Better give back the halo. However, before she thanks you, I must make it clear that there's more to my words than simply malice—"

"There is?"

"Oh, yes." Kitty Brandon was smiling again. "Very soon you will be leaving us to take up residence ashore. Now, over the past several months I've eavesdropped while you discussed how you propose to minister to the sick, and teach the infants their letters, and befriend the benighted Indians. However, I've overheard precious little about how you're going to feed yourselves—"

"*We* have our own provisions!"

"Congratulations, Mrs. Johnson, and I suppose you're about to spend the rest of your life squatting on the box lid to prevent the neighbors borrowing a cupful of sugar?" Kitty Brandon looked back at the baffled husband. "She'll have to, you know, or else when Young Mother Hubbard goes to the cupboard it will be as bare as a Derry *derrière* in winter. But to return to the more important question of—"

"I've had enough of her impertinence, Richard! Correct her!"

"Correct me as much as you like." Kitty Brandon smiled. "Nothing you can say will alter the fact that, within a few days, you're going to be entirely surrounded by the biggest gang of foister-fingers ever assembled on the face of God's earth. And you think you've seen it all on the good ship *Alexander?* Heavens, we're regular tabby cats, very commonplace burglars and cheats, nothing out of the ordinary.

"You'll need to befriend a cannibal or two because we've also brought along creatures who'll have your shadow unless it's nailed down. Even then," she went on, "I wouldn't count on finding it again in the morning when you get out of bed, if you get out of bed. Which is how those famous groceries of yours would prove to be more trouble than they're worth unless you quickly get them into whatever magazine or storehouse is built. But don't imagine your worries are at an end once the door has been triple barred and there's a sentry outside, scheming how to get inside and join the fun—"

"Come to the point!"

"I have, Mr. Johnson, I have," the government woman replied, savoring her brandy with affable indifference for others' good fortune. "You see, there's something shared by all commissaries, sutlers and storekeepers. No matter under which stone you find one, the loathsome little slugs contrive to stay plump even when everyone else has been reduced to a walking bag of bones. It's a trade secret not shared with mere mortals."

"You're not insinuating they steal the property in their charge?" Johnson snapped back.

"She would know!"

"Of course I know," Kitty Brandon agreed, looking straight across the table now, "diners and dinners, remember? Don't look so worried, you served a useful apprenticeship with Papa's raisins. You'll master the craft once you sit down to enjoy eight ounces of dead donkey, six of which are bone, one of which is gristle, the rest of which was the grocer's thumb." She stopped short. "Enter!"

An older, plainer woman stooped into the cabin. "You called, ma'am?"

"Yes, Jane. Clear away, please. And see that the captain's utensils are properly scoured: he's learning to be particular." Kitty Brandon watched while the other convict woman gathered up the crockery and put it in a wicker basket.

Jane Dundas was still the lady's maid she had been until his lordship found her copying his signature on a promissory note for seventy pounds. She was now Kitty Brandon's deputy.

"Did the cook do as I instructed, Jane? Was tonight's dinner sufficient for our ladies?"

"Yes, ma'am."

"What about the aptly named Miss Pickles? Is there any improvement in her condition . . . ?"

"Not yet, ma'am."

"Oh, hell." The younger woman considered a number of options for several moments. "I'll be along presently with Mr. Levi. He'll know what to do."

"Very good, ma'am." Jane Dundas turned to go and collided with Olsen in the doorway. She stood aside as the mate pointed at Richard Johnson. "*Kaptijn* want you!"

The chaplain followed the chief petty officer aloft. The door slammed behind them as *Alexander* rolled at her moorings. The lantern swayed on its iron hook. Kitty Brandon smoothed her dinner napkin, damped a fingertip and dabbed up stray crumbs to eat. "Any more entries and exits and we'll start to resemble *One Night at Tunbridge, or, Love's Sweet Revenge*, confounded bedchamber doors flying open and shut while we pretended to play at musical mattresses." She shrugged. "Small wonder the public threatened to burn the curtains unless they got their money back."

"I do not wish to hear about it!"

"Neither did the manager until they'd torched his playhouse as well."
Kitty Brandon folded the square of grubby linen and put it on top of
Sinclair's chart case. "However, chatting about the good old days won't
help us decide a better future, will it? I am therefore about to make the
most of this rare interlude to lay my cards on the table." She cocked an
eyebrow. "You appear to have a low opinion of me."

"I have no opinion of you."

"Tch! Another halo." Kitty Brandon smiled. "Is it not fortunate that I
do have some opinion of myself or else I might've felt resentment? As it
happens, you and I share much in common—"

"Never!"

"Wrong. We are that minority of which I spoke a few minutes ago.
We are those lions who must be swifter than eagles no matter how
impeded we are by skirts—"

"What do skirts have to do with us?"

"You'll damn' soon find out once you're sprinting to protect your
virtue." Kitty Brandon was no longer smiling. "I'd estimate we're outnumbered five to one and *Alexander*'s amiable scamps are but cut tomcats
when compared with the beasts I'm told have been unchained from the
other boats. We're in for a hot time, once ashore."

"Talk sense!"

"Mrs. Johnson, I'm talking about pack rape."

"And what, pray, is that?"

"God give me patience." Kitty Brandon shook her head. "The women's
disembarkation is going to be a rare eye-opener for you. It will also be a
tragic curtain raiser for those of us chosen to play the under parts: there
won't be a dry eye in the house after the first act. Mrs. Johnson? Please pay
attention. Regardless of what you and I have said in the past we are going
to need each other almost as much as my unfortunate girls need me. At a
pinch, if we close ranks in the colony, we'll pull through. If not? Not."

The chaplain's wife cast a haughty stare across the table. "My husband
is on the governor's staff. Nobody would ever dare harm me."

Kitty Brandon whistled between her teeth. "What's that he likes to say
to Captain Sinclair about drawing interferences from invalids? They
should be here now to enjoy the one you've just uncorked!" The convict
woman was sitting forward. "So your strong right arm is on His Excellency's staff, eh? But let's imagine he is killed, or catches a fever,
what'll be your position then?"

"How—!"

"I wager you'll be horizontal, squashed flat by the first man to rip off
your drawers, and unless you learn to smile and enjoy, your second

fantasy—that nobody would dare harm you—will be as likely as tits on a bull."

"I—!"

"Be quiet." Kitty Brandon put her elbows on the table. "I'm cutting a deal, Mrs. Johnson, fifty-fifty. I shall ensure that you and your property are spared as much trouble as possible. One of my young ladies will be in attendance as your household servant. She'll have strict orders to keep her sticky fingers off your goods while keeping others' at a safe distance, for which you'll have my word of honor. In exchange I request that you give her dinner, material for two new frocks, a bonnet for outdoor work, and a pound of soap which you will insist she learns to use every morning and every night."

"Have you quite finished?"

"Yes," Kitty Brandon replied. "I believe it to be a fair offer from which everyone will gain. Your house will be secure and at least one of my Betty Lloyds will have found a secure home. I can do no better for either of you."

Mary Johnson tilted her chin. "My husband and I do not need a thief to defend our property. Nor shall we require any 'fair offer' from a murderess. As for an Irish word of honor . . . !"

Kitty Brandon's hands remained motionless on the table top. "Your father must be rich indeed to've bought such expensive manners for you. I trust he can also swim a considerable distance without fatigue once he hears your screams for help."

"Don't be impudent!"

Kitty Brandon seemed to ignore the remark. "As a matter of personal curiosity, why do you fear me?"

"*Fear you?*" Mary Johnson's voice rose sharply. "Don't flatter yourself! I may despise your class for being so vulgar, so flashy, so cheap, but never shall I fear you!"

Kitty Brandon smiled.

Mary Johnson's fists clenched as she regained control over herself. "You have been at pains to remind us that our time together is almost at an end. Soon the colony will be established ashore and you will have to learn your place in society, Brandon."

"I love you, too." The government women's leader stood and turned in the cabin doorway. "This has been an illuminating exchange of opinions. I look forward with keen interest to observing our relative progress during the next few years. Remember, should you encounter any minor upsets, call for Papa—either the one that art in Heaven or the one in Cheapside—but don't expect too much help from anyone else. Good evening, Johnson."

20

A SHADOW walked along the wall of Phillip's marquee, his shore quarters until Government House had been roofed, and King stepped under the awning. "You called for me, sir?"

"One moment." The older man did not look up as his pen scratched across a sheet of paper on the trestle table. " 'You are therefore directed to assign Capt. W. Tench to the staff of H. E. the Govr. for the duration of His Excellency's tour of inspection at Botany Bay, viz, to translate the proceedings between H. E. and Admiral de La Pérouse. I have the honor to be, etc., etc., A. Phillip, Commodore, Royal Navy.' "

He flicked the quill aside. "Too bad your French isn't good enough, Pip. Better luck next time."

"I'd have thought yours was more than adequate, sir?"

"It is," Phillip agreed, reaching for a box of sealing wafers, "but I shall be controlling the negotiations if our French visitors have to work through a translator when I already know what's on their minds. Because the first rule of peace negotiations is like the first rule at cards, disclose everything possible about your enemy's hand while revealing the least about your own." The governor damped a wafer and sealed the latest directive to cross from the east to the west bank of Sydney Cove. "Please ensure you-know-who understands my orders this time."

"I'll do my best," King replied, warily taking the folded paper. "However, Major Ross has expressed his opinion of bluejacket officers on several occasions these past few days."

Ross most certainly had. He and Phillip were now separated by a common language written on scraps of paper. Fortunately they were also separated by a muddy stream from which both camps drew their drinking water, did their laundry, soaked their aching feet, dumped their rubbish.

"Not to fret, you'll soon be your own master at Norfolk Island." Phillip locked the writing case. "Now, is everything else going according to plan?"

"Yes, sir."

"Picked your laborers?"

"Some. I could only wish all the women were ashore so that we could see how well they'll perform in harness."

"Agreed, but it can't be done, I'm not allowing them among the men until we've built a Bridewell. There'll be the devil to pay unless we're careful. Now, is *Supply* ready to receive me?"

"As ready as she'll ever be for anyone, sir."

"Splendid, we haven't all day." Phillip pulled on his best serge coat, its white facings sponged and ironed by Bryant the previous night, its brass buttons gleaming. Although the morning was hot enough ashore there'd be a stiff breeze as the brig went down the coast to Botany, Phillip knew, as he sheathed his dress sword—the one surrendered to him on the deck of *San Agostino* after his Portuguese frigate had battered the Spanish cruiser into submission off Buenos Aires.

For a moment longer he considered wearing a set of plumpers to fill out his cheeks where the teeth had been pulled—rather like the cork inserts down the calves of his white kerseymere stockings—but decided against their discomfort, even for a meeting as weighty as this one.

"Now," the governor went on, "keep an eye on whatsisname while I'm away. I need to know everything he does and with whom he speaks while my back's turned."

King looked up at the tent's waxed canvas roof. "Yes, sir."

"Remember, he's only acting deputy, nothing more," Phillip went on, walking outside and waiting for Bryant to present him with his cocked hat.

He looked round his domain. Ross's half of the cove was a mess, as if the French navy had already succeeded in bombarding the British settlement. More trees had toppled on the parade ground. Several cooking fires had run out of control. Equipment and stores were dumped up and down the beach. Squads of convicts were muddling along with the first storehouse as Dawes's corporal of engineers kicked, caned and bashed them.

Matters were moving ahead more briskly on the east bank where efforts were being made to clear the governor's garden, to build a stable for the governor's horses, to begin quarrying stone for Government House. Meanwhile, a prefabricated residence was being hammered together by *Borrowdale*'s carpenters and a pair of items who had somehow attached themselves to the job.

Phillip set his hat on straight and started down to the shore and a waiting boat.

"A word with you, sir!" The colony's judge advocate general jumped across the stream, dressed in scarlet regimentals to comply with west bank regulations.

Phillip returned the salute. "Good morning, David."

Collins slackened his steenkirk choker with a puff of relief. "Before you depart, sir, would you sign these?" His Excellency took the charge sheets with their summaries of evidence as his legal officer went on. "Mr. Shea's picket arrested the item after curfew, trying to conceal a shirt which couldn't be accounted for."

"Our property or theirs?" Phillip asked, reading the papers as they fluttered in the light wind.

Collins shrugged. "It's even more dirty than a contractor would've sold to the public account. It must've been stolen from a companion—or gambled, contrary to regulations—so either way we've got him boxed."

"What do our informants say?"

Collins shrugged again. "It's alleged to be a first offense, but when I convene the court after lunch we'll soon flog the starch from him."

"No previous offense in the colony?"

"None that we know of."

"Then have a quiet word with this Purvis before his case comes up. Explain the benefits of cooperation."

"Is that altogether wise?" Collins replied, frowning. "Once we begin displaying lenience they'll say we're going soft. I firmly believe it's time we made an example before the rot sets in. He won't be any loss. Most unsavory."

Phillip shook his head. "As I've remarked before, David, what that class thinks really doesn't matter while we're vigilant."

"True, but—"

The governor's hand silenced him. "If our unsavory shirt thief can be turned to advantage by threatening to whip him, why not do so? If he's open to reason we'll have another informant in the convict lines and be saved his rations while he recovers from a scourging."

"I was only going to award three dozen."

Phillip smiled. "David, please remember these articles are not soldiers. Your troops might have enough beef on their bones to take five hundred lashes and still be fit for duty, but not so our average convict, most of whom look as if we ought to tie them down in a strong breeze before they get blown away. You saw what happened to the last one who had his back scratched?"

"I'd hardly say he was a typical example, sir."

"I'd hardly say he was a typical anything at present," Phillip replied, "which is why I shall continue my present policy as long as it encourages the flow of information from those who may be conspiring to steal rather more than an old shirt."

"Can I have him flogged if he won't cooperate?"

"He will." The governor finished signing the papers and put away his pencil. "Now, is that everything?"

"For the moment, yes, sir."

"Splendid. However, just before you go, I'd like your personal opinion." Phillip leaned on his sword. "Mr. King is due to leave for Norfolk Island the moment I return from Botany: there'll be a vacancy to fill on my staff. I'd rather like it to go to one of your colleagues, to bring the bluejacket-redcoat equation into balance, as it were."

"Why, thank you. I'm sure we'll appreciate that."

"Not at all." Phillip smiled. "Tench appears to be sober and industrious, with a pleasing personal manner and cultivated interests. From closer acquaintance, how do you rate him?"

Collins didn't hesitate. "I couldn't have put it better. He's a credit to the corps. And well connected, on the mother's side."

"Good. That's done. Carry on."

"Sir."

The governor returned the charge sheets and the judge advocate's salute, then walked across to the half-built stable where Bryant was watering the two mares, their foals and the colony's stallion.

The servant shuffled to attention for his master. "Still looks very poorly, sir. Still very touchy, too. Still won't let me get near that leg."

"She must've pulled a tendon coming ashore." Phillip leaned on his sword again and peered at his personal saddle mount. "Keep up the hot linseed poultices."

Bryant made a long face. "I'll try, of course, but—"

"How are the others taking to their new feed?"

"All right, I suppose. When they're 'ungry, that is."

"Not much appetite yet?"

"Not much, sir."

"It's the weather. Meanwhile, keep on trying, I'll discuss what's to be done when I return." Phillip straightened as one of the nearby carpenters climbed along the bare rafters of Government House and shrilled through his fingers. "Right-o, Phoss! 'Eave away!"

The nearest item waved back and strained on the rope which ran over a derrick block, grunting in time with his mate to raise the load of roofing shingles.

"Whoa!"

The two lags squatted in the shade again as the governor continued down to the beach.

"Captain! One moment, please!"

Phillip sighed and halted.

The chaplain joined him. "Just a few words, if you don't mind."

"Of course, Mr. Johnson, how may I be of assistance?"

"It's the service of thanksgiving. . . ."

Phillip began to frown. "But I thought we held one last Sunday, on *Fishburn*, or *Scarborough*, or something?"

"I mean general service of thanksgiving. Everyone, all together, at the same time, in the same place. Not just those who can be bothered to attend Divine Service because they're not more busy elsewhere," Johnson replied with patient slowness.

"Oh."

"Captain? Our moral standards were nil before we left England: they have become worse. Not a day passes that I don't hear of thefts and fights. I have also seen the marks of strong drink everywhere, not only on the soldiers but also on those we've been sent out to guard and reform."

The chaplain chose his next words with great reluctance. "There are also rumors of unnatural vice. Please, hear me out, because your second Garden of Eden will become a second Sodom and Gomorrah unless we act now. I absolutely insist upon an opportunity to address everyone— irrespective of rank and class—to indicate the path all must tread unless we are to suffer the wrath of God!"

Johnson scowled with frustration as Tench marched closer, his batman carrying a kit and bedroll behind him. The officer of marines saluted affably. "Good morning, sir. 'Morning, padre."

"Good morning, Mr. Tench." Phillip snapped his pocket watch shut and looked up. "Time and tide wait for no man. You can speak with me later, Mr. Johnson. Meanwhile, there's some pressing business I must discuss with the commander of the French squadron. I'll bid you a good day."

The governor signaled his tars to link arms and make chairs for himself and Tench. The chaplain watched *Supply*'s boat stroke away to the brig. Then, quite deliberately, he kicked a chunk of driftwood as far as it would fly after Phillip.

Cribb was also watching as pipes called and the commodore's pennant broke aloft. He chose a small nugget of tobacco and moved nearer the stable's makeshift door. "Mr. Bryant? Sir . . . ?"

"What?"

"When you've done with that there linseed, can I 'ave it, please?"

"What for?"

Cribb's lip trembled. "To eat."

The governor's servant pocketed the knob of baccy. "We'll see."

"Thanks, guv." The lag made a diffident smile of gratitude. "You've got class. A bloke can always tell when a gent's got class. It shows. Like the way you're worried about that prancer."

Bryant was glad of any excuse to stop doing his household chores. The master was away and the lieutenant governor had no need of, or time for, sailor servants. "O' course I'm worried! You would be." He folded his arms. " 'Orses is difficult things. They don't talk. I got to be careful."

Cribb's timid smile flickered. "Then per'aps I can 'elp?"

"*You?*"

"I can always try. I been with a few 'orses. Once."

Bryant peered down his nose the way he'd seen Mr. Ross handle saucy defaulters. "That there 'orse will kick your bleeding block off." He touched the rag and paper bandage on his own head. "See? That's what it done to me!"

"Go on, mister. Please?"

Bryant hesitated. If the mare recovered while the master was away, that would look good. But if a lag were kicked and put off work, that would not look good.

"*Please . . . ?*"

Bryant was enjoying his moment of power. "What if it stiffs you? What then, eh?"

"She won't."

"But what if it does?"

Cribb clicked his fingers. "Ben? You'll say I was 'ere without Mr. Bryant's permission?"

"Um. I suppose so."

Bryant stood aside and let Cribb into the stall. The lag whispered something and crouched. The mare whickered and shifted about but Cribb kept coaxing the hoof. Then, gently, he began palpating the heel bulbs. Bryant unfolded his arms and edged closer. "What's wrong?"

Cribb drew a splinter from the cleft of the hoof's frog, the pad of leathery tissue which should have been protected by its horny sole, and pus wept from the wound. "Gone soft. She's been too long on that bloody boat. Used to 'appen all the time, Over—" He shut up and looked up. "You'll be right, now, mister."

"Thank Christ for that!" Bryant folded his arms again. "If you'd done something wrong with that there 'orse I'd 'ave 'ad your guts for bell ropes. It's the governor's own special 'orse, it is."

"Of course, I didn't say she was going to stay right. . . ."

Bryant's arms fell to his sides. "What you mean?"

"No 'oof, no 'orse," Cribb replied simply. "Unless you want 'er lamed for good you'd better get me a splash o' turpentine to clean up."

"Right."

"And I'll need warm tar for this." He tapped the wall of the hoof.

"Right."

"Then I'd better start taking 'er for nice, easy walks to firm them trotters while you fix some decent grub. We'll need plenty o' mash and barley." Cribb gave the mare's flank an affectionate slap. He eyed the serving man. "Well? What you waiting for? Rattle along and get them things before Chippy wants me back on the job."

"Right!"

Two dark, hard, gypsy eyes watched the sort-of sailor bustle away, then Cribb peeled off the linseed poultice and dropped it into his belt pouch.

"You going to eat that?" Thorpe asked, giving himself a worried scratch.

"Not bloody likely," Cribb replied, feeling around the mare's open mouth to check her teeth and gums. "We'll rub in some baccy and trade it for grog after lights-out."

Thorpe was relieved that he wouldn't be eating cold horse plasters, yet. "That'll be tonight, then?"

"Uh huh."

"Then 'ow about we take a bit to Abe? Just to cheer 'im up?"

Cribb let the wet lips slap shut. He wiped his hands on the mare's shoulder. He looked Thorpe in the face. "No."

Thorpe stood his ground. "I reckon you ought. Abe always done the right thing by you on the boat. 'E was your mate—"

"No longer 'e's not. I've been made to look like a fool!"

"That don't change nothing!" Thorpe's finger stubbed the smaller man's chest. "When you was as sick as a dog, who got you back on your feet? Abe. And when you was going to croak, who stopped you? Abe. I know, I was there, I seen 'im!"

Cribb crossed his arms. "So what? Look what it's got me—!" The arms flung wide. He turned to take in the encircling wilderness, then let them fall to his side as he faced Thorpe again. "Even Sparrow Legs don't know where we are! First it was Bottommy! Then it was Sinny! Now 'e's shot off again! And I'll bet you a george to a pinch of shit we'll be pulling up stakes when 'e gets back!" Cribb brought his voice down to a fast, urgent whisper. "Only include me out this time. Soon as them prancers are in trim, I'm bolting for Chinaland."

"With Abe. Abe goes or I don't."

Cribb's eyes narrowed. This was the first insubordination he'd had in a year's travel with the Suffolk yokel. "What you mean?"

"Abe goes or I don't."

"You won't get to Chinaland."

"I don't want no fucking Chinaland! I want 'Ome . . . !"

"Shh! Chippy's listening!" Cribb controlled himself. "Listen and listen good. Chinaland's sort of 'alfway 'Ome. You've got to get there first before you can pick up the road to London. See?"

Thorpe did not see. He had never been a Ranger behind enemy lines. Now, more than ever, he needed familiar landmarks and friendly faces. "If Abe don't go, I don't go!"

"And if I say Abe don't go, you can bet your balls 'e don't!"

"There you go again!" Thorpe yelled through his tears. "It's always *you* want this, *you* want that, never what no other bugger wants!"

"O' course! Somebody's got to do the thinking!"

"Then you'd better start thinking about some other Chinaland because if Abe's not going there, I'm not going there, so there!"

"Shut your fucking gob!" Cribb yelled back as Thorpe shoved past, stumbling away from the stable. "Abe can go stew in 'is own juice! And you can jump in with 'im if you reckon 'e's a better mate than me!"

21

"HELLO, JOHNSON! Why so sad?" Nash asked.

The chaplain raised his face and tried smiling back. "Oh, nothing. I've just had a few words with His Excellency, the governor, Captain Phillip."

"Not too fruitful, I gather . . . ?" Nash removed his straw hat and used it as a fan, then also stood in the shade for a moment.

"Not particularly."

"It's the weather. We're all a bit on edge," Nash said. "And he is a very busy man."

"Aren't we all?" Johnson replied. "But our work won't become any less by simply declaring that time and tide wait for no man!"

"Is that what he told you?"

"Yes."

"Hardly an original turn of phrase. . . ."

"Then he left."

"Hm, I do see your problem." Nash was watching *Supply*'s topsails glide behind the promontory and flagstaff as she drew away, down Port

Jackson. "He does tend to be forever running off to some other place upon mysterious errands of state: lucky for us there's a deputy like Major Ross to handle the real business of government. At least there's one man in authority who knows where he is and what he's going to do next."

"Yes." Johnson would have had his service by now if only the expedition had stayed at Botany Bay instead of departing the moment a French ship hove into view. "I think I ought to speak with him again."

"I would." Nash nodded. "At least he'll give you a straight answer, unlike Phillip. Not that I'm saying anything against His Excellency," Nash was quick to add. "He has great burdens of responsibility to carry, I know and I sympathize, but sometimes I wonder if he's really the right man for the job."

"How do you mean?"

The gentleman exile hesitated. "It's hard to pin down, but do you think he's really 'all there'?"

"All where?"

" 'Twenty shillings in the pound'? Of sound mind? That sort of thing?"

"I—I don't know."

"Who does?" Nash arched an eyebrow. "There are many intriguing puzzles about our Mr. Phillip. You knew, of course, that he's not really a sailor?"

"*Not* a sailor?"

"He's just a farmer they've put into uniform for the occasion. That's why the major and he are always at odds. One knows what he's doing, and the other doesn't even know where he is! Botany Bay. Sinful Cove. Where next? Timbuctoo . . . ?"

"But why would anyone put a farmer into uniform to govern such a place as this?" Johnson was puzzled.

"It's the old Golden Rule." Nash rubbed his fingertips. "He who has the gold, rules. Only, in our case, he who rules doesn't much have gold yet. It was the talk of the town before I left London. Phillip's affairs are in a shocking state: but he still has connection and we're suffering the consequences."

"I—I'm sorry, but how does coming here make one richer than if one had stayed in England?"

Nash pointed at the nearest heap of equipment, under guard, under a sheet of tarpaulin. "Behold, the Temple of Mammon."

"What?"

The volunteer acting assistant storeman and paymaster shrugged. "If

I were a sporting man I'd wager one barrel in ten will either be empty
or stuffed with inedible filth—"

"*What?*"

"You saw the problems we had the other day? The food's so rotten even
lags can't stomach it. Now, why should that happen, do you think?"

"I've no idea."

"Oh, come on!" Nash chuckled with gentle amusement. "Even you
must've been tempted to slip a glass or two of water into the Communion
wine. . . ."

"But only to make it go further! The elements of transubstantiation
remain unaltered."

"Sadly, ours do not," Nash observed. "Not that I'm accusing His
Excellency of selling the stores, before we left, so that he could recoup his
losses at the gaming tables, but you've got to admit it's a peculiar
situation. I mean, it's too late to go back to the shop and complain now,
isn't it? So there has to be some shifty reason why certain people in
authority picked him rather than, let's say, Major Ross."

"Goodness, I'd never thought of it like that before. . . ."

"Neither had I," Nash agreed, "then I began helping Miller to unpack
some of our things. I tell you, it's an absolute scandal! Thank God I had
enough forethought to bring some provisions of my own, like yourself
and Mrs. Johnson. Without them we'd be hard pressed. . . ."

"Incredible." The chaplain was having to adjust to a very unfamiliar
world. "And he used to seem so straightforward."

"Don't they all?" Nash asked. "My experience of people—which is not
inconsiderable—puts me on guard against those of no apparent ancestry
who pop into positions of power. But enough of that unpleasant topic.
Look, I have a few things aboard the *Prince* and they're not all linen or
tableware. So once they're unpacked—wherever we eventually decide to
camp—why don't you and I form a dining club? Our own civilian mess,
as it were? You could bring your wife along, from time to time."

Johnson was flattered by such attention but he still hesitated to accept.
"I'm not sure that's really her sort of thing. Mary's going to be quite busy
around the house, once it's built. Besides, we've grown accustomed to our
own company since changing ships at the Cape—"

Nash displayed polite concern. "How so?"

"There's another woman on board—"

"Not *La Belle* Brandon by any chance?"

"Yes. How did you guess?"

"Now I understand your natural desire for privacy!" Nash laughed.
"You? And Mrs. Johnson? And Kate Brandon? Oh, how I wish I could

be a fly on the wall whenever you chance to be together! You knew, of course, that she was sent out for murder?"

"Yes. She told us."

"But did she tell you how she killed her victim . . . ?"

"Well, no, actually she did not. It had something to do with a lover, I believe."

"It had everything to do with a butcher's cleaver," Nash corrected drily. "And the head she split open was poor old Hardwicke's, another of His Royal Highness's closest friends. A dreadful business. She should've been swung for it a dozen times but, like our shady Mr. Phillip, she must have connection somewhere. . . ."

"Then you know her?"

"I only know of her," Nash replied. "I was present at Carlton House when it was announced that she'd got off the gallows cart, I can tell you there were some very angry scenes. 'Boy' Hardwicke was, well, close to all of us." The gentleman exile smiled bravely. "But life must go on and we shall just have to learn how best to cope with La Brandon's irrational outbursts when the moon is full, as it were. But in the meantime never turn your back on her—"

"Certainly not!"

"And our work must go on, as well." Nash replaced his hat. "I'm helping Miller straighten his muddle. Anytime you're at a loose end, feel free to stop by for a chat, I'll be either at the stores or giving the paymaster a hand."

"Thank you. That's very civil."

"Not at all. My compliments to Mrs. Johnson." Nash touched his hat brim and stepped into the heat, leaving the chaplain in the shade.

Major Ross, Captain Campbell and Lieutenant Kellow were snatching a quick lunch in the battalion commander's quarters while they planned the debarkation of artillery and munitions.

"I hope I'm not disturbing you?" Nash enquired from the marquee's doorway.

"Certainly not!" Ross beamed. "Come in, come in, do! Another seat for Mr. Nash!"

His young *aide de camp* unfolded a stool and positioned it. Nash smiled at the lad, gave John Ross his hat and stick, and took the fourth side of the table.

"Another glass!"

"Thank you, major." The visitor accepted the drink and raised it to his host. "Long life and honor! Or, ought I now to say, To His Excellency the Lieutenant Governor of New South Wales . . . ?"

They all drank to that.

Nash relaxed, accepting the plate of ham, pickled eggs and freshly baked sourdough bread which young John had prepared for him. "Please continue. I'm sure you were discussing matters of importance before I interrupted you."

Kellow grimaced. "We've only got four guns to deter the Indians, if they get too close, while keeping our labor at a respectful distance. A tall order!"

"Is that altogether wise?" Nash queried, helping himself to the mustard.

"Beg pardon?"

The civilian glanced up. "I'll bet ten to one in gold or silver that we'll no sooner have them ashore than you-know-who's going to fly back and order us to pack up again. I'm not unloading a thing from the *Prince* until I'm very sure our nominal leader knows where he's leading us."

"Aye!" Campbell shook his head. "The man's as dotty as a box o' dice! Doesn't know his own mind! Never two minutes the same! Ought to be shot! Shot—!"

"Whoa!" Ross patted the other man's sleeve. "One fence at a time."

"Shot!"

"That's enough for now, Jimmy, eat up and shut up," Ross advised his friend. He looked back at the visitor. "Would you, perhaps, have heard something I haven't . . . ?"

"Of course not," Nash replied. "I'm merely exercising natural prudence. After all, once bitten, twice shy, as they say. Not that I'd like to get bitten by Phillip," he added with a grin. "Might get rabies!"

The quip was impeccably timed. Good breeding and a manly sense of fun were always welcome guests at the officers' mess.

"Capital!" Ross wiped his eyes. "Rabies! Wait till I tell that one to—!"

Nash was horrified. "Please don't! I meant no disrespect to His Excellency! It was just one of those slips of the tongue!" He recovered his poise. "I must've been thinking about an earlier talk with the padre. Please, forget I ever said such a thing."

"Oh, aye?" Ross glanced across the table at his paymaster, then back at the civilian. "And what's our Mr. Johnson been saying that he ought not . . . ?"

"Absolutely nothing, word of honor," Nash replied, beckoning for another slice of ham. "It was just that he looked so crestfallen I had to ask what the trouble was. He replied that His Excellency and he had fallen out over some trifling thing and that he—Johnson—was feeling hurt. Then he added that, in his opinion, our present governor was nothing more than a farmer put into sailor's uniform for unfathomable reasons by persons who should know better. And that he, His Excellency, was starting to exhibit signs of mental instability, or something like that. Why?"

The three officers of marines exchanged blank glances. Ross snapped his fingers and pointed at the four empty glasses. He waited until they were refilled. "Bloody hell. Things have come to a pretty pass when even a devil-driver can spot it, gentlemen. For once he's on target. I've had more dealings with you-know-who than anyone else and I wouldn't have put him in command of anything further than I could send a musket ball. However, there's work to be done, at least by some of us, and this weather looks unsettled." He drained his second measure of rum, the only anodyne able to dull the grenade splinters which had lodged in his legs when he was barely older than his son. He stood, quite steadily. "We'll discuss this matter later, Mr. Nash."

The visitor bowed. "I'm ever your humble servant, sir."

22

"GOOD MORNING, major, you sent for me?"

"Yes. Come in, Mr. Nash, come in." The sultry weather had not cleared and Ross had alerted his men to secure their equipment. Other veterans of the Caribbean had already done so: this was hurricane weather. "Drink?"

"Thank you. But isn't it just a little early?"

"Boy!"

"Sir!"

"Squeeze another lemon. For Mr. Nash."

The two adults waited for their glasses to be charged. Ross appeared troubled. "I've been giving some thought to our conversation, yesterday."

"Oh yes?"

"I'll come straight to the point: you have a knack for uncovering others' hidden intentions."

Nash shook his head. "I'm sorry to have to disagree with you so early in the day, but you're quite wrong."

"Uh?"

"I have no such gift." The civilian gentleman smiled. "I merely listen while others speak."

Ross's face relaxed again. "Aye, well, call it what you like. It's still a gift I highly value."

"Thank you."

"There are those who think that commanding an expeditionary force is easy, that all you have to do is wear a fine suit of clothes, stick a feather in your hat and read some fancy flim-flam written by other men of straw. It is not." Ross grated loaf sugar into his lemonade. "The higher we aspire, the more others conspire."

"You also have a gift!" Nash was politely amazed at the other man's phrase.

"I knew what I was being let in for," the lieutenant governor continued in the same brooding tone. "I knew it wouldn't be easy once I accepted this appointment. I knew I'd have to mix with those who are not 'in the family' as we say. That's what we marines are, family. We look after our own: a brother officer is a brother. Even the troops have their place. Most are steady lads, with here and there a few bruised apples, but they can generally be kept sound enough by active duty."

Ross looked up again. "However, at present, New Holland holds little prospect of active duties of any kind, Mr. Nash. The finest fighting men in the king's service have been ordered to his most remote garrison where we're expected to turn farmer. Worse, we've been put under the titular head of a certain individual who barely knows how to wipe his own bum. To be blunt, unless certain steps are taken, and taken quickly, Sinful Cove will degenerate into another Port Antonio."

"I'm lost." Nash really was. "Could you please explain?"

"It's in Jamaica." Ross laid the sugar grater aside. "So was the Thirtieth Regiment of Foot. Horseguards, in London, despatched them to keep the niggers quiet. But out of sight is out of mind and the Thirtieth were both. They were forgotten, except when yellow jack thinned their ranks and fresh recruits had to be drafted out. So they mutinied and murdered their officers. My company went ashore. We took the ringleaders. I was the junior member of the court martial. I balloted the firing squads. Then we had to restore order on the plantations where the darky women and the former garrison had conspired to rebel—"

"Heavens!"

The battalion commander sipped more lemonade and wiped sweat. "A pound of powder, a spark, devastation. Port Antonio or Sinful Cove, only the names have changed, we're surrounded by combustibles and I smell fire. We'll be blown sky high unless we move quickly to stamp it out." Ross hesitated. "I suppose that our methods often appear rough and ready after life at court?"

"Not at all!"

"I wouldn't blame you if you did think that way. But bruised apples have to be stopped from turning rotten and infecting the rest of the barrel, if you get my meaning?"

Nash did. He sympathized. "Why don't we shoot them now?"

"Hn. To be effective we'd first have to clean up the three battalions of trash who've been sent out to 'work' for us."

"Oh, I see."

"I thought you might," the older man replied. "Indians I can wipe out any day. Show me a Frog and you're looking at a dead man. But it's not that easy when the enemy is among us, when the enemy threatens to become us, for although my men are volunteers they're still only flesh and blood.

"My officers are sound enough, even though young Johnstone's been fooling about. I've a first-rate sar'nt major. Most of the sergeants and corporals I can count on a while longer. But the boots are a beast of a different hue now there's two hundred you-know-whats penned aboard the boats out there—"

"The women?"

"Exactly. We're hardly ashore and I've already dealt with three cases of insubordination. That's fifteen hundred lashes and still some men try their luck. If Sparrow Legs thinks he can hobnob with the Frogs while we swing at anchor until he's built a Bridewell, you're bloody right, he is only five shillings in the pound!"

"I'm starting to see your problem," Nash murmured. "What do you want me to do about it?"

Ross set his glass down. "Jock Mason of the *Prince* hails from much the same part of the world as I. He's told me about your voyage out. He had a similar problem when there was hell below decks. You made sure he could restore discipline once every man got what he needed, in a properly regulated manner. He's beholden to you."

"What else could one do?" Nash replied modestly. "It was an ugly situation, but a word here, another there, we managed to muddle through somehow."

"Aye. Do it once, you can do it again."

Nash blinked. "I beg your pardon, major?"

"Your fifty items off the *Prince* have been reserved exclusively for my men. Pay will be off-reckoned by sixpence, like we do for uniforms and food, and receipts issued in lieu. Then, when any man fails to do his duty, his privileges will be withdrawn. A cat of two legs will have a more tonic effect on morale than one o' nine tails. But for such a policy to remain effective there's got to be someone reliable to see nobody gets more than he's entitled to—"

"You're not serious? You're not actually asking a *gentleman* to become a whoremaster?"

"No." Ross shook his head. "I'm asking you to step forward, to volunteer and help. There could be another Port Antonio once those cows get among our bulls. Consider the consequences."

Nash could think of little else. One inspired comment to Kellow had dropped so much, so soon into his own hands. And there was an amusing twist to the tale: he had been sent out to this dreadful place for failing to secure a woman of good fortune. Now it was his good fortune to be given free rein with at least fifty: the Antipodes were indeed proving to be a land of contrary fortunes!

Nash would allow the paymaster to split the five pounds, eighteen shillings and sixpence a week with the battalion commander. The civilian exile had just earned something beyond reckoning, safety. With the *Prince of Wales*'s trollops between him and the troops, and the troops between them and the rabble, Buck Nash was about to assume a position of immense security within the colony.

He managed to look troubled. "This is a very heavy load you're asking me to shoulder, major."

"We all have our crosses to bear."

"Very well." Nash smiled bravely. "Since you ask, I shall do my best to do my duty. When do we start?"

"I already have," Ross replied. "They're coming off the boats as soon as it starts to rain."

"I—I'm sorry. This has been a very trying week. Could you explain that?"

Ross pondered his reply. "I am acting governor of New South Wales, Mr. Nash. I have always been capable of acting as a governor ought. Providentially, there's a storm brewing. I am about to take advantage of it."

"Advantage? How?"

"That's my task. Just you concern yourself with keeping your side of the agreement so that my men get what they need after being cooped up aboard boat—"

"It'll be murder once the rabble joins in!"

"There'll be broken heads," Ross agreed, "but if it's not done my way there'll be mutiny in the ranks." The battalion's commander looked outside at towering thunderheads advancing off the Pacific. "When dogs rut in the gutter a good drench of water unsticks them again: let's hope to God the same remedy will work on our bitches. Because you're not the whoremonger, Mr. Nash, I am." He was gathering strength for what lay ahead. "I'll do my duty, as will the shipmasters. We're all in this together, sink or swim." The officer of marines looked up, freezing the smile on the civilian's face. "Don't you fail us. Get those sluts inside the cantonment as the rains break. My sergeants are rostering the men who'll defend the strong points while their comrades have what's necessary before taking over from them. Fail to deliver what they've been promised and I shall personally throw you to the mob as it pillages what little else remains."

23

"I'M SORRY, Kitty." Sinclair appeared uneasy and felt ashamed. "I've got my orders. I can do no more."

Her fingers clicked impatiently. "Give me a telescope."

Thunder growled. Lightning glared. The storm was moving in. Kitty Brandon disdained to notice as she steadied the spyglass against one of *Alexander*'s starboard mizzen shrouds.

Convicted morts were being disembarked from the *Prince of Wales*, were being shoved into the waiting boats, were being stroked ashore. Kitty Brandon tracked them to a waiting square of redcoats, bayonets locked, keeping back the government men as the first government women landed at Sydney Cove. The *Prince*'s chattels and their bundles collapsed on the beach behind massed infantry. Whole armies had broken against British squares on half a hundred European battlefields: Sinny's jeering, catcalling lags had no hope of breaking through as a second load of women was tipped off to join the first batch.

The telescope snapped shut. "My compliments to Miss Dundas."

Sinclair passed the order and the women's deputy overseer reported to the quarterdeck. "Ma'am?"

"The moment of which we have spoken is upon us, Jane. Kindly ask the ladies to assemble with their belongings. Captain Sinclair's men will then take us to our new home. That is all."

"I—I'm sorry, Kitty."

She appeared puzzled at his lack of spirit. "Why should you be?

You've been given your orders, I've given mine, it is best we part thus." The first, fat, wet raindrop slapped her face as she checked the troops' deployment, ashore. She returned the borrowed telescope. "Goodbye, Duncan."

Mary Johnson kept her distance. She glanced at her husband for a moment. "Our 'ladies' may not be having to carry muskets and packs, this time, but I'd say they are bearing more suitable burdens."

The chaplain nodded, counting heads as the female convicts began huddling together on the waist deck. The young and old, the frightened and bold. Rags and blankets like hoods, bundles slung over their backs or clutched in their arms. Miss Pickles's had puked down its mother's frock.

"Chin up." The woman's overseer smiled. "Miss Fitzgerald knows exactly what to do."

"Oh, Gawd—!"

"Hush now." Kitty Brandon faced her other charges. "None of us has left anything behind . . . ?"

Eleven shapes shook their heads as a curtain of hail swept across the anchorage, across the ships, across the impatient lags and troops.

The chaplain and his wife hurried to join *Alexander*'s master under a tarpaulin awning. Johnson had to raise his voice above the drumfire of ice pellets. "Can't you delay their departure?"

Sinclair cupped his deaf ear. "What?"

"This is pointless! They can wait a while longer!"

"Tell that to your governor!" Sinclair turned his back on all his passengers, free and otherwise.

Kitty Brandon flicked water from her eyes, shouldered a bag and began leading the way through the entry port, down to the waiting gig. The other women followed her as best they could, slipping, stumbling, falling between the grinning seamen who now sat at their oars.

Mary Johnson tapped Sinclair. "May I borrow your telescope, captain? It's not every day one may observe 'a rare eye-opener. . . .' "

He obliged her.

"Mary! You'll get wet!"

The chaplain's wife chose to ignore her husband's advice as she walked across to the ship's right-hand side. She held the spyglass against a taut, vertical rope and aimed straight into the open boat below.

"Give way, m'lads!" *Alexander*'s coxswain bawled through the deluge. If he got his way it would be some little while before the lobsters, or the lags, or other tars had their way with this lot, especially the Bulldog's fancy bit.

A pitched battle had broken out between competing gangs, waist deep in the water, getting ready to welcome a load of morts from *Golden Grove*. Mary Johnson watched with interest before focusing her attention again on *Alexander*'s consignment of items.

Kitty Brandon was moving even closer to the coxswain, stroking his thigh. "More to the left!"

"Wha'?" The downpour made it hard for anyone to hear.

"More to the left, damn you!" the woman repeated, pointing to the head of the cove.

"*Wha'?*"

"Idiot!" Kitty Brandon ripped her dress, baring both breasts.

"Right-o!"

The sweeps dug water, swerving the boat from the flotilla of other craft, also laden with eager men and reluctant women, bound for the west bank of Sydney Cove.

Alexander's morts were the exception. They had already begun to make new friends. Water surged past the gig's transom.

Eighty yards.

Forty yards.

Twenty yards.

Ten, five, two—!

"Now!"

Kitty Brandon's bare knuckles were dressed with brass. The cox's head snapped back. Mary Johnson's mouth fell open as Nancy Fitzgerald splintered a bottle over the man who had hoped to grope Peg Pickles and Jane Dundas hit her mark with a smoothing-iron. The other ladies of the family were also starting to clean up before landing. Fists, elbows, knees, sandbags, chunks of ballast stone, rising and falling—!

"Richard!"

The gig had careened out of control and begun to overturn.

"Hell's teeth!" Kitty Brandon abandoned her kit in the shallows and waded ashore. "Close ranks! Close ranks I say! Right face, damn you! Here they come—!"

Those lags who had lost lust's lottery at the first draw were rushing for the head of the cove, whooping, punching, tumbling over one another to be first in line now.

"The oars!" The women's commander flung wet hair from her eyes and gauged the enemy's charge. "Steady! Aim low—!"

Mary Johnson recovered herself and refocused as Nancy "Jobs" Fitzgerald covered Miss Pickles and some man's child while, around them, others of *Alexander*'s women swung their poles like battering rams. Counterattacking. Driving a wedge across the rain-sodden beach. Cutting off the redcoats who were falling back on Fort Ross, abandoning the rest of the colony to a night of rape.

Some luckless officer was bound to draw the thankless duty of commanding a rearguard action. He was now slashing left and right with the flat of his sword as the storm broke overhead. He staggered, coughing and gasping for breath as someone clutched at him.

Kitty Brandon had often fallen to her knees on the London stage. Sydney's wet sand was almost as hard, Sydney's drama was as intense, Sydney's dangers were more real. "For the love of God!" The woman refused to let go of John Shea's cloak as he tried dragging it from her grip. "Have pity, sir! Save us—!"

24

"DAMNED OLD fusspot!" Ball turned his back on Phillip as *Supply* continued her way upstream to Sydney Cove. "What's biting him now?"

"Very likely the same thing which bit him yesterday and the day before," Tench replied, joining the other young man at the lee rail, "*la grande nation* so completely at home on his colony's front doorstep. Did you ever see such a model encampment as Fort St. Louis, ex-Fort Ross? I'd say it was an object lesson to which our governor most strongly objects," the governor's adjutant added, shielding his eyes as another Indian canoe rocked past on the warship's bow wave. "The Frogs have proved to be as slippery as ever and we're coming back empty-handed because even Artful Arthur can't persuade M. de La Pérouse to formally recognize our claim to New South Wales."

Ball stuffed both fists into his jacket pockets. "What the hell d'you mean?"

Tench smiled back. "I mean that I wouldn't have missed the last few days for all the world. Could you imagine Blustering Bob trying to hold his own under the same trying circumstances? Quite hopeless. No finesse. He'd have been hurling abuse like an urchin's mud fight. It would've looked very bad for our side. However, while Arty and Foxy were lunging and feinting, this bystander noticed a number of intriguing facts—"

"Like what?"

"Our captain general is no fool."

"I could have told you that without having to mince through all your damned pollyvooing," Ball replied.

"Ah, but you belong to the same half of the king's service and you've had our governor's company since the Cape," Tench observed. "Not so I. Until only a few days ago he was a rather remote hat which I had to address, occasionally, with my own off. No longer. His Excellency not only looks like a bird of prey, he knows how to strike like one. I'd hate to ruffle his feathers."

Ball grunted something under his breath.

"What are you worried about," the captain of marines continued. "You've been cast as a humble spear-bearer, one who will spend most of his time offstage between Sinful Cove and the Enchanted Isle, ferrying an unhappy hand of pilgrims to their new prison and bringing back argosies laden with the fruits of their unwilling labor—"

"Bilge!"

"Don't complain!" Tench crossed his arms, still smiling. " 'Happy the man, and happy he alone, he who can call today his own.' I fancy you'll be enjoying many such days as the months turn into years: I'd gladly exchange all of mine ashore for a few of yours afloat. But it's not to be. Our leader has spoken: I am to lay down my spear and take up cudgels as his aide. Spare me a thought as you frolic with the dolphins and I toil among our human toads to avert open warfare."

"How d'you mean?"

The redcoat was no longer smiling at the bluejacket. "Hot blood's been spilled in garrisons less remote and more appetizing than ours. Why should we be exempt from the natural consequences of malice and gossip, envy and slander, greed and stupidity? A blind man could see that His Excellency and Ross are—"

"Mr. Tench!"

" 'Once more unto the breach, dear friend.' " The officer of marines turned on his heel and marched aft to the poop deck. He halted. "Sir!"

Supply was about to round the headland into Sydney Cove.

"What's that stink?"

Tench sniffed, frowned, sniffed again. " 'Pon my word, I'm not sure."

"Then you've never endured a summer's heat in Town: this is worse than an open privy!"

Which Sydney had become. Eleven ships had heaved their foul ballast over the side and nearly fourteen hundred survivors of the storm were now slumming on a patch of dirt hardly larger than Smithfield stockyards, back home in London. Britain's newest colony not only smelled like a tinkers' camp, it looked like one. It was one.

The anchors splashed. The gig lowered away. The officers went ashore. "Get me Hunter. Get me King. Get me Collins. Get me Ross."

"Sir!"

Phillip strode up the track to Government House. Bryant had restored the marquee to something like order and spread his master's clothes to dry on some bushes. "Um. Coffee, sir?"

"Get out."

Bryant bolted, colliding with Lieutenant King as he hurried up from the stream. "Sorry, sir!"

King straightened his coat again and paused in the tent's doorway. "You wished to see me, sir?"

Phillip turned. "What happened while I was away?"

"We had a storm—"

"So did the French."

"And Mr. Ross ordered the women ashore—"

"He what?"

"Ordered the women ashore."

"How? Why? When?"

"I'm not sure," King was quick to reply. "I was very involved with other things." With Anne Inett.

"Then he deliberately countermanded my instructions!"

"Aye, he did." Ross stood behind King, in full field order, a drill-master's cane gripped in one fist.

Phillip looked at his flag lieutenant. "Get those farm workers off your muster rolls. I shall see them the moment I'm finished with this, with this gentleman."

"Aye aye, sir!"

Ross did not budge as the young naval officer went round him. The governor sat at his camp table, flanked by the symbols of his power, the writing case and the despatch box. "You deliberately countermanded my instructions."

"Stop repeating yourself." Ross had stepped inside the marquee and was making himself comfortable on a stool.

Phillip was very close to emotional collapse after months of sustained effort. "You deliberately ordered those women ashore. Deliberately! Even though you knew there were no barracks to contain them, you deliberately disobeyed me!"

"Correct," Ross nodded without emotion. "I exercised my own superior judgment rather than blindly follow a directive issued by an officer, of roughly equivalent rank in the other arm of His Majesty's service, who conveniently absented himself when mutiny and insurrection became distinct possibilities. . . ."

"You impugn my honor! I shall have satisfaction!"

"Piffle." Ross tapped his boot with the stick. "By ordering those sluts ashore as I did, when I did, I averted another Port Antonio massacre—"

"Have a care." Phillip's voice shook.

"I did care. I still do," Ross replied. "But do you? Frankly, I don't think you're even tuppence in the pound if you seriously imagine my men are going to contain themselves until yours get around to building a Bridewell." The marines' commanding officer aimed his cane at a lagged gang, idly gaming at pitch and toss in the shade of some nearby trees.

Phillip was stunned. "That's gross insubordination."

"No, it's not. Your commission has yet to be promulgated by our judge advocate general, Captain Collins of the second battalion. By contrast," Ross went on in the same voice, "of all the effective administrative instruments within the colony, I hold the one which appoints *me* officer commanding of that same battalion, the Portsmouth division, Royal Marines. . . ."

The Royal Navy officer could sense that he was being deliberately goaded, provoked into the word or action which would present his rival with grounds to assume power in New South Wales. John Hunter had been right: two hundred bayonets were a compelling argument in any language. Phillip also knew that he himself had been wrong: Robert Ross did not invariably obey regulations.

"Dismiss. Major."

The redcoat stood with ponderous dignity. "Certainly. Sir."

Tench and Collins watched their commanding officer stroll from the tent which served as an acting Government House and waited another couple of minutes before stepping from behind the unroofed shell of the more permanent building.

They halted outside Phillip's quarters and Tench coughed. "May we come in, sir? Captain Hunter is still away, surveying upstream."

Phillip finished making an entry in his pocket book. He tucked it inside his waistcoat. He looked up, his face expressionless. "The French have learned to cope with these novel surroundings. Botany Bay is as much a credit to their ability as Sydney Cove is a disgrace to ours: but not for much longer. Accompany me."

The two younger men exchanged glances as their senior officer reached for his hat and set off down the path. A short length of wooden batten had blown away with the rest of the roof of Government House: Phillip snatched it up and continued toward the stream where a tree had toppled over, making a natural bridge. He clambered off the other end with his two staff officers and strode onto the parade ground.

Here, at least, things were moving forward in the right spirit. The marine sappers had their work well in hand. Cross-cut saws swished, axe blades bit, lopping the crowns off more trees dropped by the storm. A gang of lags and two of the colony's saddle mounts had been harnessed to one of several trunks which they were rolling away, encouraged by licks from a leather strap.

"Stan' fast, you bleeders!"

"Carry on, corporal."

"Sah!"

Phillip sighted his stick at Collins as the belt cracked, the lags grunted, the log rolled. "Memo: taskmasters, the selection and appointment thereof."

"Sir." The judge advocate's pencil jotted.

"Memo: penal labor."

Collins frowned politely. "Isn't that what we already have, sir?"

"No," the governor replied without emotion. "What we presently have is a dirty, stupid, idle rabble. I intend showing my disapproval of dirt, stupidity and idleness. If fear of the lash and the rope fail to stimulate reform, there will be an alternative. Our quarry and, perhaps, the brick field will make suitable out-camps as well as building materials."

"Sir. . . ."

They had neared a sheet of sailcloth draped between the trees to make some shade from the summer heat.

"One word with you, sir!" Andrew Balmain ducked from under the Hessian screen around his hospital's morgue. He shut the dissector like a clasp knife and dropped it into his apron pocket. "A confidential word."

"Yes?"

"As you know, we already have the flux and scurvy"— Balmain kept his voice down—"but now we're starting to get the black bile and red itch, as well. And there is one other disturbing phenomenon. . . ."

Phillip gestured for his staff to follow him as he stooped after one of the colony's assistant surgeons and straightened into the tent where some of the storm's casualties had been laid. *Friendship*'s surgeon-mate was lancing a crop of boils on one of his crewmen. There was a gurgle from the operating table as a convict wardman bore down harder on the restraining straps. Balmain stepped closer and opened his dissecting knife to scrape the sailor's neck. He held out the blade for the governor to see it more clearly. Phillip's eyes smarted with the reek of ammonia from an open bucket as he peered at several small things, like grains of boiled rice, knotting and twisting together on the bare steel.

Balmain wiped the knife clean on his apron. "The Antipodean fly would seem to excrete its progeny *in vivo* as fully blown maggots."

"The French surgeons did not seem unduly troubled, nor was I troubled by objects like that when they showed me around their work place," Phillip replied, aiming the batten at the open cess bucket under the operating table. "I suggest there might be a connection, Mr. Balmain."

"But sir, I thought—?"

"Don't think, damn you, act!" The governor stepped into the summer heat again and poked his stick at Collins. "Memo: hygiene and scavenging!"

"Sir."

The three officers strode through the curious stares of those lags who were still healthy and not yet roped to logs. Shut, expressionless faces watched from cover as the strange ge'men trespassed into a transported London slum. Phillip used the batten as a walking stick now, fastidiously holding aside fouled undergrowth as he continued his tour of inspection. "Memo: scavengers."

"I've already got that, sir."

"Then underline it. Give it the utmost urgency. Immediately after orders for the proclamation of my commission."

"And when will that be?" Collins asked, pencil ready.

"Tomorrow. Noon. Thereafter my first task will be to tell everyone precisely what I think of their progress thus far. This is an utter disgrace!" The stick hacked a track past a gnarled, fire-blackened tree, uphill from most of the convict hovels. "By God, David, did you ever imagine such useless apologies for human beings—?"

Phillip stopped. He turned, shading his eyes against the westering sun. Something had just caught his attention. Something back there, at the tree.

A canvas awning had been pegged across a low entrance hole in the hollow trunk; fuel wood had been trimmed and stacked by the hearth; the ground for several yards in every direction had been swept clear with the homemade broom which stood beside the doorway. But it was the simple field latrine which gripped the governor's interest as he retraced his steps.

Without waiting to be told or shown, some nameless item had contrived to scrape a shallow pit in the shelter of a nearby bush and heap earth alongside. There was even a bark scoop and a crossbar seat with tripod legs.

Phillip whacked his stick against the tree trunk. A shaggy head poked from the hole and peered up. "Come out! I haven't all day!"

The item did as it was told and stood waiting, bare feet planted in the dust.

Phillip pointed at the latrine. "Did you do that?"

Cribb considered this simple question and its many intricate possibilities. "Some."

Phillip checked his impatience. "Where did you learn?"

"The army."

Phillip exchanged glances with his redcoated staff officers, then looked back at the dark, closed face. "In which regiment did you serve the king . . . ?"

Cribb hesitated. Behind enemy lines he'd worn a ranger's black and green: among these enemies his best cover was to be just another bootface. "Seventh Foot."

Phillip tested the laconic answer. "And by what name were you then known?"

"Cribb. Fusileer. Sir."

The governor weighed the man and his story. Both were woefully dull but, at least, this item proved that it was possible for someone to dig a latrine without supervision: at present, around Sinful Cove, that was a high level of skill and initiative. Nor had there been any boasting claims of service in great battles which were so common among the begging classes since the war. This could be the very item the colony needed, an unimaginative donkey, accustomed to work and to obey while its betters did the requisite thinking.

Phillip pointed at the hole again. "Are you capable of digging another six like that before nightfall?"

"On my own?"

The governor reached for Collins's notebook and pencil. He jotted a couple of lines on the fluttering leaf of paper and tore it out. "Present this to the storeman. Collect six shovels. You will then locate another five hands and instruct them how to dig a latrine. It will then be a punishable offense for anyone to ease himself except at the proper place. Do that to my satisfaction and you can report back for another task. Fail to please me and I shall have you whipped. Now, repeat your orders."

"Six 'oles before sundown, then back for another job."

"Correct." Phillip waited until the reluctant lag had taken the piece of paper and then returned the notebook to Collins. "Since Ross won't bestir them, I shall. Now, memo to the chaplain: prayers, etcetera. Tomorrow's ceremony is going to set the proper tone and standard of conduct."

25

CRIBB WATCHED them go. He had six trenches to dig before dusk or else he would be next in line to get his back scratched. There was no time to waste if he was to find five—better still, six—volunteers onto whom he could unload every camp's most despised chore. "Oy! Ben—?"

Thorpe may have heard but he could not stop: he was being led toward the officers' lines under armed escort. "Uh oh! Didn't I tell 'im he'd never get far without me?" Cribb had fallen into the lonely man's trap of talking with himself. "Now look. Nabbed."

He turned and strode in the opposite direction, away from Thorpe's troubles, glancing into makeshift shelters for volunteers until he found a hollow log which had recently been improved with an empty barrel and some stolen sailcloth. "You, there, Croak? Maggot . . . ?"

"What if we are?" a voice rumbled from the log.

"Front and center, *toot sweet!*"

"Why?"

Cribb crouched on his haunches. "Want to buy a winning number . . . ?"

"Maybe."

"Then let's go! I 'aven't got all bleeding day! Sparrow Legs might change 'is mind," Cribb whispered as the last of his family from *Alexander* wriggled from their lair. He scowled. "Where's Ratbag and Squeak?"

"Scroofing." Maggot dusted himself down.

"I told you to keep a tight rein on 'em—!"

"They're both old enough not to talk to strange ge'men," Croak replied, tightening the yard of cord which held up his breeches when it wasn't looped round a contract's neck. "They'll be 'ome before dark—"

"I wouldn't bet on it! Dipper's mates 'ave promised to put a stone on our weasels! We'd better get 'em before some other sod does—!"

Maggot gripped the smaller man's shirt. "First, what about this winning ticket thing?"

Cribb sighed and smoothed the notebook page. "See that? That's Sparrow Legs' own monicker. Wrote it 'imself. Gave it to me, special."

"And what's 'e writ over the top?"

"Special orders. We've lucked a special job."

The graverobber was also an old campaigner in the king's service. "What sort o' special job . . . ?"

"You don't believe me."

"Too right I don't believe you," Maggot agreed. "After all that gold palace frogshit on the boat I'm not believing nobody. So what's so special about this lurk it's worth me and Croak believing you now . . . ?"

Cribb checked that they couldn't be overheard. To be safe he dropped his voice even lower. "We struck it lucky, right? Now, I know the job don't *look* so flash—"

"Phoss? F'Chrissakes shut up, I don't want your life story, I just want to 'ear about this job."

"That's what I'm trying to tell you!" Cribb insisted. "I tell you it's going to be a piece of piss!"

"The job, Phoss, the job."

"Honest!"

"The job. . . ."

"Latrines."

Maggot cocked an eye at the other ex-redcoat. "Titch 'as been stuck in the shitpits and now 'e wants us to pull 'im out."

"You miserable bleeders! This 'as got to be the best corner in town once I—!"

"Fuck off."

Cribb laughed uncertainly. "But we're mates."

"I've got enough gold palaces." Maggot sat on the log. "Try next door, they might still need one."

"Well, don't say I didn't give you a chance—!"

"Bollocks."

"You'll be sorry!"

Cribb marched off with as much dignity as he could muster, following the track toward the marines' cookhouse where Ratbag and Squeak were happy to do anything which let them pick through the soldiers' swill pails. It had been their vocation aboard the transport, coming out, but there is always a stiff price to pay for such choice perks: the two informers had whispered daily reports to the cook, who had then told the shipmaster about life aboard his command.

Five months out from Portsmouth, on the South Atlantic, Cribb's rival below decks—Sam "Dipper" Spillet—had opened negotiations with *Alexander*'s crew to murder their officers and sail the barque back to warmer waters. Squeak had overheard them, Ratbag had whispered to the cook, the cook had told the captain, and Duncan Sinclair had tolled the lag. Wrists lashed behind his back, the tormented pickpocket had dangled from a lantern hook while he died on the devil's bellrope. Since then there'd been no more loose talk about mutiny and the shipmaster had heard nothing more than harmless gossip from his cargo hold.

But any cove who weasels, who peaches, who pimps to Them, had better be very sure there is some other cove who can protect him from Us. Cribb could, Cribb did, his fees were high, his service good.

"Sorry, Phoss!" Squeak tried hiding a lump of wet gristle. "Um. We was told to 'elp!"

Cribb shoved past and fronted up to the cook. "I've got orders to get a couple of blokes." He flashed the scrap of paper.

The cook flicked sweat and stood back from the boiler while he tried to lip-read the governor's signature. Cribb ran a thumb round the hot ladle and sucked it clean. The cook looked up again. "Going to need 'em long?"

"All depends on Sparrow." Cribb folded the paper and returned it to his belt pouch. "Me and 'im are like this, now—" he crossed his fingers—" 'e's going to 'ave a special chinwag with me before dark. Speaking of which, your blokes game for any more stuff . . . ?"

" 'Ow much?" the cook murmured.

" 'Alf a bar." Cribb lowered his voice as Ratbag edged nearer. "Go you two cuts. What's it worth?"

The cook fanned five fingers, concealed in his apron. Cribb tweaked three more and straightened them. The cook rolled one back and shut his fist. Cribb nodded. Half a pound of the Quality's tobacco was coming ashore after dark: the marines' share of the deal had just become seven tiles of government-issue bread. Cribb's escape plans were maturing.

He turned, gave Squeak a poke to get him started and led the way across the last fifty or sixty yards to Fort Ross. The sentry returned Cribb's wink as he strode into the restricted area with his two volunteer workers and slapped the packing-crate office wall. "Shop! I 'aven't got all day!"

Nash peered round a new blanket, nailed across the entrance to keep out the dust and sun. "Yes?"

"Three shovels. Let's be 'aving them."

"You'll have to come back tomorrow morning," Nash snapped, not accustomed to this tone from that sort of person. "The stores are closed."

"So what're you doing 'ere?" Cribb replied, quite used to that voice from this sort of person.

"It's none of your damned business!"

"It is when the Big Cove's ordered me to get them shovels."

Nash scowled. "You have His Excellency's authority?"

" 'Ere."

The assistant storekeeper smoothed the scrap of paper and began copying figures into his ledger. He slowed. "You've been ordered to collect six: why are you only asking for three . . . ?"

"A bloke can change 'is mind."

" 'Blokes' can, governors do not." Nash twitched the curtain shut: the stores were closed.

The blanket ripped from its nails and Cribb stepped through. "Give me six, give me sixty, I'm still only taking three shovels tonight. Because when the governor cove tells me to do a job it gets done my way, or else I get my arse kicked, and if ever that 'appens because of something you've done I'm coming back to put your face through the floor." Phillip had told a lag but a sergeant major was telling Nash. "So let's both save ourselves a spot of bother and do what I say, now!"

The other man recovered his composure. "What did you say your name was?"

"Cribb."

"Just Cribb?"

"It's enough."

"Not for me. You must have a 'handle,' surely?" Nash continued, dipping ink. "I doubt if such a forceful identity is going to be digging lavatory pits for too much longer. I might be able to use someone like you. . . ."

"It's Phoss."

" 'Fosse'?" Nash almost smiled. The unwashed knuckleman could not only dig ditches, he knew about them in Latin!

"Phosph'rus," Cribb continued, "the stuff I use on torch jobs."

The smile died. "You're not an arsonist?"

"Sometimes. Now and then."

The storeman damped his lips. "Make your mark and get three shovels from the rack, over there."

Dirt-engrimed fingers gripped the quill, turned the loans ledger around, struck out the elegant "6" which Nash had just penned, then began drawing letters the way a Loyalist schoolmaster had taught them to scratch brickwork in a cell at Copper Hill prison camp. " 'Jos Crib III shuvls.' "

"Quite an Oxford scholar."

Cribb ignored the remark. The fingers clicked, pointing Ratbag and Squeak at the rack. "One each! Left shoulder! About face! Let's go!"

Nash made no attempt to pick up the blanket: Miller could do that. He had finally encountered the dark beast of the underclass in New South Wales. It was insolent. It was dangerous. It was everything he feared and hated.

Like many another *galant* ruffian in the Prince of Wales's circle around Carlton House, Buck Nash had often tipped handsomely to climb on the box seat of a mail coach, "holding the ribbons" while its regular jarvy taught him to spank along a highway six-in-hand. Driving was an exhilarating sport and one could be wonderfully foulmouthed with such vivid characters. However, English class lines remained as tightly controlled as the reins shared by humble teacher and noble pupil.

A gentleman was expected to be on familiar terms with his servants but those servants were required to know their place if they wished to keep that place. It was a natural order from which everyone gained something: the led were fed and clothed while they continued to fetch and carry.

This tolerant delusion had been shattered forever, like a brick flung through a mirror, when London's mob erupted from Houndsditch and Ratters' Castle to sack the city. Many individual sparks had swirled together to make the flame which finally detonated England's near-revolution. There had been Lord George Gordon's ranting against Catholics; there had been the taxes on bread and meat; the taxes on beer and gin; the taxes on candles, windows, chimneys, carriage wheels; the taxes on anything and everything which could pay for the ongoing American war. The days and nights of pillage, rape and gunfire had eventually given way to an exhausted calm, but a certain quality, a sense of security and the rightness of things had vanished from the streets of the capital, burned to cinders by malevolent little rodents like "Phosph'rus Cribb."

" 'Ullo! Been 'aving trouble with the door?" Andrew Miller enquired, civilly enough.

Nash jolted back to the present. "Oh, nothing serious. One of the clients wouldn't believe the stores were closed. I tossed him out." He stood. "Tidy up, there's a good fellow. I've something to discuss with Major Ross."

"Right-o, sir."

26

THE AGRICULTURAL future of New South Wales had been plucked from six boatloads of total strangers and herded together under guard beside the parade ground. It now stood in a defensive huddle, scratching and squinting—the tall, the short, the dull, the dim—while the Big Cove talked on, and on, and on.

Phillip's patience was wearing thin. He had explained their duties at great length, in basic English, and thus far he had not seen a flicker of understanding on any face: he could have been speaking to the trees for all the good he seemed to be doing. The governor aimed his stick at one puny item which had attached itself to a blond bullock of a young man near the middle of the small crowd. "You there! What have I just said?"

"Er, dunno, guv! But I never done it, honest!"

Phillip winced at the unmistakable cockney whine. "You're not a farmer."

"No? But I cuts corns and bunions!"

Phillip stopped himself from breaking his stick over the cringing shape. "This is hopeless, David, utterly hopeless!"

"Oh, I wouldn't go so far as to say that, sir," Collins replied, trying not to smile. "He admits that he can cut corns and bunions, surely that's halfway to cutting corn and planting onions? And if he finds it difficult to adjust, a few dozen scratches from the cat ought to sharpen his memory."

"I wouldn't count on it." Disgusted, the governor looked at the puny lag's taller neighbor. "And what work can you do?"

Thorpe pondered the question. "Sheep mostly, master. But I does barley in season, and turnips, and thatching, and ditching, and—"

"Enough!" The sun was setting, when it rose tomorrow Phillip was determined this odd-job gang would be toiling together, grubbing up shrubs and roots to level the colony's first field. The stick pointed at a bare patch of dirt on the parade ground. "Show me how you'd raise a crop on that. Come along, come along!"

Thorpe plodded between the ge'men in all their fine clothes. They halted and the three officers waited for Thorpe to make the next move. He squatted, squeezing a ball of soil in his fist, trying to estimate its loam, but the damp gray sand kept flaking between his fingers. He tried again, failed again, looked up again with a gloomy shake of the head. "She be 'ungry ground, master. We could put out a wainload of dung and marl and still she'd be 'ungry. We got to put 'er back in good 'eart first."

"And how do you propose we do that?" Phillip asked, leaning on his stick.

"Don't rightly know," Thorpe replied, scratching his bum, then his chin. "I got to think."

Phillip checked a natural impulse to hurry this item: his own farm bailiff in Hampshire was another of these Saxon oxen: Mathew Godwin could only be led, never driven. The governor controlled his irritation and looked back at the other laborers and one street corn cutter, still standing where he'd left them. They could not have been more lumpish had they been chewing cud. At least this present item recognized the need to think before acting, to which extent he stood head and shoulders above the rest of the herd.

Phillip prodded with the stick. "What's your name?"

The lag stood and wiped both hands on the gaping seat of his breeches. "Ben Thorpe, master."

"Where d'you come from?"

A year understudying Cribb in the ways of the world had still not taught him the need to lay false trails whenever ge'men got too close. "Out by Tattingstone way."

Phillip tried forming an opinion of this man's worth, based on his own experience of the Wessex pastures northwest of Lyndhurst, but Thorpe's root stock was a hundred miles in another direction, on a Suffolk heath where hovels huddled with their backs to the North Sea's gales. Ceorls from across that sea had settled Gurton Waste a thousand years before; serfs and bondmen had hoed it down the centuries. The same folk still trudged across the same hungry fields as day laborers. As Old Ben's boy, Young Ben, might have still been doing now if only his last master—the village squire—had not sent him up to London with a flock of sheep.

Paid in part with a pewter crown, Thorpe had been trapped by the city watch as he clumsily tried selling the five-shilling piece to one of the coiners who bought back duds at a discount for refacing and reissue. The woman had bolted, leaving the yokel holding ten shillings' worth of pot-metal pennies as well as the bad crown. She might have cost him his life on the gallows: instead a judge had given him Life. Transportation beyond the seas for life.

Phillip had made up his mind: this man would do, at least until they found someone better. "We are going to put out five acres this year, Ben, two of wheat, two of barley and one of the crop they call maize. Although our need is great we mustn't try to run before we can walk because the seasons here are not the same as Home. There'll also be individual plots for vegetables, but our most important task will be planting those five acres because only cereals will store to carry us through the down months."

Thorpe nodded.

The sun was almost level with the treetops. Phillip borrowed Collins's notebook and pencil again. He steadied it against the crown of his hat and signed a curt directive before ripping out the page. "That's what we call a *laissez passer*. Should anyone enquire what you are doing, show it to them and, if they still question you, come directly to me. I'll see you are troubled no more."

Thorpe folded the piece of paper and tucked it into the belt pouch copied from Cribb.

"Very well, let's have a word with your men." The governor led the way back to the other farm workers. "Pay attention, there!" The stick silenced them. "You will be taken across to Government House at first light tomorrow. There you will be shown a piece of ground which you will clear to make a field. If you have any problems, refer them to Ben." The stick tapped Thorpe on the shoulder. "Work to my satisfaction and you'll not find me ungrateful. But if any man fails to please me I shall have him whipped until he mends his ways."

Bunions wiped his nose and raised the sticky hand. "Wha' about me, guv?"

"What about you?"

"Can I go now?"

"Not yet," Phillip replied quietly. "I shall expect you to be with your colleagues when they report to the sergeant of the guard for roll call tomorrow morning."

"*Me?*" the Londoner whined.

"Yes." The governor broke his stick across the man's head. "You."

Thorpe watched the officers march off, leaving him to dismiss the workers for the night. He hitched his belt. "You 'eard that? Tomorrow. At lark fart. Now bugger off."

The other farmhands trudged away to their hutches and roosts, leaving Bunions to pick himself up. "That 'urt, that did!"

Thorpe rubbed a thumb on the bleeding scalp. "Don't feel like no bone's broke. But best Abe takes a look, I don't need you croaking yet."

"Ta, you're a gent." The corn cutter wiped his nose. " 'Ere, you really think Sparrow means it? I mean, about me 'aving to 'elp you lot to-morrow?"

Thorpe hefted the governor's broken stick. One half still made a handy length. The new taskmaster tested its grip. "If 'e don't, I do."

Bunions gave up and followed down an already well-worn track to the hospital tent as Kitty Brandon hurried into sight. She slowed and stopped. "Why, good evening, Mr. Thorpe. I do trust you're settling into your new abode . . . ?"

"Well, it's not so bad now it's not raining," he replied, reaching out to grab Bunions's shirt as the corn cutter began sidling away.

"You're both going down to the hospital?" she enquired, noticing the blood which splashed off Bunions's ear.

Thorpe nodded.

"Then while you're there would you do me a favor? *Please* speak to Mr. Levi about restoring the friendship which you and he and Mr. Cribb used to enjoy aboard the boat."

Thorpe looked very doubtful. "Why's that, then?"

"I do have my reasons," she replied. "Believe me, it is of the utmost urgency that we old friends agree to let bygones be bygones, for all our sakes. I can't speak more plainly than that, can I? Yet trying to broach the subject with Messrs. Cribb and Levi, at the moment, is like banging my head against a brick wall. You are the only intelligent man I can turn to for help. You will help me, won't you?"

"Um. Well. I can try, I s'pose."

She patted his wrist and gave him a warm, private smile. "Thank you. Good evening to you both, gentlemen."

They were further down the track when—

"Oy! Ben!"

Thorpe slowed. Cribb was heaving himself out of the ground behind a low heap of earth. The smaller man grinned brightly and hurried forward. "I was getting worried about you, mate!"

"You was?"

"Too right!" Cribb eyed the street corn cutter for a moment. "You been to the wars?"

"Sparrow bashed me!"

"That a fact?" Cribb fingered the torn scalp which the other lag was holding together. "Worse things can 'appen, as the bloke with one pin said when 'e saw both legs get shot off 'is mate." He looked back at Thorpe. "Anyway, am I glad to see you're all right! We're in luck." He reverently unfolded his requisition order for the shovels. "That's the Big Cove's own monicker. Me and 'im are like *this* now." Cribb crossed fingers.

"Why?"

"Let's show you!" He gripped Thorpe's elbow and led him toward the ditch where Ratbag and Squeak were now sitting on their shovels. "There's only three of us supposed to get this job," Cribb continued, dropping his voice, "but I'll 'ave a special word at the stores, first thing in the morning. . . ."

Thorpe poked the governor's stick at the heap of dirt. "What's it? A grave or something?"

Cribb crossed his fingers, again, warding off bad luck. "I can't tell you just yet, only me and Rat and Squeak are supposed to know." He winked. "This time we're really onto something big!"

"So'm I."

"Doing what . . . ?"

Thorpe folded his arms. "I'm Sparrow Legs' gaffer, I am."

"Get away!" Cribb poked Thorpe in the ribs.

The taller man took out his own page from Collins's notebook as Ratbag and Squeak edged closer. "This is what they call a lazy pisser. Any cove what gives me lip, now, gets told the master and that means 'e gets bashed proper, Joe Cribb."

That had already begun for the smaller man. He quietly put away his own paper. "What's it you've got to do, Ben?"

"Keep the likes of this tasking." Thorpe aimed his stick at Bunions.

" 'Ow many you got?"

"Nigh on five and twenty."

Cribb looked at his own couple of almost worthless followers, then back at the other man. "Best of luck. Keep in touch . . . ?"

"We'll see."

Cribb watched Thorpe continue down the pathway to the hospital. Shadows were lengthening across Sydney Cove. Birds, like drab brown kingfishers, were roosting in the trees, sniggering and cackling as they did every dawn, every dusk. The lag threw back his head and bared his teeth. "Sod you, too!"

Levi snipped the strand of cotton and blew powdered chalk over Bunions's scalp. "Will live."

"Ta muchly, I'm sure, but it still bloody well 'urts!" the corn cutter whined.

"What more you want for one baccy knuckle? Angel music?" The lag wardman clicked his fingers for Bunions to get off the medical chest which served as a seat under the lantern. The patient obeyed and searched around for a bit of *modongo*. Levi measured it against his own thumb knuckle, then dropped the army-issue tobacco into a plump belt pouch. "Come back seven nights and I pull the stitchings."

Bunions flinched. "I'll bet that'll cost me, too!"

Levi wiped his hands and gestured for the little *k'vetcher* to leave *Alexander*'s hospital tent before curfew: there might be other clients lurking in the shadows and there was nothing more to be earned from this broken head. If Bunions wanted free treatment that much he could always scrounge a sick chit from the orderly sergeant which would let him skip work parade and stand in line tomorrow until Balmain rowed ashore from the barque.

The patient turned to shuffle away but Thorpe hooked a finger under the laborer's belt and stopped him dead in his tracks. "Lark fart."

"I'm no good at that sort o' thing! Honest I'm not!"

Thorpe hefted the broken stick. "Lark fart."

"Oh, orright then. . . ."

Bunions slouched away into the dusk. The overseer also got ready to leave the tent but Levi stopped Thorpe with a look. "What's lark fart, Ben . . . ?"

"That's when I got to get all them out there tasking," the Suffolk man replied with a self-important nod. "I'm the 'ead gaffer now, I am!"

"No zhit?" Levi tossed the soiled piece of rag aside and made himself comfortable in Balmain's chair. "Sit down," he pointed at the medical chest. "I am curious. What is a head gaffer . . . ?"

Thorpe did as he was told, resting the stick across his knees. "That means I got nigh on two score men to show 'ow to be field taskers. And if they give me lip, I show them my lazy pisser." He took out Phillip's *laissez passer* and smoothed it in the lantern light for the other man to admire. Levi scanned the governor's signature as Thorpe went on. "I'm going to put in five acres this year—"

"Of food?"

"Ar. And wheat. And barley. And oats. And things."

Levi stood and walked across to Balmain's medicine cupboard, slipped a homemade duplicate key from his shoe and unlocked the door, then came back with two stoneware bottles in one hand, a pair of physic measures in the other. The wardman arranged the small glasses on the operating table and poured out two generous servings of surgical spirit, added a splash of laudanum to each, and brimmed them from the water cooler. "*L'chayim.*"

Thorpe warily watched to see what happened next. Levi led the way with a practiced flick of the wrist and Thorpe followed suit. His eyes popped. "Hoo! That's good belch, that is! Let's 'ave another!"

Levi finished replacing the spirit and laudanum with equal quantities of water before returning them to the security of the cupboard. He sat down again. "So, my friend, you are a man of some consequence. Five acres of food, you said . . . ?"

"And veggy gardens too!" Thorpe stopped licking inside the glass. His self-esteem was blossoming as two ounces of absolute alcohol and opium spirit chased around his belly and up his backbone. "I'm going to put in four rods o' peas! And four o' beans! And cabbages—!"

"Vegetables?" Levi interrupted with a wondering smile. "Such luck, and when luck enters the game brains score double! I am so happy for you, Ben." Thorpe wiped his mouth along a wrist as the other lag unlocked a second box and took out half a cheese, a jar of pickled eggs and a bag of biscuit. "Please, be my guest."

Thorpe never had to be told twice. He tucked into the other man's fees and perks for private, after-hours consultations, and some during the day whenever Balmain was busy treating the Quality's aches. It was doubtful who got better service, the free or the unfree, whenever Levi stood in for his nominal overseer.

The long, lean, lonely years between working in a Polish nobleman's slaughterhouse and cutting for stone in Bokhara's *suq*—then back again to Europe and a fashionable abortionist's shop in London—had given Levi a professional training unlike anything taught by the Edinburgh Guild of Barber Surgeons. And it was still delivering fresh bread and meat to his table, richly seasoned with power and payback.

Cribb had not been the only one to give him a hard time: others had been quick to taunt their discredited guide to Botany Bay's *goldeneh medineh* with its ten lost tribes of Israel in their New Jerusalem. But, as Mrs. Brandon continually reminded him, Fortune's wheel not only casts down, it also lifts up as it rolls into the future. The same faces which had jeered and spat upon him in the boat were starting to come into the hospital tent with their toes off, with their fingers crushed, with the flux churning their guts. And one way or another, they paid.

Levi made a Turkish *papirosa* from a handful of officers' tobacco, rolling it in one of the small red tissue papers which the surgeons used to wrap their prescription pills and powders. He licked the flimsy tube, pinched the ends and lit up with a contented smile. "And what's new with your fine friend, Mr. Fozzy Kripp . . . ?"

"Fucked if I know." Thorpe wolfed a wedge of cheese. "Why?"

"Just curious." Levi trickled smoke. "I notice you and he not mates no more . . . ?"

Thorpe crunched a tile of ration bread. "Know All reckons 'e knows everything. Won't talk of nothing but Chinaland!"

The *papirosa* burned hot inside Levi's cupped palm. "How's he getting there . . . ?"

" 'Orse," Thorpe replied, brine dribbling down his chin as he bolted an egg. "Reckons 'e can snaffle one and get there easy."

Levi flicked ash. "So once more we are making like *Kossaken* chasing wagons, pam-pam, with pistol guns?"

Thorpe nodded.

Levi smiled distantly. "Is this why you and he have fight?"

"Sort of." Thorpe scratched. "Joe won't never listen to what I got to say about anything."

"And what do you have to say?" the other man enquired, eyes half-shut.

Thorpe groped around for the right words. "Well, it's like this, I don't know nothing about Chinaland. And I bet 'e don't neither!"

"A good bet. Continue. . . ."

"Well, it seems to me a crust o' grub on the table is always better'n a great big pudding in the sky," Thorpe insisted with gloomy emphasis. "But Joe's so full of 'imself these days 'e won't listen to nobody."

Neither was Levi listening to anybody as the quarter guard began its rounds, beating the curfew. Other drums were never far from Levi as *Judenhetzer* tramped through the alleys of his mind, hunting Jews without a pass to stay in the city and a bribe to stay out of jail. At least, to that extent, one slept better under a tent in Sinful Cove than under tiles or thatch in Koblenz. Or Hamburg. Or Berlin.

He glanced up again, at Herr Philipp's gardener. "I'm sorry, Ben. What was that?"

"I said, I reckon this 'ere place will be all right while the grub don't get no worse." Thorpe loaded two biscuits with more of the cheese. "I never been nobody's gaffer before. It's lots better than always 'aving some clever bugger shitting on me like they done before."

"You learn quick, my friend." Levi pinched out his smoke. "As for good grub, who's growing five acres this year? Maybe fifty next? Perhaps five hundred the year after that?" The convict wardman was reaching for his lantern to go and check the hospital's foetid sheds. "Please"— he pointed at a pile of blankets—"make yourself at home. Is not right for head gaffers to sleep like beggar men in a tree."

27

KITTY BRANDON halted, standing to attention as the quarter guard began beating the retreat. It felt good to be home among the military's tents with their bells of muskets standing at each doorway on the gridwork of company streets. Here, at least, one could rest easy among some semblance of order and purpose.

A tall spar had been towed from *Sirius* earlier that day and carried ashore by nine convicts. It had replaced an earlier, temporary flagstaff and was now secured by ropes, ready for tomorrow's ceremony. Small rocks had been stacked round the foot of the pole and whitewashed by the same punishment squad which had painted the stones around the battalion's altar of drums.

She was not the only government woman living in the colony's most exclusive neighborhood: C Company's young second-in-command was keeping an even younger housekeeper who had just been sent to fetch his dinner and her rations in the same iron pot. The two women moved again as the bugler finished "Sundown."

"Red sky at night, soldier's delight," Kitty Brandon said as their paths crossed. "A sure sign that tomorrow's occasion will be one to tell the children when they grow up. Speaking of whom, how is little Rosanna . . . ?"

"Much better, thank you," Esther Abrahams replied, clearly and well: she had been a lady's maid until two cards of stolen lace brought her to judgment at the Old Bailey. "I did as you said and he gave me something to settle her cough."

"I knew he would." Kitty Brandon smiled back. "And how is Mr. Levi keeping . . . ?"

"I can't say, he doesn't speak much, and what he does say is not always easy to follow," Miss Abrahams said, shifting her grip on the pot inside her pinafore.

"I know," Kitty Brandon replied, wishing she were ten years younger and endowed with that figure, that complexion, that hair. "But please persist with your efforts. Lagged or free, we are far from home, but Mr. Levi is farther away than most. Reassure him that not all the world is unfriendly. My young ladies owe him a great debt of gratitude for what he did to ease their troubles during the journey out. However, now we're ashore and, as it were, starting from scratch. I think the time has come for us to put our heads together. . . ."

"Why?"

"Wait and see." The vastly more experienced woman patted the girl's wrist. "Now, the next time you borrow that scrubbing board from Captain Collins's housekeeper—Miss Yeates?—enquire if she would like to join us for a quiet chat. Meanwhile, if ever you require anything and I'm not available, ask Jane. During our many tribulations aboard *Alexander* I formed the highest opinion of Miss Dundas's character: a word to her is a word directly to me."

"Thank you!"

"On the contrary, thank you. My compliments to Lieutenant Johnstone. Good night." Kitty Brandon turned and continued her walk around the parade ground, following the white stones to Captain Shea's quarters.

His orderly had lit the lantern and hung it on the center pole above the empty crate which served as a writing table for B Company's commander. She could hear his cough and see his shadow on the green fabric walls as he worked. She straightened her hair, fixed a brave smile and drew the door flap. "Devil a chance you'll have of getting better while you keep pushing yourself like this!" she announced, lifting the officer's wig to kiss the bald patch underneath.

Kitty Brandon replaced the curled horsehair—rather like a gray teacosy with a plait and black ribbon down the back—and smiled with him at the comic effect as she sat on a smaller box. "You're a stubborn man, John Shea. You'll only have yourself to blame if the doctor's medicine doesn't do its stuff." She wagged a finger. "I really think it's time we had a private word with Mr. Levi—"

"Another page!" The older man groped for a piece of rag. "I'll soon be done!" He wiped his mouth. Getting drenched to the skin when the women disembarked, the other day, had not helped matters. "It's this confounded business tomorrow. By God, Kitty, did you ever see such fuss and feathers over one simple parade and review?" He tucked the handkerchief up one sleeve of his faded red tunic.

"How do you mean?"

Shea shook his head. "The Old Man's got this bee in his bonnet about the French, and how imperative it is for his commission to be proclaimed over the territory. Then, to compound matters, Ross is determined to have his hour of glory. At present both our leaders resemble nothing more than two blind men seated upon the same nag, one facing its ears and the other its rump, and both thrashing the poor brute to make it go forward!"

Kitty Brandon reached into her basket and got out Shea's best pair of white breeches, which had been laundered in the stream and dried on a bush this afternoon.

His quill was scratching again with the precision she secretly envied, looping and dotting across the paper in time with her darning needle as she tacked a new patch over his threadbare seat.

His mastery of the pen was evidence of how much he had improved himself, for Irish squires with the means generally employed others to do their scrivening while they rode to hounds six days a week and fell over drunk on the seventh. However, although heir to a bog in County Meath, he had never inherited the necessary income to lift the mortgage. The land and its peasantry had passed under the auctioneer's hammer, but the residue, after all debts were settled, was still not enough to buy a commission.

Like many another candidate officer and gentleman who hoped to repair his family's finances with prize money and off-reckonings from the regimental payroll, Shea had needed a successful war. As such he had advertised in the *Dublin Posthorn & Examiner*, announcing to the world at large that John Shea of Kilbeggan was a sure-fire prospect for fame and fortune upon the battlefield once other speculators, better britched, bought shares in his future winnings. Eventually he succeeded in pawning most of himself except for seven shillings a week of his salary and one third of whatever he could loot from the enemy.

He was now ready to lobby men of influence who could write his name onto a colonel's list of ensigns. His luck was in: the Grenada garrison had been decimated by yellow fever. More officers were needed in the Caribbean and John Shea sailed off to war. His luck was out: the sloop he was serving upon was taken as a prize by the *guardacosta* and he survived the next twenty months in the fortress of Santo Domingo before being exchanged for an equally destitute Spanish officer.

He returned to active duty three stone underweight and deeper in debt: the regimental paymaster had pocketed his pay vouchers while Shea was a prisoner of war. His prize money from the Malabar Coast passed directly to his creditors. His first battlefield promotion to lieutenant was garnisheed the day it was gazetted. Ensign Shea's second advancement, in the Mediterranean, was also sold to satisfy his owners. His third lieutenancy was won on the bloody rip-gut fence across Bunker Hill as his marines took the Rebel stronghold at bayonet point and, this time, Shea kept his epaulettes.

Twelve years or so later he was almost out of debt and desperate enough to invest in a captain's commission before lobbying for service in the South Seas. It was a calculated gamble. Warm weather might slow the rot in his lungs until he'd fought one last campaign. Then his widow could inherit a captain's share of the booty. On the other hand, if he fell in the conquest of New Holland, his widow could pledge the half-pay component of his commission if she played her cards right with the moneylenders. Either way, Mrs. Kathleen Shea would win a respite before her inevitable decline into genteel poverty.

Her husband sprinkled sand over wet ink and tapped the grains back into their tin canister. He looked up as his housekeeper nipped a cotton and smoothed the latest patch to cobble his breeches. "You're a good woman."

She understood. "I like you too, Jack."

He pushed the day's work aside. "So what's new with our wild animals out there?"

"Oh, one thousand and one bloodcurdling adventures, you may be sure. Here, give me that coat as well, I can be fixing it while you recoil from tales of the darkest villainy, of the hottest passion, of the most comical upsets—"

She helped him slip his arms from the tunic sleeves and sat down again, grimacing at its frayed cuffs and burst elbow seams. "It's no use, I'll have to direct His Excellency not to pull up the curtain: I won't allow any man of mine to walk on wearing such a costume. Heavens, tomorrow's audience will hardly be worse dressed and a more tatterdemalion troupe of tinker tosspots I could never imagine!" Her eyes twinkled kindly as she hoisted her skirt hem and cut off another patch from underneath. The colors almost matched: her petticoat had been tailored from bits of discarded army uniform in the death cell at Winchester Castle. "However, before we get onto that, I'm in need of some advice, Jack."

"Go ahead!" He stifled a cough. "Though, unless you wish to hear about scarps and earthworks, there's little of value I could tell anyone."

"You're doing yourself a disservice," she replied, licking a thread to a fine point. "You've a lifetime of experience in the world of men which I shall never penetrate. For example, consider our present plight." She succeeded in threading the needle at the second attempt and set to work on the scarlet tunic. "Here we are, a gang of castaways at the very back of beyond, more or less evenly split like red pips and black in a deck of cards. Not surprisingly, there are some kings, and some knaves, and plenty of no account. Although I'm not complaining about those which Lord Luck has dealt me," she was quick to add, "because I've a damned fine queen who's always turned up trumps in the past. Why, in normal times I could pick off tricks like that!" Her tongue clicked. "However, for some reason, His Lordship has cut a pair of jokers. One of whom I am well acquainted with, but the other is still wild and, until both have been finessed to my satisfaction, this could be a deuced tight round."

"Go on. . . ."

Shea's housekeeper glanced up from her work. "I am most familiar with our parson's wife, as I ought to be after sharing the same mattress for so many nights. Moody Mary has a natural flair for making trouble, but I'll knock the wheels off her waggon because, regardless of what she thinks, New Holland is not Old England. We've been dealt new hands. The rest of us are no longer playing by the same rules even if she persists in thinking so."

"And the wild one?" Shea set two chipped teacups on the crate before reaching for a canteen which hung, with his sword and pistols, from a nail in the tent pole.

Kitty Brandon let the tunic rest on her lap. "The assistant paymaster, volunteer storeman, and constant shadow of Major Ross. A rare combination of talents. He was aboard *Prince of Wales*, as you were. Man-to-man, what's Nash really like . . . ?"

Shea finished coughing and gestured for her to take a cup, then took the other for himself and swallowed a dose of the only draught which gave any relief. "He's English. Need I say more?"

"No, but I need to hear more."

"I'm sorry." Shea shook his head. "It's dishonorable to blackguard someone while he's not present to defend his reputation. Nash might find that a daunting task but, at least, he should be given the chance."

"Go on. . . ."

Shea warmed the rum between his palms and inhaled its healing fumes. "No."

"Jack, please, believe me, I have the most urgent reason!"

The older man reluctantly gave in. "Very well, since you ask, I do not care for his company."

"Why?"

"Because I cannot bring myself to like cheats and cowards." The officer of marines hesitated. "Perhaps, if only I'd managed to compromise on such trifling points of conduct, this life might've followed a different path, but that's all water over the weir now. Let's change the subject."

"No." Kitty Brandon had taken some long thorns and was pinning a patch over her darn. "There must be a particular reason why a man such as yourself should bear such a harsh opinion for another. . . ."

"The strongest reason in the world, my dear," the redcoat officer replied, rubbing his fingertips. "Envy. Nash appears to have the readies in abundance, but who wouldn't after eloping with an heiress?"

"The hell he did! He stole a woman."

"Surely that amounts to the same thing?"

"Only if you believe that a fork and the sausage are equal because they happen to share the same plate," Kitty Brandon replied. "But to continue, how did Nash conduct himself during the voyage . . . ?"

Shea hesitated again. "He dined at the captain's table every night, doesn't that tell you? Correction, it was poor old Mason who served at his. We weren't clear of the Channel before our exiled gentleman was running that barque any way he pleased and, if a shipmaster chooses to take orders from such a passenger, the law says that's his business. Nash corrupted everything he touched, or spoke about, which is why I made sure that, whenever I had to dine with them, I took a long spoon." The captain of marines refilled his cup. "And you'd better have one if ever there's reason to sup at the same table. It's itemized in my papers, Kitty, but for God's sake be careful how you finesse if I'm no longer here to partner you—!" He got his breath back. "A viper has more sense of honor."

"And the girls aboard the *Prince?* How did they eat . . . ?"

"As some do now." Shea sipped. "By serving my men."

"Thank you, that's all I needed to know."

"That's all I'm going to tell you," the officer replied as his soldier servant scratched at the door flap. "Enter!" The man stooped through with two dinners balanced on a box lid. "Ah, thank you, Sullivan. Place it down."

28

CRIBB HAD ambushed a rock python at nightfall: the dead snake was now coiled on a shovel blade over a low fire while he kneaded a little of his flour ration to go with the main course. Digging latrine pits had done nothing to ease his hunger but the skimpy allowance of beef, dried peas and cornmeal would have to last him until the next grub parade—and beyond if he was to hoard enough for the ride home across Chinaland.

Cribb disciplined the temptation to dip another handful of flour. Instead, he wrapped the strip of gray dough along a piece of twig and squatted nearer the hot coals. "Bastard place. . . ."

His guest kept silent, staring at his own gritty stick of bread. Thomas Barrett was the last of *Alexander*'s lags to believe that, one day, their ex-leader might be able to repay a favor. Cribb had been of use before, at sea between England and the Canaries, when Barrett was casting dud florins from musket balls melted in one of the cook's ladles. It had been Cribb who'd gulled a guard into supplying the raw materials and then into dropping the counterfeit two-shilling pieces at Rio, but the young soldier's only profit from the deal had been three hundred lashes in *Sirius*'s longboat as it rowed around the British convoy, drummers beating "The Rogue's March" in time with the cat o' nine tails.

"Yeah. Bastard place." Barrett lifted his stick and blew on the bread where it was smoldering. "So's your idea. Won't never work."

"Why not? We done it before."

"Not with this sort o' bunt," the counterfeiter said, flicking a dull metal disc across the fire.

Cribb trapped the Spanish dollar midair. "What's wrong with it?"

"Too worn, that's what's wrong with it." Barrett twisted off a bit of bread and chewed its steamy dough. "You'll never get a mold from that clunker."

"We 'aven't tried yet," Cribb said, rubbing the blurred profile of Carlos III. "I reckon it's worth a go—"

"Piss off." Barrett was always irritated whenever his professional opinion was questioned. "You'll get us both necked if you push shit like that!" Cribb crossed his fingers to ward off bad luck as the other lag went on. "Besides, what's there to buy?"

"Not much." That, at least, was true. Baccy, grog and muffin fixed everything in Sinny but Cribb had to keep the Chinees in mind: he needed a purseful of lead-alloy traveling expenses.

Barrett was eyeing the dead snake. "You really going to eat that . . . ?"

"Why not?" Cribb replied. "Just like pigeon."

"Jesus!"

The older, darker man leaned over the fire to flip the coil of meat and rearrange it on the hot iron. He ignored Barrett: there were greater problems. Sparrow Legs had come back: Sinny was going to be abandoned like Bottommy and, with it, would go any hope of a quick dash across the mountains once the mounts' hooves were in trim.

Cribb gnawed his lip and stared into the coals. There were even bigger, nearer worries. This afternoon's stoush with the storeman had not been good. Seven years in the king's service had taught Cribb that cooks, orderly room clerks and storemen matter. They can make life difficult or easy depending on how a cove goes about things. But that is when they are real storemen. Whatever, Cribb knew that his aim was off. He should have got the gent on his side, buttered him up, chucked in a few "sirs." Still, it was typical of the way things had gone since Levi fell out with him aboard *Alexander*.

Cribb knew that he had been jinxed, he no longer got anything right. The reason was obvious: with all his foreign jabber, Leafy must know a heap of *ruffi ghanee* spells. Cribb crossed his fingers again and whispered some of his own *phuri dai* Romany incantations, but they did not feel so strong this evening. Still, at least he knew the reason for his continuing bad luck.

He bit his left thumb, spat over his right shoulder to hex Levi, then lifted the shovel and snapped off a length of python. He peeled its skin with his teeth and looked at Barrett again. "Like a bite?"

The other man looked sick.

"All the more for me." Cribb nibbled the pale meat from its spine. "Ever et rat?"

"That's disgustin'!"

"So's an empty gut." Cribb sucked his fingers. "You ever rode a prancer, then? An 'orse? A nag?"

The coiner from Shoreditch squinted across the firelight. "You all right in the 'ead?"

Cribb ignored the question. He would have to do this bolt alone. Barrett would never make the first five miles to Chinaland.

29

A DRUMMER faced the dawn wind and beat the call to arms. The troops heard him, crawling from their blankets, cursing the tangled musket slings, standing to behind the brushwood palisades, staring back at the darkness. Watching. Waiting. Indians were out there. Somewhere. Watching and waiting. The horizon glowed as the sun came up, gilding the treetops around Fort Ross. The drum rolled again and weary men stood down from their posts: they had survived another night on foreign service.

Smoke began wisping over camp kettles as the troops gave a final buff and polish to their equipment. And the corporals reported to their sergeants. And the sergeants reported to their subalterns. And the lieutenants reported to their captains. And the captains fell into step, marching off to make their reports to the battalion commander.

Ross was waiting, legs straddled, an orderly at his feet, rubbing soapy water and pipe clay up his master's breeches. Their cotton twill was already shrinking in the sun's warmth: the major's toes were starting to throb but that would soon cure itself once he began putting his men through their paces.

His company commanders halted, doffing their hats. "The Second Battalion stands to arms as directed and awaits your further orders, sah!"

"Thank you, Jimmy." Ross took his time shrugging into his number one tunic which the orderly was holding open. He began buttoning it as he stepped round the corner of his marquee to check for himself.

Two hundred fighting men stood in column of route on the roughly cleared parade ground, a color party and band at their head: solid blocks of redcoated infantry behind, spike bayonets glinting, light artillery bringing up the rearguard, sappers and pioneers on the flanks. It was a balanced, an impressive display of power. His power.

Ross faced his captains again. "You would not seem to be your normal, cheerful self this morning, Shea."

"On the contrary!" The man leaned on his sword. "I've never felt better!"

"Then look it." Ross glanced at the youngest captain by age and seniority. "Everything going well with you, Mr. Tench? I trust, while you were absent from your duties here, His Excellency showed you the respect and consideration due to one of my officers . . . ?"

"Sir."

"Good. Very well, to your posts, gentlemen."

They saluted and marched back to their companies. Ross touched Campbell's sleeve and cocked an eyebrow as Shea stumbled away, racked by coughs. "One shilling will get you five the big Boghopper's not long for this world. We'd better alert Kellow, he can draw a promissory note on the pay account, fifty guineas down and the rest in annual easements. . . ."

Ross was about to let Campbell go when he glimpsed the judge advocate general trying to slip past on the other side of the battalion commander's marquee. "Mr. Collins!"

"Hell." There was no option but to change direction and skirt the tree which had been felled to clear Ross's view of the parade ground. Collins halted between the two imaginary lines which Dawes's town plan said were George Street. "Good morning, sir."

"So it is." Ross stamped both feet to keep their circulation moving as the breeches clamped his thighs like tourniquets. "It's not every day one of my subordinate officers steps up in the world. Your father was wise to buy you this appointment. Now, with yourself as the law, and young Tench shuffling the colony's paperwork, I can't imagine anything happening without your comrades being appraised of the fact first. . . ."

"Sir."

"Be mindful where your chief loyalty lies, no matter how often others may try turning your head with empty promises," Ross went on. "Comrades must come and go but the corps endures, remember that." He spoke the truth. In a quicksand world of shifting values and shifty alliances Ross had learned that he would always be on firm ground while he was trussed in leather, scarlet serge and horsehair. "Therefore, Mr. Collins, you can imagine how it angers me whenever I see the law favoring convicted items above my own men. . . ."

" 'Favoring'?" The judge advocate general frowned. "How do you mean?"

"I mean that one of Mr. Campbell's company got three hundred for stealing a shirt, yet not a week ago one of the items got off with a caution for exactly the same offense! As well you know."

"The Purvis business. Yes, it was unusual. One of His Excellency's ideas—"

"Exactly! And I'm giving fair warning I won't take any more of his harebrained ideas! Bloody hell, what kind of lunatic world is it when guards are punished more than guarded?"

"One where things are rarely what they seem on the surface," Collins replied, tersely. "Now, if you will excuse me there are still documents to prepare for the ceremony."

"Dismiss." Ross had seen a replacement audience. "Mr. Johnson!"

Collins was glad to surrender his place to the colony's chaplain, hurrying nearer, black gown flapping, a prayer book under one arm. "Yes? What is it, major?"

"Everything in order? No loose ends? I'm expecting the utmost from every man today," Ross said. "I expect you to set an example, padre. We have to instil a wholesome fear of authority into that rubbish." The lieutenant governor designate pointed at a batch of laborers who were being poked along at bayonet point by the quarter guard to witness the colony's official birth. "Others may choose to slap their wrists for theft but I want their faces rubbed into Exodus chapter five, verse thirteen, 'And the taskmasters hasted them, saying, Fulfil your works, your daily tasks, as when there was straw.' Understand?"

"It can't be done on the fifth week after Epiphany," Johnson replied, politely but firmly. "I offered His Excellency a choice of texts and he has chosen Proverbs one, verses ten to nineteen as being most apt for the occasion as well as the season." The chaplain bowed. "Now, if you will excuse me, I must attend to my duties."

Ross crammed his hat over his wig, marched in the opposite direction and took his place at the head of the column. "Battalion will prepare to advance—!"

His bandsmen jerked to attention, their left knees bent to balance the drums, elbows up, sticks level with their cockades, then struck together as the uncased standards flowered, bending forward on the wind. One young ensign carried the King's Color, the red, white and blue Union flag. The other officer of marines was privileged to steady a crimson silk banner embroidered with gold and silver thread, the laurel wreath won on the bloody beaches of Belle Isle. The battalion was honor bound to follow wherever the colors led, into cannon fog, through squalls of musket balls, by land or sea, to victory, to death, to both.

Sluggish troops quickened to the angry pulse of drums—striking, rolling, striking—as they were knocked into line by their sergeants' halberds. "Dress, damn'ee! By your right! Dress, you idle sods!"

Ross drew his sword. The fifes shrilled. Massed infantry began advancing across the uneven ground, heels crushing grit: pioneer platoons marching on the wings, their axes, saws and sledgehammers ready for any task from clearing a road to building a bridge. Four small field guns brought up the rearguard, manhandled by marine bombardiers; sponges, iron worms and rammers lashed across caisson lids; water buckets swaying under gun trails; ready to destroy or defend with shrapnel, shot or shell.

"Lef'! Lef'! Left, right, left—!"

"Dress, damn you, dress!"

"Ri-i-ight wheel—!"

The governor designate took the salute at the flagstaff as this precision fighting machine marched and countermarched. It was an impressive display of power. His power. Phillip could imagine what effect it must be having on the assembled labor and any Indian spies who might also be present: several clusters of indigenes were on the fringes, keeping their distance as Ross's troops completed the maneuver which encircled the apathetic government men and women.

Mary Johnson also felt her chest swelling with pride as the measured dignity of today's ceremonial gathered pace. She was standing on the select side of the parade ground, of course, upwind from the lags. Her husband was about to stand forth as a man of authority and she had ensured he would be on his best behavior. His gown was freshly ironed and his white Geneva bands had been rubbed clean with a damp cloth. Now, after so many humiliating delays, he had ceased being a hedge parson baptizing babies under trees or preaching at bored illiterates. He was the colonial chaplain, empowered by the bishop of London, entitled to become a justice of the peace, in due course.

The parson's wife had finally achieved her place in society. As the only free woman among the Quality she stood as far above the unspeakable Brandon—sitting to one side of the ground with the other "house-keepers"—as they were above the work gangs, squatting in the dust, picking their noses and toes.

Mary Johnson straightened her husband's hair and pulled back the black queue ribbon on the nape of his neck. "Don't forget to enunciate your vowels clearly: sometimes you're in too great a hurry."

A trestle table had been placed near the whitewashed stones around the flagstaff. On it were displayed two red leather despatch boxes containing the commissions, a copy of the relevant act of Parliament establishing the colony, the letters patent constituting the courts of law, and Cabinet's general instructions. But before any of these could be proclaimed the governor first had to affirm his loyalty to the House of Hanover. It was a necessary precaution: Phillip had not forgotten his own eighth birthday treat, a rainy morning at London Tower, watching the Scottish generals being hanged, drawn and quartered for their loyalty to the failed House of Stuart.

Johnson stood forward with the Bible. The governor rested his hand on it as the judge advocate recited the Oath of Assurance. "I, Arthur Phillip, do truly and sincerely acknowledge, profess, testify and declare, in my conscience, before God and the world, that our Sovereign Lord King George is lawful and rightful king of this realm and of all other of His Majesty's dominions and countries thereunto belonging—!"

"What they doing now?" Thorpe whispered, leaning closer as most of the lags around them lolled on their elbows.

Levi removed the twig he was using as a toothpick. "Why ask me?"

"Because you know lots o' things, that's why."

Levi shrugged. "Kings I know. Counts, margraves, prince bishops I know. Sultans, pashas, *bimbashis* I know. Emirs and khans I know. And you know what else I know? I know not one says, 'What big thing I going to fix today for Reb Abraham Levi?' when he get up in the morning. . . ."

Thorpe fell silent and chewed over this brain teaser as the officers and ge'men finished saying their long words.

"—I do make this Recognition, Acknowledgment, Abjuration, Renunciation and Promise, heartily, willingly and truly, upon the true faith of a Christian, so help me God."

"So help me God," Phillip responded.

"Horse zhit," Levi murmured to himself, shifting the toothpick to the next gap in his mouth.

Collins took another scroll from the despatch box and held it open against the wind. " 'It is the wish of His Majesty that, as soon as conveniently may be, and with all due solemnity, our said commission constituting you governor and captain general be read and published, wherein you are empowered to keep and to use the public seal, to administer oaths, to appoint justices of the peace, coroners, constables and other necessary officers. You are furthermore empowered to pardon offenders in criminal matters at your discretion—' "

"What's bimbashers, Abe?"

Levi sighed. "You looking at one."

"You . . . ?"

Levi looked to Heaven for patience, then down again. "In Turkland *bimbashi* means boss over one thousand men, like Sparrow Legs. They chop off hands, heads, pull out eyes. Everything."

Thorpe looked back at his master with renewed awe as Collins unrolled yet another document. " 'We, reposing especial trust and confidence in your loyalty, courage and experience in military affairs do, by these presents, constitute and appoint you to be governor and captain general of our territory called New South Wales—' "

Nash yawned and tilted his hat against the sun. Lord, what a bore! And Kate Brandon was acting as if this legal rigmarole was for her benefit alone, surrounded by her court of honor. Quite wasted on Shea. Not that he would be around much longer, if today's appearance was any guide, then Kellow could bid for the vacant commission. Be interesting to see how La Brandon handled that one. . . .

Collins began to fidget: Ross had finished repeating his oath of office as lieutenant governor but was still gripping the Bible and surveying his new domain. Phillip ignored his deputy and addressed the assembly, instead. "Pay attention at the back!" Some of the lags obeyed in a half-hearted way. "From this moment onward the customary laws and punishments of Great Britain are in force and will be enforced! You must know what that means or else none of you would be in the condition you find yourselves today! How and where you proceed from here will lie entirely in your hands and you'll do well to ponder the options open to you! There will be no mercy for any shirker or thief under my jurisdiction! Every man will pull his weight for the common good! And those of you who fail to grasp this simple rule of conduct will be taught it by whatever means I consider necessary—!"

"Does he not speak well, Jane?" Kitty Brandon asked, glancing sideways. "It's amazing how Mother Nature distributes her gifts. From such a shrimp one can hear a very pleasant and manly baritone, while from that addled Adonis Nash proceed pained squeaks as if his breeches had been cut too tight. . . ." Kitty Brandon folded her hands and smiled distantly at the show.

The despatch boxes were jumping about as Phillip's fist continued striking the table top. "However, those of you who show the proper spirit of subordination, sobriety and cleanliness will be allowed to wipe the slate and begin life anew! To each will be granted a tract of land and every encouragement to establish himself as a useful, productive member of society! Those are now the only paths by which you may proceed to the future. One wends across the sunlit fields of prosperity to happiness, the other goes directly to the whipping post and gallows."

Kitty Brandon checked an urge to clap as Phillip stood aside for the chaplain to take his place. "What talent!" She looked at Jane Dundas again. "Did you not observe the lyric quality of those last three lines? I couldn't have said better m'self."

"Ma'am?"

The government women's leader tapped her deputy's wrist. "Hush now, Mr. Johnson speaks."

The chaplain opened his prayer book at a slip of paper with the main points of his sermon blocked in pencil. "Brethren in Christ Jesus! Today, being the fifth week of Epiphany, we humbly take heed of King Solomon the Wise who wrote: 'My son, if sinners entice thee, consent thou not! If they say, Come with us, let us lay wait for blood, let us lurk privily for the innocent without cause: let us swallow them up alive as the grave; and whole, as those that go down into the pit: we shall find all precious substance, we shall fill our houses with spoil: Cast in thy lot among us; let us all have one purse—' "

Cribb trapped and killed an itch. "Well? What d'you reckon?" he asked Barrett.

The coiner studied the new Spanish dollar cupped inside his hands, unwilling to give a definite opinion until he'd made a trial plaster cast. "Not bad, I s'pose."

"Not bad? That spangle's the best there is!"

"Then 'ow'd you get it . . . ?"

"Never you mind." Cribb tweaked the coin back into his own safekeeping. "Just remember who's got it and who can get the stuff to make a ton more."

"You'll never let me forget," Barrett grumbled, shifting his weight to the other hip. "Anyway, what's in this for you?"

"Straight sixty-forty split." Cribb slipped the piece of silver between his cheek and teeth. "I only need enough, that's all."

"Enough for what?"

"None o' your business."

Johnson had loosened his cravat and was flapping his black gown for ventilation. " 'My son, walk not thou in the way with them; refrain thy foot from their path: for their feet run to evil, and make haste to shed blood. Surely in vain the net is spread in the sight of any bird. And they lay wait for their own blood; they lurk privily for their own lives.' "

The chaplain wished that Mary had not made him wear his best black winter suit: this Antipodean February day was distressingly warm. " 'So are the ways of every one that is greedy of gain; which taketh away the life of the owners thereof.' Put on, therefore, as the elect God, holy and beloved brethren, kindness and humbleness of mind. Be meek and long-suffering, forbearing one another and forgiving. And may the peace of God rule in your hearts. Amen."

Egyptian taskmasters flogging Israelite captives in Pharaoh's brick pits were more to Ross's taste. He made an impatient gesture at his sergeant major. The man turned, heel, toe, click. "Prime and cock—!"

The drum major twitched his baton. The *feu de joie* exploded, a running thread of musket blanks crackling along the ranks as the Union flag broke at the masthead and the band struck up "God Save Great George Our King." The bluejackets were not letting the redcoats claim all the glory: *Sirius* and *Supply* had loaded their batteries of ordnance: smoke and torn wadding boomed, drowning the marines' salute. Parrots and cockatoos shrieked across the treetops of Sydney Cove. The Indians huddled together, eyes popping as the ghostmen marched past, cymbals clashing, fifes squealing, and the lags drifted back to work.

Kitty Brandon stood up from the box which Shea's orderly had provided for her. She motioned for Jane Dundas to stay behind as she turned to address the other housekeepers. "Thank you, ladies. Until this evening, then?"

They also went about their business.

"You wished to speak with me, ma'am?"

Kitty Brandon made certain they could not be overheard before smiling at her deputy. "You must be starting to wonder why I haven't yet

found you a suitable billet with one of the gentlemen. However," she
went on, "such an appointment requires patience, discretion and more
than a pinch of luck. It's really a question of matching horses to courses,
for what suits one person does not have to agree with another, but I
promise you've not been forgotten. Indeed, you could say that I've been
saving you up for the right moment which, I am reliably informed, is
almost upon us. . . ."

"Ma'am?"

Kitty Brandon lowered her voice further. "There'll soon be a vacancy
for you at Government House, assisting His Excellency's man, Bryant."

"*Me?*"

"Can you name anyone better qualified for such a post of honor?"
Kitty Brandon was no longer smiling. "This is an opportunity of the
greatest advantage and I know that I don't have to remind you what is
expected from our ladies: how vital it is to maintain a bright, cheerful
countenance at all times; how essential it is to banish strong odors and
bad breath; how crucial it is to become indispensable to the Quality. I
also know that I don't have to tell you how desperately outnumbered
we are: please keep that in the forefront of your mind whenever you're
serving His Excellency and his staff at dinner and they believe themselves to be alone. Be a piece of furniture. And communicate with me
as often as possible when matters of substance are being discussed over
the wine."

"Just like on the boat?"

"Exactly so, but with one difference, you must be prepared to become
agreeable to His Excellency in every way. . . ."

Jane Dundas almost blushed. "How do you mean, ma'am?"

Kitty Brandon winked. "Clad in rags or bedecked with gold lace, I
promise you all men are pretty much the same under the blankets."

"But surely not with the *governor?*"

"Whyever not?" Kitty Brandon chuckled. "Heavens, if I were not so
content with Captain Shea I wouldn't mind swapping places because,
unlike many another officer of my acquaintance, Mr. Phillip appears to
be a gentleman. He also keeps his clothes tidy and his fingernails clean.
I'd say that, when your relationship ripens enough for Old Mother
Nature to do her stuff, you're going to be agreeably surprised how little
kindness you'll need to sow in order to reap a considerable connection. . . ."

"Thank you!" Jane Dundas was blushing. "I'm not sure what to
say—!"

"Then say nothing," Kitty Brandon advised. "One final word of caution, the morning after it happens be prepared for harsh words and remorse. Men make such a fuss over their confounded 'honor.' Mr. Phillip may be such a one, it's difficult to judge. But he'll certainly be aware of the gulf between your stations in society. It is at this point in the game that a woman of the world advances her interest or loses within one minute everything won during the night, for which reason I've picked you rather than anyone else in our family."

Jane Dundas smiled uncertainly. "How do you mean?"

"Let's just say that Mr. Phillip will feel more comfortable with the company of a mature, discreet woman," Kitty Brandon replied. "A pert young piece would never resist the temptation to blab about her wonderful fortune: it'd be all over the camp inside five minutes and she'd be gathering oyster shell for the lime burners before the hour was out.

"You will, therefore, give no indication of recalling what passed between you in the bedchamber. On the contrary, you will be especially attentive to His Excellency's commands and will never, upon any pretext, presume upon the public figure by means of what you learn about the private man. The greatest wisdom of all is silence. Do as I suggest and you will long remain in favor at the very center of events."

30

NASH STEPPED from the shadows as Shea's woman walked past. Kitty Brandon did not slacken her pace as the assistant storeman fell into step beside her. "Quite an impressive display of talents, was it not? Major Ross with his silent guns and Commodore Phillip with his thundering words. However, despite all the power of his oratory, experience tells me that our lieutenant governor will enjoy a more assured reign during our sojourn in the Antipodes."

"That's why you've backed him to win?"

"Why else?" Nash smiled. "It's certainly not because I enjoy his sparkling conversation, or because of anything personal I may have against poor old Phillip, but even a blind man could see that hot blood is soon going to be spilled between them—"

"To which end you're ensuring that nobody spills yours in the process," Kitty Brandon observed, pausing to allow the gentleman to remove a fallen branch which lay across her path.

"Aren't you doing exactly the same?" Nash countered, straightening and catching up with the woman again. "But take a tip from someone who knows, you've backed the wrong runner. Sparrow Legs doesn't have it in him to stay the distance. He and Ross are hopelessly mismatched. It's like harnessing a Clydesdale and a donkey and expecting both to haul with equal power." He shrugged. "Not that I have anything especial against either beast, so long as it performs, but given a choice I shall place my money on the strongest animal—"

"You always did have such a winsome way with words."

"Thank you, but we're wasting them at present," Nash replied, slowing his pace. "Can I assume that you've considered last night's proposal?"

"Yes."

"And your answer is—?"

"No."

Nash touched Kitty Brandon's arm and halted. "Would you mind repeating that?"

"Certainly." She dusted the hand off her sleeve. " 'No,' one simple little word which is simply not used often enough in affairs of this nature. Now, if you will kindly step aside, I have other matters which demand my attention."

Nash did not move. Nor was he smiling now. "I always knew you were stubborn but never did I think you were stupid. I shall allow you until this evening to come to your senses."

"I would indeed have left them were I ever to agree with your proposition. But as it happens I have rarely felt better and there is no way in the world I shall allow my ladies—"

"Ladies? They're sluts! As such they'll damn soon come to heel!"

"As I was saying, there is no way I shall ever allow my ladies to become doxies in a soldiers' brothel," Kitty Brandon concluded.

"They're that already," Nash snapped.

"Correction, they keep house for individual officers, which is quite another matter."

The man stepped closer. "Let's just get one thing clear. Major Ross has entrusted me to perform a very delicate task—"

"To be his private whoremonger? I know, I saw your first delicate performance from the quarterdeck of Captain Sinclair's command. You're all heart, Charley."

Nash controlled himself. "As I was saying, the lieutenant governor of this colony has requested me, as an especial favor, to allocate that one ration which the Ordnance Department failed to supply his troops. But

I have already spoken about that so I shall get straight to the point—"

"Please do."

"I give you until this evening. Until then my terms remain as generous as they are for the other female cargoes." Nash halted, trying to break down her obstinacy with reason, with another smile. "Surely you must see that I cannot allow you to set your own pace and your own price? You have to join me because, if I permit you to continue following your own path, it won't be long before *Scarborough* and *Golden Grove* and the rest begin going their separate ways. And should that ever happen we'd have the very crisis which Major Ross has expressly asked me to avoid—for everyone's sake."

She stopped him with a look. "You're quite serious about this? It is not enough to have the *Prince* girls, you need to dominate the entire colony, as if we were one single brothel?"

Nash hesitated. "I dislike the blunt way you put it, but there is no escaping the fact that someone in authority had better enforce order in what has the potential to become a very dangerous condition, with so many young men and so little opportunity, as it were."

"Correct."

"Then you do agree with me?"

"Naturally." She returned smile for smile. "It's plain arithmetic that, since we ladies are outnumbered five or six to one, our reception the other day will be but a fleeting shadow compared with what horrors await us unless matters are put on a business footing. It's high time we struck a deal."

"I'm listening."

"Add your numbers to mine and we'll call it quits. I shall take care of the women and you can manage the men. That is what you have in mind, isn't it?"

"It most certainly is not!" Nash's patience was being sorely tested. "Major Ross told me—!"

"Yes, yes, I've heard all that before," she interrupted with a flick of her finger. "But it is not manly to have to speak to ladies—young or old—about certain things."

"What things?"

"Precisely," Kitty Brandon replied. "You got yourself into deep water stealing the Beaumont girl: you're over your ears in trouble trying to run an orderly establishment. And that Mrs. Grimes creature you employ to do the dirty work is not much of a bargain, despite her apt choice of name. Frankly, you had better drop it all in my lap and walk away while you can. I shall see that every soldier gets what he needs, that every officer gets what he wants, and that you're left in peace to plunder the public stores until it is time to return Home to a brighter, better life. Now, what can be fairer than that?"

Nash folded his arms and blocked her path. "You will report to my quarters this evening and agree to my conditions!"

"No, I shall not, but I do see your problem," Kitty Brandon observed quietly, sadly. "Because, unless you manage to keep sweet with all those guns, and drums, and flags, an oddity such as yourself will indeed be out of his depth in Sinful Cove. It's a devilish hard path you've chosen to follow, Charley."

Nash stopped her.

"Let me go."

"Either you are with me or against me. If the former, you will come to my quarters before curfew and accede to my terms. If the latter, then take a lesson from that—!"

Kitty Brandon tried to push past but Nash had gripped her wrist, twisting it into a hammer lock, forcing her to watch one of the derelicts off *Prince of Wales*: gray hair a matted crust of dirt, toenails like black claws, the old woman's nose a diseased hole between her eyes: on her way to the lime kiln to burn more shell, to make more cement for the storehouse.

"Leave! Me! Be!"

Cribb was also returning to work, shovel slung over one shoulder, plotting how to scheme the lead balls taken from the cartridges which had made today's blanks. He heard her voice. He heeled left. He charged. His long wooden handle folded Nash like a bayonet jab. The shovel blade whirled as Cribb jumped, straddling the dropped man—!

"Halt!" Kitty Brandon ripped the rags off Cribb's shoulders, spoiling his aim before anyone in authority raised the alarm. "*Halt*, I say!"

"Good-o Phoss!" a passing lag yelled.

"You show the cheeky sod!" another man shouted, starting to hurry closer, also glad whenever a fight broke out to break the monotony.

Nash flopped about, wheezing in the dust, then rolled over to look up at this cruel land's hard blue sky. The woman might have boxed Cribb's ears but a number of similar items were now slapping him on the back as the gentleman wobbled to his knees, retrieved his straw hat, and got to his feet. "So. Our little arsonist still likes to play with fire." Nash turned, skirted around the gathering crowd of well-wishers and limped away with as much dignity as he could muster.

"Great God, what the hell d'you think you're about?" Kitty Brandon demanded, uncertain whether she ought to curse or kiss Cribb. "That was unbelievably stupid!"

"But 'e—!"

"Enough! With a reptile of that spot we kill it outright or give it a wide berth. You've contrived to do neither!"

"But 'e was touching you!" The camp scavenger squared his shoulders. "But don't you worry, I'll see you're took good care of."

"You take care of *me?*" The women's leader unclenched her fists. "Why is every man so dense all of a sudden? It must be the moon. It is I who will have all my work cut out stopping *you* from coming to an abrupt end after today's little imbroglio!"

She turned her back on the grinning lags and strode away to the officers' lines. A rather more organized squad crossed the path ahead of her, plodding down to the creek before climbing the east bank of Sydney Cove near Government House. "Mr. Thorpe!"

The work gang shuffled to a stop. Kitty Brandon beckoned their taskmaster to one side and bestowed a smile which raised goose bumps up his spine. "Allow me to congratulate you, this is indeed a considerable rise in the world. I also note with pleasure that you and Mr. Levi are speaking again." She hurried on, trying to put her thoughts in order. "That is exactly what we need. Now, do the same with Mr. Cribb."

"But 'e told me—"

"Damn what he told you, it's what I'm saying now that matters!" She checked her tongue. "I shall explain myself later, when there's a moment to discuss certain matters in confidence. Meanwhile, if there is anything you wish to bring to my notice and I am not available, a word to the governor's housekeeper—Miss Dundas—will be sufficient. She's one of us. And you may be sure we'll keep you informed about everything which concerns your important position in the colony."

"Um. When brains enter the game, luck counts double," the governor's farm overseer replied with a knowing wag of the head.

"Mr. Levi couldn't have expressed it better himself," Kitty Brandon agreed with a tight smile. "Now, back to work!"

31

"TUM, TUM, tiddle-de-dum!" Arthur Phillip felt comfortable. His private cellar had taken heavy punishment over lunch by the time everyone—even Ross—had proposed toasts to their new governor and his colony. Proclamation Day had gone off well. Very well. Splendidly well. Immensely well—!

Phillip waved an airy hand for Bryant to be quick about lighting that confounded lantern. The marquee door flap fell shut. Still humming to himself, the ruler of the empire's largest and latest territory felt in the right mood to bring his journal up to date: it was a chore which had better be done while the sense of well-being lasted.

He straightened his spectacles, nearly knocked over the inkwell, dipped his quill. "Sydney Cove, Thursday 7th Feb'y, 1788. Being assembled in one place, the garrison, labour, etc., etc., paid respectful notice while formal possession of New South Wales was effected in due form. Upon the completion of which all indicated their loyal affection for the Crown before His Majesty's plenipotentiary retired with his staff to mark the event in a manner befitting the occasion. Winds, variable. Sky, clear. Temperature, 84°. Barometer, 29.60."

Phillip was now at liberty to continue his ongoing correspondence with Mr. Secretary Rose. He smoothed a fresh sheet of paper and gathered his thoughts as he went over this momentous day, point by point. "My Dear George. The deed is sealed, signed and delivered. This vast new land is ours. God Save the King.

"Considering the haste with which the ceremonials were conceived after my return from visiting M. de La Pérouse (of which more later), you would have been most agreeably impressed with the spirit of the occasion. Even Major Ross (who is not bearing up well under the rigors of foreign service) exerted himself so that a smarter body of troops could not have been found in any of His Majesty's dominions. Not that my lieutenant governor was acting alone, of course, and I wish that something tangible be done for Captains Tench, Shea and Collins. The astronomer royal's young protégé, Wm. Dawes, is also one who merits advancement as a position becomes vacant—"

The governor stopped writing but did not look up as his man tiptoed in with freshly scorched coffee and burned biscuits. "That will be all, Bryant."

"Begging leave to speak, sir? I just 'eard there's to be a servant woman 'ere, or some such."

"Well?" Phillip dipped his pen. "What of her?"

"Is it I'm not giving satisfaction?" Bryant shifted his weight to the other leg. "I always done my best! It's not easy, cooking and things."

"How does your head feel?" Phillip glanced up from his work. The servant blinked at this unexpected question as his master went on. "The last time you annoyed me it became injured soon after. You've removed the bandages: the effect must've worn off."

"No offense, sir! It's just that I—!"

"As for engaging a housekeeper," Phillip continued, ignoring the flustered apologies, "I'd have thought you'd welcome an opportunity to be quit of these chores." He flicked his quill at the coffee cup.

"Sir?"

"I do not require an able-bodied man, on full rations, to boil a kettle."

"No, sir?"

"That is why you're being replaced," Phillip went on in the same remote tone. "I am assured that Mrs. Whosit is an excellent cook and a proficient laundry maid: you are neither."

"No, sir."

"However, you appear sturdy enough to devote some energy to grooming my horses and managing my garden—"

"Garden, sir?"

"The exercise will do you good. Unless, of course, you'd prefer to be returned to general duties on the t'gallant yards?"

"No, sir! Not me, sir!"

"In which case you'll begin digging and watering a much larger patch of vegetables from which we shall all supplement our rations in due course." The governor prepared to go back to his own work. "It will set a good example to those others with time on their hands and untilled soil at their doors. Dismiss."

The flap fell shut. Phillip dipped ink again and tried composing his mind after this interruption, but his good humor had gone. Cursing under his breath he returned to the more urgent task of shaping policy half the globe away. "Concerning our colony's internal affairs, today's assembly allowed me to address the troops and convicts *en masse* for the first time and, I am pleased to say, their demeanor throughout the ceremony was an agreeable contrast to their previous behavior.

"I am confident that, as they learn to recognize the gravity of our condition, there will be a marked improvement overall. Being far removed from the tippling houses, brothels and gamesters which brought them low in the first place, I would make a small wager that we are now in an ideally primitive state for the reformation of criminal impulses. For how is it possible to steal money where there is so little to be stolen?"

Phillip paused to sharpen his quill nib. "My internal arrangements are likewise suited to the suppression of the criminal element. If *divide et impera* is the guiding rule of rulers, my subjects have been most assuredly divided. With one hand I direct the guards, and with the other I control the guarded, and both have been well seeded with informants to check the disaffected. If only it were as easy to control their appetites!"

Phillip glanced at the daily ration tally pinned above his work table, dipped the quill and began a fresh sheet of paper. "May our resupply be not delayed for any reason. Despite the severest economies I cannot expect to hold out for more than another two and a half years at our present allowance of fourteen-ounce pounds, but I state the obvious. Sufficient to say that I am confident our nation will never neglect her destiny in these southern seas, to which end you may assure our allies in Parliament that every man in New South Wales is doing his utmost for the common good, with thrift and industry our constant watchwords."

The governor hoped he was not laying it on too thickly, but George Rose was going to need all the supportive evidence at his command if the New Holland List was to pass next year's budget review reasonably intact. "One thing only is lacking and that is the presence of old friends. This colony, despite its immense size, feels like a man o' war where one is forever conscious that every gesture, no matter how minor, is the subject of gossip by subordinates. Happily the new Government House is almost finished and I shall soon be able to enjoy rather more privacy than this tent affords.

"As you can imagine, it is not easy being oneself under such conditions. May it not be long before we can again ride up Lyndhurst Hill and see others passing down the Solent, outward bound for distant waters, by which time I shall have traveled enough—"

It had been a long day. The claret was taking effect. Phillip abandoned the letter, dragged back the blanket and collapsed on his cot.

32

COLLINS CAME up the track to Government House. Bryant heard the crisp slap of a sentry's salute outside the door and hurried to bow like a major domo as the judge advocate entered, then straightened to bustle away and announce this morning's first visitor. Collins hardly noticed the fellow. He strolled round the bare antechamber, rapping its framework with his knuckles, eyeing the exposed roof beams, for this matchwood and tar cloth shed was not only the governor's new home, it was also the colony's secretariat, treasury and law court.

Collins wished he could look forward to winter in such comfort but an apathetic gang of lags had yet to finish building his hut. He had stopped issuing threats and left his housekeeper to ensure that its foundations were dug deeply enough to hold up the walls: the lopped poles and woven twigs ought to be daubed with wet clay from the brick pit by tomorrow evening. Building standards were much stricter, now. The first officer's hut to be raised had collapsed when Ross slammed its door, burying him under a heap of grass thatch.

Bryant returned. " 'Is Excellency will be out presently!" He hoped the new servant woman would hear who was still the senior underling.

Collins did not notice. He was busy studying his own reflection in the chamber window, one of five—all in Government House—which were the only panes of glass between Java and Chile. Collins grimaced at himself. Dawes had insisted that the Pacific was a fertile mission field, embracing one third of the globe, when they spoke in the mess a few nights ago. By his own reckoning it was just sixty million square miles of damn all, whose only value was to put the greatest possible distance between Collins and his wife in Portsmouth.

The high endeavor of Proclamation Day was another fading memory. Yesterday's squalor was today's filth was tomorrow's epidemic as autumn threatened Sydney Cove. The judge advocate felt the leaden ache of isolation and there was little relief out on the anchorage where the convoy was readying for sea. *Supply* had left for Norfolk Island. The others were slipping away. Soon the last barque would tug downstream, catching her trade wind for Canton and Home, leaving Collins behind to go about his duties in a village of hovels—the hub of mirth, culture and enlightenment on a desert island almost the size of Europe.

" 'Morning, David."

Collins turned from his reflection as the governor came in from the bedchamber, still buttoning his coat. He tried to smile. "Good morning, sir."

"Well." Phillip sat at the trestle table and nodded for his legal officer to take the other stool. "What's on the agenda for today?"

"The usual. Theft and quarrels. Oh, there was one amusing incident," Collins added, trying to put a bright face on the day's work. "One of the women off *Charlotte*-the-harlot stole a flatiron last night. When the alarm was raised she ran away and tried hanging herself, but they managed to cut her down and the surgeon tapped a pint of blood." The judge advocate opened his despatch bag. "I'll have her flogged once she can stand again."

"What a curious thing to take. Any idea what she could've wanted with a flatiron?"

"None at all, though I doubt it was to keep her linen smooth and white."

"Neither do I." Phillip took the charge sheets which Collins was placing on the table. "Well, at least our informants are performing rationally." The governor was assessing last night's harvest of crime. "This report seems straightforward enough. Don't get too technical with witnesses: the brickyard can use him."

"I'd rather it didn't, sir," Collins replied, following the older man's finger. "I think we ought to neck that item. He's been nothing but trouble since we arrived and an execution would have a tonic effect—"

"No doubt it would," Phillip interrupted, "but I have a greater need for at least another twenty thousand bricks if those storehouses are to be finished before winter. Our provisions must be thiefproof and weatherproof or else we'll all suffer the consequences."

"I know, sir, but I still believe that this particular item's greatest value would be stretching a rope in public," Collins persisted. "Moreover, it's time we spared some consideration for the troops."

"Oh . . . ?"

"The sergeants are reporting a falling-off in standards," the judge advocate continued. "The troops are grumbling. They say that convicted thieves get off with lighter punishments than do free guards. Now, if we neck one for them—"

"David, we must've been over this ground a dozen times already," Phillip snapped. "The articles you refer to are simply in no physical condition to survive a session at the flogger's hands. End of argument."

"Try telling that to one of our men when he's had five hundred and someone else is getting fifty for no less a crime!" Collins controlled himself. "This disparity of punishments is dividing the colony, sir."

"Aided and abetted by Ross, I do not doubt," Phillip said, scowling. "I require bricks. This item will earn his bread by doing work, not loafing around the infirmary on convalescent rations. The same goes for these ones here and here—" he tapped more names on the charge sheets— "they can grub up tree stumps and haul wood, it'll be the first honest work they've done in their misbegotten lives. While as for this beauty, here, she can reflect upon her sins at the lime kiln."

"As you direct, sir." Collins plainly disapproved as the Old Man finished signing the summons to convene these trials later today. "Will that be all?"

"For the moment." Phillip tossed his pen aside and sat back, fingers steepled. "Concerning more immediate matters, I've noticed that Captain Shea is still on the sick list. This is becoming too frequent for my liking.

I assume my deputy is playing the happy huckster with a certain forth-coming promotion . . . ?"

"Yes."

"Who'll get it? Anyone we can trust?"

"Kellow, sir."

"Damn. Still, if a paymaster can't afford rank, who can?" Phillip shrugged. "Very well, keep me informed as things develop."

Collins clicked his heels and left Government House. Phillip was about to reach for his own hat and follow him on a tour of inspection when Bryant trotted in from the back garden and, again, stood to attention by the door. He jerked it open as the sentry outside presented arms to a senior officer. "Captain 'Unter, Your Excellency!"

Phillip put out a hand as *Sirius*'s commander crossed the threshold. "Welcome home, John. Be seated."

"Thank you, sir."

The governor looked at his manservant. "Back to the weeds."

"Er, aye aye, sir!"

Phillip waited until he and Hunter were alone and could speak freely, then looked back at the travel-worn officer who had just spent the last week probing for their elusive inland river. "You've eaten?"

"No, not yet."

Phillip tugged the string which ran through a hole in the scullery wall at the back. Jane Dundas wiped her hands clean and smoothed her apron before answering the bell. "Your Excellency?"

"What's in the larder for Captain Hunter?"

"Well, although it's not rations till tomorrow, there's some baked fish with onion sauce."

Phillip glanced at the other naval man. "What d'you say?"

"I'd say it's the best news I've heard in a very long time," Hunter replied. "And if you could see your way clear to being generous with the pepper. . . ."

"It'll be a pleasure, your honor. And to drink?"

"Tea."

Jane Dundas straightened from her curtsey and went out to fan the fire under its rolled tin flue, several yards from the flimsy, flammable Government House.

Hunter took off his coat as Phillip opened the field notebook which the other man had laid on the table. He flicked pages, checking new figures and sketch maps. "Doesn't look as if we're going to find a branch of that river close to camp." He glanced up. "And there are no brooks to drive a waterwheel. What about a tide mill instead?"

"Little chance of that."

"Then how the hell do the Indians fill their granaries?"

"They don't. I've yet to see any evidence of cultivation," Hunter replied, bending forward to indicate something on a penciled sketch. "There are just some bark huts or hunting lodges, here, and a few fishing canoes, but otherwise things remain much as before—no temples, no ruins, no fields, nothing. And if there are any great chieftains or kings out there, they're making themselves uncommonly scarce. Or their domains begin further west beyond the mountains." He flicked the sketch map again. "If there's a third alternative I'm blessed if I know what it could be."

"That's nonsense! There's got to be *something*, if only we look hard enough!"

"Yes, trees, beyond which stand ever more!" Hunter shrugged helplessly. "For once I'd say the lords commissioner knew what they were about when they promoted the story that we've been sent here as a form of outdoor relief for the criminal classes. It'd be difficult to imagine a place more suited as a jail. Who needs iron bars when nature's provided countless acres of wooden ones?" He looked up from the brown splotches of age on his wrists. "I'm sorry, you've enough problems without me adding more."

Phillip stood and went to the empty packing case which served for a sideboard in Government House. He replaced the stopper in one of his decanters and returned with some madeira. Hunter took it and half-emptied the tumbler at a single draught. "Thanks. I needed that."

"I know. It's unlike you to be so cast down." The governor returned to the other man's notebook. "Now, what's this business you've marked at the head of navigation?"

The wine was reviving Hunter's spirits. He bent forward again. "It could be farmland. As near as I can judge it's deep loam and thinly wooded for a change, so there'd be little work needed to clear it. A fort could be built on this hillock—" Hunter pointed at his sketch—"to cover the landing area and become base for further advances toward the mountains—assuming that's your intention, of course."

"It most certainly is." Phillip began polishing his spectacles with a scrap of wash leather. "We must spare no effort to establish relations with the local kings, whoever and wherever they may be." He slipped the glasses on his nose and returned to a neat column of calculations opposite Hunter's sketch map. "Hm. There must be about fifteen miles of navigable water between our cove and this farmland. So, once our shipwrights build barges and skiffs, the two settlements will be connected by

a natural canal system and we'll have bypassed the forest here and here."
Phillip tapped paper with his pencil.

He was brightening at the prospect of action. "Let's both take a look
at it before winter sets in, then we could detach more of our numbers and
let them plant crops for next year as a further insurance against disease
and that sort of thing." The governor stopped short, waiting until his
housekeeper had finished setting the table.

Jane Dundas held the empty tray against her front. "Will that be all,
gentlemen?"

"Yes, thank you." Hunter felt inside his coat pocket for a knife and
fork as the government woman went back to work in the scullery behind
its thin pinewood partition and Phillip tried some of the tea. He pushed
it aside. He had lost the taste for the drink since serving with the
Portuguese navy in Brazil. It baffled him that anyone in his or her right
mind could drink this slop when they could savor coffee.

"Delicious!" Hunter smacked his lips and breathed out. "So, how's
our military colleague been keeping while I've been absent?"

"Mercifully quiet," Phillip replied. "This might be a prudent time to
leave him to his own devices, briefly, before winter confines everyone to
quarters."

"Is that altogether wise?" the other naval officer asked, putting his cup
aside. "Remember what happened when the women were disembarked."

"I'm not likely to forget in a hurry." Phillip watched his friend begin
the delayed breakfast. "However, my deputy is engrossed with building
that wretched stone hut for himself. If we're lucky he'll demolish it like
his last dwelling and save us the trouble of raising a tomb. Speaking of
which, Shea's sick again."

"When was he not?" Hunter forked at the meager serving of fried
beans which Jane Dundas had added to his ration of fish. "The poor
devil's been dying by inches since we left Portsmouth."

"All the more reason for us to inspect your new farmland, now," the
governor replied. "The rains are coming apace, hardly the best season for
a man in Captain Shea's state of health. The moment he's off the battalion
strength we'll have Campbell and Kellow versus Tench and Collins, with
you-know-who holding the balance of power. . . ."

"What a damnable mess." Hunter had laid his knife on his plate and
was reaching for the teapot.

"Not so." Phillip consulted some papers. He glanced up again. "I
believe events are unfolding quite satisfactorily. Shea's imminent departure should be encouraging our garrison commander to bide his time.
Instead, as you once reminded me, our Mr. Ross tends to preen himself

in the shaving mirror while he admires the manly, masterful features of Robert, Lord Ross of New Holland."

"Yes?"

Phillip smiled briefly. "He should also reflect upon the fact that the equally bellicose Robert, Lord Clive, eventually destroyed himself with his own razor. And an oversharp tongue."

"Hm. . . ."

"Quite." Phillip tapped the papers together and turned them face down. " 'Getting ahead like the Quality' can become a headstrong, headlong rush for the nearest precipice unless we occasionally pause to see what snares our rivals may be stretching across the paths of glory."

Hunter had stopped eating. "Is that what you're doing, sir?"

"Me? Certainly not. There's no need while he persists in attacking Tench—"

"*Tench?* But I thought he was the fair-haired boy!"

"Not any longer."

"Why?"

Phillip shrugged. "It's a complex matter. I've been informed who lit the fuse and what her motives were, but there's no need to heap further fuel on that bonfire of vanities. Sufficient to say that my deputy has this unhappy knack of talking himself into trouble with his subordinates. And in my experience of such men, the more they lash out, the more quickly they entangle themselves in nets of their own making." The governor smiled. "Which leaves us free to get on with our own business, like inspecting this place of yours at the head of the harbor."

33

"THAT'LL BE ALL." Johnson marked his prayer book with the quartermaster's receipt for eight ounces of flour, the burial fee in a barter economy. "Close the grave."

"Right-o." Cribb sat on an overturned wheelbarrow in the shade of a nearby tree: the colony's scavenger was also its sexton. "Um. What's it cost to get spliced? Church proper? With all the trimmings . . . ?"

"The authorized fee for celebrating a marriage is established by act of Parliament at two shillings and sixpence, although nowadays it seems as if half a pound of flour is considered sufficient," the chaplain added. "Please close the grave."

"But what if a bloke's got no grub to spare . . . ?"

"Simple charity would not allow such a consideration to stand in the way of a properly solemnized Christian marriage," Johnson replied, hurrying to get away from this clearing by the brick field track, away from its flies, away from its smells, away from the ever-lengthening row of raw earthen mounds.

"You don't mean you'd do it free?" Cribb asked with a disbelieving shake of the head.

"Yes. Now, do you think—?"

"But that's not right! It's not fair. I'll bet it costs quids to buy all that book learning and such. You can't just give it away. I mean, what's 'alf a crown or 'alf a pound of bread when the job's got to be done proper?"

"If only more of my parishioners thought the same." Johnson tucked his gown and book under one arm.

Cribb's shoulders had slumped. "Me and the girl want to do the right thing, sir, but it's not easy sparing a bit off the rations once you chuck out the bone, and the maggots, but we'll save up some'ow. Don't you worry, we'll do the right thing, fair and square."

"Is it you who wishes to be wed?"

Cribb hid a timid smile. "Well, we sort of been thinking about it, yes."

"Then allow me to congratulate you." Johnson had forgotten the droning blowflies, at least for the moment. "Marriage is an honorable estate, a sure defense against all sins of the flesh," he went on, warming to his task.

"Of course, it's still early days," Cribb cautioned. "She's one of the best but the bloke I share digs with, Tommy Barrett, 'as gone and took a shine to 'er as well. But I reckon I can get Peg to go for me if I can show 'er I've a proper bread chit to get spliced church regular."

Johnson nodded in time with this sad little tale, told in a dialect almost as foreign to him as Latin or Greek. "I do understand. At times these women can indeed be most unreasonable."

"You're not wrong there, sir," Cribb agreed, man to man in a world of wily females. "Of course, Tommo's a good mate, I won't say nothing bad against 'im, but so's the mort. She's special, see? We'll make a go of things once we can get regular spliced, church proper, mister and missus. But first I got to some'ow get a spare bread chit. . . ."

The useful little item's smile was reminding Johnson of his duty to the poor and lowly. On impulse he took out the bookmark. "Accept this with all my best wishes for your future happiness."

Cribb was aghast as the chaplain held out the slip of paper. "For us? Oh no, I couldn't!"

"Please. I insist."

"Oh. All right." Cribb swallowed hard, smiled bashfully and accepted the chit. It vanished inside his belt pouch, joining the other ration receipts being hoarded for the long ride to Chinaland. "You're a regular gent!" he called after the chaplain.

Johnson was not listening. He had another marriage to concern him: his own. Mary was no longer the compliant helpmeet he made his wife just over a year before: she had become very difficult and moody of late; he did not know what to make of her. And that was not all; the same insubordinate spirit seemed to be affecting everyone else around him.

The first convict assigned to dig and water the chaplain's vegetable patch had been half-blind and ruptured, the second a habitual liar, drunkard and thief, and the third laborer had been taken away to the quarry after performing unnatural vice. Johnson was now having to get up at dawn and hoe his own garden before the sun became too hot.

And there had been a very unpleasant scene, in public, between one of the soldiers and a corporal. The trial had been acrimonious as well. It was said that Major Ross wanted the soldier shot by firing squad. Johnson hoped not. If it were true then he'd have to be present, and he had never before officiated as a chaplain at an execution. The longer such a duty could be delayed, the better.

The colony's chaplain hesitated on the edge of the encampment. For a moment he considered returning home for lunch in the canvas and branchwood shanty he shared with Mary. Instead he continued walking along the beach, away from her complaints about the accommodation, about the climate, about the company, about the governor, about himself.

The days were drawing in and the evenings growing more chilly, but noontide was still hot enough to stop most work ashore, even if the remaining shipmasters were impatient to embark their ballast once the last cargoes were under cover. Dawes's marine artificers had a different set of priorities; they were taking a midday snooze in the shade of the first brick building to be almost completed in New South Wales, waiting while a convict work gang stripped another load of bark shingles for the roof.

" 'E's not 'ere!" Corporal Drury shouted at the civilian devil driver, silhouetted in the doorway, peering around the storehouse interior.

"Then where is Lieutenant Dawes?"

"Somewhere else." Drury shut his eyes again.

Johnson quickened his pace again as he continued toward the small shed which stood apart on the western promontory of Sydney Cove, facing a wide sweep of open sky to the north. The observatory had become his substitute for the junior common room at Magdalene College, Cambridge. He smiled with relief. Dawes, Tench, Nash and himself had turned it into their own dining club—the Literati—as a congenial alternative to the officers' mess and Mary's monologues. Collins and Balmain were associate members and tended to stop by from time to time. As did the governor. Phillip had already brought his dinner over to the observatory on a couple of occasions to escape from Sinful Cove by scanning the planets through his astronomer's four-inch telescope.

The more down-to-earth Johnson had made an equally exciting discovery inside the little shed: the handful of other enquiring minds in the settlement actually held him in some awe. He was their university graduate, their Latinist, their arbiter in learned discussion about books and ideas. Around the rest of the campsite he might only be the resident God-guesser, tolerated while he preached at illiterates, but once under the observatory's thatched roof he became a man of respect again.

Richard Johnson tried to maintain a proper attitude of humility whenever men of the world sought his opinions, but it was never easy. Watkin Tench often gave an impression of cynical amusement at that world's folly, especially when reading aloud from his book, correcting the manuscript as it advanced chapter by chapter. On the other hand, William Dawes more than compensated for his company commander's pose. The young veteran had revealed himself to be a man of firm principle, of inner strength, of Christian values, with whom the chaplain was delighted to share his skills as a scholar while they toiled together on the first English-Indian lexicon.

The officer of engineers was determined to improve his future prospects by earning a fellowship of the Royal Society for his work in New Holland. The observatory also doubled as a laboratory and construction office now that Sydney's town plans were pinned to its walls, and the other work surfaces were cluttered with plant presses, a microscope and slides, folios of botanical drawings and bunches of dried specimens for Dawes's patron, Dr. Nevil Maskelyne, FRS.

A sentry was lolling in the shade, guarding government property from the government's convicted servants. He opened an eye as the chaplain walked past. Johnson halted in the sudden gloom and peered around the hut. "You there, Dawes?"

"Over here!"

Johnson stepped nearer the drawing board as his eyes accustomed themselves to the half light. He looked over Dawes's shoulder. "Has anyone said where the church is to be built, yet?"

The officer of engineers shook his head. "I'm afraid not."

The chaplain hesitated a moment, then lowered his voice. "Do you think it would make any difference if I said that I am willing to consecrate my first parish to St. Phillip?"

Dawes smiled up at his friend. "If a few lines on an otherwise blank sheet of paper can become 'George Street' and 'Pitt Street' to win political advantage half the world away, who knows what the right choice of name might not achieve closer to home?"

"Then you think I should try?"

"Why not?" Dawes brushed the ants from his lunch on its piece of pudding cloth. "What have you to lose? What do you have to gain . . . ?"

"A properly constructed church. And a school. And a library," Johnson replied with a determined frown.

"And His Excellency's favor, you won't get the other three without first winning that, I'm afraid."

The chaplain clenched his fist. "One would think a church was a self-evident necessity."

"Not if one were trying to build a thiefproof store before the winter rains began in earnest." The young officer took his slab of cold pease pudding and started to eat. " 'Render to Caesar the things that are Caesar's.' I'm sure, if you treat our governor with the consideration due to his office, he will eventually reciprocate with the respect due to yours. Here endeth the lesson."

Johnson had sat on one of the packing crates which furnished the little shed. "If only I were as confident as you appear to be, but one hears so many stories about him. Nash says—"

Dawes brushed his lap. "This is your first time overseas, is it not?"

"Er, yes. It is."

The young veteran's face twisted into another scarred smile. "Don't believe everything that everyone tells you. Gossip and malice are as natural to garrison life as fleas are on a private's collar. Indeed, if I were a gambling man, I would wager silver to gold that it's only a matter of time before Mr. A calls out Mr. B to settle a point of honor with pistols or the dueling blade."

"That is a terrible thing to say."

"Agreed," Dawes replied, using his finger to dab up a few stray crumbs of his lunch, "but such is life on foreign service in the glorious profession of arms. However, returning to more constructive paths, I would treat Nash's stories *cum grano salis*. Right? His Excellency has always dealt with me in a fair and friendly manner," the lieutenant of marines went on, licking his finger clean. "I could wish I had served under more bluejacket commanders who were as sensitive to the feelings of their redcoated subordinates as is Commodore Phillip. Here endeth the second lesson." Dawes sat back on his stool. "Now, to work, what new things have you learned from the Indians?"

Johnson felt around his pockets for a notebook recording his latest finds. Most of yesterday afternoon had been spent at an encampment of savages about half a mile west of Sydney Cove. The chaplain had stayed there for several hours, quite alone and unharmed, squatting on a fallen branch while the chieftain of the small tribe touched objects and patiently named them for his ghostman guest.

"Mary was rather displeased when I got back so late," her husband explained, searching through his notes. Dawes felt that it was not his place to comment about another's domestic life as he got ready to copy more words onto a master list pinned beside the street plan of Sydney Town.

"Ah, here we are," Johnson was smiling again. "*Dalangar* means 'dirt' or 'sand,' I'm not sure which at present."

"Uh huh."

"*Guwai*—though it sounds like 'go away!'—actually means 'come here.' "

"How curious."

"Isn't it?" the chaplain agreed, watching his friend's pencil as it printed with a mapmaker's precision. "And *jurun* is definitely 'salt' or 'savory' according to context. That is to say, it seems to serve as a noun, or an adjective, or it can be conjugated with an auxiliary verb."

"Good." Dawes glanced up. "Next?"

"*Bagal*," Johnson replied, reserving his greatest enthusiasm for this discovery. "It appears to be one of those pieces of bark they use to carry fish and things: 'bowl' or 'tray' I suppose we should call it. In fact they showed me how to make one," the chaplain said, riffling through his notes, searching for the correct entry. "I'll show you next time I pay them a visit."

"Please do." Dawes's pencil was ready. "How's it done?"

"Very simply but elegantly." Johnson had found the page. "First they go over to those big rocks where there are beds of sandstone lumps and chips; you've seen them? I couldn't tell the difference between one or the other, but the *wujungir*—the menfolk—seemed to find it very easy, almost as if they were entering a smithy or workshop of some kind.

"Anyhow, they select one of the larger pieces and one of their number clasps it between the soles of his feet while he uses another lump of stone to shape it into something like a hammer or axe." Johnson smiled at the memory. "It was another of our Antipodean paradoxes, something so crude in effect and yet so economical in concept, not one movement too many before achieving the desired result.

"Now, while all this was going on, someone else had taken me to a tall tree with wonderfully smooth bark and indicated that I should watch closely while another of the *wujungir* took the axe—*bumbja* I think he said—and struck the tree, working outwards and downwards in two curved lines until they met again at the bottom. Then another man stepped forward with a different stone and a piece of stick which he had shaped to a point and, with only a couple of light taps, peeled off the bark which he then trimmed with his teeth—"

"Good Lord."

"They then took the bowl over to a fire," Johnson concluded, "hardened it in the hot coals and, less than half an hour after starting, they had finished a perfectly serviceable utensil from little more than a few lumps of stone, some bits of stick and a tree."

"Crude, indeed." The engineer had laid his pencil aside and was wistfully toying with a pair of brass dividers which marked a page in his book of mathematical tables. "You certainly have the knack of communication, Richard. That is something else I must master before I can go forth and teach."

"You will," the chaplain insisted with an understanding smile. "As I told Mary last night, we've been called to this place to exert ourselves and to alleviate the discomforts of our less fortunate brethren which, in a minor way, I did after they'd finished the *bagal*. You should've seen the astonishment when I showed them how to use a steel hatchet! They immediately saw how much quicker than stone it is, and anyone can use it to shape a utensil without then having to chew off the rough edges."

"They certainly appear to be ready pupils," Dawes agreed, using the dividers to step off imaginary distances across his drawing board.

"I'm convinced they are," Johnson nodded. "Perhaps we should also take along some spare shirts and hats? They could then see for themselves how much more comfortable they'd be in this climate."

"Perhaps." Dawes slapped a large, grayish-green bushfly, its proboscis quivering, thirsty for sweat, hungry for blood. He scraped the dead insect on the heel of his boot and glanced up again. "Confounded things. If only we were birds we'd be feeding on the fat of the land instead of, well, whatever it is we're doing."

"Yes, they seem to be hatching everywhere at present. I think there must be more rain on the way."

"Then let's hope it doesn't cloud over before I've finished this evening's observations," Dawes replied, shoving both hands into his breeches pockets and moving across to the telescope, poised on its heavy wooden tripod. He halted, shoulders hunched, distracted. " 'In somer seson softe is the sonne'? Hardly! And Autumn doesn't seem to be much better."

The astronomer had begun loosening the retaining screws, swinging the long brass barrel to aim it through an open window hole. "You know, Richard, our dusky neighbors are not the only ones who have to cope with paradoxes in this contrary land. For example, consider the intricate assembly of lens, prism and mirror which permits us to view the macrocosmos of God's heaven by night. Nothing alters but the perspective when we peep into the microcosmos of our own little hell by day. . . ."

" 'The fault, dear Brutus, is not in our stars, but in ourselves,' " Johnson chided gently, joining his friend as the other man focused his attention around the drowsy, soft haze of a cooking fire on the opposite bank of Sydney Cove.

"That's what troubles me," Dawes said, squinting hard into the eyepiece. "Anyhow, it shouldn't be too long before *Alexander* is outward bound for a happier place, a better clime. Her spars are dressed and swayed aloft," the officer of marines continued, inching his telescope sideways to study the barque's rig. He glanced back at the chaplain. "Like a look?"

"Thank you." Johnson took his place on the stool as the other young man untied a tobacco pouch and loaded a long-stemmed pipe.

"See anything interesting?"

"Not especially," the chaplain replied, crouched at the eyepiece now. "Everyone seems to be asleep. It must be this weather."

Dawes hung a smoke ring in the air. "I wonder if they really are?"

"Are what?"

"Asleep. Off guard. Heedless and uncaring." Dawes had folded his arms to lean against the wall. "Has it never struck you how much like an English millpond this Sinful Cove can be? On the surface, all so quiet and unruffled. But down among the weeds and rubbish, minnows flee from pike as bigger fish eat lesser fish and so *ad infinitum*." The astronomer had straightened again to see better through the open hole. "Speaking of big fish, here comes Tench and I'd say he was anything but sleepy. Minnows beware!"

Johnson immediately swung the telescope and shortened its focus.

The sentry gathered his wits and snapped to attention, musket at the slope, hand smacking butt, saluting as the redcoat officer strode nearer. Tench pointed at a tree one hundred yards from the observatory door. "Get over there and don't move until I order you to come back."

"Sah?"

"On the double!"

"Sah!"

Tench halted inside the observatory entrance. Fists on hips, he glared at the two men standing by the telescope. "And I trust you are well satisfied with today's work, Dawes?"

"Sir?"

"Don't play the innocent with me. You know damn well what I am referring to."

"No, I don't!"

"My father's profession."

"Uh?"

"I told you, and you alone, that he was a schoolmaster. Now it is common gossip. It has just been used, by our battalion commander, to ridicule me before the entire mess!"

"Oh, God."

"Your damned, sniveling, creeping prayers are as worthless as ever they were!" Tench yelled, closing the gap between himself and Dawes. "You, you sanctimonious shit. But I shall have my satisfaction, pistols or swords, once I've dealt with Ross I will send you to deliver your prayers in person!" He swept books off the nearest shelf and thrust them under one arm.

"Please!" Johnson rushed forward. "What's wrong?"

"Everything." Tench replaced two volumes on the shelf. "However, there are proper procedures for making amends. I am going to shoot Major Ross. And then Lieutenant Dawes."

"You can't mean it!"

"Get your hands off me, padre! This is none of your business!"

"It is! It is! I have never heard such dreadful—!"

"Out of my way."

"No!" Johnson clung to both doorposts. "I won't budge till you explain this, this—!"

"Richard?" Dawes opened his eyes again. "Stand aside. The answer you seek concerns only Captain Tench and myself."

"No!"

Tench dropped the books as he snatched for his sword, but his belt had been empty for more than ten minutes, now. "God damn you all!"

"Blasphemy!" Johnson was no longer gripping the door frame.

"Richard! Enough!" Dawes lowered his voice. "Captain Tench has every right to be enraged."

"What?"

"I betrayed his confidence. I—I told you, his father was 'a humble village flaybum,' not a Welsh squire of substance. But I swear to God that I never breathed a word to anyone else!"

Johnson swayed for a moment. "Mary."

"Surely you never told your wife?"

"Only in the strictest confidence!"

"Oh, God . . ."

Tench turned at the observatory door, the books under his arm again. "Honor does not allow me to call a lady to account. Nor will I soil my blade with your blood, sir. I shall consider myself satisfied after you have taken a whip to that woman."

"Captain!" Johnson implored, moving forward. "Stop! One moment! Please listen!"

Tench knocked him aside and stepped into the drowsy afternoon light.

34

"AND YOU SAY the men are still grumbling?" Ross asked his sergeant major.

"Yes, sir," the other veteran of many battles replied, rain splashing from his cocked hat, puddling on the floor around his gaiters.

Ross said nothing. The troops' morale was a constant worry, as was the lime mud which barely held together the stonework stacked around him.

"It's the punishments, sir," the sergeant major continued. "And them morts."

"Too much of one? Not enough of the other?"

"Yes, sir."

Ross twitched his cloak and moved nearer the hearth. "Very well, get back to the lines. Keep your ear close to the ground. And present my compliments to Mr. Nash at the commissary."

The battalion's senior noncommissioned officer clicked his heels and crouched out into the weather.

Rose pointed at an empty tumbler. His young *aide de camp* tilted the gallon jug which served as a decanter in the lieutenant governor's mansion while his father paced up and down the single room, trying to ignore the wet dribbling through the grass thatch, onto the canvas ceiling, down the raw walls.

"If only the profession of arms was as straightforward as it's imagined by some, life would be so much simpler. War's bad enough, but peace is hell, boy." He took the tumbler and sat by the fire to heat the Brazilian *agoardente*. "What do you do with fighting men when there's no fighting to be done?"

"Don't know, sir!"

"Then you'd better start knowing." Ross puffed out the crown of blue flames which fluttered round the rim of his glass. "It's not all beer and skittles being a king's officer. The enemy you might only face once a year, but your troops will face you every noon parade, fit to fight and fighting fit. Trouble is, there's only so much close-order drill you can busy them with before they go stale. At least, on campaign, we can keep the buggers marching."

"Sir."

"Still, if we play our cards right, this New Holland might be the making of us yet," Ross consoled himself, sipping the hot rum. "Never forget, Major Robert Clive—later Lord Clive of Plassey—returned Home a nabob. Worth millions."

The aide to Major Robert Ross was never going to be allowed to forget. A day might dawn when he'd become the second Lord Ross of Glenure, with a seat in the country and a seat in Parliament, but for the moment he remained an apprentice officer with wet feet and short rations.

Someone tapped on the door. The boy opened it. Nash stepped past. "Good afternoon, major. You asked to see me?"

"Aye. Sit down. Drink?"

"Er, just a small one, thank you. With water." Nash watched carefully to see that his instructions were carried out. "Long life and honor!"

"You won't enjoy much of either unless I get all the women you promised," Ross responded. "I thought there was supposed to be fifty, at least?"

"There will be, I promise. It's just that, well, there's an unaccountable spirit of insubordination which needs to be curbed—"

"How much longer have my men got to wait?"

Nash spread his hands. "A few days? I promise you, everything will be exactly as we agreed, once I've brought *Alexander*'s drabs to heel. Why the sudden impatience, major?"

"Because my men know their pay's being off-reckoned but a goodly number have still to get what they're paying for!" Ross snapped back.

"They're ripe for mischief and I've enough on my plate without you loading any more troubles!"

"So I've observed."

"And what's that supposed to mean?"

"Tench is demanding a court of honor—"

"Tench can demand whatever he bloody likes!" Ross said. "He'll never get it! His cronies are under open arrest with him and the rest'll follow Kellow's lead if it comes to a verdict!"

"Are you sure?"

"Uh?"

"Let's imagine for one moment that such a court doesn't go quite as we hope and, instead, it upholds Tench's honor," Nash replied quietly. "You're going to be called out by his seconds and, almost certainly, shot dead or run through."

"I'll see him in hell first! I've put better men than him six feet under!"

Nash was not impressed. "That I do not doubt, when your aim was steadier. But now, unless you elect for grapeshot, I doubt if you could hit, let alone pip, the ace of spaces at twenty-five yards, left hand or right. Tench can, Tench does, consistently!"

"By God, take care, sir!" Ross reared above the smiling, self-assured civilian. "That's what undid Tench! Lecturing *me* on the limits of authority! I put *him* in his place, too! His mother was had by some Taffy baronet! There's no other way a flaybum's boy got ahead so quickly—!"

"So he has influence!" Nash was no longer smiling up at the older man. "And who the devil d'you think is pushing him now? Urging him to put a bullet through you to serve another's interest?"

The sweat chilled on Ross's face. "Sparrow Legs?"

"Bravo! At last, the penny's dropped," Nash murmured. " 'The grave's a fine and private place, but none, I think, do there embrace,' or make provision for their family's fortune by using their authority as a colonial lieutenant governor. . . ."

Ross's eyes narrowed. "Just what is it you're trying to tell me, Mr. Nash?"

"I am advising you to be very, very careful, major," the civilian gentleman replied. "Despite what you may think, the present incumbent at Government House is no fool. Remember, he has connection among the Pitt Interest. He must know what your ambitions are, especially after that little fracas with Hunter off Africa, and he's going to make sure you don't inherit his shoes by emptying yours, first."

"Bloody hell."

Nash flicked the remark aside. "We are surrounded by his spies and toadies: every lag he remits from the lash is one more name in his little black book. Why else do you think he's so lenient? And I know for a fact that certain of the women are actively spreading slander about you, but I'm taking care of that. However, all is not lost, we still have loyal followers who wish you to succeed to the governorship and I meet them almost every day as they pass through the stores. Indeed, one of our most reliable informants is a chap from Shea's company, a very sound man, Asky by name. But, as I was saying, you must be on your guard against further attempts to provoke you into a position where another of your officers—Collins, perhaps?—could become a cat's-paw for a certain naval gentleman on the other side of the harbor."

"Bloody hell. . . ."

Nash shrugged. "I'm sorry to be so direct, major, but I assumed you knew that was their plan? I mean, if you're killed in a duel everyone's hands will be clean. Captain Campbell will then be declared incompetent by a board with the judge advocate general in the chair. Shea will take his place as the nominal battalion commander, until he pegs out. At which point Phillip's adjutant, Tench, assumes that responsibility as well. Meanwhile, that other naval captain, Hunter, assumes your lieutenant governorship. Phillip's pawn to king, bluejacket checks redcoat in three moves, end of game."

Ross was shaking with rage. "I'll see them all dead first."

"No, you will not," Nash contradicted politely. "You'll act as if you knew nothing. Instead, you'll pay heed to those who are still loyal to your interest."

"Uh?"

"For instance, that Asky I mentioned a few moments ago. The moment he steps up to corporal he's entitled to use a woman whenever he likes, not just once a week. Now, I have reason to think he'll not be unmindful of this favor because, whenever he stands guard at Government House, he stands very close to the wall. And he has an excellent recollection of the many things he overhears. . . ."

35

"GOOD MORNING, sir."

" 'Morning, David." The governor was already at work behind the table, wearing his watch coat to keep out the chill. Bryant had tried to light a small, portable iron stove but the damper needed attention: smoke still leaked around the lid. "Not too fresh for you last night?"

"Not at all." Collins stopped rubbing his hands and sat down at his usual place. "It got a bit nippy once the skies cleared but, if that's the worst we ever experience, it'll be a good campaign."

"Thank God someone thinks it possible," Phillip commented, sitting back in his chair. "At the moment I feel more like poor mad Tom o' Bedlam than one of His Majesty's captains general. Wherever I turn I see dirt and disorder, and whenever I turn someone seems to be trying to stab me in the back. The very last thing I need at present is open warfare among my officers!"

"I couldn't agree more with you," the judge advocate said, opening his despatch bag, "but we're at a complete stalemate. Tench is adamant about the court of honor to clear his reputation, half the staff are under arrest with him and so ineligible to serve upon it, and the other half are watching Kellow's lead. As for the original bone of contention—that damned court martial verdict—Ross will never budge in his demands and regulations prevent Tench from ordering a retrial until London gives an opinion."

"London? But that'll take years!"

"Yes."

"This is absolutely preposterous! I will not have my deputy snarling at his officers—half of whom are confined to quarters!—while some damned clerk in Whitehall decides whether or not to brush the cobwebs off his elbow! And that's final!"

"I'm sorry, sir, but as things stand at present we have no option."

"That's absurd!" Phillip's fist hit the table. "No effort must be spared to resolve the matter! Understand?"

"Oh, I understand all right, but do the parties in conflict?" Collins replied, taking out the morning's crop of crime and punishment from his bag.

"David?" The governor leaned forward and composed himself again. "I know that many of your corps resent interference from my side of the king's service, but if there's something I can do to help—unofficially—you will let me know?"

"Thank you, sir. That's very good of you to offer."

"I can hardly do less." Phillip shrugged. "Despite everything Major Ross has done to provoke me, I desire nothing so much as to see him and Tench resolve their difference. Quickly. We must consider the effect all this must be having on those we are supposed to be guarding."

"I know, sir. The atmosphere in the mess has become very unpleasant."

"I can imagine." Phillip sat forward. "Now, what's on today's agenda?"

Collins laid three papers on the table and turned them around for the governor to read. "Two D and D's—drunk and disorderlies—and one theft from public stores."

"Stores?" The governor's mouth tightened. "How? Where? Whose?"

The judge advocate checked his facts. "Three pints of oatmeal, two pints of peas, seven pounds of hardtack, four pounds of meat, six ounces of butter—"

"But that's a full week's rations!"

Collins pushed the summary of evidence for Phillip to read. "They were issued for one of Shea's men yesterday afternoon. When he returned to quarters shortly thereafter the rations were gone. However, one of our informants had noticed suspicious circumstances and guessed where they might be hidden—"

"Name?" Phillip was taking out his pocket book and pencil.

"Ah, Purvis. Jeremiah Purvis, ex-*Alexander*."

The governor made a memo to authorize the customary ounce of tobacco for vigilance. He looked up again. "Proceed."

Collins shrugged. "What more is there to say? It's the usual story. Once Corporal Asky had discovered the loss of his rations he alerted the sergeant of the guard and they searched this Barrett's shelter. Most of the food was recovered, less an amount which had already been consumed by the accused. Of course, the fellow denies ever being anywhere near the corporal's tent."

"Don't they all?" Phillip drummed his fingers for a moment. "Barrett? What's he like? Can we use him?"

"I hardly think it'd be worth the effort, he's a thoroughly bad lot."

"Which one isn't?" Phillip went silent again. "Breaking military lines and entering quarters. Stealing and eating a guard's rations. This is starting to sound like a capital offense to me, David."

"I agree."

Phillip leaned forward. "Get onto Dawes. Get those damned storehouses finished and get everything under lock and key while there's still anything left to protect."

"And Barrett?" Collins kept his voice neutral. "Shall I pass sentence of death? It'd have a beneficial effect on the troops," he added. "I'm sure most of their malingering and grumbles have been fomented by the differing scale of punishments: they're also bored by the lack of action or apparent purpose in being here. However, once we neck this Barrett item the law will be seen to be impartial. I'm sure an execution would do much to raise the men's spirits. . . ."

Phillip had begun signing documents to convene the trials at Government House later that day.

"Shall I hang him, then?"

The governor nodded.

"Thank you. And the other pair? The drunkards?"

"Fifty lashes and ninety days, quarry or brick field."

Collins tapped his papers together and replaced them in their bag. He stood, acknowledged the housekeeper's curtsey and strolled into the crisp, autumnal sunlight. He spoke to nobody but, long before the judge advocate had put the available officers' names into a hat and drawn those who would sit in judgment after lunch, the word was out that Thomas "Spangles" Barrett would be topped that evening.

The coiner's stock soared: he was about to become the first cove to stretch a rope at Sinny. It was a considerable distinction. Others would dance on air later, of course, but Barrett's reputation stood on firmer ground as the quarter guard marched up to Government House with the three accused men.

Twenty minutes later the guards marched away with two coves winking and grinning at the large crowd of well-wishers, while the third prisoner—his hands trussed, a musket shoved under each armpit—was carried like a sedan chair at the head of the triumphal procession.

They splashed across the stream and halted at the improvised prison stockade, a log with a chain and padlock, roughly halfway between the parade ground and the incomplete storehouses. The two drunkards were sent back to work until it was time for their scourging. Only Thomas Barrett was now officially allowed to be idle, slumped on the log while his ankles were secured to the other end of the chain. The duty sergeant detailed one of his men to stand guard until sundown when the entire colony could be mustered to see justice done.

Cribb waited until it was all clear, then marched up to the sentry and unfolded the dog-eared piece of paper which had Phillip's signature on the bottom, ordering him to draw shovels from the public store. "Special orders. Got to give 'im a bit of grub." He jerked a thumb at the weeping prisoner and slipped a tiny nugget of baccy into the soldier's tunic pocket.

"Right-o." The redcoat stared ahead, murmuring from the corner of his mouth. "Be quick about it."

"Bene cove." Cribb hitched his belt and walked up to the shape on the log.

The condemned man wiped his nose with a shaky hand. "What the f-fuck do you w-want?"

"Somebody 'as got to see you're being took care of." Cribb groped inside his shirt and pulled out a small rag bundle.

Barrett ignored the two bits of hard-tack and a hunk of pickled pork. "F-fuckin' bastard!"

"Who is?" Cribb squatted in the dust, one eye on the prisoner, the other cocked for trouble from officers.

"That slimy m-minge Dick Asky!" Barrett sobbed. "Reckons I pinched 'is rations! Swore it on a B-bible, 'e did! And it's all your fault!"

Cribb blinked. "Now what've I done wrong?"

"Them things was for you! I b-been got!" Barrett lunged for the other man's throat but pulled up short at the end of his chain. "I'd be right if you 'adn't made me take your pitch in that fuckin' tree!"

"Chrissakes! It was *you* what put the clamps on me for somewhere private!" Cribb spat back. "I been sleeping rough every night you've been cooking them clunkers! And I fixed you enough stuff to make thirty, not including the good 'un, so where's my split?"

"G-get fucked!" Barrett howled, overwhelmed by his own loss.

"But I need 'em!"

"Psst!" the sentry hissed.

Cribb was gone by the time the colony's devil driver halted at the prison log. Johnson carried the communion wafers on his prayer book. This was his first execution. He damped his lips. "Thomas Barrett? I am ordained to bring you comfort in this, your hour of affliction. But first, I must know if you are a communicating member of the Church of England?"

"Wha'?"

Johnson wished himself far away. Instead, he spread his black gown and joined the condemned man on the log. "My son, your time is brief. I must direct your gaze to that which awaits all as we pass from this world to appear before the Judgment Throne—"

"But I never done nothing!" Barrett wiped his eyes with the back of a wrist. "I'm the wrong bloke. Honest!" He clutched the chaplain's sleeve. "I never done nothing wrong! Tell 'em, please!"

Johnson tugged away. He was finding this very hard without the prisoner making it any more difficult. "Our Heavenly Father knows the innermost secrets of every heart. He will understand. Believe me—"

"I been grassed! Got at!"

Had there been time, had there been a choice, the chaplain would have spoken quietly, hopefully, reassuringly. But there was no time for compassion, there were no choices. A spark of repentance had to be struck and blown to raging heat if the condemned man was to enjoy life everlasting. But first, Barrett had to sense the full burden of a misspent life before he could dissolve the hard crust of sin with hot tears.

"My son. Listen. Your time is short. All are accursed who err and go astray from the Holy Commandments. Return therefore to our Lord God with all contrition and meekness of spirit, bewailing and lamenting, acknowledging and confessing, seeking to bring forth the fruits of repentance—!"

"I never done nothing wrong!"

"For now is the axe put unto the root of the tree so that every one that bringeth forth not good fruits is hewn down and cast into the fire!" the chaplain promised, close to tears himself. "Oh, my son, believe me! It is a fearful thing to fall into the hands of the living God! It is written in Scripture that He shall pour down fire and brimstone upon us poor sinners! Then shall appear the wrath of God in the day of vengeance—!"

"They want Phoss!" Barrett moaned, burying his face in his hands.

" 'Then shall it be said unto them, Go, ye accursed, into the fire everlasting which is prepared for the devil and all his demons!' " Johnson wiped his palms and threw an arm around the other man. "Repent! Take up the easy yoke of Christ Jesus! Seek with a contrite heart the Holy Spirit so that Our Redeemer will deliver you from the extreme curse of those who shall be set on the left hand of God! Pray most earnestly that you will be set upon the right when He takes possession of His most glorious kingdom—!"

Barrett's shoulders quaked. "The f-fuckin' cunts!"

Others were also persevering with their duty against great odds.

Collins intended that his first public hanging would be carried out with all the pomp and majesty of the law in action. The battalion's flogger had presented himself to the judge advocate's hut for instructions. Collins had delivered them. The redcoat had folded his arms and replied that he would never stoop to neck a convicted lag. Collins had compromised his principles as an officer and gentleman by adding half a pint of rum and an ounce of tobacco: both had been refused, a clear signal that Ross had been the first to give this man his orders for the day. Not only were the marines now refusing to supervise the laborers, they were not going to kill them, either.

The afternoon's sandglass was trickling in the quarter guard tent and, thus far, all Collins had managed to assemble was one condemned man. There was still no executioner. And there were no gallows. The judge advocate snatched up his hat and went for a quick walk around the settlement. But this was not England with her comfortably shaped oaks,

this was New Holland where most trees soared high before throwing out
a branch.

Swearing under his breath, Collins scrawled a note to Captain Walton
of *Friendship,* requesting the urgent loan of one spar and one carpenter.
Both were promptly rowed ashore and the merchant seaman agreed to rig
his beam between two trees on the edge of the parade ground, cash in
advance, plus the cost of the beam which had been set at a scandalous ten
pounds sterling. "Can't never be used on ship again," Chippy said,
cheerfully shifting his quid of baccy to the other cheek. "It'd be jinxed,
see?"

Collins saw. He could also see the sun westering over the inland ranges
as the quarter guard's drums drew excited crowds of lags from all parts
of the settlement, except the quarry and the brick field. A few Indians
were being encouraged with gifts of old hats and beads to come along,
to watch, to learn, to tell their kin what happened to troublemakers.
Assuming Collins ever recruited a hangman.

He marched over to the pair of drunkards who were now stripped naked,
waiting to be flogged before the evening's main attraction. "I am empowered to remit your punishment, you don't have to be whipped—!"

"Gor' bless your lovin' 'eart, sir!"

"You're a regular ge'man!"

The judge advocate silenced them. "However, in exchange for clemency, one of you will volunteer to carry out the execution!"

Their grins faded. The lags shuffled their feet. Collins clenched his
sword hilt. "Refuse and I shall charge you both with insubordination!"

Ross was seated on a canvas stool, thoroughly enjoying the spectacle.
He looked up as his senior company commander clicked heels. "D'you
see that, Jimmy? Piss weak. That's what being on Sparrow Legs' staff
does to a man."

Campbell shook his head in agreement. "All stand to order, present
and correct, sah!"

Ross could see that, too. His troops—less those guarding the quarry
and the brick field—had crossed their muskets to form a human box in
front of the gallows, penning the happy crowd which was standing on
tiptoe to get a better view.

Cribb had given up any hope of ever getting his thirty counterfeit
dollars from Barrett. The God guesser was still on the log, still exhorting
the wretched man to repent and be saved. Instead, Cribb was now
crushed at the back of the crowd, watching Nash and Asky in the
shadows, behind the stores.

Cribb's bowels ran cold. Sinny had begun to feel like Copper Hill prison camp where informers had bred like flies on dung, and where the commandant, Caleb Ledyard, had also flogged and hanged forced laborers. It was time to bolt. Bugger the clunkers, he would go without them. Sparrow Legs' man had said something about there being a recce' in the direction of Chinaland. It was just possible, if he slipped Bryant enough, he could tag along as odd-job man to the officers' orderly.

Phillip had chosen to absent himself at Government House, which now made Ross the senior officer present. He stood and strolled across to join the judge advocate general. "Having trouble, Mr. Collins?"

"Neither of these damned scoundrels will volunteer to be hangmen!" Both had already earned two hundred strokes apiece, in weekly doses of fifty—given with the heavier, military cat o' nine tails—for wilful disobedience of a lawful command.

The lieutenant governor snapped a twig in two unequal halves and held out both fists. "Choose!"

"Wha'?" the nearest man whined. "Aagh!" His luck was in, the fist which had just decked him held the long twig, it was last night's drinking companion who was tonight's executioner.

The other lag's legs buckled. Ross gripped his hair. "Get started."

" 'Is mates'll croak me!"

Ross nodded at the setting sun. "If he's not hanged by the time it touches that treetop, I'll have you killed myself, with a thousand lashes at the triangles."

He let go of the lag's scalp.

The man fell. His crime had been too much drink. For that he was now being condemned to an outcast's life of contempt and danger as the colony's scragger. "I c-can't! I never 'ung nobody before!"

"He's never been hanged before."

Richard Johnson stood in front of Barrett, surplice flapping, hoping to shield him from the sordid squabble. Ross was less sensitive. He cocked both of his pistols and leveled them at the lag's snotty face. "The sun's setting."

The man wobbled upright, beaten, but first he had to serve his friend with the first installment of fifty, arms roped around one of the trees which supported the gallows beam. William Balmain was today's duty surgeon. He kept the tally of blows, ordering a halt at ten sets of five chalk marks on his slate. The last of the screaming Indians ran away as the doctor began treating raw flesh with pickling salt.

Collins waited until a proper sense of decorum had been restored, then took out the death warrant while the regimental flogger taught their novice hangman how to pinion a prisoner without wasting too much cord. "Thomas Barrett! You have been tried and found guilty of stealing rations for a week, the equivalent of another's toil for seven days! This detestable and abominable offense leaves no alternative but the only sentence which reflects the horror of your crime! Let all take heed therefrom! God Save the King!"

Two makeshift ladders had been propped against the beam from opposite sides. One of the marines helped Barrett up his ladder by jabbing him in the rump with a bayonet. Scragger dragged himself up the other ladder to meet his victim at the top. Nobody had thought to blindfold the condemned man, nor had he been given the usual St. Giles's cup of rum. "Sorry, mate!"

"And f-fuck you, too!"

" 'I am the resurrection and the life, saith the Lord!' " Johnson's eyes were squeezed shut. " 'He that believeth in me, though he were dead, yet shall he live! And whosoever liveth and believeth in me shall never die—'!"

Ross nodded.

The battalion's drummers struck the "Rogue's March."

Barrett's ladder twisted.

36

JOHNSON LAY on his sack of dry bracken and stared up at the darkness. Rain pattered across the canvas roof. He felt diminished. A consecrated priest had broken the Sixth Commandment. And the killed man was still hanging out there, toes pointed, eyes popped, awaiting Christian burial.

The chaplain dressed at sunrise and left his wife in her blankets but she was awake by the time he returned to their shed. The breakfast fire needed fuel. The oatmeal ration was sour and insufficient. The ants had found a way into the sugar. The governor had failed to supply a domestic servant who would not pilfer—!

Richard slapped Mary's face. Twice.

He was not the only person acting out of character as he trod behind the sexton's wheelbarrow, along the Brickfield Road, away from camp. One of the government women was flouncing about, hands on hips, tossing her curls in plain view of everyone. "—An' I'll bleedin' well do what I like, when I like, Mrs. La-de-da Brandon!"

"Come back this instant!"

"Nyah!" The younger woman stuck out her tongue and screeched with laughter.

"By God—!"

"Pig's tit!" Nancy Fitzgerald flung up her skirts, spun around and stuck out her arse. "Kiss that goodbye!" She gave a pert little curtsey and skipped toward the military lines where a crowd of admirers waited, clapping and whistling.

The chaplain reached the small clearing where his sexton had already prepared a grave. Barrett's clothes had been stolen during the night, of course. Cribb gripped the naked ankles, twisted them over the edge of the hole and tried arranging the stiff limbs.

"As a condemned individual, should he not be facing downwards?" Johnson asked, peering into the shallow hole.

Cribb straightened. Slowly. "I seen 'undreds o' blokes, Over There. Some was face up, some was face down, and some didn't 'ave no faces, or arms, or legs, up or down." He thrust out the shovel handle. "If you want it done different, do it yourself."

The civilian opened his prayer book at a dog-eared page. " 'We brought nothing into this world, and it is certain we can carry nothing out. The Lord gave and the Lord hath taken away, blessed be the name of the Lord—' "

The curtailed burial service was soon done. Cribb spat on his palms and got ready to close the grave as Johnson left.

Kitty Brandon waited till he was out of sight and stepped from behind a patch of scrub, quite recovered after the first open rebellion against her authority. She joined the sexton. "A bad business. And yet they say he protested his innocence to the very end."

"Gutless sod." Cribb drove his shovel into the mound of loose earth.

"That's as may be. Of greater importance now is the question of whether or not he spoke the truth. For if he did," Kitty Brandon went on, "it would indicate those rations were planted to entrap another. In which case, but for the grace of God and the greed of the late Mr. Spangles Barrett, you were due to choke yesterday. Not that it would've surprised me. You have a rare talent for antagonizing people. Indeed, you've managed to do little else since we landed—"

"Now look 'ere!"

"Be silent. You were grassed. We must ferret the nark who fingered you," the woman went on in the same flat, expressionless voice. "We might start with a certain Jeremiah Purvis, ex-*Alexander,* whom I am reliably informed is to be awarded an ounce of tobacco for services rendered."

"Ratbag."

"Correct. Such an abject apology for a man would never have the nerve to do a job on his own account. You will ask for the name of his latest owner. When he's told you, tell me. Omit the details. I shall then decide what further steps are necessary."

"It'll be a regular treat. . . ."

Kitty Brandon began to leave the graveyard. On impulse, she turned and walked back. "You're in mortal danger. Lose no further time, speak with Mr. Levi and Mr. Thorpe no matter what it might cost in hurt pride because, without allies, you're already a dead man!" She glanced at Barrett's flyblown face. "Luck like that never happens twice."

The time had come for Johnson to show that a civilian gentleman could have a code of honor and duty no less demanding than a military officer's. He took a deep breath. "May I come in?"

Tench was stripped to his breeches, a towel knotted round his neck, completing his toilet. He looked over one shoulder. "Oh, it's the padre."

Johnson took that as an invitation to stoop inside the daub and wattle hut. "I accept responsibility for what I did, concerning Lieutenant Dawes's confidence. I stand ready to make amends in whatever way gives you satisfaction."

Tench laid the razor aside and splashed cold water from the bucket. "How?" He dabbed himself. "With communion wafers? At ten yards?"

Johnson's face stiffened. "There's no need for childish abuse. I am sincerely apologizing, as one man to another."

"That excludes your wife. A pity."

"Mary has nothing to do with this!"

"I'd have said she had everything to do with it," Tench replied, flicking the towel. He reached for his shirt. "My reputation, which took me ten hard years to win, was destroyed by your wife at a single blow. If she wishes to make amends, present her with my compliments and tell her to go to the top of a windy hill. There let her rip open a cushion and shake it quite empty. I shall consider the account closed when she's recovered every single feather and sewn up the bag again. She will then understand the damage she's done to me and, *en passant*, her husband."

"Me?"

"Of course. You've hardly stepped out of this verbal cesspit smelling like wild violets!" Tench buttoned his cuffs. "After all, whose devoted companion is now the recognized village scold and gossip? So, if you will excuse me, I have duties which require my attention—"

"I'm very, very sorry."

"Doubtless you are, but what difference does sorrow make?" Tench replied, tucking his shirt. "The wretch you despatched to Heaven last night must've also been very, very sorry. And I've no doubt you tried to get him to apologize for his misdeeds. But would he be any less dead had he confessed for every sin since Adam's?"

Johnson remained silent.

"Then your apologies are of no earthly use." Tench reached for his wig. "Now, please go."

"But we can't leave matters the way they are!"

"Who said we were?" Tench shrugged into his tunic. "I have an officer's right to a court of honor and, despite everything that drunken boor can do to deny me, I shall have my reputation restored either by public retraction or blood."

Johnson shook his head with despair. " 'Pride goeth before destruction, and an haughty spirit before a fall.' Please, I humbly beg of you, reflect! Seek in your heart to find compassion for a very human lapse! Dawes is distraught at the consequences of his one thoughtless action—!"

"And yours. Now, good day to you, sir."

Johnson stood his ground. "I will not go! You pervert the truth! Nothing so trivial as 'reputation' can ever be worth a single human life! To say otherwise is a blasphemy!"

"You want the truth, eh?" Tench reached for a bundle of foolscap sheets on his desk. He removed the lump of rock which served for a paperweight and scanned the top page. "Pay attention to this. It's an account of yesterday's business, written for Messrs. Debrett of Piccadilly." He paused. " 'The time was fast approaching when violations of public security could not be restrained by lenience and admonitions. A desperate and hardened rogue, Thomas Barrett by name, was detected stealing a large quantity of provisions and brought to trial on the 28th of the month. His Excellency was pleased to approve the punishment most dreaded by all which was duly executed at a little before sundown the same day.

" 'The prisoner who, hitherto, had remained indifferent to his fate, began taking heed of our chaplain's exhortations and confessed the enormity of his offense before mounting the ladder with upcast gaze. After urging all present to take warning from his end he was duly launched into eternity. Throughout this melancholy spectacle the Reverend Mr. Johnson acted with commendable steadiness tempered by Christian charity and compassion.' "

The chaplain wiped his brow. "It was nothing like that."

"Of course it wasn't!" Tench replaced the piece of rock. "You had your eyes shut most of the time. You repeated yourself on at least two occasions. The miserable little runt you were trying to convert to purity of heart died bleating obscenities. Our hangman was even more scared and incompetent than his victim at what was, frankly, the most botched execution I've ever witnessed!" Tench crossed his arms. "Now, which version do you wish printed? Mine? Or the truth?"

"I—I don't know!"

"Happily I do know. You'd prefer the Bishop of London to read mine because the truth, as you term it, would make you the laughingstock of England. Therefore, in the balance between trivial reputation and solid veracity, even a minister of religion will press his thumb on the scales to influence their relative weights."

"That's a false analogy!"

"The hell it is," Tench snapped back, "but don't worry, I'll do the decent thing, lie. Because I am aware, even if nobody else is, that what's said or written in haste upon this abomination of desolation will be considered at leisure in London! Why else do you think I am demanding a court of honor? Because I wish to risk my life in the unlikely event of Ross holding his pistol steady? Because I enjoy the prospect of wounding Dawes?"

"I cannot say, it's all so very confusing!"

"On the contrary, it is all so extremely simple. Unless I restore my reputation here, I'll be socially dead there, in London. Further promotions will cease and I shall have no alternative but to do what . . . ?"

"I—I don't know."

"Neither do I." Tench unfolded his arms and reached for his empty sword belt as a corporal and private halted outside the officer's hut, ready to escort him through the day, a sign to all that he was under arrest, his movements restricted by higher authority. "I have but one trade, Mr. Johnson; take that from me and I am ruined. I might raise about eight hundred pounds for my commission, less what I owe, say three hundred pounds clear, enough to buy a decent mount, a brace of pistols and a black vizard. At which point I'll be equipped to turn highwayman on Hampstead Heath as an alternative to begging in the gutter. 'Spare a penny for a poor solja fallen on 'ard times! What give 'is all for King George against them dirty Rebels! Gor' bless your loving face, ma'am . . . !' " He picked up his hat and straightened the regimental cockade. "Thank you, no. I prefer taking my chances in front of Ross and your friend. Now, step aside, my keepers await me."

The chaplain watched the three redcoats march away, then turned and put the officers' lines behind him. He gave his own home a wide berth and continued along the track to the observatory where he could be alone, but he was still out of luck, Dawes was packing some equipment.

Johnson stepped inside the former dining room of the Literati Club. "I'm most awfully sorry, William. I tried."

Dawes finished wrapping a specimen jar. "You didn't really think he'd change his mind?"

"I hoped I might make him see reason."

"He did. It's that our reason, his and mine, happens to differ from yours."

Johnson shook his head again. "There are things I no longer understand as well as I should."

"Richard, you are a civilian, a free man, we are not." Dawes rested on the edge of his work table for a moment. "There's a world of difference. We are soldiers, 'jealous in honor, sudden and quick in quarrel, seeking the bubble reputation even in the cannon's mouth.' For us to act otherwise is not possible, no matter what we may personally feel, because when one has so little, honor is everything. Strip that from us and we are left almost naked against an indifferent world of civilians." Dawes hesitated. "I'm afraid that Captain Tench is only acting as I would, were I in his place."

"But what if he perseveres with this madness? What if he—how do you say?—calls you out?"

"I shall do my duty as I am honor bound." Dawes straightened. "Until which moment I shall try to leave a respectable body of work to mark my stay in New Holland. Pass me the magnifying lens and that absorbent paper, please."

Johnson watched them go into the knapsack, with the specimen jar and flower press. "William. I'm coming with you."

"But there's no provision been made for another on the expedition."

"I shall ask His Excellency. Immediately. You and I must work on our lexicon and grammar."

Levi was working on his English alphabet, copying labels from Balmain's salve jars onto the surgeon's slate before rubbing them out again with his sleeve. He did not notice Kitty Brandon enter the dispensary until she coughed. "Oh! Sorry—!"

"Please. Remain seated." She smiled back. "It's just that we haven't heard much of you, recently. I thought I'd see how you were getting along."

Levi laid the slate to one side. "I eat. I sleep. I live. Is enough."

"Then at least one man has his head screwed on the right way," she observed, leaning against a roof pole. "Speaking of other things for the moment, have you had time to form an opinion about that fellow in the stores? Not Miller, the other one, the one they call 'Mr. Nash'. . . ."

Levi's face was impassive. "Sometimes I talk when Dr. Balmain send me there. Then I say, 'Good morning, your honor. Lovely day, your honor. Be happy, your honor.' It makes him feel good."

"But what about yourself? How do you feel?"

"Does it matter what I feel?" the surgeon's assistant countered with a shrug.

"It might. To me."

"Then to you, I tell. From so high"— Levi held his hand level with his knee—"there has always been some Big Cove saying 'Come here! Go there! Eat zhit!' Is not a good feeling."

"So you don't care much for him?"

"Let me answer this way," Levi replied. "In London they going to neck me. Why? Because I help a girl. But who is it who sends such girls to 'Dr. Achmet'? It is fine English gentlemen like your Mr. Nash. So who should they hang?"

"Thank you. I'd better be getting along—"

"One moment." Levi raised his hand a fraction of an inch. "What we really talking about is the stiff-necked, big-mouthed Mr. Fozzy Kripp. Yes?"

"Yes."

"Then give him this advice, from me, it cost nothing. That neck is going to get fixed unstiff unless he learn bloody quick to say 'Good morning, your honor. Lovely day, your honor.' There is much I do not know," Levi went on quietly, "but one thing I do know. This is not New Jerusalem and I was wrong. But so is he if he thinks to go to Chinaland because I been to Tashkent, and Bokhara, and places, and still they not Chinaland. One thing more," Levi added, raising his hand another fraction. "Our fine major of the sergeants has rag for brains if he thinks he going Home from here when he don't even know where here is. *Nu*, Ben has brain for brains because he tell me, 'While there's good grub I like it here.' That's thinking! We eat, we sleep, we live. What more does Fozzy want, a knot under the chin?"

37

PHILLIP STOOD at the window and savored his breakfast coffee. Another barque was being fumigated before her papers were sealed: by this time tomorrow *Friendship* would be off the coast, northward bound for Canton and Home. It was a prudent measure to burn sulphur and tar below decks. Last week two women stowaways had been smoked out and flogged aboard *Golden Grove* and, no doubt, more would be discovered in the crew's quarters when *Alexander* shortly took her leave.

The governor looked up at the morning sky: today promised to be crisp, invigorating, perfect weather for inland travel. Even the small vegetable garden in front of Government House was returning to life after the months of summer, he thought, watching his housekeeper ladle washing water along some rows of beans.

Phillip approved of her thrift. It was another sign that he'd chosen well. Dundas was undoubtedly the best from a very mixed bag of chattels. A former ladies' maid, and it showed.

He did not need to remind her to put on a clean apron before serving dinner—tasteful spreads which were infinitely better than anything scorched, burned or destroyed by Bryant in the past. Nor did she smoke a pipe, or pick her nose, or spit on the floor as so many of the other female items would have done. She was not even light-fingered with his rations inside the pantry and, thus far at least, had not touched any of the trifling copper coins which he had left lying around his bedchamber. Moreover, she appeared to have a surprisingly trim figure as she bent over the small green shoots, rather like a younger sister of Mathew Godwin's wife, back on his Lyndhurst estate.

Phillip swirled his coffee, ready to finish it, then stopped. A sentry had been assigned to the garden to protect its vegetables. The marine had hurriedly adjusted his tunic and was volunteering to help Dundas fill her bucket. They spoke for several moments before the housekeeper went down to the water hole, alone. Phillip's face relaxed and he finished the tepid drink with a jaunty flourish.

Jane Dundas stood to one side as Captain Tench and his escort strode up the track. The officer acknowledged her curtsey, returned the sentry's salute and raised his fist to rap on the front door of Government House, but Bryant was ready to snatch it open from inside. " 'Is Excellency awaits you, sir!"

Tench walked past the major domo and clicked his heels.

"That'll be all, Bryant. Continue inspecting the cabbages for caterpillars."

"Er, aye aye. Sir."

Phillip waited until the door had shut. He smiled. "Thank you for attending me so promptly, Mr. Tench. Coffee?"

"Yes. Thank you, sir."

"Sugar?"

"Please."

Phillip served the other man, then refilled his own cup and motioned for Tench to take a seat. "I'll come directly to the point. I've been told several versions of your *contretemps* with Major Ross but, thus far, I've chosen not to intervene. I had rather hoped you could resolve your differences without the mediation of a third party, especially one from my side of the king's service." The governor shook his spoon dry and took more sugar from the unlocked canister. "Sadly, that does not appear to be happening so I'm being drawn into the conflict, whether I like it or not. However, before I give a decision, would you mind telling me your version of what happened?"

Tench put his cup down. "Well, sir, you'll recall that I was president of the court martial which tried Marine Hunt for striking Corporal Dempsey and calling him a Chatham sodomite?"

"Yes."

"Well, the previous day, I'd endured a harangue from Major Ross on the gross inequality between convict punishments and those awarded to our men. With that in mind," Tench went on, "I directed the court to take a lenient view of what was obviously a dispute fomented by the principal witness, one Nancy Fitzgerald, and so we handed down a balanced judgment. Hunt could either apologize to his corporal or receive one hundred lashes in lieu thereof. Whereupon Major Ross ordered me to convene another court and pass a more severe punishment as our leniency would further undermine good order and military discipline—"

"But that's illegal."

"I know." Tench controlled the shake in his voice. "I informed Major Ross that no man can be tried twice for the same offense, once it's recorded, whereupon we were ordered to surrender our swords to the quarter guard. As president of the court I was singled out for especial abuse. In addition to my father's profession, the reputation of Sir Wynne Williams was dragged through the mire and treated with public contempt. The inference was that . . . was that his interest in my mother, and myself, was. Was of. Was of a particular nature."

"You said nothing which could be construed as insubordination?"

"It was not possible. Major Ross had rendered me incapable of further speech. Sir."

Phillip walked behind his desk and slowly sat down. "No reasonable man can deny your right to satisfaction. Indeed, had you not demanded a court of honor, your position in the corps would've been compromised. However, in such matters there is always a danger that one word can cast a dark cloud over far brighter horizons. . . ."

"Sir?"

The governor steepled his fingertips. "Our Continental neighbors have raised *affaires d'honneur* to an art form with the most impressive rituals and codes of behavior. We British, by contrast, tend to be more pragmatic. That was brought home to me when we paid our visit to M. de La Pérouse. Remember? On the one hand there was poor old *Supply* which appeared like a coal barge alongside *L'Astrolabe*. On the other hand were the Frenchmen, models of precision in everything they undertook."

Tench shifted uneasily as the older man went on in the same thoughtful voice. "There's no doubt the *messieurs* can beat us hands down any day when it comes to devising intricate systems and profound methods to regulate every nuance of human behavior. I envy their gift! Who wouldn't? My opposite number has been provided with no less than six chronometers to navigate his two frigates. John Hunter brought in nine vessels with only a broken pocket watch and a log line. Ball and I found our way here by dead reckoning and an occasional lunar sight." Phillip smiled, amused by something intensely personal. "And yet, for all the resources of *l'Académie française*, which of us carried off the prize?"

"I fail to see any connection with my honor, sir."

"Appearances can be deceptive, Mr. Tench," the governor replied. "What may seem to be an admirable model may, upon closer examination, prove to be impractical. The French have a dangerously brittle feel about them. While everything functions, they'll function superbly well. But let one piece fail and everything stops dead in its tracks: they could soon be in for eventful days. But that's another matter.

"We British are different. Like *Supply* we can appear rough and ready in good sailing weather, but let a storm threaten and something break, we can generally tie a knot and sail on. It's the one quality which most infuriates our neighbors: in a perfectly ordered world we should lose more often than we win, but we don't. The secret is our national genius for compromise, our ability to grasp the whole rather than become obsessed with rigid rules."

"Sir." Tench damped his lips. "With all respect, you've never been held up to ridicule and told that you'd be better employed as a village flaybum!"

"No?" Phillip studied the backs of his hands. "That's another thing which struck me aboard *L'Astrolabe*. Unlike France, Britain can accommodate all sorts from all walks of life, if they're willing to exert themselves. Why, in our social muddle it's even possible for the son of a schoolmaster to govern the empire's largest dominion."

Tench blinked. "You?"

Phillip nodded. "The jealous have called me all manner of names to my face, just as they're doing now behind my back, but they've never stopped me reaching any objective I've set myself."

"But he said my mother was—!"

"A close friend of Sir Wynne Williams?" Phillip enquired. "How fortunate. Promotions cost money as well as talent and connection. To be born with all three is to be lucky indeed! Perhaps that's the reason Major Ross is so consumed by envy?" The governor leaned forward. "Continue upon your present path and you could make lieutenant general with a knighthood and military list pension. But do something rash, like wounding or even killing your commanding officer, and it will never be forgiven or forgotten when future appointments are being discussed. 'What's said or written in haste upon this abomination of desolation will be considered at leisure in London. . . .' "

"So you've also spoken with the padre."

"Of course. Mr. Johnson is my chaplain too, you know, and he's starting to cope with great difficulties. I trust as much can be said about you when the time comes to include a certain recommendation in my despatches to the Admiralty."

"What recommendation?"

"That's my business."

"Sorry, sir."

Phillip ignored the apology. "Major Ross has agreed to put his case in writing. You will now do the same. I shall add a covering note before despatching the matter to merciful oblivion somewhere in Whitehall. Meanwhile you'll be released from arrest, in exchange for which you will drop all demands for a court of honor. I would suggest that, when your sword is returned, you make a brief speech of acceptance. Let magnanimity of spirit be your theme: you'll find that it will win more regard than you've lost."

"Is that an order, sir?"

"Good heavens, no!" Phillip stood. "Over the years I've observed that difficulty either makes a man or breaks him: you don't seem to be the sort who fractures easily. Now, if you'll excuse me, I can see Mr. Collins coming up the path and there are still some matters I must attend to before going away."

Tench clicked his heels. "Thank you, sir."

"Thank you, Mr. Tench."

The two officers of marines exchanged salutes in the porch. Collins walked into Government House and the door swung shut. "Any luck?"

"Water finds its own level," Phillip replied. "Now, you're quite clear what must be done while I'm gone?"

"I have your instructions." Collins began opening his bag.

"So has Ross. Gave them to him personally when we hammered out the compromise last night. It remains to be seen if they're carried out, though." Phillip arranged some papers on his desk, then shoved them back in their original order. "I am so weary of that man's damned obsessions. 'Inca diamond mines'!" The governor made a helpless gesture. "At the very moment when everyone, regardless of rank, ought to be digging the ground to fill his belly, my deputy only wishes to dig it and fill his pockets with pretty lumps of stone! But don't let's dredge over that again. D'you have those things for me?"

"Right here, sir."

Phillip scanned the receipts and documents, made a few minor corrections and signed his name. "That'll clip my deputy's wings while my back's turned." He flicked a paper with his fingernail. "Keep a firm rein on him."

"Easier said than done, sir."

"True,"— the governor reached for his plain brown civilian coat— "but I'm sure you'll devise ways to keep him bogged in routine. Ah, I see my traveling companions are assembling outside, let's join them." Phillip shouldered his fowling piece, the water bottle and a haversack. He stepped onto the porch and returned Hunter's salute. "All present and correct, John?"

"Ready, aye ready, sir."

"Splendid." Phillip inspected the short line of ration bags and pieces of scientific equipment which had been slid out for his approval. With prudence there ought to be enough hardtack for himself, Hunter, Dawes and Johnson, to supply a week's march into the wilderness. And enough over for the five marine guards, his manservant and the item recruited to be everyone's odd-job man. "It's a pity about the horses, John. A saddle mount and pack animals would've more than doubled our endurance, but better luck next time." He snapped his fingers at Bryant. "You've left directions for them to be fed more oats?"

"Aye aye, sir!"

"Good, then shall we—?" Phillip stopped. The quarter guard's sergeant was hurrying from the west bank. He halted, hat off to the senior marine present.

"What is it, Fitch?" Collins asked.

"Still no sign o' that there bolter! Permission to send out a patrol beyond the picket line? Sah!"

The judge advocate shook his head. "Permission denied."

"Sah!"

Phillip waited until the redcoat had marched away. "Who's tried escaping this time, David?"

"One of the cook assistants. Failed to return after going out for firewood. We did a sweep at first light this morning but he'll soon get tired of his own company and slink back like the rest."

"Flog him." Phillip was more concerned with his own excursion beyond camp limits. "That'll not only cool his ardor for travel but serve as a warning to everyone else who daydreams of gold mines in China. Damned stupid rumor!"

Collins saluted and stood easy as Phillip led the way downhill to where *Sirius*'s cutter had laid alongside a temporary landing of rock and planks. He went aboard and sat in the stern while everyone else fitted where they could find a place. "Whenever you're ready, Evans."

38

THE COXSWAIN obeyed and his men bent to their sweeps until an easterly breeze could be caught off Point Maskelyne. The oars swung inboard as Evans loosened the cutter's sail, put over the helm and began tacking past the observatory, steering inland for the head of Port Jackson.

The governor remained impassive as he viewed the passing scene. He knew that every shade of feeling would become the subject of gossip among the tars, among the redcoats, perhaps even among the lagged items—one of which seemed to be dozing at the foot of the cutter's mast. Phillip knew that those in authority can never be too careful in public, but all the same it was a blessed relief to be quit of the colony and its endless bickering. At least for the next few days.

There was now no risk that the lieutenant governor would be able to exploit this absence. Ross could hatch as many plots as he liked with Campbell; both men were now entangled in a net of their own weaving. At least half the officer corps sympathized with young Tench's stand, and most of the remainder could be counted upon to stay neutral until they had seen which way the wind was blowing after Shea's commission went up for sale. Ross had played his best hand, and lost—

"I said, this is where I saw them last time," Hunter repeated, pointing inshore at a small flotilla of native canoes, floating like lily pads near a mud flat while dark shapes crouched, spearing fish.

"Interesting."

Sirius's commander was under less pressure, he could even afford to smile occasionally in public. "You've never seen such ill-found craft in all your life, just sheets of bark tied up with vine at both ends and a few bits of branch for ribs. If you and I were to try paddling one we'd overset it within moments, but those people over there handle them as if they were born to it." Hunter shielded his eyes against the sun's glare. "Would you like me to bring one closer so that you can take a look?"

"No, thank you, I'd prefer to make camp before dark. Too much time has already been wasted."

"It won't take more than five minutes, sir," Hunter persisted, "and a description of their primitive customs will excite favorable comment in London. . . ."

"Oh, very well then, but not too many and not too close." Phillip took the plugs of greased rag from his shotgun barrels.

Hunter ordered the coxswain to furl their sail while he flashed a mirror at the nearest canoe, then held up a small piece of red cloth, fluttering it in the stiff breeze. "That'll do the trick."

This time it did not: the Indian fisherman dropped his spear and began paddling hard for the shore.

"Perhaps you'd like me to try hailing him?" Dawes volunteered.

Hunter scratched his head. "If you think it'll do any good."

The young officer of marines turned to his civilian friend. "The second person singular, present tense, imperative mood of *guwai*?"

"Prefix *dabidgi*, add infinitive."

"Thanks." Dawes cupped his mouth. "*Dabidgi-guwai! Dabidgi-gu-wai-i-i!*"

At which the entire flotilla scattered, hiding wherever dense mangroves stalked into the water. Phillip replaced the plugs in his gun, Evans hoisted the sail again, Dawes shrugged at the chaplain, Hunter coughed drily. "Perhaps it's some kind of religious festival? They might not want us around, today."

"Then I trust they don't have many such occasions on their calendar if this is their usual response to our overtures," the governor replied as they began moving again. "It is not the intention of Parliament to throw good money after bad despatching shoddy labor around the globe once tractable local servants can be recruited. Therefore," he went on, looking directly at Dawes, "*my* intention is to make contact with their kings and chieftains without further delay, so that proper relations may be entered into."

Cribb's eyelids flickered, then shut again. He was snug while Bryant was mug enough to deflect the wind coming over the back of the boat. As for the Indians, the best of British luck to them, they would need it if this lot ever collared 'em for servants. And as for the Big Cove's big words, who cared? He had never been a gypsy nypper on the run, on the make, on the take.

Cribb dozed. It had been a busy night. He felt tired but good. This was the way to get around, the ge'man's way, the easy way Home. Too bad about the prancers. Specially the little mare. If only she hadn't took bad eating local grass, Cribb could have been halfway to the mountains this time tomorrow, cantering easily with all these grub bags lashed across her crupper. And that fancy gun stuck like a dragoon's carbine in the scabbard. And its bullets. And powder. And the Big Cove's watch, purse, pocket compass too.

The lag stifled a yawn. Still, once back in Sinny he would know which road to take. Another private word with Mrs. B., a quick leg up in the saddle and they would not pull rein till they hit Chinaland. Then she would understand why he still had not bothered to talk with Leafy or Ben. There was no point. There were not enough nags to go round for everyone to bolt. It was that simple. Anyhow, they could not ride, they had said so, tons of times, on the boat. Besides, they were doing all right for themselves. They were not having to dig graves just to win a crust—

Cribb knocked wood for luck and muffled another yawn: it had been a long night's work.

"Oy! Bugger off!" He rolled clear as the coxswain's mate trampled past, the sail dropped in a heap and the cutter ran aground. They had reached the head of navigation and the sun was now only six or seven fingers above the forest, by Cribb's estimate, as he waded ashore with the expedition's breadbags.

"You there!" Bryant aimed a finger at the convicted item who had paid four ounces of tobacco for the privilege of being here this afternoon. "Look lively!"

Cribb dragged their boat's mast onto firmer ground where the sailors were lashing oars together. The mast was propped against these makeshift crutches while the odd-job man gathered rocks to pin down the sail which had been thrown over the ridge pole to shelter the officers.

"Now get the wood!"

Fuel was scarce around what seemed to be some kind of stamping ground for the local Indian tribe. Several large fireplaces were scattered among the paperbark trees, each one surrounded by a deep compost of kangaroo bones, fish heads, mussel shells and human dung. Cribb widened the range of his reconnaissance as he gathered twigs and worked closer to the officers.

The governor and his entourage stood on the river bank, studying an eel trap—a rough weir of stones piled across the river at its narrowest point. "We can demolish it easily enough," Phillip agreed, "but how much further could we proceed by boat? From the rate of flow I doubt if there's a confluence upstream." He turned as the odd-job man worked past, scavenging bits of driftwood trapped among the stones. "I therefore propose to establish a defensive base here which can be used to run a series of traverses inland until we intersect the major river system. Then we can build a permanent outpost for trade with the peoples beyond the mountains. Meanwhile, this place might serve for a corn mill if we quarry enough rock to raise a sluice." Phillip stopped short. "Mr. Dawes? Just what is that you're doing?"

The young officer of marines was crouched by the waterside, riffling gravel and sand inside his canteen's tin cup. He straightened. "Searching for mineral specimens, sir. The curator at the Royal Society insisted I took every opportunity. There may be traces of gold—"

"Enough!"

"Sir?"

"I've had more than enough idle speculation about gold, and diamonds, and China, and God knows what else from those who ought to know better! It's hard enough for me to get such items to scratch the ground for their daily bread!" Phillip controlled his temper as he pointed at the odd-job man, still gathering wood on the weir. "If such a foolish notion ever took root in their stupid minds they'd fritter their puny energies digging for gold, surely the most useless product this land could ever produce!"

"How do you mean, sir?"

"Mean, Mr. Dawes? I mean that gold cannot be eaten, gold is too soft to be worked into tools, and under our present circumstances gold is impossible to spend! It is the very epitome of dross. You will be better employed digging our colony's only wealth, its soil. Come!"

The young man reluctantly emptied his canteen into the shallows and followed as the governor took a spade from their boat to begin sampling the ground. The odd-job man watched them go away before starting to sample the beach, idly scuffing along, wriggling his toes in the wet sand to feel where the nuggets were nesting among the dead cockle shells.

Phillip had more luck, working upslope through the undergrowth, digging pockets of loamy earth, and Hunter's opinion was confirmed by the time the officers walked downhill to camp at last light: this location would be most suitable for gardening once the trees were knocked over, the roots grubbed up, the ground broken.

Nor had the marines and sailors been idle. A low redoubt of spiky brushwood had been planted around the campsite to defend it during the night and a picket posted while the other men skewered their beef rations on ramrods to grill by the fire.

Phillip returned the sentry's salute and stepped inside the safe area. He nodded at Hunter. "An excellent choice, John. Tell me, did you name it on your previous visit?" The other man shook his head. "Very well, let's do it now. It's time I commemorated my close neighbor, Mr. Secretary Rose of the Treasury. George and I have been on very cordial terms since he was invalided out of the navy, back in 'sixty-three."

This was enough to qualify the choice of name as Phillip took out his spirit flask and proposed a toast to the settlement of Rose Hill in Cumberland County—already claimed for the king's younger brother—in the colony of New South Wales. All present—except the convict, of course—drank to their future health and prosperity in cognac or rum, according to their standing in colonial society.

39

"I SHAN'T be long, Miller."

"Right-o, sir!"

Nash shut the ration ledger and went over to the pork barrel, searched under its scummy brine until he had found a ham which turned the scales at nine pounds, then stowed it in an empty bread bag.

The stroll across camp was splendidly invigorating, quite unlike an autumn day in England with its dying leaves and misty melancholy. Here, in this New Holland, the sun was diamond sharp. The air crisp. The leaves aromatic, pungent.

Nash was smiling as he approached the chaplain's residence. "Good morning, Mrs. Johnson!"

She straightened from a seed bed near the shanty door and brushed her fingers clean. "Good morning, Mr. Nash. My husband is not home."

"So you're planning a surprise for his return?" the polite, attentive gentleman enquired. "Tell me, ma'am, what is that you're cultivating?"

"Hollyhocks. I brought the seeds. From England."

"What exquisite taste," Nash concurred. "I'm sure they'll delight him, too."

"Yes. It'll be more like Home."

Nash replaced his hat and moved out of the direct sun, into the shady overhang of split bark shingles. "I envy any man such a generous, thoughtful companion as you, ma'am. However, 'Nor yet unenvy'd, to whose humbler lot, falls the retired and antiquated cot; its roof with weeds and mosses cover'd o'er; and honeysuckles climbing round the door. . . .'"

Mary Johnson looked up from the bare path, trimmed with lumps of sandstone taken from a former Indian encampment near the rocks. "Had I been told, before we came, that I'd envy such a cottage as the one you've just described so eloquently, I—I would—"

"Please, do not distress yourself!"

The chaplain's wife tried to compose her emotions again. "Forgive me, I've not been myself, recently. I do so endeavor to make the vicarage a presentable dwelling for my husband, but the perversities of nature delight in thwarting my every attempt."

Nash smiled with simple, unaffected sadness. "I know how you feel."

"Do you?"

"Yes, and it reflects the greatest credit that your sensitivity is offended by the harsh contrast between this unfeeling wilderness and our own dear land. . . ."

Mary Johnson was being brought closer to tears.

Nash put a finger to his lips. "Please, allow me to finish. It is only proper that you should feel disconsolate. As a gentleman even I cannot remain unmoved by the profound melancholia which pervades this desolate place."

"Yes!"

"I know how much you suffer." Nash looked around with brave resignation at the surrounding loneliness. "Where are the majestic oaks of a boundary hedge, beyond which stretches the vicar's glebe, rich acres gladly tilled by villagers who claim it a privilege to serve . . . ?"

Mary Johnson's eyes brimmed over. "W-when Richard said he wished to be ordained, I did so hope he would solicit his university for such a living. Instead, Mr. Wilberforce prevailed upon us to come—here."

Nash shifted the ham to the other arm and waited for her to recover.

"Don't be too hard on him, ma'am, I'm sure your husband made the correct decision."

"But—?"

Nash ignored the timid interruption. "Although I've not yet had the honor of dining with the patron to whom you refer, I do count several other members of Parliament among my dearest friends—General Burgoyne, Mr. Sheridan the orator and playwright, and Mr. Fox who advises the prince of Wales on matters political—and everyone speaks with unstinted praise for Mr. Wilberforce. He is the very model of a Christian English gentleman. Please, allow me to continue," Nash said, raising his hand to silence the woman again. "By obliging him now, you can surely anticipate a choice preferment when you return Home."

"Then you think it's possible?"

"Not possible, ma'am, assured," Nash smiled. "Why, Wilberforce must have several benefices of his own to bestow, not counting parishes in the gift of noblemen with whom he's formed connections. And if either course fails, you may always count upon me to exert what modest influence I have with His Royal Highness—"

"Oh!"

"Because, contrary to the spiteful rumors which certain disaffected interests like to spread, our prince of Wales is also a model Christian gentleman. I have often seen His Grace of Canterbury at Carlton House, deep in conversation with His Royal Highness. Therefore, it must be only a matter of time before your husband gains everything you wish. An assured income of several hundred pounds a year, a parsonage more like a bishop's palace than a mere rectory, and surrounded by every embellishment which human eye can lend to nature's palette, rich with the tones of England's incomparable autumns. . . ."

"Oh, thank you!"

"No, ma'am, thank *you*," Nash replied, straightening from a bow. "During my association with Richard I have formed the highest regard for a true scholar and a loyal gentleman, for he often speaks warmly of your support in these trying times." Nash hesitated. "If only the Literati were still in existence, or could be restored, what a blessing that would be, but it seems most unlikely now." He hesitated again. "I was present when Tench abused Richard and William: a terrible scene."

Mary Johnson said nothing.

Nash chose his next words with care. "Something overheard at the time suggested you may even have been instrumental in the original quarrel. . . ."

"It was an accident!"

"Of course," Nash replied, "nobody in his right mind deliberately spreads falsehoods and rumors, but a slip of the tongue is entirely human and understandable. . . ."

Mary Johnson trembled. An unguarded gang of lags was passing the vicarage fence. One shape slowed to check its rows of peas climbing their sticks, assessed the woman's lonely hut, then caught up with the other prowlers again.

"I said, an honest slip of the tongue is entirely human and understandable," Nash repeated.

"It would never have happened had I not spoken to Major Ross about Richard's commission of the peace!"

Nash frowned. "I don't understand?"

Mary Johnson damped her lips. "Captain Phillips has shown scant regard for my husband's position in society. We have yet to hold a service of thanksgiving. And Richard has yet to be made a justice of the peace."

"Of course, but what's that to do with Tench?"

"I—I hoped the lieutenant governor would help, when I indicated that an important post of honor—the governor's adjutant—had gone to, had gone to the son of a mere schoolmaster's wife."

"One, moreover, who had abandoned herself to a minor Welsh baronet?" Nash enquired quietly. "Thank you for taking me into your confidence, it clarifies much which I've found puzzling in this affair. You were absolutely right to demand those perquisites of office to which your husband is entitled by education and breeding. As for that other matter, I have also been deeply hurt by Tench's deception. When first we met he seemed such a gentleman. And yet, throughout it all, he was laughing at us behind his hand, as liars are said to do. Indeed, he reminds me very much of another person with whom we are both acquainted."

"Who?"

"Your fair traveling companion aboard *Alexander*. . . ."

"The Brandon woman?"

"Who else?" Nash smiled. "Like Tench, she is also a most accomplished liar—"

"In which way?"

Nash shrugged. "Take your choice. You knew why she was transported, of course?"

"She murdered her lover!"

"No."

"I—I beg your pardon?" Mary Johnson blinked.

"She most certainly did not murder her lover," Nash replied firmly.

"But everyone says—!"

"Ma'am, 'everyone' is rarely the most reliable source of information," Nash cautioned in a severe tone. "Sir James Hardwicke was also one of my parliamentary friends, a honored and trusted member for the county of Hampshire, when and where he was murdered by the Brandon woman. That much is true, at least. But as for them being emotionally attracted, I hardly think it likely that a gentleman of his standing would associate with a common playhouse actress!" Nash checked his tongue. "Yet, despite everything she did, I can still find it within myself to pity her—"

"Pity! Why?"

"She's mad."

"Mad?"

"Insane," Nash elaborated quietly. "She labors under the delusion of being Mr. Sheridan's half-sister. She also puts on airs about an imagined relationship—on the wrong side of the blanket—with M'Lord Brandon's relict. A pure fabrication, of course, but she uses it to establish a hold over anyone ignorant enough to believe her, like your husband's sexton, for example. But, in truth, she is just an Irish dancer fallen upon hard times." Nash raised his hand, stopping the woman's interruption. "Which is where poor old Hardwicke made his fatal error of judgment—"

"How?"

Nash shrugged expressively. "She concocted an excuse to see him while he was attending to his constituency in Winchester. I suppose she imagined that, because of his connection with Mr. Sheridan, she might solicit a minor part on the London stage. When James politely declined to interest himself, she produced a dagger and stabbed him. Through the neck."

"How awful!"

Nash nodded. "I feel his loss most dreadfully. There are still moments when I believe it's a nightmare figment of the imagination, then I see Kate Brandon, brazen as ever, and I know it to be true. It puts me on my guard because, no matter how frank and open she appears to be, her mind could suffer another collapse and she could kill again at any moment—"

"We shared the same mattress!"

"God watches over His servants, ma'am."

"I knew she was evil, but this is even worse than I thought!"

"You have absolutely nothing to fear from her," Nash hastened to reassure her. "It is quite evident to me that you and she must have cohabited on civil terms. Even in her confused state of mind she regards you as a friend. That's why I go out of my way to remain on speaking terms with her—you may've noticed how we exchange a few pleasantries from time to time?—because I have no intention of waking up with my throat cut!" Nash chuckled. "Believe me, whenever she comes for her rations, I am polite and guarded in my dealings with her. Speaking of rations, I took the liberty of saving you an unnecessary walk." He shifted the ham from under his arm. "Please, take it with my compliments."

Mary Johnson did as she was told.

The assistant storeman straightened his sleeve. "You'll find it somewhat above the normal allowance but Richard will be absolutely exhausted when he returns home: a few tasty bowls of broth will do much to restore his spirits. Meanwhile, put the Brandon woman quite out of your mind. Had she intended to murder you she'd have done so on the boat." He stood back a few paces, eyeing the Johnsons' walls, then stepped inside the hut and tried its door.

Nash came out again, smiling. "Just keep that wedge in place at night, and bar the shutters, and you'll have absolutely no reason to worry, I promise you. Now, I must about my business. Your servant, ma'am."

He straightened and strode away.

40

CRIBB AWOKE cold, stiff and hungry. He rekindled the fire from last night's embers while Bryant prepared to heat the scraps of dinner for his master's breakfast. The marines finished polishing their buttons, badges and boots as Phillip ordered the sailors to return in seven days' time. Bryant commandeered two of their oars: the flat blades sat comfortably on his shoulders in front and the round looms, uncomfortably, on Cribb's at the rear as tentage, bread bags, water canteens, Dawes's botany box, butterfly net and insect-killing jars were loaded onto the poles between the bearers.

The governor slung his fowling piece, checked the compass bearing again and began counting paces inland with Hunter. At one thousand for every half mile traversed, they could start filling the blank sheets of their notebooks. Dawes and Johnson marched behind with the hatchet, blazing a trail and passing occasional remarks. The marines crunched along on the flanks in open skirmishing order, hobnails skidding over bare rock, still hoping to catch some Indians unawares.

Cribb plodded in time with the governor's servant, as if they were in the winding column which had tramped south from Montreal before being swallowed up by the wilderness of the Iroquois Confederacy. The lagged convict had still been wearing boots then, not strips of sacking wound like gaiters above his bare feet. But hard campaigns are humbling experiences. And these redcoated guards could not patch their split soles forever, Cribb knew, treading on Bryant's shadow as the sort-of sailor grumbled along in front. The day would inevitably come when there would be little or no apparent difference between free and unfree men in New Holland's wilderness.

Cribb smiled.

Things had been much the same Over There once the fitful trickle of British supplies stopped reaching the American warfront. Tarleton's Rangers, officers and troopers alike, had slashed and hacked their way across the Carolinas clad in green rags and shreds of blue uniform stripped from the enemy dead.

Young Joe Cribb had entered that lifetime almost naked, wearing a shirt and empty cartridge pouches, rum brave, bayoneting the Rebel gunners at Saratoga. Old Joe Cribb had called it quits two thousand days later, cold sober, hunched in the trenches of Yorktown. But at least he was better dressed. The French colonel's creamy buckskin breeches had fitted a treat and Cribb would have been wearing the officer's boots as well if only the shard of shrapnel had not struck too low, completely ruining the waxed black leather by the time their new owner had cut the seams to try and dig out the mess inside them.

Cribb grimaced.

That aside for the moment, he knew that he had come out ahead in America, just as he was certain to come out ahead this time once he got to Chinaland with a bag of nuggets. Half the gold would be left for setting himself up in London, but the other half of his winnings was going straight into the best feed the Chinese could serve up, and wouldn't Mrs. B.'s eyes sparkle then—!

Phillip had panted to a halt. The morning was getting warm. He shrugged off his coat, crushed the metallic green fly which was trying to sip sweat from his nose, and looked at Hunter. "A most agreeable excursion, is it not? You see that hill?" He pointed. "I suggest we lay a direct course for the summit. From there we ought to be able to get a bearing on the river. And towns."

Hunter saved his breath. He judged they were now upon some nameless ridge overlooking an inland sea of rolling treetops, while in the far distance stretched a gray-blue rampart of mountains. Closer to hand a few hazy smudges of smoke marked possible Indian villages or hunting camps. Otherwise there was nothing. No mighty rivers. No walled cities. No great roads to the interior. Just countless biting, scratching, crawling, itching insects. And the occasional kangaroo which bounded away as clouds of gaudy birds screeched overhead.

Phillip cocked his gun and swung, punching two charges of shot through a flock of rainbow-lorikeets. One of the redcoats was sent off to retrieve his officers' dinner. The party resumed its track downhill, into the spicy, astringent emptiness of the bush.

Cribb marched with the five dead birds near his face, swaying and twisting on the oar like little hanged men. He crossed his fingers and looked away: there were more immediate worries as this reconnaissance patrol headed for Chinaland.

The assistant storeman was the most urgent, the most puzzling.

Sneaky sod, grassing a bloke with nicked grub just to get him stretched. A normal cove would have flattened his head with a lump of rock, but such ge'men always reckon they are cleverer. Still, Ratbag had been quick to cough up the whole story once a knifeblade began playing with his scalp. Apparently it had been Nash's plan to croak the camp scavenger on the gallows so that no other lag would ever forget what happened to "impertinent little firebugs" who dared to stoush a gent for putting the fumblers on—

Cribb stumbled, clutching the oars as the expedition slowed to another halt.

So far they had been steering across open woodland which almost seemed as if someone were deliberately keeping it clear with controlled fires, Phillip thought, flicking sweat from his eyes. But if that was the case, this barricade of spearwood and thornbush must have been left intact as a natural hedge, for some reason.

He put away the handkerchief. "Well, John, what now? Either we chop our way through or tack our way around. Which do you suggest?"

"Blowed if I know." Hunter mopped his face and let the neckcloth flap loose over his open waistcoat. "It might only be a few yards thick. Or it could stretch from here to Jericho."

Phillip considered the options as the rest of his followers found shade under a tree. "You know, I can't help wondering if our Indians aren't more subtle than we're giving them credit for being. This could be some kind of covert, rather like the ones we use for driving partridges back Home. Can't you imagine a shooting party lying in wait at one end while the villagers drove game toward us?"

Hunter shook his head. "If we allowed them that much common sense, why haven't we seen any agriculture? Or industry? Or commerce? Or indeed anything?" He shrugged. "I'd say we're in for a long walk either way we choose to go."

"Let's see." Phillip was using his notebook as an improvised plane table. He took a sight to starboard and noted the bearing. "Forward, gentlemen."

Dawes and Johnson stood. The marines shouldered their muskets. The bearers took up their burden.

"As I suspected!" Phillip announced some minutes later, halting at a gap in the hedge where a number of broken throwing sticks and slender, kangaroo thigh bones littered the ground. Several appeared to be fresh, the governor thought, looking round at the empty silence. "Well. Now all we have to do is extract the reciprocal bearing, count two hundred and eighty paces, and resume our previous course. We rest at midday for half an hour." He snapped the watch shut, slipped the timepiece inside his waistcoat pocket and resumed counting steps.

They stopped ten minutes earlier than planned, at a rocky outcrop among silvery shrubs ablaze with golden pompoms—rather like mimosa, Phillip thought, remembering his months in the south of France during the recent war. Dawes snipped a small twig and stored it in his hatband with some other botanical specimens while Phillip took out his pocket knife to notch the bark and see if it would ooze a useful gum during lunch. He cautiously tested a leaf to see if it was edible or could be brewed to make a nourishing drink. "Ptah!"

There was a boggy pond in a cleft of sandstone, slicked with seepage and moss. Dawes swept it clear with a fallen branch, combing away the fleece of slime before refilling his canteen, then took one of the shot cockatoos around the pool to Johnson.

The chaplain had kicked off his shoes and was soaking his feet: one of this land's large red ants had attacked him, clamping its jaws through the Englishman's thick woolen stocking; his ankle throbbed and burned.

"Feeling better, now?"

Johnson tried to smile. "Yes, thank you."

The naturalist opened his satchel, took out a roll of instruments, selected a narrow scalpel and slit along the bird's stiff legs. "Hold the claws." Johnson did as he was asked, watching closely as the other man peeled off the skin—rather like a purse—and cut away the body at the neck. The carcass was put aside for tonight's meal. Dawes chose another tool, similar to a sharpened egg spoon, and scooped the cranium's soft tissue before dusting the skin with a mixture of saltpeter and crushed peppercorns. Then he wrote a label and rolled it inside the slim package until the bird could be properly mounted. "There, I think that ought to please Mr. Locke."

The chaplain rinsed his fingers in the pool. "Who's he?"

"The curator at the Royal Society: his disapproval could be very damaging. A bit of an old tyrant but an absolute gold mine of information once he learned I'd managed to get on the expedition to Botany Bay. For instance, have you ever really looked at a simple feather . . . ?"

Johnson wriggled his toes underwater. "Not especially."

"Then it's time we continued your education in the natural sciences." Dawes was an engineer officer by necessity but a teacher by vocation. He put his lunch down and reached into the satchel for a magnifying lens. Somewhere along today's track through the wilderness he had tucked a large, grayish brown feather into his hat, with the other specimens. "Behold, a scapular from that galloping cushion, Sir Joseph Banks's *Dromiceius novaehollandiae* which, for the sake of economy, we shall now term the emu. Observe the complexity of its structure—"

Johnson squinted through the glass. His friend was no longer bantering as he went on, "From the central shaft, or rachis, you'll see, on each side, a row of barbs which bear curved barbules. Correct? Now, observe how the rearward barbules carry small barbicels which hook onto their neighbors' to form the light, flexible structure we take so much for granted whenever we set pen to paper."

"Goodness!" The chaplain had forgotten his aching feet. "Who'd imagine so much could be contained within such a small space?"

"More persons than evidently you think." Dawes put the feather back in his hat and leaned into the shade. He dusted ants off his food. "We're privileged to be here. There are *savants* in Europe who'd gladly pay a thousand in gold just to be in our shoes today, with or without blistered feet."

"And I could think of someone here who'd pay the same amount to travel in the opposite direction, if I were able," Johnson replied, trying to jest. He failed, never comfortable whenever he needed to reveal an inner feeling to anyone. "I'm sorry, Bill. If only I could share your enthusiasm for this country. But I can't."

"Why not?"

Johnson shook his head. "I don't know."

"Buck up, the sun's shining."

"That makes no difference. It can shine as hard as it likes. I still feel like it's November. No, please, allow me to finish," he hurried on. "I suppose it's just another of this land's horrid paradoxes that one can feel icy cold around the heart even when one is feverish hot, and so alone even when one is surrounded by good company." He bit his lip. "Everything here is so wrong! Look at that confounded New Holland dromedary of yours! A bird so big and ugly it can't even fly! And look at these awful trees, always the same gray, never green like proper foliage!" The chaplain made a helpless gesture. "Oh, if only I'd listened to sense, not sentiment. . . ."

Dawes nibbled a dry grass stem. "I do understand how you feel, Dick. It affects all of us to a greater or lesser degree, but we must resist the temptation to brood over our condition. Because those things you find so repugnant are, for me, the main purpose of being here at all." He spat chewed grass over one shoulder and looked back at the chaplain. "Nobody's asking us to make this a permanent home, we just have to make the best of a bad job until we can return to England.

"Speaking personally, opportunities to build a worthwhile reputation come but seldom in peacetime. You're more conversant with the ins and outs of a vicar's life, but military men like myself have to seize every advancement which presents itself, because what are our alternatives? More wounds? Death in battle or under the surgeon's knife? Or, at last, to 'succeed' like Ross?"

The amateur naturalist might have added more but Phillip had finished comparing notes with Hunter. He stood again. "Forward!"

The bearers took up their load and the party continued, holding a northwesterly course across broken, wooded country through the stifling, airless forest.

Cribb plodded in silence, remembering every axe mark which Scarface blazed: they would come in handy once her ladyship and himself were trotting this way. Good riding country. Open enough to get up a quick lick, away from Indians. The black buggers were all around, of course, flitting like shadows between the trees, keeping out of musket range. So long as they did that there would be no hard feelings.

But their water hole did not look so flash. Nor was the fodder growing around it. Not enough guts to feed a prancer. Sparrow Legs ought to have known better. He should have brought a string of Romany nags, Welsh cobs, ponies able to clop along all day on a bite of grass and a boot up the arse—not regimental chargers with their bottomless hunger for oats, and bran, and mash, and fancy stuff.

Still, so long as they got her ladyship and himself to Chinaland, they would be able to rest up until it was time to move on to London.

Nobody else, least of all Richard Johnson, had as much reason for hope as the hours toiled past, broken every thousand paces to sample the soil and collect more inedible vegetation for Dawes's press. Leaves, bark and twigs were all they were collecting. The Indians had vanished, and with them had gone any words which might have made sense of this empty, alien silence.

Johnson shivered, wiped sweat and prayed that he wasn't hatching a fever. The relief at leaving Mary behind had turned sour. His feet hurt and his blanket roll felt as if she had deliberately packed a housebrick where it would chafe his shoulder. His tricorn hat kept slipping from side to side and his coat flopped open, flapped shut as he limped in Hunter's footsteps.

The chaplain tried to revive his spirits by reviewing the moral precepts of Demokritos. " 'Pleasure and pain alone determine the happiness which dwells not in herds or stores of gold but in the soul, the dwelling of our *daemon*. Thus, the best that any man can hope to achieve in this world is to pass his life with as much joy as possible.' "

Johnson decided to contemplate the soulful homilies of St. John Chrysostom, instead. " 'So long as we behave like sheep, we are victorious. Even if ten thousand wolves surround us, we shall conquer. But the moment we become as wolves, we are conquered, for by so doing we shall have spurned the Good Shepherd.' "

He gave up.

In happier days he had drawn much comfort from the classics and the church fathers, but their words were losing the power to reach out and touch him among the dust, and flies, and heat. The Antipodes might be offering Dawes the opportunity to better himself, but he was only a soldier who happened to share some cultivated interests. However, no matter what he might say to the contrary, Dawes would never understand the deep ache which comes after one has been cut off from tradition. And ritual. And the support of equals.

Johnson was struggling with an internal giddiness which threatened whenever the thermometer registered one hundred degrees in what the calendar and common sense said were winter; whenever items like the sexton replied in their insolent, nasal yowl and he felt powerless to reprimand them; whenever he strove to keep his stability on a landscape where oak trees bore pine needles, where grotesque creatures abounded, where a malignant nature triumphed over human reason—!

He squeezed his eyes tighter and tighter and tighter to block out the scorching void. Johnson was discovering that the limits of his vocabulary were the limits of his universe. While he could think, and read, and speak in Latin and Greek he was a free citizen of a world which spanned two thousand years. But the moment he opened his eyes again he would be reduced to brute savagery by a mouthful of guttural—!

His toe snagged a thin rootlet, stretched across the track like a tripwire set to snare poachers. He pitched flat on his belly. "Ohhh!"

"Come along, padre." Hunter put out a hand for the winded man to grip and climb up. "Worse things happen at sea."

Phillip took advantage of the landlubber's clumsiness to take another bearing, then ordered the odd-job man to dig another set of holes. "What d'you think, Dawes?"

The naturalist rubbed the abrasive soil between his palms. "Blowed if I know what to make of it, sir. It appears to support such a profusion of plants yet, at the same time, one has the feeling that one acre wouldn't raise a single radish."

Phillip also let the soil trickle away. He dusted his hands on the seat of his breeches. "Forward!"

The bearers stood, gripped their oars and the governor resumed his line of march. "Not much further now! We shall camp on the summit tonight. It'll be another opportunity for you to make useful observations for the astronomer royal, Dawes. We must do everything possible to get you that fellowship. Besides, Sir Joseph expressed a particular interest in Botany Bay and its environs, when last we spoke." Phillip was glad to talk while Hunter counted this half-mile section of today's march. "Tell me, is it all that difficult to tack an FRS onto your name . . . ?"

"I can't say yet," the younger man replied, shifting his loaded satchel to the other shoulder. "It's a considerable honor, of course, and not bestowed lightly. One's patrons must be convinced that a worthy contribution has been made to the sciences. And even then it's by no means certain the other fellows will cast their votes in one's favor."

Phillip looked rather disappointed. "Oh, well, good luck anyway. But assuming you win, what'll you do? Stay in the king's service or try something new? Didn't I hear recently that you would like to become a schoolmaster?"

"Yes. Very much so. If I'm spared that long."

"You will be." The governor ducked under a low branch. "It'll serve nobody's interest if the protégé of Sir Joseph Banks and Dr. Maskelyne meets an untimely end while under my command. Moreover, unlike certain individuals, I happen to hold schoolmastering in some esteem. I would hate to see it deprived of a likely recruit just because of a few hasty, ill-considered words."

Phillip shortened his pace as the ground angled upward through more timber and thornbush. The evening breeze was losing its heat. Another flock of birds swept overhead. "Look, John! Ducks! Didn't I say there'd be a river soon! Come on, everyone, best feet forward!"

The governor was least laden. He made it to the top well ahead of the rest and was waiting impatiently as the main party toiled nearer.

The scrub was still too dense for a clear view inland but a solitary tree had grown on the summit, bent by the prevailing winds off the Pacific. Phillip took Dawes's hatchet and commanded the odd-job man to drop his load. He pointed at the foot of the tree. When the item was stooped, rather like an ostler earning a tip by helping a gentleman to mount a horse, the governor stepped onto his shoulders, gripped the lowest branch and chopped out a pair of notched footholds.

Phillip's years as a seaman, on the yards of a man o' war, served him in good stead now as he shinned up the smooth gray bark to the topmost fork of the lookout.

"Can you see anything, sir?" Hunter called aloft.

The other man did not reply. He was holding his breath and the spyglass, squinting against the sunset, determined to be the first man in history to see the river, to see the city's gilded spires, to see the snow-capped ranges of the interior.

"What is there—?"

The governor said nothing. There was nothing. No marble temples. No distant towers. Nothing.

41

"THAT'S ALL, sar'nt major. Dismiss."

"Sah!"

Ross waited for the door to shut, then looked back at Campbell and Kellow. "So there you have it, gentlemen, yet another act of gross disobedience. Not that I'm surprised, you can't expect the finest body of troops in the king's service to turn farmer and still remain trim as gamecocks."

"Aye!"

"That's true, sir, but what can we do about it?"

"Do about it, Mr. Kellow? We can stop the rot, that's what we can do about it!" The battalion commander stuffed both hands into his breeches pockets and continued pacing around the antechamber of Government House, wig off, shirt-sleeved, deeply troubled. One of his corporals had been struck with a garden fork. The offending marine would be disciplined, of course, but the underlying canker would not be cut out as quickly or easily.

The men were bored. They were stale. They were resentful. They were surrounded by even more bored, stale and resentful objects. But at least the Second Battalion, Portsmouth Division, had a legitimate cause for grievance. They'd embarked for prize money and glory, fighting the French and the Indians in a South Sea paradise where ripe fruit fell from the trees and ripe women fell to the ground, eager for whatever Jack Tar and Tommy Lobsterback could serve up.

Instead, they were being ordered to plant vegetable marrows and potatoes in Sinful Cove, and their only relief—apart from the normal delights of sodomy, or watching someone else get the lash—was being doled out by a handful of dockside scrubbers who were charging famine prices for what they could not have given away, back Home.

"We're pit terriers, not poodles." Ross stared through the window at an almost inert landscape where a few lags and redcoats wandered about, without purpose, without pride, without spring in their step. They were not even marking time, they were just filling in time until a relief convoy came to take them back to the world. "What we need is the taste of good raw meat between our teeth. . . ."

"Aye!"

"Shut up, f' Christ's sake, Jimmy!"

"Aye!"

"It's not enough that Sparrow Legs tried making us turnkeys, now we're supposed to become bloody gardeners as well," Ross added. He resumed his pacing. At least, while he was acting governor, he could use Government House until Dawes's artificers had weatherproofed his own mansion. They could then get back to the stores and roof those before winter. "And that Nash hasn't kept his bargain: he promised me fifty, at least!"

That was the rub. The Royal Marines had barely half that number of women to themselves and this basic shortage was causing bad blood. The men could see that every officer had a housekeeper, that the sergeants and corporals had access at will, but many privates had none—even though their pay was being docked for it, along with their boots, uniform and ration money. Meanwhile, not a few of the remaining morts were being used by the lags they had met aboard boat, and some had even finalized the arrangement in front of the chaplain, which had further reduced the number in circulation. "Bloody hell. . . ."

"Captain Collins," Jane Dundas announced with a token curtsey near the door.

Ross was distracted by other, more urgent matters. He looked at Kellow again. "My compliments to Mr. Nash. Get him here, *toot sweet*."

The paymaster exchanged salutes with the judge advocate as a sentry slapped his musket sling for both officers. Collins continued inside. " 'Morning, sir."

"More paperwork, more likely," Ross grumbled. "I'd hardly know what to do with my time if I didn't begin every day signing a bagful of invoices, and prescripts, and orders. I'm buggered if I know how my predecessor ever stepped outside to take a pee."

"Sir?"

Ross hunched his shoulders. "So what's new today?"

"Well, at least our bolter's been found," the judge advocate replied, quite used to his commanding officer.

"Which one?"

"The cook assistant. Purvis, ex-*Alexander*."

"One hundred. No, better make it two. This thing's becoming a habit."

"We could make it a thousand lashes, sir, the deterrent value would still be nil."

"What the hell d'you mean?"

"He's dead."

"Then good riddance." Ross was in no humor to mourn the loss of a lag when the colony's minority of free men were ripening for trouble.

"His head's been pulped by an Indian warclub," Collins went on, "but not before they'd tortured him."

"Oh. Then sit down, Mr. Collins, tell me more."

"That's pretty well all there is to say. When I went out to view the *locus in quo*—"

"Talk bloody sense!"

"It's a legal term, sir."

"Oh. Well?"

"When I viewed the corpse it was spread-eagled behind some rocks, just off the Brickfield Road," the judge advocate concluded.

"They got that close to the settlement, eh?"

"Yes."

Ross turned to his deputy. "What did I tell you? Sneak-thief heathen! If I've told Sparrow Legs once I've told him a hundred times, we'll either be a second Port Antonio or another Fort Detroit, mutiny or massacre, you mark my words!"

"Aye!"

Ross looked back at his law officer. "So what, in your learned opinion, should we do next . . . ?"

"I've prepared the papers for a coronial enquiry." Collins opened his bag. "If you'd care to peruse them and sign—"

"I do not care to peruse them. Nor am I going to sign anything."
The judge advocate blinked.

"In my opinion Pervert, or whatever his bloody name was, could not
have been more useless, alive. But dead?" Ross began to smile. "I think
he might kill several birds with one stone." The acting governor sat
down behind Phillip's desk. "Because your 'coronial enquiry' is just
another excuse for more paperwork and it'll conclude that one of our
laborers was murdered by an Indian or Indians unknown, which I know
already. Left unanswered will be the question of what to do next. . . ."

"You mean the funeral? Without a chaplain?"

"I mean nothing of the sort! If he's at the brick field he's near enough
buried as far as I'm concerned." Ross leaned forward. "I mean that I am
going to punish the Indian or Indians unknown. I am going to take
Shea's company, which has been getting very slack recently, and tone
them up with an extended route march."

"But the governor said—!"

"Mr. Collins? I am the governor."

"Sir."

"Captain Campbell will remain behind as my deputy and you will
make it your especial task to guide him."

"Sir."

"Tench's company can be given extra picket duties to make up the
numbers and show the lags we mean business. It'll also take him down a
peg or two after last night's fal-lal speech to me in the mess."

"Sir."

Jane Dundas coughed. "The storeman."

"Show him in."

Kellow led the way and Nash glanced around the interior of Government House, the first time he'd had an opportunity to do so. He smiled
brightly. "Good morning, gentlemen."

Ross leaned further forward. "Where are those jam tarts you promised?"

Nash was puzzled. His face cleared again. "You mean the certain
articles we spoke about, earlier? Everything's coming along splendidly,
believe me!"

"Why should I? However, this is your lucky day, Mr. Nash. I'm
about to leave camp for a short while. When I return every woman off
Prince of Wales will be actively engaged in her duties for my men—"

"But some are already married!"

"I only want full measure, Mr. Nash, I'll let you make it up how you
like. Now, stand aside." Ross got to his feet. "Mr. Kellow? You're acting

captain, B Company. This is your chance to show us what you'll be like once they're permanently yours."

"Sir!" The paymaster clicked his heels and followed his leader into the sunlight.

Nash breathed out and looked at the judge advocate general. "What do you think all that's about, Collins?"

"I'd say one third of our troops are about to be reminded that digging a garden isn't such an onerous task, after all; that I am about to assume the daily routines of running a garrison cum prison camp; and that you are about to recruit more women, willing or otherwise."

"It won't be easy! Some are very wilful!"

"My dear Nash, military life was never meant to be easy." Collins removed some documents from the desk as Campbell knocked over the inkwell. "Now, if you'll excuse me, I'm about to be kept rather busy. Good morning."

It was almost a good afternoon by the time B Company stood to arms in full field order. Ross counted heads as he rode up the column and its corporals reported to their sergeant, and he reported to the acting captain, and Kellow spurred forward to report to the major. Young John Ross was on the third saddle mount, about to win his first campaign certificate; without several of these to his credit he could never hope to buy accelerated promotion from ensign to lieutenant. The rest of the colony's horses were hitched to a pair of guns behind the color party, while the balance of the field artillery was left behind the bastions of Fort Ross in case the Indians sensed an opportunity to attack or there was an uprising among the lags.

Ross stood in the stirrups and swept his sword at the forest. "Forward march!"

Tench stood in the shade as seventy infantrymen crunched up George Street toward the Brickfield Road, past a few gangs hauling logs, man-handling stumps, clearing plots for winter wheat. The near-naked laborers watched apathetically as their guards marched away upon some errand, greatcoats and camp kettles strapped to bulging knapsacks, leather stocks buckled round necks, black spatterdash gaiters buttoned up gray flannel breeches.

"David? D'you know what I'm going to do once I get back Home?" Tench enquired, leaning on his sword as the fighting patrol faded away into the bush.

"No. Surprise me."

"I'm going to sell my commission and lease the mastership of Bedlam: I could run a madhouse at a tidy profit, easily." Tench loosened his steenkirk choker and unbuttoned his waistcoat now that dress regulations would be relaxed for the next few days. "Another couple of years' training and I'll be well on the road to retiring a wealthy and respected burgess of London. There's hope yet. Come, let us celebrate with lunch at the observatory and, for dessert, we can shred Baffled Bob's reputation, consuming each succulent morsel *con gusto*."

"That's laying it on a bit thick!" Collins laughed. "The major knows what he's doing."

He did not.

By midafternoon Ross had penetrated further into a wilderness than he had ever sortied before. The road to Lexington Common may have been more hotly contested but at least it had traversed some farmland where a man could march straight ahead through the bullets. Not so this latest expedition to search out and destroy his nation's enemies. The compass needle swayed in time with his mount's plod as the column of redcoats wove its way around and across monotonously open woodland, between and past scrub, over razor grass, under lawyer vines, into deep gullies.

The infantry were now hauling two field guns while cursing artillery-men tried leading horses which had never been broken in as draft animals. The engineer section had been reduced to carrying everyone's surplus equipment as well as their own tool kits. Not that their leader was free of troubles, even if he was sitting down. Ross had fought most of his campaigns from the deck of a man o' war, not a saddle. He was out of practice. His seat was tender. The hot leather was galling his thighs.

"Halt!"

Ross slid off the mare and slackened his breeches where they were sawing him in half, then addressed the next problem—how to defeat a thicket of spearwood thrown across his line of march. "Mr. Kellow!"

"Sir?"

"Advance the sappers!"

"Sir."

The ten strongest men in B Company peeled off their tunics and began chopping a path through scrub so thick and whippy that an axe could hardly be swung, and when it was its blade bounced on impact. Mean-while, their comrades prepared to repulse Indians.

Ross hitched his scabbard and made a tour of inspection where the marines knelt, bayonets fixed, muskets sloping forward. Behind them reared a wall of undergrowth which would prevent a stab in the back, but the battalion commander was less confident about his flanks and vedettes.

He halted, shading his eyes, surveying a killing field unlike any he'd planned in Canada, or the Caribbean, or on the limestone crags of

Gibraltar. This forest was not to his liking. Nor were the tangled shrubs, ablaze with flowers between the threatening rocks. Honey-eaters and jewel-like finches shot from blossom to blossom through the drone of insects and the click of cicadas. Indian marksmen were probably slithering closer, like their allies the snakes, the spiders, the scorpions, the mosquitoes, the chiggers, the ticks.

Ross turned. A corporal was reporting to the sergeant who was reporting to Kellow who was marching to his major. The two officers exchanged salutes. "Obstacle cleared. Ready to proceed, sir!"

The column had advanced ten yards in thirty-six minutes, very good time in such country. Ross shut his watch, mounted and gave the horse a sharp kick in the ribs to get her moving. "Forward!"

The punitive expedition followed their leader into the breach and out onto another sand plain of scrub, and grass, and vines, and gullies. Only now, the silent tree trunks around them were striped with evening shadows, confusing to the eye, bewildering to the other senses.

Ross lost patience with the erratic compass and began marching by instinct and the setting sun as it curved around the northern horizon, unlike its accustomed track on the other side of the equator.

The battalion commander sighted his first Indian village at dusk. "Skirmishing order! Fix bayonets! Advance!"

B Company, the Second Battalion, the Portsmouth Division, the Royal Corps of Marines, stormed through the derelict shelters without loss.

"Well done, Mr. Kellow! We'll soon have your men as trim as gamecocks!"

"Sir!"

"Water the horses."

Ross was still pacing around the battlefield when a corporal reported to the sergeant, who reported to the acting captain, who reported to the major. "Corporal Drury begs leave to report an occurrence, sir."

Ross followed the young officer across the cleared village. They halted. An Indian woman had been partially cremated. A man and child lay rotting under a lean-to of boughs and twigs.

The three ghostmen looked down. Ross swished the flies which swirled around his wig. "Aye, well, interesting."

Kellow ventured closer. He took a charred stick from the pyre and poked a crust of black scabs on the woman's left leg, most of which had escaped the flames. He glanced up, worried. "Smallpox?"

"Stuff and nonsense!" Ross silenced him before their troops caught the rumor and lost their improved spirits. "It's quite evident to me that we're looking at the victims of a domestic upset! Such things happen all the time among primitive folk. Come, let's make bivouac for the night."

The senior officer marched back to where his men were drawn up in four ranks, awaiting further orders. Ross gave them: the entire force was to move to a better defensive position some hundred yards upwind.

Drinking water still remained a problem, though. The horses had made short work of the seepage which had accumulated in a rocky basin since the last hunting party had migrated from the village.

"Kellow!"

"Sir?"

"Deepen that hole! There's got to be more water."

It was long after dark before relays of men from Drury's platoon finished jarring their crowbars against surprisingly tough sandstone. They had sunk a dry well to waist depth. It would now hold about two hundred gallons after the next rains.

Meanwhile, the rest of the troops had not been idle. They had slashed the undergrowth and piled thornbrush to funnel attackers onto the sentries' bayonets if the Indians attempted to massacre them during the night. It would be a close-fought battle, wooden clubs against clubbed muskets; chest to chest, knee to knee, rip, kick, stab in the moonlight. "Double the guard. And pass the word that it's a hundred for every man whose water bottle holds less than six pints in the morning."

Ross stood by his word. One of the sappers had slaked his thirst during the night. He was lashed to a tree and flogged. Water discipline had been restored.

Ross continued a tour of inspection while his men razed the defenses to prevent them falling into the enemy's hands. As he hoped, as he had expected, as he needed to believe, there was considerable evidence of Indian gold mining among the rocks. He hurried across drifts of stone flakes, waited until he was sure everyone else was busy with other tasks, then quickly stuffed his tunic pockets with discolored lumps of quartz: the first nabob of New South Wales had repaid the Indians for their theft of his half guinea, back on the beach.

Ross rejoined his men, drawn up in column of route, awaiting further orders. Their commander aimed his sword at the twig village. "Burn it! And deny this to the sneak thieves." He kicked dirt into the empty waterhole. His servant held up the mare's droopy head as he mounted her to oversee phase two of his attack plan.

The sergeant took a burning branch from the breakfast fire and went downhill.

Ross kicked his mare forward as dry twigs and bark litter rumbled into flame behind him. "Double march!"

42

"ALL THINGS considered, a most satisfactory reconnaissance," Phillip insisted.

Hunter ducked his head as their cutter luffed off Point Maskelyne and the crewmen got ready to row the rest of the way into Sydney Cove.

"After all, we have found the river," Phillip went on.

Hunter still said nothing. In his personal opinion they had found a meandering ribbon of muddy water choked by dead timber swept downstream on winter floods. By no stretch of the imagination would it ever be the St. Phillip they had slogged so far, so long, so hard to discover, and so the honor of its name had gone to the president of the Board of Trade & Plantations in London, Lord Hawkesbury.

"Yes, I'm convinced that, once a wagon road connects it with Rose Hill, our colony will become the granary of the Pacific Ocean," its governor concluded with a confident smile.

Dawes avoided his eye. Johnson looked down at his bare feet and wondered how he could ease shoes over the blisters before hobbling ashore. Bryant slumped against the mast, more like a shipwreck survivor than a pioneer who had been far and seen much. The odd-job man dozed in the shade. Cribb had been halfway to Chinaland and back, easy, and once he was mounted nothing could stop him finishing the trip. "Tarleton's Lantern" would be floating high over the ranges tomorrow night, full and round as a five-guinea piece, lighting the way for him. For Kitty Brandon. For Home.

Cribb stretched, yawned and smiled as the coxswain's mate coiled the painter. His shipmates tossed their oars and carried the governor onto dry land. Phillip replied to his adjutant's salute. "Everything resolved satisfactorily, Mr. Tench? I see you are wearing your sword again."

"I did my best, sir."

"Splendid." He turned. "Come, gentlemen, let us go to my quarters where we can—" He stopped. "David? What the hell's that? Over there?"

The judge advocate shut his eyes. "It would appear Major Ross has also chosen this moment to return."

" 'Return'? Return from what?"

"He did not inform me, sir. However, I believe he decided it lay within his jurisdiction to punish the Indians. . . ."

A column of troops was lurching down George Street from the Brickfield Road as lags downed tools to laugh, to whistle, to hoot at their unlucky guards. The only other time Phillip had seen fighting men in such bad shape had been at Forte São Paulo when a company of *bandeirantes* came home two years and three thousand miles after failing to plunder the Spanish treasure house of San Luis Potosi in the Andes.

Ross was still in command, though no longer in the saddle. Nor was anyone else. Their stock of oats had failed the previous morning, the mounts had been fed what seemed to be a native vetch or pea, an hour later all five horses were dead.

Phillip gripped his gun and charged up the beach before Kellow could dismiss the men to their lines. "I wouldn't." Tench touched Collins's elbow to stop him following the governor.

"Bloody massacre!"

"You cretin—!"

"Murdering heathen!"

"You killed my horses—!"

And Cribb bolted, straight for two sappers with a mate's arms hooked around their necks.

Levi watched from the shade of the morgue's doorway as the odd-job man sprinted past. "Ben? I smell trouble."

"Ar?" The governor's gaffer was wetting his hands before sitting down to an early dinner with Dr. Balmain's assistant. This novel use for water was something else which Levi demanded if the farm overseer was to continue sharing the same quarters. Other outlandish customs included not snorting his nose clean wherever he liked, and never pissing on the ground indoors.

"Big trouble."

Thorpe grinned back, rubbing both hands on his hair. "The master'll give tons better'n 'e gets, never you worry!"

"*Putz!*" Levi elbowed the other man from the bucket and took the pat of wet clay which served instead of soap. Then stopped. Kitty Brandon was hurrying down the path from the officers' lines. Levi beckoned her into his private dining room and offered Balmain's chair. "You eat yet?" The offer extended to a grilled mullet, basted with olive oil from the medical supplies, garnished with cress grown in the one place least likely to be burgled around Sinful Cove—the morgue.

"No, I must make haste. Kindly oblige me with another of your draughts for Mr. Shea."

The convict made a helpless shrug. "For you, anything, but if the *doktor* find I doing his work for the Quality too—pfft!"

"You may count on my absolute discretion," she replied quietly. "I would prefer Captain Shea drank your concoctions than lost any more blood to that leech Balmain, doctor or not."

Levi bowed in the formal, continental manner which had greeted many masked clients inside Dr. Achmet's Magnetic Consultorium. "To-night."

"Thank you." Kitty Brandon had changed her mind. She took the chair, arranged her skirts and sat at the head of the long, scrubbed table. "Time no longer favors our interest, gentlemen."

"What you mean?"

The government woman kept her voice low: some of Balmain's regular patients in the neighboring shed might still be conscious after their treatments with emetics, purges and paregorics. "Campbell's elevation to the governorship presented Nash with a unique opportunity to tighten his grip on the rations. Our ladies are now being threatened with slow starvation unless they quickly change sides."

"But the master's got back 'ome now," Thorpe reported with a loyal wag of the head.

"What difference that make?" Levi countered.

" 'E can give as good as 'e gets, that's what!"

"Phui!"

"Direct your attention to our own problems!" Kitty Brandon had command again. "Even Mr. Phillip's position could soon be under challenge. If Nash has his way the troops' discontent will force the creation of a military council—"

"How you know that?"

"Feminine intuition, Mr. Levi," Kitty Brandon replied as quietly. "It's the custom for overseas garrisons to prefer their own officers as governors. When Ross assumes control of New South Wales he'll have done nothing more than many another presented with the same golden opportunity. Only in the case a certain civilian rat will have scurried around all the dark corners, preparing the way, first. And when that's done, we're done for."

"You thinking something?"

"Yes."

"What?"

"I'm thinking it's long overdue Mr. Cribb rejoined our interest. I'm thinking that neither you, nor Mr. Thorpe, nor even myself have the touch to execute a certain delicate task—"

"No!" Levi's fist struck the table. "You know what that *vyzoso* call me—?"

"I've been told till I'm heartily sick of hearing it!"

"Name me one reason why I now got to help that, that big-mouth *Kossak!*" the wardmaster demanded, still pounding the morgue table.

"Your own neck."

43

PHILLIP GLANCED up from a sketch of Rose Hill as Collins came in for their daily conference.

"Good morning, sir."

" 'Morning." The governor snapped his fingers at Dundas on her way back to the kitchen. "Coffee."

The judge advocate had worked with the Old Man long enough to recognize profound depression: it was one of the character traits they had in common. He dropped his despatch bag on the table and sat down. "I had a few words in the mess, sir. The opinion is that you did the only thing possible—"

"No, I didn't. It was a disgraceful scene. In public."

"True," the younger man had to concede, "but we all marvel at your restraint, given the extreme provocation."

Phillip hunched his shoulders and contemplated the large black blot which had somehow appeared during Campbell's brief reign.

"The coffee, Your Excellency. . . ."

He looked up at his housekeeper's kindly face. "Thank you."

Collins waited until the woman had left again, then helped himself to a cup. These morning conversations were among the few perks in an otherwise thankless round of duties. The governor had bought a plentiful stock of coffee beans in Rio: other officers were already experimenting with toasted biscuit crumbs or local teas stewed from dead leaves.

"I'm afraid it's going to be a very full agenda, today." Collins opened the bag. "There's a capital offense topping the list."

"Hn! Tell me about it."

"Oh, just the usual theft, once there's a full moon to see by and deep shadows to hide in." The judge advocate was separating an order to convene the criminal court, turning it round so that the governor could follow the summary of evidence if he wished. "Fortunately a Marine

Dukes, assisted by Corporal Asky, was able to recover the two linen undershirts, a week's rations and a pewter snuffbox almost immediately." He pointed at the paper. "Asky's name is scratched inside the lid and it'd been pledged for a loan from Dukes, from whose tent it was taken. The sergeant of the guard conducted a search once the alarm was raised and found everything freshly buried in the said item's bivouac—"

"Who vehemently protests his innocence."

"Don't they all?" Collins replied.

Phillip sipped coffee. "Name?"

"Cribb, ex-*Alexander*. He loiters round the military lines, cadging odd jobs. That's how our informants connected him with this particular theft," Collins explained, holding the paper steady as the governor's quill hooked, scratched, dotted.

The prisoner whistled a flat, tuneless march between his teeth as he was brought to Government House under close escort. His only taste of justice, apart from a brief appearance at the Old Bailey, had been as the orderly sergeant at courts martial in the colonies. Those had been even more abrupt than the English law of London: the accused were generally stood against the nearest tree, wearing a blindfold, or broken by relays of floggers.

Cribb had no reason to think that the same system of justice would hand down a different verdict as today's orderly sergeant gave him a shove in the back, straight through the door, halting him at a chalk line in front of five officers. The orderly room clerk sat to one side of the table, ready to take the minutes of proceedings. There was nobody else. It was going to be Cribb's word against last night's sergeant of the guard, "Scratcher" Fitch, Corporal "Dirty Dick" Asky, and Marine "Chimney Chops" Dukes.

Collins rapped the table with a wooden gavel. "Regulations direct me to instruct you on the *pro forma* duties of the president and members of this court. Our task is to determine the guilt or innocence of the accused as to the charge or charges upon which he has been arraigned and, if found guilty, to determine the appropriate sentence. The fact that a charge or charges has or have been preferred against him should not be construed as *a priori* evidence of guilt. The determination of guilt or innocence must be based solely upon the weight of evidence and can only be arrived at after resolving all material issues of fact. Thus it is our duty to maintain an open mind, free from prejudice or bias. God Save the King."

The captain, two lieutenants and two ensigns took their seats. Collins picked up his convening order and looked at the nondescript item squashed between two marines, muskets tucked into their sides, staring straight ahead. "You are entered as Joseph Cribb, number 437 on the scale of rations, ex-*Alexander*. It is alleged that, on the night of the seventeenth, instant, you did break bounds and feloniously enter the quarters of Marine Peter Dukes from whence you stole two linen undershirts, a quantity of food, and one pewter snuffbox, all of which were duly recovered from your customary place of abode, thereafter. How do you plead? Guilty or not guilty?"

"I never done—!"

"Be silent. You will have ample opportunity to present your point of view." Collins glanced at the clerk. "Enter that as 'not guilty'."

"Sah."

The court president looked at his orderly sergeant. "Call the first witness."

"Sah!"

Sergeant Fitch stamped in and held the Bible while the oath was read to him.

Collins picked up a very commonplace snuffbox. "Do you recognize this?"

"Sah!"

"Where did you first see it?"

"Freshly buried in the ground under the accused's shelter, sah!"

"Do you recognize any other articles?" Collins asked, running his finger over some biscuits, two threadbare shirts and a large piece of cheese.

"Sah!"

"And where did you first see them?"

"Freshly buried in the ground under the accused's shelter, sah!"

The judge advocate sat back in his chair. "Was the accused present at the time of your discovery?"

"Sah!"

"What were his reactions?"

"Cut up real rough, sah!"

Collins glanced at the clerk again. "Enter that as 'resisted arrest'." He looked back at the convict. "Do you wish to question the witness?"

Cribb studied Enoch Fitch. "Well, at least you kept your word this time. You reckoned you'd get me, on the boat. Now, just 'ope the bloke who promised to pay you remembers to kick back the doings. . . ."

"Sah! I protest!"

"What is the point of your question?" Collins asked, steepling his fingertips.

"If I got to be grassed, I don't want to go cheap, that's all," Cribb replied.

"Strike that from the record: the remark is irrelevant."

"Sah."

"Call the next witness."

Corporal Asky stamped in and gripped the Bible. Collins held up the snuffbox. "Do you recognize this article?"

"Er, sah!"

"Where did you last see it?"

"This morning, freshly buried in the ground under the accused's shelter, after I give it to Marine Dukes after 'e loan me some baccy, that'd be two days ago, just after evening muster to be exact, sah!"

"Does the accused wish to question the witness?" Collins asked.

Cribb sucked a tooth. "Oh, all right." He looked at Asky. "You always was a terrible rotten liar, even on the boat. One o' these days it'll get you in real trouble. . . ."

"Strike the accused's remark from the record. It is irrelevant. Call the next witness."

Asky left the courtroom and Dukes clutched the Bible, swearing to tell the truth, the whole truth and nothing but the truth, so help him God.

Collins held up the snuffbox. "Do you recognize this article?"

"Sah!"

"How did it come into your possession?"

"Er, Corp'l Asky let me loan 'im some baccy till next rations, that'd be two days ago, just after the evening muster, and I sort of took it till 'e could give me baccy back, then it got stole last night and this is the first time I seen it since, sah!"

"Does the accused wish to question the witness?"

Cribb looked deep into Dukes's shifty eyes. "You're even worse than Dirty Dick. If they was raffling the Bank o' England for best liar you'd be lucky to win the shit'ouse seat with a stinker like that. . . ."

"The court will come to order!" Collins hammered the table until his brother officers had restrained their mirth. "That remark will be stricken from the record! Let the witness withdraw and the accused enter his defense!"

Cribb also promised to tell the truth, the whole truth and nothing but the truth. "It's all lies." He looked along the row of gray, horsehair wigs and shaven faces. "It's plain as daylight why I've been framed to wear a rope collar. I'd say it all started back about the time we was waiting on London River. Terrible cold it was, as you'd remember. So one of the traps, Marine Asky as 'e still was, though 'e usually answers to 'Dirty Dick,' wants to use a mort—"

"The accused will confine his remarks to the events of the past few hours."

"Oh, them?" Cribb mused. "Nothing special about the last few hours, for me at least. The last few days are different, though, that's when I was 'elping Mr. Phillips and the other ge'men, so there'd 'ave been plenty o' chance to plant the dibbins where I dossed and nobody would ever know they was there—till they got found again."

"Are you insinuating these articles were buried deliberately to incriminate you?" Collins asked, flicking the evidence in front of him.

"You mean there's some other way they could've got there?" Cribb replied. "Strikes me that since I didn't nick 'em some other cove did, unless they dug a little tunnel like moles and sort of popped up in my roost by accident."

"The court will come to order!" Collins slammed his gavel down. "A pert tongue will gain you nothing! This is a court of law, not some common bawdy house!"

"Oh, sorry, ge'men, I must've come to the wrong place."

"Order! Order I say!" Collins sat forward. "Are you telling us that you are so well fed and clothed that you would never stoop to acquiring food and clothing by illegal means. . . ?"

"You mean pinch 'em?"

"Yes."

"O' course I bloody would."

"Ah—!"

"But not from Dirty Dick or Chimney Chops," Cribb went on. "I mean, a bloke might catch something nasty if 'e wore them shirts. And as for eating anything Scratcher touched first, no, thank you very much!"

Collins pounded the table until he had everyone's attention again. "Those remarks will be stricken from the record! The accused will stand down! I shall now direct the court!"

The judge advocate controlled himself as Cribb left with his escort. "We've heard Sergeant Fitch describe how he discovered these articles in the quarters of the accused. We've heard Corporal Asky identify the snuffbox which he pledged with Marine Dukes for the loan of some tobacco. And we've heard Marine Dukes testify how he lost certain articles, including the snuffbox. A clear line of events connects the accused, the evidence, and the witnesses.

"Our sole task now is to weigh their relative truthfulness. On the one hand we have a senior and junior noncommissioned officer of the corps, entrusted by us with responsibilities above the average. And we have the testimony of Marine Dukes, a veteran of the Savannah campaign, with eighteen months' war service aboard HMS *Resolute*. On the other hand we have the flippant 'wit' of one Joseph Cribb, convicted at the Central Criminal Court, London, and sentenced to penal servitude for life for theft and arson. Need any more be said?"

The judge advocate looked along the row of faces. "Very well, let's start with our junior member. Ensign Woolcot, how do you find the accused, guilty or not guilty?"

"Guilty, sir."

"Ensign Bruce?"

"Guilty, sir."

"Lieutenant Wade?"

"Guilty, sir."

"Lieutenant Stanton?"

"Guilty, sir."

Cribb was marched back to the chalk line.

Collins finished writing something and glanced up at the prisoner. "From the evidence presented to this court it is plain that you deliberately planned and carried out a felony which, had it been successful, would have deprived a member of the defense establishment of his rations in addition to certain personal belongings. By so doing you would have weakened the colony's power to retaliate to the extent that Marine Dukes would have been unable to perform his duty. Therefore, you not only committed a theft, you harbored treason. Clearly this offense must be punished so that others do not fall for the same fatal temptation." The judge advocate paused. "Joseph Cribb. It is the unanimous verdict of this court that you be taken from here to the place of execution where, at a time to be stated, you will be hanged by the neck until dead. God Save the King."

"Is that all? Can I go now?"

"Order! Order, I say!"

The escorting sergeant gave the condemned man a gentle nudge. "Come on, chum."

Cribb walked into the sunlight. Head erect, shoulders square, he paced along the line of redcoats who waited to take him back to the lock-up. He halted at the first man, inspecting him from gaiter buttons to cockade. "Ten days pack drill, sar'nt!" Then the next man. "Get a shave!" Then the next. "Your firelock's a bloody disgrace, soldier, shine it!"

The sergeant tapped him on the shoulder. "Save the laughs for later. After work. Come on. . . ."

Levi stood alone in the shade of the morgue, watching the procession pass the hospital before dispersing at the improvised prison. The condemned man stretched out on the ground and made himself as comfortable as an ankle chain would allow. A marine guard stood easy at each end of the log.

"*Goteniu.*" Levi shook his hands dry. He had enough problems of his own without taking on a lost cause like Cribb's. The hospital's population was increasing steadily, men and women alike, in spite of the number who took their final discharge up the Brickfield Road.

Levi's responsibility was the male ward, a long shed thatched with cabbage palm and clad with slabs of bark. This was a plum perk in a village where most worked for up to sixteen hours a day on sixteen ounces of food—less spoilage, spillage, theft and the storekeepers' thumbs on the scales.

The competition for a few days' rest in hospital, even on half-rations, was fierce. The opportunities to make a profit were limited only by the size of a patient's tobacco cache, which had given Levi great power. And great risk. His was a dangerously exposed position for a foreign Jew to hold for too long. And there were constant border skirmishes between the male ward and the female, only a few yards away, behind its hessian flyscreen which did little to keep out prowlers after dark.

Levi's rival was the one-eyed Mrs. Martha Grimes, midwife and procuress of Portsmouth Town, despatched to the colonies for failing to stay sweet with the local justices of the peace. She had taken the lesson to heart. Long before her arrival at Sinny aboard *Prince of Wales* she had marked Charles Nash as being a ge'man with a future. Once they settled into their new homeland Nash had rewarded her foresight by seeing she became the matron and hospital storekeeper.

The competition for a few minutes' rantum-tantum under the blankets was intense, the chance to profit only limited by the garrison's daily spirit ration, and Mrs. Grimes's power was even greater than Levi's.

He turned his back on Cribb's troubles and went inside the morgue to attend to his garden.

The surgeon's convict aide was still watering cress on its damp blanket in the corner when Ben Thorpe panted to a stop inside the doorway. "They going to neck Joe!"

"So what's new?" Levi replied, checking that he was leaving enough of the old crop to seed another generation of salads next week.

"But they going to 'ang Joe!" Thorpe yelled, waving the stick he normally used to urge his workers.

"Please. I hear." Levi straightened. "What you want me to do? You want me to go to Mr. Kripp with a file, say to the soldiermen 'Excuse me your honors!' and cut him free?"

"B-but we can't just let 'em 'ang Joe!"

"Why not?"

"Because we got to do something!"

"What?"

"Something!"

"Sure, sure."

"I'm going to do something!"

"Good."

"Um, I'm going to do it now!"

"Ben?" Levi affectionately patted Thorpe's arm. "You are good man. Strong man. But it all stops when it gets to where your mouth is. From there up what you got for brains?"

"I—!"

"Listen. They going to hang Joe. Too bad for Joe, too bad for Mr. Spangles they don't do it first, but that's life. Now—"

"I'll show all you clever buggers what I got for brains!"

"Ben—!" But Levi was talking to himself.

Phillip's gaffer was off to see the master. He crossed the stream and trudged up the path to Government House. A sentry slapped his musket and aimed the bayonet at the intruder's naked chest. " 'Alt! Advance one and be recognized!"

Thorpe rummaged inside his belt pouch and took out the scrap of paper which had appointed him to be an overseer. "I got to see the Big Cove. Quick!"

The sentry glanced over one shoulder. "Corp'!"

The guard commander paced out of the bark shanty which sheltered His Excellency's protectors for the next twenty-four hours. "What's your 'urry, tiger?"

"I got to see the Big Cove!"

The corporal took the piece of grubby paper. "Wait." He went inside Government House. He came out. "Right-o, in you go. . . ."

Thorpe folded his *laissez passer* and sidled through the doorway, hat in both hands. He came to a halt: Phillip was about to be served a late luncheon. There was a fresh tablecloth over the ink blot. A china plate, wineglass and cutlery had been laid for one. An empty pickle jar held a sprig of flowers.

"Yes, Ben?"

"Begging pardon, master." Thorpe shuffled his hat brim from hand to hand.

Phillip understood these Saxon peasants, stubborn, loyal, durable, but woefully slow-witted. He smiled, encouraging the man to continue. "Yes?"

"It's Joe."

"Joe?"

Thorpe looked down at the waxed floorboards between his bare feet. "Joe's my mate and it's not right."

Phillip squeezed the high, curved bridge of his nose. "Ben. I've had a very trying time recently. I still have much to do. Would you mind getting to the point, please? What's not right?"

Thorpe's voice trembled. "You really going to 'ang Joe, m-master?"

Phillip sat back. "This Cribb is a friend of yours?"

Thorpe nodded uncertainly.

"And you've taken time from work to plead for clemency? To ask me to spare his life? Is that it?"

Thorpe nodded again.

"And you realize I can have you whipped for leaving the fields without permission. . . ?"

Thorpe made another dejected nod.

"Then he must indeed be a friend." Phillip reached for the carafe which his housekeeper had been chilling inside a porous earthenware crock of water. He measured a glass, took a sip, looked up again. "I'm sorry, there's nothing I can do."

"Master—!"

"There's nothing I can do for the simple reason that your friend has been found guilty of a very serious theft at a time when larceny is rife. If we don't punish him others will be encouraged to steal what's not rightfully theirs. And if that happens we shall all suffer, won't we?"

Thorpe nodded.

Phillip took another sip of claret. "At times like these it's more humane that one pays the supreme penalty of the law than many should risk their lives. It's unfortunate that your friend was the one. I do wish I could offer you more comfort." He put the glass down. "Now, concerning the maize crop, are we irrigating it sufficiently?"

Thorpe nodded.

"It wasn't looking so good when I inspected it this morning. Put out more dung: it is vitally important we germinate enough to harvest seed for next season. And I require that fallen timber to be reduced to ash and spread on One Tree Field before the winter rains: there must be wheat in the barn next year," he added. "Very well, that is all, dismiss."

Thorpe bumped into the door frame and left Government House.

44

NASH SPOKE with the guards. They moved away from the prison log as he strolled nearer. "Well, what a surprise. Our little arsonist in trouble?" The assistant storeman tilted his hat and smiled. "Who was going to put my face through the floor? And now who's at my feet, instead? Tell me, how does it feel to be so close to death . . . ?"

The prisoner slowly opened an eye. "Oh, difficult to say. Tell you what, let's change places. Then you'll know."

Nash nodded. "They told me you were a comedian even after you'd been condemned: I see what Collins meant. But you've no one to blame but yourself, you know. It was incredibly stupid to leave camp for a week."

"Case of second time lucky?" Cribb replied. " 'Ere, make yourself useful, for once. Shift over." He flicked a finger, moving the other man's shadow so that it fell across his own face. "That's better. That sun's a bit 'ard on the eyes."

"In your predicament I'd be eager to see it for as long as I could." Nash was still smiling, still looking down at the fire-raiser. "When it reaches those treetops you're going to be 'topped,' as they say, though unlike you I'm rather looking forward to the experience."

"Uh?" Cribb wriggled himself more comfortable, leaning on one elbow, looking up at the gentleman.

"It's true. So are the troops. They've not been happy, recently. 'Some good raw meat' is what they need and that's what they're going to get. You should satisfy them for a few more days until their other appetites are catered for." Nash paused. "However, I'm having you killed for a rather more personal reason. Can you guess what that might be, Cribb?"

"Because we 'ad that bit of a stoush back in the stores?"

"You flatter yourself! Try again."

Cribb was baffled. "I know you don't like the look of my face, but even a rotten prick like you wouldn't croak a bloke just because of the way 'e looks and talks."

Nash considered the prospect. "Actually, I would. I'd gladly hang every last one of your class—"

"Then who'd do the dirty work?"

"Those who remembered their places, of course, which is doing the dirty work. You forgot. However, I might've been disposed to excuse your insolence had it not been for one further reason. . . ."

"You mean I done something else wrong?"

"Not yet. Nor will you, now. But you might have done after that bitch Brandon ordered you to murder me."

"You're off your perch!" Cribb laughed. "Jesus, she'd never do a thing like that! She's a lady."

"She's a bitch. A sly, underhand—uuuf!"

The flung rock took Nash in the crotch. Cribb's free arm swung over, following through, dragging the bowed man into a heap. The guards struggled to prise the heaving shapes apart. Nash would eat very little for the next several days: Cribb's thumbs had almost met behind the other man's windpipe.

"Phoss! F'Chrissakes! What you trying to do?" one of the redcoats pleaded, frightened in case an officer had noticed the tussle.

"Job the sod."

Kitty Brandon had focused her man's fieldglass on the prison stockade across the parade ground. She rammed the tubes shut. "I'm going to the hospital."

"I! Feel! Much improved!" John Shea coughed from his cot.

"All the more reason for me to see Dr. Balmain now." She tied the sunbonnet under her chin, took her basket to appear busy and strode away. *Alexander*'s surgeon was on duty this afternoon. She curtseyed. "Captain Shea's compliments, he is feeling much improved and wishes to thank you in person. . . ."

William Balmain smiled back. "Why, thank you kindly, ma'am." A summons from any member of the commissioned officer corps, even if it was only a penniless Irish captain, had immediate priority for a naval warrant officer. Balmain put a clear beaker into his bag: he would need it to scry his patient's urine, the color would show how much further blood had to be tapped to clear the morbid humors affecting Shea's chest.

Kitty Brandon watched him go, then went into the morgue. "Stay seated," she commanded Levi. "Miss Dundas informs me that His Excellency's mind is quite made up: Mr. Cribb hangs. It's time for the light infantry."

Levi put aside his practice alphabet. "You want me to go? You think the Big Cove take notice of a Jew *karabelnik* the Mrs. Grimes call such bad names?"

"Enough of that twaddle!" Kitty Brandon hitched her skirts and sat on the edge of the dissecting table. "Within four hours Nash wins, we lose, do I make myself plain?"

"Always you do that," Levi replied. "So what you want me to do about it?"

"Get Balmain off his arse. Get him over to Government House the moment he returns from the butchery he calls 'treatment.' "

"With what reason?"

"Mr. Cribb is the best, the only scavenger this pest hole has had to date. Get Balmain to say that Mr. Cribb is worth more alive than dead—"

"You want *me* to do that? I put one foot wrong and the Mrs. Grimes—!"

"Fail to move both feet smartly and Mrs. Brandon will do far worse!"

"Oy. Will not be easy. I must think."

It would not be easy. William Balmain was only one of the six surgeons in the colony who bled the living and cut open the dead. In the tight, enclosed, jealous world of hospital life he was not at the bottom like James Callam, who had come out on the brig *Supply*, but neither was he at the top, like John White who had come out with the governor's entourage aboard the frigate *Sirius*. Levi tended to rank his man about halfway up, or halfway down, depending on how tetchily Balmain was behaving at the time.

Some days were worse than others because the young Scot was poor, not ragged poor, but shabby poor, forever condemned to wait in the antechambers of power while better-connected colleagues strolled past, to the manner born. This had been sufficient reason to volunteer for duties in a remote penal camp where—with a pay scale based on tuppence a month for every name in his care, plus a bounty of five guineas a year from Queen Anne's Chest to buy his bandages and salves—there was only a slim margin of profit to be earned. He was facing an uncertain old age unless he worked harder to improve his connections at Home.

But that was not proving easy, either. As an apprenticed surgeon's mate, roughly equivalent to a ship's carpenter in the Royal Navy, Balmain was not in the same social class as a university-trained physician, a lack which Levi had soon learned to exploit. By now, a respectful "*Doktor?*" was sure to steer William Balmain in the desired direction, especially if a member of the Quality was waiting at the end of the path, and particularly while a skilled convict was happy to drudge around the wards, free.

Theirs was a business partnership which not even the one-eyed Martha Grimes had yet split asunder.

Levi smiled respectfully as the younger man returned to the hospital with fresh blood on his hands. "*Doktor?* I been thinking. . . ." And ten minutes later Jane Dundas announced another unexpected visitor to Government House. "Mr. Balmain, Your Excellency."

"Oh. Very well. Show him in." Phillip laid his book aside. "Yes?"

The surgeon halted, hat under arm. "I beg leave to present the sickness and mortality return, sir."

"Can't it wait until the end of the week?"

"I think not, sir." Balmain laid his sheet of paper on the table. "You will observe that we have a visitation of the red itch and putrid scab again."

"Then do something about it."

"I wish I could, sir, but the scavengers *pro tempore* are less than wholehearted in their approach to work. I had to get one flogged while you were away, traveling with the regular one, after a patient was found to have been interred at less than the regulation depth."

Phillip considered the list of figures; they supported his own, private fears: the settlement was teetering on the brink of an epidemic unless there were soon a winter frost to freshen the bad air. "Very well, get the Orderly Room to drum up another work gang."

"I've already done so, sir, but they say I've had my quota for the month. Besides, it's not numbers we need, it's willing hands."

Phillip spread his own in a way which reminded Balmain of the hospital's convict assistant. "So you expect me to produce them from my pocket?"

"Er, no, sir, though in a manner of speaking you could produce one very easily."

"Oh?"

"I speak of the one under sentence of death. Before he accompanied you upon the expedition he was the best we had. Nothing was ever too much trouble for him. If only—"

"Mr. Balmain. You haven't come this afternoon to plead for the life of this Cribb person?"

"Not exactly plead, sir. I merely wish to see the sanitary arrangements properly directed again." Balmain knew he was walking a very fine line between advancing his interest as a conscientious subordinate and retarding it by annoying the governor. "Isn't the S and M list cause for active concern, sir?"

"Yes, but your answer is 'no.' We may be threatened with a plague of red itches and putrid scabs but we are already infected by thefts which, unless quickly brought under control, will overwhelm what little moral health we have left! I'm doing what you do when confronted by a rotten limb, lopping it off to save the rest of the body." He picked up his book. "Close the door as you go."

Jane Dundas watched the surgeon pass her kitchen window. She picked up an empty bucket and followed him down to the stream. Kitty Brandon was waiting by the laundry area. "It's no use, his mind's quite made up!"

"Damn. Time for the heavy guns. To your post, Jane." Kitty Brandon picked up the empty working basket and strode back to the hut which she kept for John Shea. Her handiwork was everywhere, from the gray flannel curtains to the red patchwork quilt which covered her man's camp bed. He looked terrible, a cadaver striped with chinks of light through the wall beside him.

"You're looking better, Jack." His housekeeper smiled at him. "Dr. Balmain thinks you should try walking again for a little exercise, to keep the blood moving around."

Shea nodded. "Thank you, Kitty. It's such a nuisance, being here. Young Kellow, has much to learn." He sank back against the straw bolster and recovered his breath. "Can't put old heads, on young shoulders, you know."

"I know." She squeezed his arm. "It'd be a far happier world if only we could, but it's only experience of that world which gives a man the Roman sense of duty which is your reputation in the king's service."

His face had regained some color. "Duty and honor, while a man has them, he has everything—!" Shea smothered the heaving cough. "While there's duty! And honor."

Kitty Brandon bit her lip. "We need you, Jack."

The color drained away. "Who does?"

She hesitated. "There's been a miscarriage of justice. An innocent man is to be hanged this evening."

Shea let her sit him straighter. "Tell me. About it."

Kitty Brandon outlined the case while she began dressing him in his regimentals. Even so, twenty minutes had passed before he was ready to try passing the doorway. His sword hung loose in its scabbard, to lean against. Across the uneven parade ground. Over the shallow stream. Uphill again to Government House. His face glistened with sweat as he returned the sentry's stiff salute.

Jane Dundas was at her post. "Captain Shea, Your Excellency."

"Good God!" Phillip stood as the officer of marines tried to click heels. "Please, another chair! And bring that brandy!"

The two gentlemen sat, waiting for the decanter. Phillip covered his empty glass with his palm but nodded for the other man's to be filled. He watched Shea restore himself with a stiff draught. "Only the most urgent errand could have brought you. How may I be of service?"

"Thank you, sir." Shea wiped his mouth and tried to bow from the waist. "It is my duty to stop a miscarriage of justice. An innocent man is to be hanged this evening."

Phillip arched an eyebrow. "Cribb?"

"Yes, sir."

"What about him?"

Shea had little enough breath to sustain his own life: he had to be brief when pleading for another's. "There's a strong suspicion that hostile elements have planted evidence so that a man, loyal to us, will be seen to be destroyed by us. If this happens we'll have driven a sap under our own defenses and be sitting upon the mine set by those enemies to whom I refer."

Phillip considered the shades of meaning. "You know, until this afternoon I couldn't have told you who was our camp scavenger, nor did I care so long as the work was done neatly, quickly and regularly. However, it seems that from such a menial position, this Cribb has contrived to interest a surprising assortment of people." The governor sat forward again. "You say that evidence has been 'planted' to incriminate one of our supporters?"

"I believe so, sir."

"Pardon me saying so, Mr. Shea, but it all seems rather Oriental to me: what would be the purpose of such a plot?"

The officer of marines put away his piece of rag. "I can't say, sir, but cliques and cabals are as natural to garrison duty as bad pay and poor rations. Both are breeding grounds for rebellion against authority."

"Point taken. Very well, what evidence have you to set against the sworn testimonies of—" Phillip peered at one of the papers uppermost in front of him. "Sergeant Fitch? Corporal Asky? And a Marine Dukes?"

"Their names are sufficient, sir." Shea paused. "I could say more but it's not honorable to speak ill, even of such men, unless they are present to defend themselves."

Phillip pushed the paper away. "Surely you can see that I have no alternative but to let the sentence stand? Unless I have verifiable evidence that a perjury has been committed, the execution must proceed. Not to do so would be to show weakness and lack of resolution at the very moment when our troops and laborers are preparing to go into winter quarters, the very season when conditions will become even worse and those cabals redouble their efforts. Because, contrary to popular belief, I am quite aware of what's happening in my command.

"There's also the matter of principle at stake," he went on. "Not to continue with this execution would be to introduce an element of chance into the system of justice over which I preside. It would reduce our court to a tombola, a lottery where numbers are drawn and punishments awarded instead of prizes. That's hardly the best foundation upon which to build an enduring society, is it?"

Shea's face glistened again. Phillip rang for his housekeeper. "You take one arm, I'll take the other, I think it best if he lay down for a while." They half-carried Shea into the governor's bedchamber and stretched him upon the plain bed. Phillip shook out his blue serge cloak and laid it over the dying military officer. "Take your ease, Mr. Shea. You're no trouble."

45

JANE DUNDAS took the bucket and hurried to where Kitty Brandon was going through the motions of scrubbing a pair of breeches. "Captain Shea's done his very best, but it's no use!"

Kitty Brandon pushed herself off her knees. "Thank you, Jane. Return to your post."

"But what more can be done now?"

"Fight!"

The woman may have believed there was still a battle to be won but Cribb was under no illusions. The governor's signpost had been carried from the carpenters' yard and hoisted between two trees near the prison log. Scragger was now on the ladder, trying to tie a noose. The condemned prisoner sighed, stuck two fingers in his mouth, whistled. "Oy! Bring it 'ere!"

The executioner obeyed. "What's up, Phoss?"

"You've not learned a bloody thing about this job since you topped Tommo."

"But I never done it on my own before."

"You're not doing it on your own now," Cribb said, slapping the log and inviting the unhappy hangman to sit down. "Look, I must've necked a good dozen, Over There. Spies, mostly. And you know what I learned?"

"Wha'?"

"The big 'uns croak sweet; it's us little buggers die 'ard: it's something to do with the weight. So you know what I used to do?"

"Wha'?"

"Measure the doings from neck to ankle, then put on six inches for luck." Cribb stood, stretching his neck. "Go on, slip it over! Crissakes, if you're too scared to touch me while I'm warm, what's it going to be like when I'm stiff?"

Scragger did as he was told and fitted his client by marking the drop with another knot.

"And rub on a bit of tallow," Cribb said, palming a handful of tobacco to pay for the privilege of a quick death. He sat down and watched the executioner return to work, then wearily shook his head. "What a cow of a day. . . ."

The guard was being changed. Another pair of redcoats stamped past, equipment clinking, slapped their muskets and took up positions. Their corporal marched over to inspect the iron bezel ring around the prisoner's ankle. "I done what you asked, Sarge," Drury reported, standing easy for a few moments.

"Thanks, Ted." Cribb groped under his shirt and untied his body belt. He undid one end of the rag tube and poured out the rest of his tobacco. "See the lads get this. Tell the drummers to start as I give 'em the nod. And none o' that 'Rogue's March.' Sound the Advance. Same as we done, as we done Over There."

Drury clicked his heels.

The work day was drawing to a close.

Thorpe left his fields early. The two sentries ignored him as he plodded nearer the log, a mattock slung over one shoulder, ready to be returned to the stores for the night. "Joe. . . ."

Cribb looked up from the sandy gravel. " 'Ullo."

"Just you 'old that there chain still against the wood!" Thorpe whispered, starting to heft the heavy blade.

"Thanks, mate, don't bother." He jerked a thumb at the redcoats. "You'll be stuck so full of 'oles they'll never know which was your arse and which your mouth. Besides, where's there to bolt to?"

"B-but I can't just do nothing!"

"Strewth, there's tons you can do." Cribb tried to give the other man a playful punch. "Start by wiping that nose: you'd think it was you they're going to twist off."

"S-sorry, Joe."

"So'm I. But, as the little piggy said when 'e sat down to boiled bacon, enjoy it while you can."

Thorpe nodded dumbly. "I'm sorry I called you all them things."

"Nyah, I've 'eard worse. Look, get rid of that bloody chopper before you do yourself an injury. Then grab a good seat before the crowd gets too thick." Cribb made a bright wink. "Go on! Bugger off!"

Thorpe did not see Levi pass the other way. The convict wardmaster spoke a few words to one of the sentries and waited until Cribb had steadied himself again, then turned and stepped up to the log. "What do you want me to do, Joe?"

Cribb motioned him to share the seat. "Look after Kitty."

"What then?"

"Croak that sod." Cribb was looking across the parade ground to where Nash and Asky were standing, laughing.

Levi nodded again. "Will be pleasure."

"Nh! I wish I could be 'ere to 'elp finish the job. Still, you can bet your nuts I'll be out there somewhere, giving you a shout and shove when you need it most."

"I know. Will be like the time on the boat, when I stiff the Mangler. Sure, later we say bad things, but was nothing." He stood abruptly. "You are good mate. Go in peace."

Cribb watched him stride back to the morgue where an autopsy had been booked. A new regulation from Government House authorized a credit note of two shillings and sixpence on the stores for every post mortem; competition was fierce among the colony's surgeons: Balmain had worked hard to secure this one.

Kitty Brandon waited, out of sight, until the prisoner was ready to receive another visitor. She smiled at the sentries, arranged her skirts, sat on the log. "We did our very best: nobody could've done more. Mr. Thorpe, Mr. Levi, even Captain Shea have all put in good words with His Excellency. However, be prepared for the worst when Captain Collins returns."

"Thanks." Cribb took a deep breath. "I been ready a long time. Mr. Grim's an old mate. Don't get no easier, though."

She patted his wrist. "You are a very proper man, Mr. Cribb. I know you won't disgrace us."

Cribb looked at her for the first time. "Sorry I've not got much." He fumbled under his shirt and pulled a leather-thonged pouch over his head. " 'Ere. It'll bring you luck."

"Yes. Of course. But what is it?"

Cribb tugged the drawstring and took out a strip of dirty red silk. "I 'ad a mate, the first time I bolted. Good bloke. One o' the Sixty-Second's color party, as we went up to the guns, on that bloody ridge." Cribb steadied his breath. "In the end we 'ad to chuck it. But they never got our colors."

She knew. She had seen it. In General Burgoyne's bivouac the night before Britain's army laid down its arms at Saratoga. The American

Rebels could take the wrecked wagons, and the smashed firelocks, and the broken men, but they would never capture the regimental battle honors. The flags' ashes had been scattered, on the squally wind, in the darkness. Later, it had been rumored that some banners had been secretly torn up and kept by the survivors from their color parties.

"You 'ave it. Nobody else cares."

She gripped the piece of silk and stood. "You will need to be alone with the chaplain."

Johnson approached with his prayer book and box of communion wafers. He had to cough twice before the ex-gravedigger looked up again.

"I'm so very, very sorry to see you brought to this condition."

"So'm I."

The chaplain sat beside the condemned man. "My son, listen. As you know, I am ordained to bring comfort to all in their hour of affliction, but first I must enquire if you are a communicating member of the Church of England . . . ?"

"No."

Johnson nodded. "Our Lord will understand. His sacrifice at Calvary was for you. But to enjoy Life Everlasting I must hasten to direct your attention to that which awaits everyone as we pass from this world to appear before the Judgment Throne."

"Uh huh."

The chaplain persevered. "Believe me when I say that all are accursed who do go astray from the commandments of God. Return, I beseech you, to Him who knows the innermost secrets of every heart. At this extreme moment we need to lament our sins if we are to bring forth the fruits of repentance—!"

Cribb stopped him with a shake of the head. "Look. I don't like 'urting your feelings, right? But I don't think this makes a blind bit of difference."

"I—I beg your pardon?"

"This don't make no difference," Cribb repeated, simply. "I must've seen a ton of blokes get it. Most of my mates got it in Americky. And, I suppose, I got one or two. Didn't seem to be much time for thrones and fruit, then."

"But to die unrepentant is to endure hellfire's eternal agonies!"

"You mean I've more to come?"

"What?"

"Saving your presence, you really 'ave got it all wrong," the condemned man insisted. "It's a burning shame they won't let me come back and tell you what it's like, if it's like anything. Because, if there's more after this place, it's got to be better. And if it's nothing, well, that's it."

Cambridge University had not prepared Richard Johnson for theological debate with a hedgerow gypsy. Luckily for him, the battalion was starting to muster on the parade ground in front of the gallows: subalterns pointing their swords to direct the excited crowd of lags, sergeants leveling their halberds, corporals raising their canes.

The judge advocate checked the arrangements and marched up to the makeshift prison. "Ten more minutes, padre." He snapped his watch shut and continued down to the stream, across the bridge and up the opposite bank.

Jane Dundas saw him approaching. She left the kitchen window and went through to the antechamber. "Captain Collins, Your Excellency."

The governor did not look up from his work as the colony's legal officer rapped his heels together. "Is it ready, sir?"

Phillip took his time removing his spectacles. He sat back. "David? I've been giving some thought to this evening's business. Now, earlier today you said that the task of a court of law was to weigh the truthfulness of an accused man against that of his accusers. You were right, of course," the governor went on, "but only insofar as you went. You overlooked another, higher purpose for the laws we execute."

"Sir?"

"I refer to the preservation of authority and discipline, the maintenance of those standards without which the rabble would overwhelm us in a single night."

"Yes, but—?"

Phillip's look silenced him. "We are both acquainted with the realities of life for the great majority, back Home. I believe someone once described it as being 'poor, nasty, brutish and short.' And recent events in the capital, when that pyromaniac Gordon inflamed the mob's passions, support such a low opinion of our citizenry."

Collins looked down from the ceiling. "Of course, sir, but this evening—"

Phillip ignored the interruption. "I'm not entirely convinced we are any more familiar with the realities of life closer to home, namely in that transplanted slum which I can see and smell from my bedchamber window. We hardly brought the cream of English society with us to the ends of the earth and I've no reason to think that my subjects' lives are less poor, nasty or brutish, even if I do have to shorten some upon occasion."

"Sir. I told the padre we had ten minutes. Please may I have the execution warrant?"

The governor shifted a paper and picked up his quill. "How simple it must seem from the other side of this table. All I need to do now is write my name and the law will do the rest. And you are right, it is easy, because it is of no concern to me whether or not this Cribb item lives or dies. However, it would concern me vastly if it were ever proven that he was a piece of cheese—rather like that which it is alleged he stole from Messrs. Fitch, Asky and Dukes—and that instead of catching rat we have trapped our own fingers."

"Sir. I told the padre—!"

"I heard you first time." Phillip was studying the trial transcript again. "Last year, in Rio de Janeiro, I had the honor of an audience with His Excellency the Viceroy and Captain General of Brazil. During the course of our initial conversation, Dom Luis warned me about such an event as the one we now face."

"How could he?"

"Perhaps he knew more about the art of government than I did at the time?" Phillip leaned back, stroking the quill across his fist. "I'd gone to the Palace of Justice to plead for one of Ross's men, some numbskull who'd tried passing bad coin to the locals, a capital offense, of course. I was not overly concerned about our stupid bootface but I was most anxious about the effect all this was bound to have on Anglo-Portuguese relations. Do you know what De Vasconcellos told me?"

"No, sir. I do not."

"He told me that my man had been 'framed,' I think that's the correct term, by certain enemies of the royal government in Brazil. They were waiting for our marine to be burned at the stake, for if he were, the pro-French cabal in Rio would have taken an important trick. But, on the other hand, if a British soldier were reprieved after Portuguese citizens had paid the supreme penalty for the same crime, Dom Luis's rule would be further undermined, sapped, if you prefer, from below. Either way he straddled the horns of a dilemma."

"I fail to see any connection. Sir."

"You would if you were sitting this side of the table," Phillip replied, still stroking his knuckles.

"But I've promised the padre we'll be ready in ten minutes and it's getting dark."

"So I observe. I have also observed an execution by firelight."

Ross had, too, and he was planning another. "Bloody hell, Jimmy, this is preposterous!"

"Aye?"

"Aye! That weathercock Collins and Sparrow Legs are up to no good, you mark my words."

The crowd was also restive. They were late for dinner and nobody would be dismissed until the ladder had been jerked away from the figure trussed at the foot of the gallows. Cribb had given up trying to move his arms, which had gone numb under Scragger's clumsy pinions, and Johnson had given up trying to strike hot tears of repentance from the flinty little face at his side. Instead, the chaplain was praying silently and earnestly. He stopped. Collins was striding through the dusk, a white paper fluttering in one fist.

Some of the crowd gave a half-hearted cheer but were shut up by the rest who were straining to hear the sentence which would kill Cribb and allow them to go.

By tradition the hangman was drunk. He swayed and almost fell over as the judge advocate brushed past and halted in front of the condemned man. The paper rustled. "Joseph Cribb! Having been tried and found guilty as charged, it is the pleasure of His Excellency to extend the royal clemency. Your sentence of death is therefore—"

"Hooo!" Scragger clapped both hands over his mouth.

"Your sentence of death is therefore commuted to fifty lashes and thirty days' hard labor in the brick field. God Save the King."

"Bloody hell, didn't I tell you?"

The crowd also felt cheated. Free time had been wasted for nothing. Rocks, clods of earth and sticks lofted over the heads in front, pelting the hangman. The marines were furious, too, but at least they could have some fun with their musket butts, restoring calm while Scragger untied his client.

The hangman took the lash from the drum major.

There were murmurs of approval from the fancy, in the first few rows, as Cribb stripped off his duds. Here was a cove who looked good for a "tickle" of a hundred strokes, or even a "feel" of two hundred. A "scratch" of fifty should be a piece of pie for a bloke whose back and shoulders had been "plowed" in a prisoner-of-war camp.

"Um, Phoss? You got to be tied to the tree. See?"

"Nackers! I'll take 'em straight. And do us a domino."

The murmurs turned to whistles as the game little number faced the crowd and crossed his arms, waiting for Scragger to lay on, switching the cuts left, right, left, right, slashing a diamond pattern of welts, weals, wounds.

"Forty-eight! Forty-nine! Fifty!" Balmain marked his slate and struck off the tally which had just earned him a sixpenny bonus for dressing the raw flesh with salt and mutton fat.

Cribb wiped his face with a sweaty wrist. "Is that all? Can I go now?"

46

"FIVE? But I told you—!"

"The rest are coming," Nash insisted in a husky voice.

"Hn!" Ross looked straight ahead as he marched up the Brickfield Road, his garrison cloak swirling in the damp, morning light. "They're coming all right. You've too much to lose by reneging. But *when* are they coming?"

"Soon."

"How soon?" the battalion commander insisted, ignoring the stench as they passed the graveyard.

Nash covered his nose with the muffler he wore against the quinsy which, he said, was still troubling his throat. "Some of the women still ply their trade as if this were London. However, I can promise a fresh spirit of subordination once a few last obstacles have been removed."

The two gentlemen lapsed into silence as they trudged through dank, autumnal undergrowth.

Sydney Cove had been planned as a prison without walls, but even an open jail needs a separate area for its hardest cases, a whispered name to calm the other inmates. This was one of the few administrative details which the governor and his deputy had ever agreed upon: both felt the need for an area of strict regime confinement if they were to rest easily after dark, and supplying it had been one of the very few tasks which Ross had gladly undertaken since landing in New Holland.

He was a regimental officer, used to ordering men forward to penal companies in war, or sending them back to punishment stockades in peacetime, which gave him experience above the ordinary. Sinful Cove now had three calming influences—the quarry, the lime kilns, the brick field. And every lag knew that, no matter how terrible the main settlement was bound to become, there would always be somewhere worse unless he shut his face and did a government stroke, the minimum unit of work which kept a cove off the triangles and on the rations. The colony was now producing blocks, cement and bricks for next year's building plan. And Ross's men were more obedient now they could earn a spell of guard duty at places where a man could have some private fun.

Nash enjoyed it, too. Whenever work was slack in the stores and he could entrust Miller to look after their interests, the assistant storekeeper and paymaster accompanied the visiting justice of the peace around the punishment camps. There was something appealing to a person of his tastes and refinement to see the insolent, the stubborn, the upstart, being humbled, being reformed, being taught his or her place in colonial society. And Ross, for all his surliness since returning with the punitive expedition, was always glad of company from the Quality, and free legal advice.

They were approaching the brick field. The lieutenant governor had done well in so short a while. Beyond the fence of sharpened pickets stood two raised sentry boxes on roughly cut bush poles, one either side of the clay pit, so that at no time were any of the reconvicted convicts out of sight.

Another of Ross's refinements were the four planks buried in the ground with a fifth as the lid, held shut by boulders. Saucy items spent a day or two inside the Box. There was also a log which had been rolled under a bough from which hung a pulley and rope. Any item who stepped out of line could have his feet tied to the sleeper to stop him leaving the ground when his wrists were dragged into the air by three guards, and a fourth flayed the taut ribs with a tomcat—the military lash—studded with pistol shot. A few yards away stood the stocks—two planks with notches where ankles could be trapped and padlocked—and the pillory.

Ross had full authority to order any of these penalties during his inspections as the visiting justice. The only power which Phillip had reserved was the noose. It was still mandatory to send any item who struck a guard down to the main settlement for execution: which is why no convict had yet struck a guard, or given cheek, or attempted an escape. These offenses were punished in private, by the guards, and never appeared in the Orderly Book which Ross initialed.

"Hmm, they certainly appear busy enough, Mr. Nash."

The kiln chimney, tunneled into a rocky outcrop, was shimmering with heat fired with billets split by items who could be entrusted with an axe. And they appeared busy on a flat patch under the tarpaulin shelter where wet clay was being rammed into molds and dried until the bricks could be stacked for firing. And they were appearing busy at the pug mill where men clutched each other, stumbling up and down, pugging muck, chopped straw and water.

The System certainly appeared busy.

"May I check that one again, major? I'd like to see he's still being treated properly."

"Aye." Ross stepped away to initial another uneventful page in the guard hut.

Nash beckoned a trusty to step to the regulation six-feet distance between free and unfree. "Bring him up."

"Yuss, guv!"

Trusties stood at the pinnacle of power on the brick field: those who dug the raw clay with their bare fingers crouched at the bottom. They worked naked in all weathers, except for the rag gut string which held up their ankle chains. It was the Pit which came closest to Exodus chapter five, verse thirteen for Ross, and it was fear of the Pit which permitted the garrison's officers to rest easy after dark.

The trusty kicked an item up the ramp which led to ground level from the widening pond of rain, piss and shit.

"Hello, Cribb. Still another twenty days. I do hope you're being treated all right. . . ."

Two dark eyes looked out from sockets like caves.

Nash smiled into them. "Don't do anything silly. Oh, and before you return to work, your 'lady' wishes to inform you that her privileges have been withdrawn: she can no longer gossip around Government House kitchen anytime she pleases." Nash made a gesture of dismissal. "You'd better go: you can't afford to miss your tally."

Cribb could have taught the gentleman much about work quotas, here in the brick field and there in America where he had been chained to an anvil, just as Caleb Ledyard could have taught Ross a few refinements to camp life. As for Kitty Brandon's news, that had been known since yesterday.

A network of lurks, perks and payoffs flourished both sides of the guardhouse. The same detail of troops which escorted the swill tub into camp also brought the ointment pot for those, like Cribb, who had raw backs. The larger bits of contraband were sunk to the bottom of the tub under skilligalee boiled with old oatmeal. The smaller pieces were burned in the salve jar which Levi filled each day with sulphur and beef dripping. And whispers of news weighed nothing.

The Other System did not appear busy. It rarely appeared at all.

"Mr. Nash!" Ross snapped his fingers and beckoned.

The sentries stood to attention.

The two visitors left for home.

They parted at the edge of camp and Nash went into the store to tell

Andrew Miller to boil the tea kettle in the annex which served as their office and quiet area.

"Er, begging leave," the storekeeper said, "but Lieutenant Kellow sends 'is compliments. You've got to see 'im, urgent."

"Thank you, Miller, I'll attend to that presently. Tell me, has the Thorpe item been in for his things yet?"

Miller checked the loans register and shook his head.

"Then perhaps we ought to jog his memory. Send a runner."

"Right-o, sir."

Thorpe squelched in from the fields, a scrap of canvas dragged over his shoulders against the weather, and reported to the stores. Nash was alone behind the desk now that his nominal superior had been sent off on an errand to the observatory. "Come in, Ben."

"You want to see me, master?"

"Yes. I'm told you'll be needing another bushel of seed for planting. When do you want me to issue it?"

"Um. Well. We're still a-clearing that there patch. Soon?"

"Soon it is," Nash agreed. "We'll have everything ready for you to put a mark on the receipt." The clerk sat forward, elbows on the bare planks. "There's not another Ben Thorpe in our village?"

"I don't think so."

"Ah, then it must be you."

"Me?"

Nash smiled briefly. "Just a silly rumor. Something about His Excellency becoming displeased about something. Personally, I'd be sorry to see you lose your job—"

"Lose my job!"

Nash shook his head. "There's no need to worry, it's only a rumor, you know how they buzz around, never the same for two—"

"But it's not fair! I always done the best I can!"

"Ben. It's only a rumor, right?" Nash frowned slightly. "Of course, where there's smoke there can be fire, sometimes. Are you positive you haven't done anything to displease His Excellency?"

Thorpe was scratching himself now. "I don't think so!"

"Then you've nothing to worry about, have you?"

"No, master."

"Are you quite sure?"

"Sure, m-master?"

"Well, sure you haven't kept back some beans which you were told to bring to the stores? Or forgotten a pumpkin which you found later that same night . . . ?"

"I was 'ungry!"

"Shh!" Nash put his finger to his lips and glanced around to make sure they were still alone. "Ben, I understand. What you did was foolish but hardly the sort of crime which could earn you thirty days in the Pit and dismissal from your position. Although, look what's happened to that woman from your boat, the one who used to look after the soldiers' laundry. Wasn't she caught thieving? And where is she now . . . ?"

Thorpe gulped miserably.

"So it could even happen to you," Nash concluded. "You must be more careful. There are many others who'd give a lot to have your privileges. Speaking of which, I'd be less active with that stick: there are some who'd also give a great deal to have you under their fist, for a change."

"But I only done it for the master, master!" Thorpe was bewildered and alone as his secure world of warm food and dry blankets began to fall apart.

"I know that, but does His Excellency?" Nash enquired fairmindedly. "Memories are always shortest where they matter most and I am reliably informed that he did not take kindly to your interference in that business last week: 'damned insolence' I think he called it. You shouldn't have gone to Government House, it was very stupid of you. His Excellency had been about to reprieve your friend: your presumption nearly cost Joe his life. I'd be much more careful in future," Nash went on in the same concerned voice. "In fact I'd take a good look at myself before it was too late—"

"Too late?"

Nash nodded. "You've more enemies than you think. There's the Jew, Levi I think his name is, you should hear what he was saying behind your back about your brains! And there's Captain Shea's housekeeper: the less said about her the better. And there are others. You need real friends, particularly among those who count, the people you can count on whenever you need a helping hand." Andrew Miller was coming into sight from Point Maskelyne. Nash gave Thorpe a reassuring pat. "Don't take it so much to heart! Remember, when you're in trouble, come and see me first. Even if His Excellency does decide to whip you for stealing that pumpkin I'm certain Mr. Ross will put in a good word on your behalf, once I've explained the facts to him. Off you go and I'll have that seed weighed for you to collect later."

Thorpe blundered past Miller and ran away into the trees as Nash and his colleague prepared a tasty lunch of kangaroo pie, baked to perfection by a marine who had been a pastry cook before enlisting for a life of greater excitement and adventure in the king's service.

"I'll be down at the hospital if anyone asks for me," Nash said, folding his napkin. "I'll then see Mr. Kellow about that other business." He reached for his coat and stepped into the weather again, following a muddy rivulet which crept across the camp through the surviving undergrowth.

The autumn rains had done nothing to improve the hutches, the coops, the hovels which now made up the greater part of Sydney Town. Only the public buildings, like its stores and hospital, were anywhere near a reasonable standard.

"Good afternoon, sir." Balmain half-stood.

"Thank you, doctor." Nash was glad to duck into the dispensary and shake his hat. He took the other chair, sighed with relief, stretched out his legs. "That's better! If only the rest of it were as good as your hospitality, this would indeed be a good afternoon."

"How do you mean?"

Nash hesitated. "Look, in my work—like yours—one hears so much. A word here, another there. Most are baseless, in fact I'm sure some are downright lies. And yet, having discounted all that, there'll always be a *residium* of facts which were straws in the wind, so to speak."

The younger man was nodding in time with these measured, considered, cultivated words.

"Doctor? If I were you I'd have a few words with the women's matron," Nash advised, lowering his voice. "There'a a rather worrying story going around which concerns your male wardmaster, the foreigner, whatsisname, Shylock. Get to the bottom, sort it out before His Excellency gets to hear officially, and then has to deal with it himself. I mean, such things look so deuced bad on a record of service, don't they?"

47

NIGHT WAS falling. Rain was falling. Kitty Brandon was coming down the track to the officers' lines, a bundle of firewood under each arm. The housekeeper stepped into Shea's quarters, elbowing the door shut. Water leaked through the thatch, between the warped boards, around the sheet of oiled paper which served for a window. The interior of this one-room shed was as wet as its surrounds.

"There!" Kitty Brandon fed the makeshift hearth and blew its embers to a cheerful heat. "That's more like home!"

Her man lay under a piece of sailcloth rigged across his cot. "Please. Sit. Talk."

"Of course, but don't fatigue yourself, you've got to rest."

Shea waited for her to wipe the water from his face. Then he spoke, slowly, saving each breath. "I regret much. I should have been, a better husband. And father. But I had no choice. Tell her that."

"Yes. Of course. Exactly as you've told me."

Shea shut his eyes. After a while he opened them again. "It will not be easy. Alone. Among the heathen blacks." He shut his eyes. "Think kindly, of me. When you go, Home. Please."

"Yes. Of course. Often."

The eyes opened again. "Find, a good man. Not safe."

Kitty Brandon stood. "I won't be a few moments. Dr. Balmain can mix you another drink—"

"No. Listen. My things, will be sold. See they don't cheat, Kathleen. Don't go. Yet."

The rain eased and stopped about the midwatch of the night. Kitty Brandon could still hear the man's labored breathing between the plip and splash of wet rolling off the roof. The night light flickered in the draughts, wavering against the bark slabs. Few of John Shea's former tenants had ever lived, or died, in a more wretched hovel.

"Kitty . . . !"

She was dressed, she was ready, she lit the lantern from the slush lamp, she hurried into the night. A sentry challenged her, then stood aside. The dispensary was in darkness. She crouched where Levi sprawled, snoring. He woke up quietly as she squeezed a finger below his ear. "What you want?"

"Captain Shea's sinking fast," Kitty Brandon whispered back. "He may rally again in the morning. Give me another dose to get him that far."

"*Shpilkes.*" Levi tried sitting upright, rubbing his face and neck.

"Get me another dose of the damned medicine!"

"Shh! The Mrs. Grimes has heart of a rat and ears of a mouse!" Levi hissed, awake now. "I got no medicine. I got nothing. *Doktor*'s orders. I put one toe wrong, one time more, it's the Pit."

"Blazes!" Kitty Brandon looked around for other help. "Mr. Thorpe? Where the devil's he hiding?"

"He still not back."

"Oh, God. . . ."

Levi had other, more urgent problems. He lit his lantern from hers and went into the darkness. Balmain's new residence stood about seventy yards away, where the sea breeze generally touched shore before reaching the hospital and the morgue. The convict explained his errand to one of the sentries who had a contract with the surgeons to protect their compound after hours, and went up the pathway of whitewashed rocks to another bark shanty.

Balmain did not sleep alone on Wednesdays. Once a week he could afford to employ a young, rather pretty pickpocket—Gillian Webster, ex-*Scarborough*—who had found a new vocation in domestic service with the colony's six medical men.

"Gnnn? Wh'uzzat?"

"Your honor? Captain Shea presents his compliments and, with respect, wishes to inform he is dying." Levi then bowed to the other person in the bed and turned his back while Balmain dressed.

48

BRYANT TOOK the coffee, tested the temperature of his master's shaving water, then gathered together the towel, the soap, the razor. "Back to your work, Jane!"

The housekeeper obeyed as the major domo paced from the kitchen and rapped on His Excellency's bedchamber door, making the matchwood walls shake.

"Come in, confound you!"

"The weather glass is no longer falling. It might get better tomorrow, sir."

Phillip waited for his man to arrange the toilet things on the plank which served for a washstand, then climbed out of bed, rolled the sleeves of his nightshirt and adjusted the shaving mirror on its nail by the window frame. This daily ritual reminded him of the months when he had done exactly the same things at the Bower Anchor tavern, while assembling his fleet off Portsmouth.

Phillip studied the stranger who regarded him from the mirror. The past year and a half had not been kind to either of them. The swarthy, confident English gentleman who used to greet him every morning was now the Old Man to a thousand-odd castaways, an old man with a pleated face and frosty white hair. Only the eyes had not changed. They were still brown, still heavy-lidded, still shrewd.

Phillip smacked the razor up and down his leather strop while he looked out at the misty anchorage—the sum total of his life's work. The convoy was gone, now. HMS *Supply* was at Norfolk Island, unless she had sunk. Only *Sirius* remained, readying for the most uncertain, the most hazardous voyage in her long years of service.

John Hunter was going to catch a westerly wind across the Pacific; was going to try and double Cape Horn; was going to try and reach the Cape of Good Hope; was going to try and strike a bargain with the Dutch; was going to try and fill the cranky old frigate with fresh supplies; was going to try and complete a solo voyage around the globe before famine wrecked the colony.

Phillip looked into the mirror again, rubbed his wet shaving brush on a knob of yellow soap and tried to raise a feeble lather. The odds were against HMS *Sirius* ever being sighted again once she cleared Port Jackson. If Hunter returned to Sydney Cove he would be the second commander to circumnavigate the Antarctic. James Cook had been the first, ten or eleven years earlier, when he led two snug barques among the ice floes and polar gales. John Hunter would attempt it alone while Arthur Phillip was left alone to cope with theft, murder, mutiny.

There was a sudden scuffle outside the window. "Now what the hell's wrong!" Phillip flung open the catch and shoved his head into the raw morning air.

The corporal of the guard and two sentries were bashing some Indians who had slipped through the patrol line from Botany Bay. "Bugger off! Shoo!"

"*Djirabali! Garindji wingala nai!*" Graybeard shouted back.

"What appears to be the trouble, corporal?" Phillip demanded.

"*Baribun!*" Graybeard saw the chieftain of the other coven of white ghostmen whose sorcery had driven the fish and game from his people's mother.

The first magician had given him a hat trimmed with silver brocade, as a token of submission, before going back to the sunrise. Also a scarlet loincloth and a medal with "*Louis XVI Roi de France et de Navarre*" on one side, a laurel wreath and "*Les frégates du Roi de France, La Boussole et L'Astrolabe, commandées par M. de La Pérouse*" inscribed on the reverse.

The large bronze disk dangled on its ribbon around Graybeard's neck as he knocked away the English corporal's grip and stamped across the Government House potato patch to demand that these wizards be gone, as well. He slapped his shrunken belly, then pointed at one of the women, suckling a sickly infant. "*Danan mam dubajin birin!*"

Phillip squeezed his eyes shut: today was getting off to a very bad start.

For a moment he considered sending for Dawes or the chaplain to come and act as an interpreter, but sign language would save time by explaining what his tone of voice could not. "Be silent!" He tapped his own belly, then pointed at the redcoats before sweeping his hand to include the rest of the settlement. "I, have, nothing, more, to give! You have been given all the blankets and rations and presents I can spare! The needs of my—!"

"*Gunambu nanja nimbin!*"

"I said be silent!"

"*Djirabali—!* "

"Corporal!"

"Sah!"

"Disperse them! But don't go too near that child, it looks infectious."

Phillip withdrew his head and snapped the window shut. He ignored the screams. Experience had taught him that making gifts to the Indians was very much like throwing money at a crowd of beggars. He could have presented the old troublemaker with the keys to the storehouse and it would have made no difference; by this time tomorrow there would be another hundred hungry faces jabbering outside the window, and about one thousand empty bellies conspiring on the other side of Sydney Cove.

The governor of New South Wales had completed the inevitable descent from affability, through irritability, to hostility by the time he tugged on a warm coat and slammed the bedchamber door shut behind him. "Hell—!"

The prefabricated door frame fell out and just missed his head. The local termites, which normally took a century or so to demolish one of their native hardwood trees, had taken to and were taking apart the pinewood frame of Government House.

Phillip had very little appetite for work as he sat down at his table and wondered where to begin.

Jane Dundas carefully opened the other door as the judge advocate made his usual, punctual appearance. "Captain Collins, Your Excellency."

"Good morning, sir."

Phillip glanced up. "Why?"

"Oh, nothing in particular. Just a figure of speech."

The governor waited until their watery coffee had been served. "Begin again. Give me some good news. Make this a good morning."

"Actually, we don't have much."

"Try harder."

Collins looked up from his untasted cup. "Jack Shea's dead."

"Well, if that's the best you can offer, spare me the rest." Phillip put his cup aside for a moment. "You've alerted the orderly room?"

"They were expecting it. Full honors will be paid. After all, Captain Shea is—or was—the first gentleman to die in the colony."

"Someone had to start, I suppose." The governor hunched his shoulders. "Very well, signal to *Sirius*. Parade our bluejackets and fire a minute gun until the business is over. You can also ask Mr. Hunter to donate that coffin we use for a cupboard in the great cabin. It will be a token of our respect to a gallant redcoat."

"Thank you, sir."

Phillip said nothing: where John Hunter was bound there would be no need for a handsome, elmwood box if he died at his post. And it would be a bad omen for the coffin cupboard to be brought into Government House. "I'm sorry?" He looked up sharply. "What was that?"

"I said, there's a Mrs. Kathleen Shea and young daughter, back Home. We'll auction his things and deposit the money with his papers. I'm sure I speak for everyone in the mess when I extend, to you and our naval colleagues, a cordial invitation to be present. . . ."

"Thank you. We accept. Put me down for five guineas."

"Thank you, sir." Collins had the subscription list drawn up, His Excellency's name at the top, of course. Now he had to approach his own battalion commander and Ross would have to make an equal or better contribution from his own very shallow pocket. Shea's death had also bequeathed another delicate task. "There's the matter of his housekeeper. She'll have to come off B Company's rations and be put out of his quarters."

"Who'll get them?"

"Kellow. He's overdrawn his pay account by fifty guineas and stood guarantor for the balance in his capacity as the paymaster. . . ."

"Damn."

"What about the housekeeper, sir?"

Phillip made an irritable gesture. "I'm sure she's more than capable of fending for herself. Thus far I've seen no woman in the colony who's lacked for attention. I am dismayed, disgusted would be a more apt word, at the way in which several of our gentlemen—of both services, I'm not being partial or naming names—cohabit with their housekeepers. Openly. Doesn't anyone realize the deplorable standard it sets for the rest of the colony? Why, only yesterday I saw young Johnstone dandling a baby on his lap while his concubine took her ease! Nobody can persuade me that the Archangel Gabriel suddenly appeared at the foot of their bed one night, etcetera, etcetera!"

Collins owed a duty to at least explain a brother-marine's housekeeping arrangements. "Actually, sir, the child belongs to Mrs. Abrahams, not Lieutenant Johnstone."

"I don't care. It looks wrong. Now, do we have any other business to discharge?"

"Yes, quite a lot. I'll get—"

Phillip stood, stopping the other man from opening his bag. "It can wait. I'm going for a long walk and I do not wish to be disturbed, by anyone."

49

ROSS STOOPED lower, peeping through his window's shutter as Phillip sloshed past, hat brim pulled down, wet cloak swaying. The lieutenant governor straightened again and peered over his son's shoulder.

The eleven-year-old veteran had almost recovered from his first campaign. Sitting up in bed, he was writing with charcoal on one of the wooden boards which he scraped clean, then dipped in whitewash, every night, ready for the following day's schoolwork.

"Hn!" The elder Ross was not impressed with the English clergyman's curriculum of mathematics, grammar, logic, theology and Latin. Real schoolwork had been the iron-fisted regime of the Reverend Archibald McMurdo, dominie and tutor on the Earl of Bute's estate where only a handful of many crofters' sons earned a place on the school bench, either sitting along it or being stretched across it while the schoolmaster's leather taws flayed bums.

Ross took his aide's work and scanned it for error. Disappointed, he handed back the arithmetic exercises and stepped nearer the fire to kick some heat from a smoldering log. "You'd have had pencil and paper by now if we'd been Home, on general service." He gave the fire another kick. "Frog Indiamen being plucked like ripe plums off the Channel. Enough prize money to buy a mansion. Instead, what've we got? A croft such as the least of your grandfather's tenants wouldn't have housed a pig in. . . ."

Ross turned, lifting his coat tails to the dull crackle of heat. A sound roof, a hot fire and a grumble were among the few pleasures of life in New South Wales. "Now the best we can manage is to sell the Big Boghopper's commission, take our cut and give the rest away to his bloody widow woman." The battalion commander nodded at the desk where a stack of paper awaited his attention: topmost were Shea's pay receipts, less Kellow's off-reckonings for creditors in London and Dublin. "The fool hardly owned the breeches he stood up in, when he stood up, which was seldom enough. Even his buttons are pledged to the Jews. He must've thrown money round like a man with ten arms. They'll never say that about me, though!"

Ross jiggled the pieces of Indian gold ore which only left his pocket when there was no risk of anyone else seeing them. The biggest lump of quartz had become a talisman. Ross would bide his time with the present occupant of Government House until the roads dried out again and a full-scale campaign could be launched inland, under a new governor's command. Gold was there for the taking and the present lieutenant governor knew who would be taking it.

He glimpsed his housekeeper. "You!"

Nancy Fitzgerald poked her head around the open doorway which connected the scullery with the main body of the hut. "Yes?"

"Where's breakfast?"

"You et it last night."

"Then get over to the bloody stores and tell Nash to advance more on next month's ration!"

The pert young thing flounced into the weather.

"By God, boy, there are times when I'm astonished at my own moderation." Ross had stepped back to the fire and lowered his fist. " 'You ate it last night.' What the hell did she think we were going to do with a handful of birdseed and two small fishes? Feed the Five Thousand?"

His aide was used to these bitter monologues. There was no other member of the family with whom the lonely man could share his dreams of a brighter, better future. The convict girl knew how to coax a brief, warm release but only hard, cold gold would ever ease the heartache of jealous poverty.

The boy watched his father go over to the shutter again and squint into the weather to see how his breakfast was coming along. "Bloody hell. . . ." The Fitzgerald item had just passed Sparrow Legs and the devil driver, conspiring together in the shelter of the storehouse doorway.

Phillip twitched his collar and moved nearer the wall. "I'm sorry to lose Mr. Shea, padre. Although he was never in the most robust health, he was always upright and honorable in his dealings. I never heard him make a malicious remark about anyone or complain of his station in life:

a truly Christian attitude which many, better situated than he, could learn from. I suggest you take Two Corinthians, chapter eight, verses two and three as the text for today's business."

"Of course. If you insist," Johnson replied stiffly, always annoyed whenever others, with less learning, presumed to tell him how to run his affairs. "However, you've raised an issue of fundamental importance."

"I have?"

"Yes. Not to put too fine a point upon it, Mr. Shea is—or was— Irish," Johnson observed. "It is a well-known fact that many of that nation are openly Papist or secretly backsliders." The chaplain frowned with concentration. "Due to his infirmity I did not expect him to attend Sunday devotions and I was never disappointed. But, even when he was *in extremis*, I was never summoned to his bedside. Therefore, how can one say with any certainty that he should be buried with the blessings of the Church of England?"

Phillip had been leaning on his stick while the other man spoke. The naval commodore now drew himself erect. "Captain Shea fell on the field of honor. Had he died in the Colonies, or the Caribbean, or the East Indies, or at any of the thirty-eight major engagements where he faced the king's enemies, there would have been no caviling over doctrine. His personal relationship with God is a private matter: his public relationship with me was another. He will be despatched as befits a British officer and an Irish gentleman. Good day, sir."

The chaplain was left alone in the rain.

An iron gang clinked past with bundles of roofing shingles slung over their backs and chests, like a mule train, Corporal Asky strolling beside them with a long switch of spearwood, shouting the pace.

Johnson squelched the other way, along a sodden track which led to Point Maskelyne. There, at least, he might find congenial company. Not only had he been unjustly reprimanded for doing his duty, his wife kept blaming him as her belly swelled. He stooped inside the observatory but he was still out of luck: it was empty.

Cold, lonely, dispirited, the chaplain sat on one of the boxes of botanical specimens and opened Bishop Wheatcroft's *Grace Abounding* while he sought to compose a homily for this afternoon's funeral. He stroked the volume's calfskin binding. If he shut his eyes he could almost be inside his room at Magdalene, again. Before he married Mary. With a brisk fire in the hearth, and good books within reach, and a plentiful supply of candles—

Johnson brushed his cheeks and ignored the pencil marks which were young Ross's next dictation test. He turned forward to the flyleaf, instead, where his college tutor had penned an ode after learning that one of his students was to go as a missioner to the South Seas.

> *The Lord who sends thee hence will be thine aid,*
> *In vain that lion, Danger, roars.*
> *His arm and love shall keep thee undismay'd,*
> *On stormy seas and far off shores.*
>
> *Go! Bear the Savior's name to lands unknown,*
> *Tell the Southern World of His wondrous Grace,*
> *Energy divine thy words shall own,*
> *And draw untaught hearts to seek His face.*
>
> *Many in quest of gold and empty fame,*
> *Would encompass the globe or venture near the poles,*
> *But how much nobler thy reward and aim,*
> *To spread God's word and win immortal souls!*

Tears splashed the ink.

50

KITTY BRANDON followed her man's cortege up the Brickfield Road, slow-marching to the boom of minute guns and the thud of a side drum. She stood at the back, head bowed, while the chaplain spoke briefly and to the point. She came to attention as the firing party discharged its flat patter of shots over the grave. She remained behind when the battalion's kettle drummer rolled a brisk paradiddle and the troops tramped back to camp. She waited until the sappers had filled the hole, smacked the mound into shape and clanged a head board in place with a spade blade. And then she went home.

"Well, Jack, I hope the company's better wherever you now are," Kitty Brandon told the empty room as she laid a handful of dry bark on the hearthstone. She swung a kettle from its trivet, as twigs began crackling, and put out one of the teacups.

The water had barely started to bubble when she raised her face from the tabletop and quickly smoothed her hair: a detail of troops was halting outside. A sword pommel struck the door. "Open up!"

Kitty Brandon lifted the catch. Robert Kellow moved forward, a drawn sword under his cloak. "Yes . . . ?"

"I have orders to take the inventory of Captain Shea's effects!"

"May I see them?"

"What?"

"The orders."

"Out of my way!"

The marines stood guard while Kellow, an orderly room clerk and the duty corporal went indoors.

Kitty Brandon frowned. "Mr. Callow? A less charitable person than I might think you've been given verbal orders to be as deliberately offensive as only a military officer knows how."

Corporal Drury hid his grin behind a showy cough as the young officer aimed his gloved finger at the woman. "Get your things and get out!"

" '*Get out*'? Ah, now I understand why Major Ross had to despatch six men—seven if you could be included—to throw one widow lady onto the streets," Kitty Brandon observed, quietly. "He was afraid I'd throw you out, instead."

Kellow chose to ignore her insolence. He continued moving around the hovel, calling out the articles for tomorrow's auction. "Curling tongs, brass, old. Wig, gray, much the worse for wear. Breeches, flannel, two pairs of. Stockings, black cotton, three of—feh! Cups, tea, cracked, two of. Plate, eating, tin. Jar, tobacco, empty. Papers and journals, various." He directed the clerk to parcel them together with string for safekeeping at Government House, the colony's only archive and legal deposit.

"Stop—!"

"Surely you can't have changed your mind about ejecting me from my home?"

"Certainly not!"

"Then I may leave—"

"Come here!"

"Mr. Callow, kindly make up your mind. Either I go, or I stay, for not even I can do both at the same moment."

Drury hid another grin.

The convicted woman was allowed to keep her skirt, her bodice, her sewing kit and two hair ribbons. The rest was tossed in a heap on Shea's blanket.

"That candlestick was given to me, Mr. Callow."

"My name's Kellow!"

"Perhaps, perhaps," Kitty Brandon mused, rolling her things in a bit of rag, "though only your mother knew for certain."

The eviction of an officer's housekeeper was an event to enjoy. Corporal Asky stood with Nancy Fitzgerald as lags from the *Prince of Wales* capered around on all fours, yelping and coupling in a mock dog-fight to entertain the crowd. The pack turned, dashing at Shea's woman as she stepped into the raw afternoon.

"Sic the bitch! Go on, boys, sic 'er!" Asky laughed as Ross's housekeeper scooped up a fistful of muck: the crowd screeched for more as the bespattered woman stood in the doorway, proud and erect. One of the dog-men reared, ready to lick Kitty Brandon's face clean with a slobbering leer. She twisted at the hips and kicked away his knees, dumping and jumping him, heels first, a Dublin street fighter's "slap."

The pack scattered.

Levi was about to start a bowl of *krupik* with shreds of meat stirred into the boiled flour soup. His spoon stopped, halfway to his open mouth. "Lady? You look bad!"

"Not so bad as I feel." Kitty Brandon accepted the stool which Levi hurried to push her way. "May I shelter here for the night?"

"Why you need to ask?" He put the spoon in his bowl and pushed them her way, too. "Please. Eat."

She shook her head.

Levi rested his chin on both fists. "So why you not home?"

"Major Ross requires the hut for Captain Shea's successor. Lieutenant Kellow is a young man, anxious to prove his worth to those above him, which generally involves discomforting those below."

"Then you sleeping here." Levi gestured around the dispensary. "I get bed somewhere."

"No. Thank you. I need somewhere quiet. Where I shall not be disturbed."

"In the sick house you want to be alone and quiet?" Levi pulled a long face.

"I shall stay in the morgue."

"No!"

"Is it presently occupied?"

"No, but—!"

"Then there is no problem," Kitty Brandon concluded in the same flat voice. "What harm can the dead do that the living haven't already achieved? Enough. I have spoken. Tomorrow we shall talk but tonight I must be left alone."

Levi sighed. He gathered up his own bedding and followed her. She was right, the house of the dead was the least likely to be disturbed after dark. He followed her into the morgue and laid his things at her feet.

She nodded. "I thank you with all my heart. You are a friend."

The convict wardmaster bowed and left to search for a patient who no longer required a blanket and a bag of bracken. Kitty Brandon waited until the door swung shut on its leather hinges, then lit the slush lamp. She placed the tin pan of melting tallow at the head of the table and took out her sewing kit. She felt among the hanks of thread. Kellow had not found the military button she had been going to stitch on Shea's tunic.

Kitty Brandon tried polishing its dull brass with the hem of her skirt. It was so little to show for a life honorably led, bravely endured, fought to the end. His regimental colors had been paraded up the Brickfield Road, but it was here they were needed most. Now.

The woman hesitated, then undid the front of her dress. Cribb's pouch hung between her breasts. She slipped its leather thong over her head, tugged open the drawstring and smoothed the strip of scarlet silk. The Royal Marine button was displayed on that, crown and laurel uppermost. John Shea's wake could proceed with dignity.

Time passed.

The lamp's flame shook as squalls of rain swept across the camp, beating against the morgue's walls. It almost blew out as the door creaked open, then steadied again as it shut. Cribb stood in the shadows, chains muffled with sacking, a guard's cape around his shoulders.

"Get out." Kitty Brandon's eyes were wet and distant.

Cribb moved closer.

"Get out."

He set the physic glasses at the head of the dissecting table, then the alcohol, the laudanum and the last of Levi's ration hoard. "Abe says they eat and drink at these things in Po Land, like we do."

"Get out."

The man tilted two measures of spirit and presented one to her with surprising gentleness. He upturned a bucket and sat down where Shea's feet would have been. "We done it for my gran'. *Phuri dai* Romany she was."

"Get out. I wish to be alone."

"Well, you're not." He looked around the windowless shed with its hessian flyscreen, high under the roof. "You never left me in the lurch. You never run away from us, Over There. I'm sticking by you now."

"I want—"

Cribb pushed her glass nearer and raised his own. "Captain Jack, one of us. Not like that pimple squeezer, Yellow." He sipped his drink, letting its fire trickle down his throat. "Ted told me."

Kitty Brandon wiped her eyes. She drank and breathed out. "You are too polite. Kellow is dogshit. Ross is the dog. Nash tosses the bones. Give me another."

Cribb refilled her glass and shared out the bits of cheese on scraps of ration bread. "Eat up."

"I'm not hungry."

"Eat up. We've got to keep in fighting trim. There's a little job we got to finish. . . ."

She began to eat.

The mud around Cribb's eyes flaked as he smiled at her. "Just as soon as I'm out of the Pit I'll see it's done, special."

"Don't be so sure he's going to let you out," she replied, her voice empty except for hatred.

Cribb's smile died. "What you mean?"

"Why else do you think he keeps bringing you up to see you're being 'treated all right'?"

"Why . . . ?"

"Because, within the next three days, you are going to be taunted until you lash out at him—as you did once before—only this time it'll be Major Ross you strike. And there'll be no reprieve from the governor. So don't say you weren't warned." She hesitated, picking her words with care. "Don't raise your eyes to look at him, no matter the provocation, for there's a form of smile which brings out the devil in the less fortunate, and there's a tone of voice which is deadly.

"We only play at it in the theater. One has to be born to rule to have the knack of superior breeding such as our fine abductor of heiresses can assume. Which means that you must become less than the dirt you wallow in, Mr. Cribb. It will not be easy, for such as yourself, but hold fast no matter what he says or how he says it." She paused. "If you do, if you come out alive, we'll be ready. But it will be done my way."

"What?"

"You heard me. If Nash killed you, man to man, I'd accept the outcome. But I shall never allow a coward to murder by proxy. Meanwhile," Kitty Brandon touched the button on its piece of grubby red silk, "these will remain above my heart until the day I die, a reminder of two very proper men—"

"One."

"What?"

"One." Cribb's voice had the abrupt, flat crack of a sniper's shot. "If I'd bolted for Chinaland, you was coming. I know we've not always seen eye to eye, but you stuck by me when it looked like I was done for. That's what counts with a bloke." He'd crossed his fingers. "You and me. We're like this, now."

"Wait a moment." She smiled uncertainly. "Don't I have some say in the matter?"

"No." Cribb filled her glass to the brim and raised his own. "To us. Shoulder to shoulder. Back to back. Eye to eye . . . ?"

The woman hesitated while she considered all the available options at Sydney Cove. Then, quite deliberately, she raised her glass as well. "To us. Joe."

Cribb bundled the remains of their meal under his cape for the rest of the coves in the slave barracks. He stood. "Ted's waiting."

"Take care! Please."

51

"It's very decent of you to call, doctor. Something to keep out the damp?" Nash enquired.

"Why, thank you kindly." Balmain rested his bag on the stores counter and took the tumbler of *agoardente* braced with cinnamon, sugar and hot water.

"You know, I've always had boundless admiration for you gentlemen of the medical profession," Nash continued, making himself comfortable in the storeman's chair. "There have been times when I wished I'd followed the same exalted path instead of doing law. It seems to me that you manage to combine the deepest learning with the highest resolution: quite a paradox, is it not?" Nash sipped his negus. "What was that I once heard? A surgeon-physician must have 'the eye of an eagle, the heart of a lion, the touch of a lady'? Speaking of which, I see you've trapped a rare specimen recently! How's she taking to the harsh realities of a garrison hospital after living the life of luxury up in the officers' lines . . . ?"

"You speak of Mrs. Brandon?"

"Yes, I believe that's her present name," the assistant storeman and paymaster replied, "though around London she had a number of other aliases. However, I've no doubt she'll buckle down and do a good job, but be on your guard, her behavior can be erratic at times. Not that I'm saying anything personal against her, of course."

"Of course." Balmain finished his drink. "Speaking for myself I consider the colony to be fortunate to have acquired her services."

"Oh . . ."

"Yes. She and I first became acquainted, professionally, when Captain Sinclair took ill aboard the boat. In my opinion, had she not tended him as she did, he would have perished long before we reached Rio." Balmain put down the empty glass. "I need hardly add how impressed we were by the way she nursed Captain Shea through his last illness. Her attitude to duty, under the circumstances in which we now find ourselves, is worthy of the highest encomiums."

"I am relieved to hear you say it, doctor. Which is why I'm distressed to be told these stories from so many conflicting sources—"

Balmain shook his head. "As we say in the medical profession, *expositio que ex visceribus*, which means we must stick to the visible evidence, not just hearsay."

"A most excellent precept," Nash murmured. "However, never forget 'Ex paucis plurima concipit ingenium. . . .' "

"Er, that's in *Galen's Anatomy?*"

"No, Sir William Blackstone's *Commentaries on the Laws of England*," Nash replied. "Freely translated it means we may learn much from only a few hints."

Balmain reached for his hat. "Aye, well, good day, sir."

"Good day, doctor."

The storeman smiled as his guest went out into the foul weather, turned left and followed the track downhill to the creek which was now a muddy brown torrent spilling into Sydney Cove.

A work party of lags leaned against the current, up to their armpits, holding the rickety bridge while long poles were wedged against its struts.

Balmain shuffled along the planks above their shoulders and continued uphill toward Government House. He rapped on the door.

"His Excellency regrets that he is unable to receive visitors until further notice," the housekeeper announced, politely, firmly.

"That's what I've been informed, Mistress Dundas." Balmain tried squeezing past to stand in the dry. "Is he not feeling well?"

She remained politely firm. "I am not qualified to comment on His Excellency's state of health."

"But surely—?"

"He has informed me that, when he wishes to be bled, or cupped, or given a clyster, he will send for Mr. White, or Mr. Arndell, or Mr. Considen, or Mr. Bowes, or yourself. Good day, sir."

"Who the hell's that?" the governor shouted as Jane Dundas shut the door.

"Mr. Balmain this time, Your Excellency."

"Damned vultures."

Phillip had caught a chill at the funeral and awarded himself a few days in bed to recuperate. He was sitting up, now, red woolen nightcap askew, boat cloak draped around his shoulders for warmth while he finished some private correspondence. He coughed. "Do something about *that* wretched thing."

Jane Dundas knelt by the stove and tinkered with its damper to stop more smoke leading into the bedchamber. Phillip reached under his blankets and pulled up his nightshirt to polish his spectacles. The rain rattled against the window beside his head and more water dribbled down the limewashed sackcloth which hid the termite tracks from floor to ridge pole.

"More rain, less bricks, more chance we'll all be living in a barrel like whatsisname, Diogenes." The governor replaced his spectacles. "Kindly leave me to get on with my work before everything, literally and metaphorically, falls on top of my head."

"Yes, sir."

But Phillip's heart was not in anything this afternoon. It was costing him too much effort just to slow the inevitable collapse of morale in the settlement. The pickets had nowhere to dry off their greatcoats and leggings as they huddled inside bell tents and shanties, gambling their rations and rum at pitch and toss, bored and listless, waiting to go Home. Only the main public buildings and a handful of officers' huts were complete and even they would hardly survive this winter as green wooden planks warped, shrunk, cracked. Only increased effort in the quarry, and brick field, and lime kilns could stop Sydney Town from retreating into next summer like a defeated rabble.

"Oh, God. . . ." The governor trapped a wet snort and folded his soggy handkerchief.

It was almost the first anniversary of a warm summer's morning when he'd been entertained on the roof of another governor's mansion, in Teneriffe, celebrating His Majesty's royal birthday. Soon it would be another June 4 and the British monarch would be another year older, assuming he was still alive and of sound mind. Not that either had seemed likely when the last despatches from London had reached Phillip in Rio. George, prince of Wales, was now almost certainly on the throne and would have made a clean sweep of his father's administration to install his own political creatures.

A hostile committee of scrutiny would await Mr. Pitt's governor in New South Wales once he was recalled to account for the deposed prime minister's aborted Pacific empire. Phillip's annuity of five hundred pounds would be the first item struck from the Treasury accounts by Messrs. Fox, Burgoyne and Sheridan, he knew. Arthur Phillip also knew that he would be lucky if he were allowed to retire to a modest farmhouse to prepare his *Voyages,* assuming a publisher could obtain the necessary license to print them. Even then he would have to bear the cost of publication, of course, after passing a subscription list around his few remaining friends.

Phillip trapped another sneeze.

He hoped that the birds and animals and other freaks of this New Holland would arouse some curiosity, but not one person in ten thousand—unless he or she had grossly perverted tastes—would ever wish to read about Britain's transported menagerie. One specimen had recently taken his entire week's ration of flour and made sixteen flat griddle cakes. Minutes later, the still raw dough began fermenting in his gut. The convict died later the same night, a bloated and loathsome mess after a surgeon cut him open at the hospital.

And that had not been the only instance of swinish behavior among the work force. Instead of leaping at this second chance to cultivate the virtues of thrift, industry and sobriety, tempered by a cheerful and willing obedience to their betters, the great majority were loutish, idle, thieving, sly, stupid—!

"Captain Hunter, Your Excellency."

Sirius's commander walked through, his sea boots splashed with mud. "I trust I find you on the mend, sir?"

"So do I. Sit down."

Hunter dragged the packing case which served for a chair in the viceregal bedchamber, but which now held Shea's papers until they could be sorted for despatch to London, and moved closer to the stove. "Who'd ever have thought that New Holland, in winter, would be so much like Edinboro' in summer?" he smiled, kneading his fingers by the hot iron box.

The quip fell dead.

"Coffee, gentlemen?" Jane Dundas enquired from her place in the doorway.

Phillip made a gloomy nod.

"Please," Hunter added. "And if there were a tot of something in both cups I'm sure it would not go unappreciated. . . ."

She curtseyed and returned to the scullery.

Hunter transferred his smile to the gray man propped up in bed. He was looking at the squire of a displaced village where an average of two cottagers a day were wheelbarrowed up the Brickfield Road. Phillip could easily be the next to follow Shea. At which point the assumption of power, smoldering since Hunter and Ross confronted each other off Africa, would detonate.

Sirius's commander was a troubled man despite every effort to hide it. If Phillip died after the elderly frigate slipped her moorings for Capetown, the lieutenant governor would assume the full powers of a captain general. There would be no demoting Ross after *Sirius* returned from Africa. If she returned.

Hunter dropped another billet of wood through the stove lid and put down the poker. "I had a few words with young Tench earlier today."

"What the hell does he want now?"

"Nothing especial. He just feels we should know the troops are broody."

"When were they not?" Phillip replied. "I long ago came to the conclusion that Tommy Lobsterback is never so happy as when he's utterly miserable. I could serve them plum pudding on silver platters and they'd find something to pick fault with."

"That's not his opinion, nor mine," Hunter said, kicking off his boots and warming his toes, too. "We're primarily concerned with keeping the men in a reasonable state of readiness in case it's necessary to guard the powder magazine, the public stores and the artillery park before, let us say, Captains Campbell and Kellow get their marching orders. . . ."

"Oh."

Jane Dundas brought in her tray, set out the cups of coffee stiffened with rum, and retired again.

The governor waited until they were alone. "What's he suggest, John?"

"It's no suggestion," Hunter replied, wrapping his palms around the hot cup. "There's more than the usual hanky-panky with the troops' off-reckonings in the paymaster's office. They're being deducted for what Kellow's accounts describe as 'laundresses,' although the men are still doing it by hand, as it were."

"We're talking about the brothel?"

"What else?"

"Surely that's a simple enough thing to organize?" Phillip said, reaching for his own drink. "There's never any of this fuss at Portsmouth Point when the fleet's in."

"Sinful Cove is not Portsmouth."

"Really?"

"And there's another matter which Tench has brought to my attention," Hunter went on, ignoring the governor's sarcasm. "Rumors and gossip are hopping around like fleas. It's his opinion that trouble is brewing, somewhere. I've sensed it myself. So have our own bluejacket officers. Whatever's behind it, the women certainly aren't behaving as one would expect—"

"And how, pray, does one expect a woman to behave?"

"Damned if I know," Hunter shrugged. "I could never afford to get wed while there was a chance, so they're all a bit of an enigma to me, but I'd have thought they'd be only too grateful to move in with the troops for protection—"

"Surely they have?"

"Only some. It seems there are a lot of unofficial liaisons among the convict class. And those who remain unattached appear as if they're being manipulated by someone."

"*Manipulated?*"

"Blessed if I know what the proper word is, but that's Tench's opinion when every one of the free whores charges his men the same elevated price for her services. And if the troops offer even fractionally less, it's refused, point blank. Take it or leave it. They're behaving like a ring of dockyard contractors, bidding for government supplies," Hunter explained, trying to give this problem a man's depth and understanding.

"That's ridiculous! Why, in Portsmouth, I'm told it's each doxie for herself and the devil take the hindmost!"

"This is not Portsmouth. . . ."

"Rubbish! Tench must be imagining things!"

"That's his hope, too," Hunter replied. "Because, unless there's a change for the better, and soon, his men are going to take the law into their own hands—"

"I thought they already had?" Phillip observed tartly.

"Taking by force that which they can't obtain by barter," Hunter concluded, "in which case we'll have mutiny among the guards and a general insurrection among the rest."

"Oh."

"Speaking personally," Hunter went on, "it's high time we did something to jog them along, to get their minds onto something more constructive. For example, it'll soon be His Majesty's birthday, the first week of next month, which would be an excellent excuse for a general celebration."

"Something like a dinner for the staff? Bonfires? Music?"

"Why not?" Hunter replied. "It'd have a tonic effect all round."

"Why not indeed?" Phillip agreed. "I wonder if Tench would be interested? He's a bit that way inclined."

"I think he might be, if you asked."

"Very well, I'll have a word with him. And thank you for bringing that other business to my notice. I'll give it serious thought: we can't have convicted harlots setting the pace, as it were. Do let me know what else you hear, John. On this side of the cove one is rather isolated from the mainstream of events."

"I most certainly shall." Hunter had pulled on his boots and was standing again. "Now, if you'll excuse me, I have to be aboard before dark."

Phillip watched the burly, dependable man go, then reached for his pencil. But evening was drawing in. It was getting hard to see the paper. He summoned his housekeeper. "A light, please."

"Certainly, sir. And would you like dinner now or later?"

Phillip considered the offer. "What is it?"

"Braised pigeon in pickled cabbage, with white onion sauce and dumplings stuffed with fried beans. I've also soaked some apple rings with raisins to make a pie, if that's to your liking . . . ?"

It most certainly was. Bryant had served the same uninspired rations day after week after month. Since his promotion to outdoor duties the cuisine inside Government House had improved beyond measure.

"Now, please."

The governor congratulated himself as the woman went back to her duties. He had chosen well. Her service with a titled family was evident in everything she undertook. Dundas was quiet, attentive, honest and discreet—essential virtues in a personal servant who might otherwise spread slander. Phillip was confident that she was not the source of a recent outbreak of malicious rumors. Utter nonsense, of course, but the more outrageous the lie the more people wished to believe it!

But his housekeeper would never stoop to gossip about her employer behind his back. She was not the type. That was probably why she had fallen foul of the law in the first place. The muster list said that she had been convicted for forgery, but Arthur Phillip knew something about life behind the park gates of those five-thousand-acre domains.

It would have been impossible for an attractive woman to serve in such a household and not run foul of internal politics: just like Sydney Cove. It was easy to imagine the trail of misfortunes which had led her so far from Home. Almost certainly it had begun when she refused to consort with a son of the family: such things happened all the time in those big houses. There must have been one almighty struggle over the bed before she escaped with her virtue intact—

The governor recovered his composure as his housekeeper brought dinner on a trap. She stretched above him and hung the lantern over the bed. "There. I trust that's to your satisfaction, sir."

"If you made it, I'm sure it will be." Phillip spread a clean napkin across his lap and lifted the piecrust to peek underneath. "Delicious!" He glanced up. "Jane, is it not . . . ?"

"Er, yes, sir."

"Your speech is not that of a Londoner. Tell me, where did you come from?"

She hesitated. Then, quietly, sadly, "I was born and raised in Bristol though my father was from Ulster."

"And you entered service with which family?"

"The Reverend Doctor Willoughby's, of Bath, with whom I remained upwards of five years before his youngest daughter married well and I accompanied her to London."

Phillip forked the dinner and wiped his lips with the napkin. "So how did you come to be transported?"

"I—I'd rather not say, sir."

"Why?"

She remained silent.

"Why . . . ?"

Jane Dundas took a deep breath. "After the war there was little call for the books and charts which my father printed for the sea trade. We fell upon hard times. Although my mother had once been a seamstress to the Quality she was now unable to help as her eyes had grown dim."

"Go on. . . ."

She shrugged helplessly, the first time Phillip could recall glimpsing a personal emotion behind the trained exterior of his servant. "I—I had often helped my father do copies and letters during the course of his work. It was not difficult to make what they call a draft, upon my mistress's bank, instructing it to send seventy pounds to Bristol." She looked down at the floor. "I was foolish."

Phillip could only marvel at the commonplace decency of such commonplace folk. This woman had risked the gallows to help her family. Justice had been swiftly done, of course, but her crime had been prompted by the highest motives.

"Thank you for being so frank," the governor replied. "If only others in our colony were so forthcoming, it would vastly ease my load."

Phillip hesitated, then put his dinner aside, barely touched. "There are some who envy me this lonely eminence, but if only they knew what a burden it is, to be forever called 'His Excellency.' If only they knew how often it feels as if I've taken vows of poverty, chastity and obedience to become His Majesty's viceroy."

The governor looked back at the woman as draughts swept the bed-chamber and the lantern swayed on its hook. "There are many nights when I would gladly surrender all the honor, all the power, all the glory just to have someone who would listen, without criticizing, without complaining, while I spoke of the day's events. . . ."

Jane Dundas returned a diffident smile. "Please don't sound that way, sir. There's a lot of us, out there, who bless the day we were put in your charge. Because we know you're not like those other gentlemen. Right from the very start we could see you would be kind to us. And fair—"

Phillip was groping for his handkerchief again: this damned cold had weakened him more than he realized. His eyes were blurring. "Go."

The alarmed housekeeper stepped closer. "What is it, sir?"

"Go!"

"My poor, dear master!"

Sleet rattled the window pane.

Wind beat against the walls.

The stove glowed.

52

BRYANT'S BACK ached and there were blisters on his palms. Swearing, he shouldered the hoe and limped away from Phillip's personal garden. A wintry sun broke through, there were patches of sky between the scudding clouds, but the former butler at Government House was in no humor to notice or care about an improvement in the weather as he joined a line of idlers waiting outside the storehouse.

Nash looked up from his ledger. "Why, what are you doing there, Mr. Bryant?"

The gardener's back straightened and he went straight to the head. "This thing's got to be the wrong size." He propped the hoe against the counter. "It's too 'eavy."

"Mm, I do see what you mean," Nash agreed. "Definitely the wrong size." He turned. "Take over for a moment, Miller."

"Right-o!"

"This way, Mr. Bryant. Mind the step." Nash led the way between tiers of ration casks and boxes of equipment to some racks of tools which stood among coils of rope and tubs of tallow, replacement wheelbarrow spokes, leather bags of seed, rolls of cabbage netting and bundles of candles. "Oh, dear, we're out of the smaller size. Look, try this one, I'm sure it will fit you once the handle is trimmed here, and the blacksmith narrows the blade—here."

Bryant felt much better as he swapped one iron hoe for an identical iron hoe. "Thank you, sir. You're a gent."

"On the contrary, thank you. I am merely doing my duty. You have a problem and it's my pleasure to help you solve it. Just as you do for His Excellency, the man we all so admire and respect—" Nash stopped short. "We do respect and admire him, don't we?"

"I s'pose."

"Heavens. What's the matter, Mr. Bryant?"

"It's that bleedin' woman!"

"Oh," Nash sighed. "Would you like to get it off your chest?"

Bryant would. Bryant did. And what Bryant didn't know his imagination supplied.

"This is terrible!" Nash agreed as the manservant panted to a halt. "Who would ever have thought it of His Excellency! But your secret is quite safe. I'm astonished. I simply don't know what to say except that you must go back to work and behave as if nothing's happened," the assistant storeman and paymaster went on, still shaking his head with utter disbelief. "In the meantime, if you ever wish to unburden yourself to anyone, don't hesitate to come here."

"Thank you, sir!"

"It's the very least I can do for a man who's been so badly treated. Come. Mind the step. And on your way, collar young Ben Thorpe, please. He's out on One Tree Field, I think. Tell him to see me immediately."

"Aye aye, sir."

Nash patted Bryant's shoulder at the door, then took over from Miller at the desk. He was still dealing with the day's tally of grumbles and complaints when Thorpe plodded up the track. "Come in, Ben!"

Miller resumed his place on the high stool as Nash led Phillip's gaffer back to the quiet area. "I am pleased with your progress: the sugar ration will be raised to four ounces, next week."

"Thank you, master!"

"However, I require an additional service," Nash went on in the same voice. "You remember what I told you about Cribb? Well, despite everything, they're turning him loose this morning. Let's hope he's learned his lesson but one can never be too sure with that sort. They're not always responsible for their actions: they get easily excited. I need someone steady, someone like yourself, to keep a close eye on him. Get him a place in your work gang and let me know how he behaves."

"Ur, right, master."

"Now," Nash continued, "I notice that you are still living apart from that Levi individual."

"Ar."

"A pity. I want a close eye kept on him, as well. You are to let bygones be bygones. Understand? Go through the motions of befriending him again. And tell me what his movements are."

"Um, well, I can try—for another ounce?"

"Tobacco or sugar? You can't expect both."

"Sugar!"

"Good man." Nash laid a hand across Thorpe's shoulder and led him to the door, then reached for his hat on a nail behind the desk. "I'm going over to B-Company, Miller. I shan't be back before lunch."

"Right-o, sir."

Nash whistled a sprightly tune as he strolled through the moments of crisp sunshine. It was a strange land where a winter's day could be more welcome than one in summer: where, true to the contrary nature of things, a profusion of flowers bloomed on the remaining trees and shrubs, where an abundance of parrots flashed across the settlement from forest to forest, screeching and chattering.

"Good morning, Kellow, this must be what they mean by the expression, 'the air was like champagne.' " Nash accepted the stool and sat down. "Not that I can remember popping a bottle at White's or the Pineapple Tree which made me feel quite so stimulated. I'm sure there'll be days in foggy London when I may even look back on Sydney Town with just a *soupçon* of nostalgia. . . ." He was looking round the hut's interior. "Settling in all right?"

"Yes, thank you," the other young man replied. "Anything had to be an improvement on that tent."

"Agreed, but I still think a lick of paint is what we need in here. And we'll change those dismal curtains: they look as if someone cobbled them from old breeches. I'll have the necessary stuff sent over this afternoon."

"Thank you kindly—"

"Not at all. Speaking of improved style," Nash went on, "your mess steward was over to replenish the liquor cupboard. He had to show me the account book and I couldn't help noticing that celebrating your promotion had added a tidy sum to an already extended bill: I do hope you're not sailing too close to the wind?"

The battalion's paymaster smiled as he shook his head. "The troops are booked to get their winter kit soon, on paper at least."

"Ah, that's all right then." Nash was relieved.

"Besides, M'Lord Pitsligo is a kinsman," Kellow added, watching the English gentleman's response to that.

Nash was suitably impressed. "Then we've no worries about payment: I'm so delighted. Actually, although poor old Balmain hails from the same part of the globe, he has nothing like your fortune or connection or else he wouldn't be in his present pickle. Have you noticed with whom he's 'connected' now . . . ?"

"No. Who?"

"Shea's relict, no less!"

"Good Lord! Really?"

"Yes. Can you imagine? La Belle Brandon dancing the blanket horn-pipe with him!" Nash chuckled. "Of course, he can only afford to enjoy the Webster woman once a week so it makes a kind of sense to go where he can, when he can. It's all supposed to be very chaste and professional, but he was setting his cap at her aboard the boat, coming out. I'm reliably informed there was very nearly bloodshed between him and the captain, whatsisname, Sinclair. The fair Brandon was egging them both to further her ambitions because she can be *very* devious. . . ."

Kellow was nodding. Fresh news was always welcome in the mess after dinner had been cleared, the cards cut, the corks drawn and the first bottles sent round the table.

"He's playing with fire," Nash continued, "rather like His Excellency, but that's another matter. You knew, of course, that Balmain's light o' love murdered one of the Hardwicke boys in a fit of pique? Same thing, pure jealousy—"

"No!"

"Split his head open, from crown to chin, with a butcher's cleaver. Terrible scandal, you must've heard? I'd have hanged her there and then but, as they say, the devil looks after his own. Or, as we prefer to say in the law, *qui semel est malus semper presumitur esse malus in eodem genere*: 'Once a criminal, always a criminal in the same way.' " Nash shrugged. "Frankly, I wouldn't be in—or out of—Balmain's breeches for a thousand guineas a night. Sooner or later he's going to rouse the Old Adam, or Mother Eve, within the breast of his charming bedmate and awaken with his throat cut."

"Good God!"

"I'm sorry, but I thought you knew? I'd say it's bound to happen, sooner or later. I mean, take the case of poor old Shea," Nash said, getting ready to stand and leave. "Did he fall? Or was he pushed? We'll never know for certain. But one thing which can be proved beyond any shadow of doubt is the amount of time our Mrs. Deadly Nightshade spent at the hospital dispensary, toward the end. And who should happen to be lurking there whenever she was present but Shylock, dispensing his strange mixtures to help Shea sleep. . . ."

"One moment! Sit down, please. How do you mean?"

Nash reluctantly obeyed. "Look, Kellow, this is in the strictest confidence. For your personal protection, that's all. Not a word of this must leak out or else I'm going to wake with *my* throat slit by that Cribb animal: he's as thick as thieves with the other two murderers—"

"Of course, of course, but what's this you're saying about Jack Shea?" Kellow interrupted, leaning forward.

Nash spread his hands. "You be the jury. You consider the facts. Draw your own conclusions—"

"Yes."

"Captain Shea's health was improving steadily until Brandon inveigled her way into his housekeeping. Brandon starts to procure sleeping draughts from Hemlock—who, incidentally, was sent out for administering potions to young damsels in distress—and Captain Shea's health takes a sudden turn for the worse. I, meanwhile, was doing everything in my power to tell Balmain what was happening right under his very nose but, strangely, he did nothing. Eventually Captain Shea dies, our sawbones inherits his housekeeper, and they are now living happily ever after—he believes."

"Good God, that sort of thing happens *here?*"

"My dear friend, the world at large is not composed of honorable military gentlemen." Nash stood again. "As our chaplain would say— and Heaven knows he must be an authority on the subject with such a virago sharing his bed—'All wickedness is but little to the wickedness of a woman.' " He looked around the hut. "If these walls could only speak, what a tale they would have to tell. . . ."

"Indeed!"

"Still, at least you're on your guard, that's all that matters. Just be careful the Brandon bitch doesn't try smarming any more of your colleagues. Meanwhile, when I send that stuff over I'll include a padlock for this door—"

"Please do!"

Nash left Shea's old quarters in even better spirits than he had stepped inside. This was indeed a most stimulating day and it would not be over until the last candle was huffed out in the officers' mess and Kellow had been carried home to bed by his batman.

53

" 'I LAY DOWN on the grass, which was very short and soft, where I slept sounder than ever I remember to have done in my life, and, as I reckoned, about nine hours,' " Jane Dundas read aloud, turning the next page of *Gulliver's Travels*. " 'When I awakened, it was just day-light. I attempted to rise, but was not able to stir: for as I happened to lie on my back, I found my arms and legs were strongly fastened on each side to the ground; and my hair, which was long and thick, tied down in the same manner.' "

"Sounds more like Sinful Cove than Lilliput," Phillip commented, also sitting up in bed, both eyes shut, happy to be resting them after a day's work. "Go on, please."

" 'I likewise felt several slender ligatures across my body, from my arm-pits to my thighs. I could only look upwards, the sun began to grow hot, and the light offended my eyes. I heard a confused noise. . . . In a little time, I felt something alive moving on my left leg—' "

"Ross."

Jane Dundas smothered her giggle and tried concentrating on the story. " 'Which advancing gently forward over my breast—' "

"Declared, 'Bloody hell, what do we have here?' "

"Stop it," she laughed. "I want to see what happens next!"

"Sorry."

"You're not."

"Word of honor . . . ?"

She composed her face and tried to be serious. " 'Moving up my left leg . . . came almost to my chin; when bending my eyes downwards as much as I could, I perceived it to be a human creature not six inches high—' "

"I told you so!" Phillip grinned, glancing at his companion. "Young Billy Rose was right. He said I'd find the book useful in the Antipodes, when he presented it to me, just before I left Home. Every single word has been true thus far. We've hardly begun and there's already been a famine, disease, drunkenness, a shipwreck and now the plotting of lesser mortals. I dread to think what's going to happen next!"

"I'm going to put out the light, that's what's going to happen next," Jane Dundas announced firmly, marking the page with a slip of paper before placing the book on the packing case near the fire.

"Just another chapter, please?"

"If I read now, you won't have any tomorrow night—"

"Why?"

"Because we've only two inches of candle to see us through to the end of the week," the housekeeper replied, opening the lantern to snuff and trim the wick.

"You've been to the stores?"

"Mm."

"And?"

"There's a shortage of candles."

"Shortage? Why . . . ?"

Jane Dundas had rolled to face the wall. "It's the rats. Mr. Nash says they've eaten several dozen and we'll have to pull our belts in."

"He knew who you were?"

"I—I think so. Not that I've ever asked for special allowances whenever I've collected our rations, just as you instructed me to."

"Hm." The governor was also easing under the blankets, facing the other way to enjoy the stove's soft glow. "Rats, eh?"

Jane Dundas said nothing.

Arthur Phillip said nothing. His stormy marriage with 'Lotte had taught him to be content with very little from a woman. Now, in his fiftieth year, he felt as if he had crossed a wild mountain torrent and gained the other side reasonably unharmed. Nowadays he could either rest in the shade of the rocks and watch others get tossed around by the fury of their passions, or he could gently amuse himself in the shallows.

The choice was his, now. And Jane Dundas was his choice. She had become a comfortable, undemanding warmth beside him through the long hours of the night. She was the plain, unadorned reading voice with its pleasant, West Country burr. She was a hint of lavender water on clean bed linen. She was discreet, she was dependable, she was Jane.

Phillip stifled a yawn. His eyelids drooped.

54

A LANTERN glowed in the morgue where Levi had brought the drink, Thorpe had smuggled a pocketful of boiled potatoes, and Kitty Brandon had brought the remains of His Excellency's evening meal.

She raised her glass. "Welcome back, Joe."

All drank to that and sat down at the dissecting table to celebrate his return from the living dead. Cribb ate little and slowly, the way he had survived previous prison camps. Kitty Brandon's eyes twinkled at the guest of honor. "Eat up. 'We've got to keep in fighting trim. There's a little job we got to finish. . . .' "

She folded her hands and looked around at the other members of her innermost family. "Which brings me to the second reason for this evening's convivial gathering. We're neck and neck with Nash. His neck or ours. It's time he went."

None of the three men contradicted her. They had learned to listen whenever she spoke in that tone of voice. Her face was impassive. "I often discussed Captain Shea's journals while he was alive, especially those entries which referred to Nash, and Captain Mason, and certain matters of consequence aboard the *Prince*. Without exception they revealed that our rival has one defect—"

"He's still breathing."

"For a short while longer, Mr. Levi," she agreed. "However, first I propose to step backward in imagination and consider the object of our concern, an object which the world at large either fears or fawns upon." Kitty Brandon could have been a judge summing up before passing sentence.

"Nash is witty, he is well connected and, when required, he can be quite charming company. In other words, he combines low cunning with high intelligence. However, despite those several advantages, he cannot overcome one fatal flaw—his own fear. Now, I can't say I altogether blame him: it cannot be easy playing the fine gentleman before an audience of men who are anything but gentle and women who, in spite of my best endeavors, are rarely ladies."

She raised a finger, silencing Cribb. "Nash confessed as much to me when first we landed and he had to leave his sanctuary aboard *Prince of Wales* to cope with this new, if temporary, home. 'Black lice' he called us. An apt description. Some of our fellow adventurers do give one reason to need friends, or else why are we four together again? But to continue. Nash is a coward surrounded by those he knows are his natural enemies. As such he is eaten hollow by fear, but not fear of what's happening to him—which is nothing but good, at present—but fear of what might happen the moment he stops telling lies.

"A proper man, a man of mettle, advances to meet his enemies, knowing that all owe a debt to nature which must be repaid. But a coward is haunted by specters of a hundred deaths." Kitty Brandon shrugged. "As Captain Shea remarked *apropos* certain things, he often noticed the same worrisome trait in young officers before their first engagement.

Most lived to master their fear, at least in public, once the guns began to speak, but our Charley has never been put to the test—"

Cribb scraped mud from his face. "Look, no 'ard feelings, but let's stow the gab and stiff the sod. Right?"

Levi brushed aside that unhelpful remark. He leaned into the lantern's glow. "Lady. You telling something. What?"

She nodded. "I'm saying that Nash is now too well entrenched behind lines of falsifications. I'm saying that, while he remains surrounded by an admiring clique of the garrison's officers, we have no chance of beating him, because he is expert at molding bullets for others to fire. And yet, despite all, I believe I can see a spark of hope in the gathering darkness—"

"Let's just get on with it!"

Kitty Brandon ignored Cribb's muttered interruption. "I believe there is hope because all cowards need to be forever puffing themselves up with lies. Ours is no exception. He needs to play center stage, preening his feathers in the cracked mirror of public regard. Moreover, he never knows when to leave well alone, or else why does he covet the handful of girls we care for?"

"Look—!"

Kitty Brandon looked and Cribb fell silent again. "God knows there are enough of his breed in the profession," she continued. "There's not a troupe of jugglers which doesn't have its own Charley Nash greasing the balls so that he can whisper what a shame it is that poor old so-and-so's lost his touch." She shrugged. "Eventually they get themselves so tied in knots, twisting tails and telling tales, they don't know if they're Arthur, Martha or neither."

"So what we going to do?" Levi murmured.

She smiled back. "Applaud his efforts."

"Ur?"

"What?"

"You heard." Kitty Brandon was about to pass judgment. "Nash must be given every chance to play the lead and befog the truth until it is time to cue him off. Because, in my experience of these matters, those persons who matter most stay mostly out of sight. We are the distant voice which directs our playhouse kings to make their entries, to strut their tiny parts in tinsel crowns, and then to exit at the appropriate moment."

"But 'ow?" Thorpe was plainly worried.

"With a bloody pickaxe, that's 'ow!"

Levi shook his head. "Won't do, Joe."

Kitty Brandon cocked an eyebrow. "And why do you say that, Mr. Levi?"

The dark, Levantine profile was looking at Cribb, instead. "Why you think Nash all the time trying to hang you?"

"To croak me, what else?"

"Horse zhit. Anytime he want he can snap his fingers and get you stiffed like you done Ratbag." Levi snapped his own fingers under the other man's startled nose. "But what good's that? Like the lady say, he is always needing to be big with the mouth so he can shout, 'Look at me, world! See what a *macher* I am! Jump when I tell or I kill you like I kill that flea Fozzy Kripp!' "

" 'Ere—!"

"So, like you, he is full of horse zhit," Levi concluded. "*Nu*, to be a real *macher*, you got to be different to regular coves. Is not enough to bash a head with the shovel and blame the black men, because that frights nobody. So, next time I help croak a bloke, every other bugger is going to take off the hat to *me* and say, 'Yes, your honor!' when I look at him, or else all this is fart talk."

Levi looked around at his listeners. "So I was wrong, this is not New Jerusalem? Too bad. But one thing I learn bloody quick and you'd better learn, too, this is new land where all—cove and gent—are the same dirty and hungry together. Will not be for long. No matter. By then I am eating good. Because there is one thing more than money. There is one thing more than women. There is even more than grub, and that's respect. Because, when a cove's got respect, he's got all the grub. And all the morts. And all the money . . ."

Kitty Brandon broke the short silence. "Thank you. I could not have described our condition more clearly myself."

"Ar, it's easy enough for all you clever buggers to talk like that!" Thorpe banged his fist on the table. "You can drive a 'orse to water, but 'er got to want to drink, first!"

"Correct." Kitty Brandon made a brief smile. "Therefore, we shall encourage Nash to do something entirely in character, something which has always worked for him in the past, but which this time has an unexpected outcome, rather like stepping on a floorboard only to find himself in the cellar—or world—below."

55

"ABOVE ALL, this will be a happy occasion, Mr. Tench," Phillip went on. "Their morale is terrible. Their attitude to themselves and their surroundings is abominable. Indeed, I have just been informed about an unofficial unit of labor called 'the government stroke' which appears to be the merest fraction this side of total immobility. However, we shall persist in our endeavors. I am resolved that His Majesty's birthday will be marked by the open hand of generosity on our part and a renewed sense of purpose upon theirs."

"Really, sir?"

Phillip nodded. "I've reprieved those two wretches condemned this morning: they can be marooned on the rock for a month."

"Pinchgut?"

"Is that what they're calling it?"

"I believe so."

"Splendid, the lesson is being learned." The governor stood. "You have complete freedom of action, Mr. Tench. Rope in whoever you need, draw on the necessary stores. I am counting on you to transmute our human dross into a more worthwhile substance. Offer them the carrot or apply the stick, whichever gets results."

Tench smiled. "May I borrow that phrase, sir?"

"Of course." Phillip stepped round the table and reached for his walking cane. "Speaking of which, I'd like to have a chat about publishers, when you can spare me a few moments. I understand you sent off your book aboard *Charlotte* . . . ?"

"Yes."

"Splendid news. I do wish you the very best of luck with it." The governor reached for his hat, as well. "You'll let me have the subscription list when it's circulated? I'm sure George Rose will be eager to get two or three copies. Perhaps more."

"Why, thank you, sir!"

"My pleasure." Phillip turned in the porchway, acknowledged the other man's salute, then turned left and went to inspect progress at Government Farm—a crazy quilt of gardens enclosed by hurdles which failed to keep out hungry lags, stray sheep, rootling pigs, bounding kangaroos, creeping caterpillars, slugs, thrips, snails, slimy mildew and black blight.

Tench strode the other way, across the stream and into the main settlement. An experienced regimental officer, he knew that his next duty was to delegate authority and the work. But to whom? It was easy enough to mobilize a platoon and dig a sap or raise an abatis: it was something else to confect a joyful occasion with threats of the lash. What was needed most was someone who could be handed the broad picture and left to fill in the details. Ideally a person with a proven ability to orchestrate concerts, and assemblies, and plays.

Tench quickened his pace toward the hospital, returned the sentry's salute and ducked into the main ward of the men's wing. "Good morning, ma'am."

Kitty Brandon straightened, flicking hair from her eyes. "Good morning, Mr. Tench."

The captain of marines counted the changes since his last inspection of the garrison sick quarters. The ill, wounded and dying now lay on stretchers of old sacks, lifted off the bare earth on wooden poles cut from the surrounding bushland. Thick whitewash had been daubed along the split timber walls to reflect some light into this dismal shed. A rope hung under the rafters, airing relays of blankets and bed clothing. Most of the patients were cleanly shaven and it was even possible to breathe indoors, Tench realized.

He inclined his head. "I fear that my request will seem rather frivolous, ma'am. I doubt you can be spared from these duties."

"Spared? For what?"

Tench folded both hands around his sword hilt. "It's His Excellency's wish that the royal birthday be marked by an assembly: he hopes it will do something to revive our spirits before the rigors of winter depress them further. He's honored me with a request that I produce a suitable entertainment. Now, our talent is rather limited, but I feel we ought to be able to do somewhat more than link hands around a bonfire. . . ."

"I should hope so," she smiled back. "And what is it you have in mind?"

"I'm not altogether decided," Tench replied. "I'll have a word with the bandmaster, that should be good for a few rousing tunes. I also know that some of our chaps have reasonable voices. And, no doubt, we could put on two or three skits. However, we ought to try and involve everyone, not just the military. Indeed, I was wondering if you knew of anyone who could drum up a little enthusiasm from the Great Unknown . . . ?"

"You mean from among us convicted burglars, cutthroats, drabs, stranglers, footpads, graverobbers, etcetera?"

"I'm sorry."

"Why should you be? I've never apologized for any action which brought me hence." She patted his wrist. "Come, if we are to be co-directors of the most sumptuous spectacle in the brief, inglorious history of New South Wales, we must agree to call a lag a lag and not, alack!, a lackey. . . ."

He was laughing with her. "I am ever your humble servant, ma'am. It is my good fortune to have been asked to arrange this celebration. Is it not truly said that, 'Against ill chance men are ever merry'?"

"I believe that to be true," she agreed. "However, captain, it is my ill chance to've been somewhat restricted by orders from Major Ross, so there's devil a chance of anyone being merry if I can't leave this hospital to busy myself elsewhere." Kitty Brandon paused. "How do you suggest we overcome the problem . . . ?"

"I shall speak directly with His Excellency: I'm sure he'll sign a general pass."

"Then we've a partnership," she replied. "You obtain the necessary paper and leave the rest to me."

Tench bowed and left with a spring in his step, as did Kitty Brandon once she had the governor's *laissez passer*. She produced it for the sentry guarding the bridge, and for the corporal at Government House. "I've been sent with some medicine for His Excellency," she explained, holding up a bottle of water.

The redcoat grunted and let her proceed to the kitchen area.

"Good morning, Jane. May I ask you for a considerable favor?"

"Of course." The housekeeper wiped floury hands on her apron.

Kitty Brandon stood much closer and explained herself. Jane Dundas thought hard, then nodded.

"Good. And how is His Excellency keeping . . . ?"

"Much recovered."

The younger woman smiled as well. "I've often observed that, when all else fails, there remains one potent remedy which will arouse a man unless he's already a corpse, and even then I wouldn't bet on it until the coffin's been nailed shut. Anyhow, I am delighted to see that our patient is responding to treatment."

They both smothered their laughs.

Nash was not laughing when Corporal Asky reported that Bitch Brandon had been awarded a pass to go where she pleased, and that she had promptly used it to visit her deputy at Government House. "Damn! How did she get one?"

"Dunno, sir! But it looked all right to me!"

Nash controlled his unease. "What did they talk about?"

The marine fingered his scruffy chin. "They was whispering, like, but I did 'ear something about corpses, and coffins, and 'Is Excellency getting the treatment, then she give 'er the bottle—"

"Enough!" Nash clicked fingers. "Miller? I have to go over to B Company on urgent business."

"Right-o, sir."

The assistant storeman and paymaster did not return to his duties till after lunch. He had hardly settled down to faking the month's flour consumption when Thorpe came in from the fields. "Yes? What do you want?"

"Um. That corn seed, master. You got 'er ready yet?"

"Yes. Come inside. Mind the step." He led the way to the back of the stores. "I trust we can look forward to a bumper harvest next year: there'll be considerable belt-tightening unless your men start pulling their weight: don't let them slack. His Excellency is known to be angry."

"Y-yes, master."

"What's the matter?" Nash scowled. "You're not your usual self, today."

Thorpe's lip trembled. "I don't know what to do! They're all on at m-me!"

"Oh. Who's troubling you, Ben?"

Thorpe wiped his nose along both wrists. "First there's 'er ladyship—"

"The Brandon woman?"

"Know All, she is, like Joe and Abe, too," Thorpe replied. "Everybody reckons they got more brains than me."

"I can't imagine why," Nash sympathized with a tight smile. "I have always found you to be a fruitful source of knowledge. Pray continue."

Thorpe took a deep breath. "Well, it all begun at the secret meeting—"

"Where?"

"The 'ospital."

"What happened?"

"Well, Mrs. Know All said as 'ow you'd got to go because you was neck and neck with 'er."

A pulse throbbed on Nash's temple. "Do you know what she proposes doing about it, Ben . . . ?"

Thorpe looked abject. "Joe said 'e was going to croak you with a pickaxe. Then Abe said it was better to get you stretched, or something. Then she begun talking all fancy and told us we'd be 'earing more—"

"When?"

"Don't know."

Nash made another brittle smile. "You've done well. I shall review your sugar ration. Now, you must pretend that nothing's happened but, the moment you hear something new, come to me. Understand? No matter how trivial or unimportant it may appear to you, I must know, immediately."

"Yes, master."

"Very well." Nash pointed at a sack of maize. "Back to work."

Thorpe obeyed and trudged away from the stores.

He had to use his stick on Bunions: the little Londoner had yet to learn that a dibber makes holes in the ground to plant seed and that corn had to be drilled in straight rows between ring-barked trees. Cribb led the gang, nodding over his hoe, breaking clods of earth, mixing them with ash to put some heart into the barren soil. Curtains of rain drew over the clearing, drenching guards and lags alike. The afternoon dwindled down to a wintry twilight. The muster roll was called, tools were shouldered and everyone shambled back to camp. Another government stroke had been struck off another government day.

It was Levi's turn to boil a stew for the other three members of the family. Thorpe grumbled about the smell as he washed his hands. Cribb told him to shut up and move over while he rinsed the muck from his own neck. Kitty Brandon watched them slosh and snort around the bucket before joining the men at a makeshift dining table in the hospital annex.

"Well," she said with a controlled smile, "I trust it has been a profitable day?"

"No more'n usual," Thorpe muttered.

"Wrong." The woman's smile never wavered as she tweaked two pieces of paper from the neck of her dress. The first one she held up for a moment. "This is a general pass which allows me to go where I please, whenever I please, while we decide how to sling this tiny pebble which will level our Goliath flat upon the earth. . . ."

Kitty Brandon passed the second paper around the table. "Captain Shea, God rest his gallant soul, had many months in which to observe our opponent, aboard the *Prince*. What you are reading now is but a small sample of those things which Nash and Grimes did with the connivance of the shipmaster. Damning evidence, I think you will all agree."

As it happened, none of the men could read what had happened aboard the transport coming out from England, but there was no denying the obvious power of such elegantly penned words on a page ripped from an officer's journal.

Kitty Brandon took the paper back and laid it aside. "However, as rouge and rice flour are to us in the profession, a few additional words are to Captain Shea's papers. As you know, Miss Dundas has an excellent eye and a steady hand, she was glad to improve our evidence with the five or six extra lines which I dictated while you kept Asky entertained, Joe—"

Cribb was emphatic as he shook his head. "I still don't like it. Let's keep it short and sweet, the army way, the only way."

She raised her finger. "It will work like a charm once Jane replaces this"— the finger tapped the forged entry—"among Captain Shea's effects. Then all we need do is instruct some dependable survivors from the *Prince*, because Nash was unwise to annoy those ladies who were no longer so young or so able to work for him, and we'll be ready for him to step on that floorboard we spoke of—"

"I said let's keep things simple," Cribb repeated in a hard voice. "Stow the gab and stiff the sod, my way."

"No," she frowned, "this will work. Once the ladies have learned their parts they will be ready to testify that what is on this paper is the truth, the whole truth, and nothing but the truth. His Excellency will only need to spend a few minutes interrogating our witnesses and the cat will be properly out of the bag.

"The aptly named Mrs. Grimes will be the first to crack: she would do anything to save her hide. As for Nash, he'll be deuced lucky to get out of the Pit inside a twelvemonth because, and I know this for a fact, the governor is quite aware of what Major Ross and Nash are hatching on the sly. Joe? I'm deadly serious. While Captain Shea's journals are safe in Government House, ready for a committee of investigation, we are safe. I promise you there's enough 'gunpowder' in them to blow our enemy to smithereens and back again—"

"Short and simple."

"We'll see." She stood. "Tomorrow will be long and busy as I help Captain Tench arrange our entertainment. I must bid you a good night, gentlemen."

It was a good night for at least one gentleman.

Nash was dozing inside his hut at the back of the stores, well fed, warm and dry. The duty picket had finished grand rounds and the troops' lantern was bobbing away into the drizzle.

Water plipped off the stores' roof.

A twig snapped.

Nash groped under his pillow for a life-preserver as someone urgently scratched at the shutter. "Who is it . . . ?"

"Me, master!"

The assistant storeman held the candle at arm's length and slid the bolt. Thorpe stumbled through the open doorway. He was alone. Nash lowered the cosh. "Well?"

"They're doing it, master!"

"Doing what?"

"I don't know! But it's all this 'ere—!"

Nash snatched the paper and skimmed Shea's characteristic handwriting. Then he went back over it line by line, word by word, comma by comma. He looked up. "Can you read, Ben . . . ?"

"Read? *Me?*"

Nash distanced himself further from the peasant's damp, doggy odors. "So. What is it proposed to do with this, this tissue of lies?"

Thorpe scratched his belly harder and scowled with concentration. "Mrs. Know All reckons bossy boots Dundas is going to improve that there evidence, then put it back with them other papers, then tell some old morts off the *Prince* what they got to say, and if they do you won't be out of the Pit in a twelvemonth because of what you and Major Ross done on the sly. And there's enough gunpowder in Government House to blow you to smithereens. And she's safe while the captain's papers are safe for a committee, or some such."

Nash was tapping the paper with his fingernail.

"Um? Can I go now, master?"

"Yes, yes. Be off with you, then."

"And the thing?" Thorpe asked with a nervous bob of the head. "She's going to use it soon, she said, so she's got to find it where she left it. . . ."

Nash dragged his attention back to the present. He hesitated a moment then returned the torn page. "You have done well for yourself, tonight. I shall not be unmindful of your service after we have disposed of our enemy."

"Thank you, master!"

56

"WHAT THE HELL are you doing here at this hour of the night, Kellow?"

"I'm sorry to disturb you, sir! May I come in?"

Ross nodded. The Fitzgerald item moved aside, still holding the tin slush lamp, still holding her frock together.

"I need a few words, sir. Alone. . . ."

Ross climbed off the straw mattress and pulled on his breeches. He jerked his chin at the housekeeper. "Take a walk."

"Suit yourself!"

The two officers were left alone—except for the young aide, who was pretending to sleep in the far corner of the single room—but Kellow still kept his voice to a whisper. "There's to be an insurrection."

"Who by?"

"The convicted items."

"Go on. . . ."

"His Excellency is to be poisoned. So are we. Then they'll seize the guns, join forces with certain of our troops, and march inland. For China."

Ross leaned closer, sniffing the other man's breath. "Have you been on the grog?"

"Sir—!"

"Mr. Kellow. I have no idea what o'clock it is back in the civilized world but this has been a very long day for me. Poison, eh? An uprising, no less? Our servants and men decamping for China? Who, may I ask, says so?"

"A most reliable informant. He has contacts everywhere."

"Mr. Kellow. As I learned at Port Antonio, we don't shoot the whole bloody regiment, just its ringleaders. And why? Because the generality of mankind are content to be led like lambs to the butcher's knife." Ross's voice was starting to rise. "I have also encouraged my own informants among the convict class and, thus far, not one has been able to convince me that any of our abject apologies for human beings could display enough initiative to seize hold of his own cock let alone seize an armory and then face cold steel!"

"But they have! They have a leader! There's a Ranger sergeant! Out there—!"

Ross stopped tucking his shirt. "Sit down, Mr. Kellow. Let's begin at the beginning, again."

57

"SAR'NT MAJOR!"

"Sah?"

"Despatch a runner to Mr. Nash's quarters. Get him here at the double."

"Sah!"

Ross drummed his fingers on the table top and continued brooding over the notes from last night's talk with Kellow. Without looking up, he spoke to his son. "You're about to see what we do when troops go stale and start conspiring behind our backs."

Nancy Fitzgerald was impatiently waiting for him to clear a space so that she could lay breakfast. The lieutenant governor waved her away to the scullery as Nash hurried up the path.

"You particularly wished to see me now, major?"

"Where the hell are those women?"

"I gave you another four on Monday!"

"Which means that my men are still twenty-eight short of the agreed total."

"But—!"

"You recall what I said I'd do to you if ever you failed?"

"I resent the tone of your remark!"

"You can resent whatever you bloody well like," Ross replied, starting to stand, "because there's going to be trouble in the convict lines. Within the next couple of days we'll have another Jamaica mutiny. Only this time it'll be my marines siding with the darkies—!"

Nash was quick to recover. "Control yourself, major."

"Uh?"

"I'm disappointed, shocked, that a man of your experience would be taken in by rumors of unrest and poison—"

"So you've heard them, too?"

"Of course I have. People are forever coming into the stores with malicious gossip. I've learned to shut my ears; I would strongly recommend you do likewise. Now, unless there are further matters you wish to discuss, I am going to finish my breakfast before opening the stores."

Ross stopped him with a look. "Are you by any chance acquainted with an ex-Sergeant Major Cribb?"

"I never associate with that class of being."

"You ought."

"Why?"

"Because Colonel Tarleton's man has been here, among us, all the while. . . ."

"So?"

"You still don't understand what I'm referring to, do you?" Ross said.

"Not particularly! Is this some kind of elaborate joke?"

Ross shook his head, slowly. "That nondescript little item who used to masquerade as our scavenger is about to lead a mutiny, Mr. Nash. And, if we allow him to proceed, blood will be shed. On both sides."

"I don't know what you're speaking about!"

The battalion commander sat down again. "Pay attention to me, Mr. Nash. My troops are about to get their 'laundry allowance.' They will then be amenable to discipline. And I shall then be able to take the necessary steps with our laborers. Am I making myself plain, Mr. Nash?"

"Not entirely. If one scavenger poses such a threat to your men, have him arrested."

"Mr. Nash? Never, *ever* presume to tell me my duty," Ross replied. "Your only purpose in the colony, now, is to tell me when my troops will get those women."

The civilian gentleman shrugged. "I may be able to let you have them the day after tomorrow—"

"Try harder."

"But—?"

"They will be allocated tomorrow. At the noon parade."

"It's not that easy!" Nash snapped back. "I'm in the midst of some very delicate negotiations! You'll wreck everything I've been working for these past several weeks!"

Ross was standing again. He leaned forward, again. "Mr. Nash? You will deliver those women. Tomorrow. At noon."

58

NASH WALKED away from the lieutenant governor's mansion, then quickened his pace once he was out of sight. He had a duplicate key to the stores. The sentry watched him open up rather earlier than usual. Nash shut the door again, from the inside, and hurried over to his desk. A wad of receipts and time-expired passes were spiked on a wire hook. The assistant storeman riffled through them until he had Cribb's original order for six shovels, returned for cancellation by the brick field orderly room after the prisoner had been searched and ironed.

" 'Morning, sir. Bit early, aren't we?"

"Good morning, Miller." Nash casually tucked a grubby scrap of paper inside his waistcoat pocket. "His Excellency is determined to make this a joyful birthday for His Majesty. We'll be rushed off our feet by conflicting demands from those who've been ordered to amuse everyone from the governor downwards with their amateur theatricals, tonight."

Miller nodded as his deputy finished weighing half a pound of lentils, tipped them into a cloth and knotted the corners. "The chaplain has a ration voucher he wishes to exchange for two pounds of bread or the equivalent," Nash explained, walking toward the open door. "It seems his wife is becoming very fussy with her food."

Miller nodded again. "They're all the same when they get that way. I remember my missus before we 'ad our first nipper. Could never get 'er enough pickled 'errings to eat!"

Nash laughed, sharing a manly joke as he left the stores, then strode across the parade ground toward the chaplain's quarters as the colony started to enjoy its first public holiday since Proclamation.

A bonfire was being stacked in the center of the open space, an easy entertainment to arrange with so much fallen timber littering the ground, while a fatigue squad from B Company finished whitewashing the rocks around the flagstaff before starting on those marking the officers' lines.

"Good morning, ma'am." Nash halted beside the bed of hollyhocks. "I trust this is not an inconvenient moment?"

A wan face looked through the open door: pregnancy did not agree with Mary Johnson.

"I've taken the liberty of entering one and a quarter rations against your name," Nash went on, smiling as he held out the lentils. "We must keep up your strength, ma'am."

She hesitated, then accepted them. "Thank you. You are very kind."

"My pleasure." The gentleman replaced his hat and prepared to leave. "If only all our womenfolk had your strength and forbearance. Sadly, that is not the case."

"No?"

He half-turned away, then changed his mind and faced her again. "No, it is not, and I'm unsure what can be done about it. Perhaps I ought to ask your advice?"

"Yes, of course, if you wish, but how could I possibly help?"

Charles Nash was still uncertain how he should approach a very sensitive issue. "I am distressed to remind you of a most unpleasant topic, especially at this time, but you really are the only person I can rely upon for unbiased opinion—"

"Yes?"

He took the plunge. "Did you not spend two months in the company of that Brandon woman?"

"Yes."

"Now, we both realize that she can kill irrationally, in a fit of rage. But would you say she was the sort who could administer poison?"

"Poison!"

"Shh!" Nash glanced around to make sure they were not being over-heard. "Please! Calm yourself! It's only a rumor."

"What is?"

"That Captain Shea did not die of natural causes but, instead, was poisoned by his housekeeper—aided by the hospital Jew and our former scavenger who, Major Ross assures me, is really a violent arsonist."

"I would believe anything of that woman!" The color had returned to Mary Johnson's face. "As for arson, I saw them burn down Papa's shop!"

"Shh!" Nash was becoming alarmed at the effect of his simple ques-tion. "We must never allow personal antagonisms to cloud our better judgment! This is a matter for cool heads, not hysterical emotion."

Mary Johnson controlled her breathing. "I believe that woman poi-soned Captain Shea."

"Wrong." Nash was severe. "One may say with accuracy that Mrs. Brandon is, in your opinion, *capable* of administering an arsenic or phosphorus powder, grain by grain, in Captain Shea's food. It is quite another matter to prove it in a court of law, even though I have been shown a paper—allegedly from the said officer's journal—in which he appears to have voiced a suspicion that his health was being undermined—"

"I believe her capable of any deceit!"

Nash shook his head. "I do hope you're wrong, ma'am. This could lead to some very unpleasant questioning of witnesses to the crime. You must keep this to yourself, understand? Meanwhile, I shall give it further thought. Perhaps, tomorrow morning, I shall have the necessary evi-dence to place before His Excellency? He can then go through Captain Shea's papers and form his own judgment."

Nash turned as the chaplain walked up the garden path. "Good morn-ing, Richard. I've just taken the liberty of anticipating an extra mouth to feed on our scale of rations. Fortunately, as some come into the world, others depart."

"It is indeed very kind of you to consider us," Johnson replied, shifting his prayer book, gown and box of communion wafers under the other arm.

"Not at all." Nash smiled. "I assume you'll be at this evening's entertainment?"

"I think not. Mary is not her usual self."

Nash measured the distance from the chaplain's dwelling to Gov-ernment House. He smiled again. "I do hope you reconsider. They tell me it will be very, very good, and by no means vulgar in tone. Our

Mr. Tench is going to do us proud. Anyhow, I must hurry back to work. Your servant, ma'am."

Nash straightened, shared the smile with his two civilian friends, and strode away across the parade ground.

Sirius's mainsail had been slung between the trees a few yards from where the gallows beam was raised, when required, and more canvas was being hung to keep off the showers which might dampen tonight's enjoyment.

Nash slowed to a halt.

Someone with an impudent sense of humor had cadged a pot of red paint and lettered THEATRE ROYAL along a plank before stenciling a decorative border of chain links. This professional touch was now being swung aloft by the frigate's bosun, tiptoe on a scaffold of other planking while Tench's coproducer gave directions.

"Well, hello, Kate."

She turned, exhilarated. "Well. Hello, Charley."

His smile faded. "Kate? My offer is still open. There's ample room with the rest of us for you and your followers. Why not do the sensible thing? Come over, please? Events are moving our way, not yours. Let bygones be bygones because, despite what you may think of me, I'm not a malicious man. I can't bear a grudge."

"Heavens, I never thought you could." She was also serious, now. "So you're allowing me time to reconsider?"

"Of course." Nash reached out and touched her. "Let's forget our differences and begin again, assuming your original offer still stands . . . ?"

"Which one?"

"That you'd look after the 'ladies' while I looked after the stores. . . ."

"That's the way you want it?"

"Yes." He shrugged. "If we agree to play our cards right we can live on the fat of the land and you'll return Home with me when my time's up. You don't belong among these people, Kate. Once we get back to London I'll have a word with Dicky and we can go into partnership. Indeed, I've already sketched the title scene of *Hellish News From Afar, or, The Fatal Shore*, in which you will be the misunderstood heroine. I shall be your long-lost sweetheart who's smuggled himself aboard the fleet to be with you in New Holland, and we'll smuggle ourselves home—through China—in the third act. It'll be a triumph!"

Kitty Brandon brightened as his words took shape in her mind, as well. "That's a stroke of pure genius. We'd be the first to stage such a daring plot—"

"Quite. I'll have a word with Tench," Nash went on, heartened by her obvious interest. "Debrett's will get his book next year but he can do a gloss which we can sell for a shilling, at the door, once we get back—"

Her face was radiant. "Charley, you have missed your vocation! I can see it all as if it were spread before me! Over there's myself, wrongfully convicted for an act performed by you—motivated by the highest ideals— to protect an Important Personage. Now, smitten by remorse, you disguise yourself as a common sailorman so that you can rescue me from the cannibal kings of Botany Bay. However, at first I don't recognize you until chance reveals you to be my own dear heart. Meanwhile, during the intervals, we can have a chorus of boys dressed as these comic animals, jumping around. And a couple of knockabouts with funny accents. And a dark villain who desires me all for himself to the extent that he challenges you to a duel with wet sponges! And we can put on a charivari of Chinees in their funny hats!"

"Brilliant invention—!"

"But that's not all!" She laughed with him. "We'll really give the crowd their money's worth when we hold a hanging, a bit like Punch and Judy's, to top off the show while we two lovers elope!"

"*Bravissimo!*"

She caught her breath. "Charley? We're partners."

"You really mean it? You'll let bygones be bygones?"

"Tch! Let bygones be bygones, I say. What's past has passed and it's the future we should both be concerned about, now. Speaking of which," she went on with a brisk toss of the head, "I had better finish this job for Mr. Tench or else there'll be ructions."

Nash was smiling with open admiration. " 'As in a theatre the eyes of men, after a well-grac'd actor leaves the stage, are idly bent on him that enters next. . . .' You really are in your element with these sort of things, aren't you?"

"Of course," she replied with a knowing wink. " 'The play's the thing wherein I'll catch the conscience of the King. . . .' "

"Dearest Kate, be assured here is one devoted admirer who awaits with breathless anticipation the outcome of your endeavors, tonight."

"You'll be present, then?"

"But of course!"

"So we can expect to see you among the Quality?"

"Just try keeping me away!"

"Away? Or awake?" Her eyes twinkled.

He laughed.

They parted.

59

THE FIRST royal birthday in New South Wales was exceeding Phillip's hopes. Tench's program had been planned with flair and attention to detail. The battalion paraded under arms at noon and a *feu de joie* rippled along the ranks of muskets as the flag inched aloft and the bandsmen struck up the national anthem. The bonfire blazed and collapsed into a hillock of glowing embers: the lags' grog ration was bartered, gambled, stolen and—once in a while—drunk to the long life of the Third George.

Jane Dundas oversaw the officers' wine from her pantry at Government House. Tench capped one of Dawes's quips with a line from *Much Ado About Nothing* as Ross tried to propose the loyal toast before Phillip could take the credit: Kellow volunteered a couple of young ensigns to escort their battalion commander back to quarters where he would sleep better than under a bench.

The governor waited until they returned, then stood at his end of the dining table, smiling and indulgent. "Gentlemen? Your attention, please." There were several coughs, a few belches, near silence.

"Today's festivities remind me of that last occasion when I had the honor to celebrate His Majesty's birthday. It was, you will recall, while we were the guests of His Excellency the governor of the Canary Islands, Don Luis de Branciforte.

"Looking back from my own vantage point, as the captain general of a more extensive colony, I cannot believe that only one year has passed since we dined on the roof of the *presidio* in Teneriffe. So much has been achieved. It is impossible to credit that a mere twelve months separate us from those strangers, for so we would surely appear if we could but return in time to view ourselves, then.

"Consider what we have achieved, redcoat and bluejacket alike, as we've hauled together for the common good. Do you not remember how we began our modern Odyssey with eleven vessels? And how, eight months and half the world away, we delivered those same craft, safe and sound, as directed by His Majesty's command? Ours is an achievement unparalleled in history. But that was only the start of our *anno mirabilis*.

"A town has been planned. The rule of law and civilized conduct has been established among brute savagery. Commerce and industry, thrift and sobriety will advance as our line of settlement extends westward from

Rose Hill and eastward from Norfolk Island. Indeed, no matter how we view our labors, they are breathtaking in scope and heartwarming in the courage they display—!"

The governor waited for his staff to settle down again.

Phillip smiled at them, his fingertips resting lightly on the table. "Long before we next celebrate this happy day, I am supremely confident that we shall have even more reason for our mutual satisfaction. During the months ahead I can see broad fields of wheat rippling in the sunlight. I can see orderly streets of brick dwellings taking shape. I can see the energetic gait of purposeful citizens. I can see the future beckoning us to strive, to achieve, to live together—!"

Jane Dundas was hurrying round the table, replacing empty bottles with full ones.

"Gentlemen. I ask you to charge your glasses and be upstanding for the loyal toast."

Everyone stood to attention as best he could.

"His Britannic Majesty George the Third. King of Great Britain, France and Ireland. Defender of the Faith. Duke of Brunswick, Luneburg and Hanover. Arch-Treasurer and Prince Elector of the Holy Roman Empire. Sovereign of New South Wales!"

Some of these resounding titles were the husks of glory. But Phillip's officers were saluting the substance of power as they raised their glasses to an unspoken empire of which Sydney Cove was now the most distant, the most recent outpost.

60

THE GOVERNOR and his staff were in excellent spirits by the time dusk settled across Sydney Cove and they had strolled under the awning to take their places along the front row of benches, seats and chairs.

Sirius's riding lights were hoisted to port and starboard of the stage and most other lamps in the colony had been commandeered to illuminate an area where lags and marines, men and women, lolled, squatted, crouched behind the Quality.

The bandmaster twitched his baton and struck up "God Save the King" for the seventh time since breakfast, encoring with a medley of patriotic airs to set the mood. The applause turned to sighs and lingering groans as tonight's mistress of ceremonies swept into view.

Kitty Brandon had trimmed a straw bonnet with blue ribbon, borrowed enough cheesecloth to tie a soft *fichu* across her shoulders, and adapted a pink muslin skirt by gathering up the hem with yellow paper flowers. She was sixteen thousand sea miles from the other Theatre Royal's dressing room and wardrobe but nobody noticed or cared as she sank into a deep curtsey and the entire audience rose to its feet.

Kitty Brandon was radiant as she straightened to face Phillip, now seated with Hunter on his right hand, Collins on his left.

> *"Honored sir, I heard one critic say,*
> *He'd try to coax some moral from this play.*
>
> *The moral's plain enough, cried I, with one accord*
> *All social happiness rests with you, our noble lord!*
>
> *Through this bold drama due loyalty will gild the crown,*
> *As you, by its command, rule o'er our town.*
>
> *Can one doubt? This small stage will prove it so,*
> *Thus hence curs't melancholy and let foul misery go!*
>
> *And in their place, may all bask*
> *In the sun of humor, till we end our task. . . ."*

The mistress of ceremonies curtseyed again, acknowledging more thunderous applause.

The loyal ode had been freely adapted from Julia's epilogue in *The Rivals*, a role which Richard Sheridan had refused to give his bastard half-sister but which she'd learned in any case, just to spite him.

Phillip nodded enthusiastically as Hunter leaned across to say something.

Kitty Brandon scanned the crowd. Cribb stood near one of the lanterns, somewhat to the back, wearing a bright red *diklo* neckerchief for the occasion. Nash was nowhere to be seen near the Quality in front.

"Friends!" she continued. "To assist us in our duty of dispelling foul melancholy, it is my singular pleasure to welcome that veritable Vesuvius of vivacity and vibrant virtuosity in the vernacular verbal arts, Mr. Samuel Crocker! Direct to our sunny shores after satisfying the most discerning judges of form at the Old Bailey—!"

Bunions was a natural first turn, a whip-snap Cockney. He capered on, winking, grinning and slapping his thighs.

"Did you 'ear the one about the county bloke what come up to London? O' course 'e wasn't used to paved streets and suchlike so, when a dog run out to take a bite from 'is leg, 'e tried to grab up a stone. But they was all rammed in the ground. So then 'e said, 'What a queer place to live! They tie up the stones and let the dogs loose . . . !' "

Dawes looked at Tench.

Bunions waited for the crowd to settle down again. " 'Ow does a poultry dealer earn 'is living? You give up . . . ? *By fowl means!*"

Phillip looked at Hunter.

"Then there was the bloke in a threadbare coat. And 'is mate asked 'im if it was sleepy. 'Why you asking that?' said the first bloke. And 'is mate answered, 'Because it don't look like it's 'ad a nap in seven years . . . !' "

The crowd loved him.

Bunions was in his element. "Anyone 'eard the one about the tapster what sold a noggin o' ale to a ge'man? So the gent blows off the froth and, straightway, the tapster gives 'im a regular fourpenny one, right on the conk! And the ge'man says, 'Ho, what are you a-doing of that for?' And the tapster says—wait for it—*'Blow for blow . . . !'* "

The comic trotted off, twirling one finger and grinning down at the Quality.

"Did you think that was humorous, John?"

"I suppose it all depends on your point of view," Hunter replied, "as the highwayman said when he leveled his pistols."

"Oh."

"Thank you, Mr. Crocker!" Kitty Brandon returned to center stage. She scanned her audience. Nash was nowhere to be seen. Nor was Cribb, now. "Assist me to welcome that marvel of manual manipulations and dazzling dexterities, Mr. 'Thumbs' Perkins, one of His Majesty's brave lads!"

The royal marines gave their mate a huge ovation as he began juggling with burning sticks, wrapped with oakum dipped in tar, a happy knack he'd acquired over the years handling cannon linstocks. Still applauding, Kitty Brandon whipped him off before he set fire to the scenery.

"That was rather well done, John!"

"I'd like to see him fool around on any vessel I commanded!"

"Oh."

The mistress of ceremonies was in place again. "Drama! Mystery! Thrills—!"

She stood aside with a flourish as a dapper young cove, ex-*Lady Penrhyn*, proved that he had lost none of the deft touch which had earned him fourteen years penal servitude for emptying pockets around London's bear-pits. In rapid order he produced a string of colored bunting from one ear, played a pack of cards like a concertina, crowed like a hen and squatted to lay a ball of rag tied to resemble an egg.

The crowd whistled and cheered.

"I'm sorry, there really wasn't much choice," Tench apologized.

"On the contrary, I think you've both been most successful," Dawes disagreed. "If our object is to raise their spirits, I'd say you're doing just that—"

The bluejackets' cheers were redoubling as Kitty Brandon presented *Sirius*'s bosun—a stocky veteran of storm, fire, shipwreck and battle—gold rings in his ears, baggy black pants flapping, tarpaulin hat tilted at a rakish angle.

The petty officer balanced an empty bottle on his nose, no easy thing for a man in his condition, and lurched at a popular version of "Villikens & His Donah."

"Oh, no—!" Kitty Brandon squeezed her eyes shut.

The marines and the lags were of a different opinion as Bosun bellowed out his first verse.

> *"Ow-w-w down in Stepney an 'arlot did dwell,*
> *The saucy young cow, I used 'er so well,*
> *Then one foggy ev'ning these things come to pass,*
> *She pulled up the window and stuck out 'er arse!"*

Phillip looked stunned. Collins looked down at the floor. Hunter looked at the canvas overhead. Kitty Brandon thumped the sailor on the shoulder, trying to distract his attention.

Weaving unsteadily, Bosun caught the bottle and replaced it as the greater part of his public belted out the refrain. The bandsmen picked up the tune, leading the chorus. The mistress of ceremonies could do no more. She withdrew to the wings and let human nature run its course.

> *"Now-w-w a nightwatchman was just passin' by,*
> *The surly old sod was eatin' a pie,*
> *Then 'e looked straight up at the sky,*
> *As a steamin' 'ot turd got 'im smack in the eye!"*

Phillip coughed into his fist. Tench studied his fingernails. Kitty Brandon gritted her teeth. Campbell rolled about, slapping his knees. The bottle fell again. Was caught again. The song was on again.

"So-o-o the idle old bastard was blinded for life,
Wiv twenty-four kids and a slut for a wife,
Now on the corner you can still see 'im sit,
Crying 'Spare me a penny! I'm blinded wiv shit!' "

The mistress of ceremonies gripped Bosun's ear with fingers like farriers' tongs and steered him off, through a barrage of cheers. She returned, smiling bravely, and scanned her audience. Cribb had not returned. Levi could not be seen. "Thank you, Mr. Higgins! That was an unexpected diversion. And now, if it's true that 'Music has charms to soothe a savage breast' prepare to greet those two musical charmers, the inimitable Croak & Maggot—!"

The contract strangler and freelance graverobber were really quite talented. Maggot thrashed the spoons, clapping them between palm and thigh, while his mate squawked on a gum leaf cupped between his thumbs. Their repertoire was limited but none of the six-hundred-odd lags cared. In a world unevenly split between Us and Them, it was good that We were equal to the traps, and the ge'men, and suchlike rotten scabs.

As indeed many of the lags were.

The next turn was brilliantly performed. A solo acrobat who did backward flick-flacks from a standing jump, walked on his hands, turned elegant cartwheels and danced on a slack rope, valuable skills which had made him one of London's most nimble cat-burglars until he'd booked to dance on another rope outside Newgate, had been reprieved because of an administrative muddle, and then been despatched to Botany Bay instead.

Kitty Brandon stopped scanning her audience and began smiling again. "Thank you, Mr. Bliss! With such agility it would indeed be folly to be wise! And now, I beg leave to announce the moment we've all been waiting for—the Interval! A welcome pause to rest and refresh ourselves with the generous bounty of His Excellency the governor, aided by Captain Tench, C-Company's illustrious commander!"

The cooks had to use their ladles like truncheons to establish order as everyone scrambled for a place around the steaming cauldrons of hot gruel, sweetened with sugar and spiked with rum. Most of the lags and all of the military carried their wooden bowls or tin pannikins wherever they went, day or night. Those whose mess kits had been stolen, had to rent one from the more astute citizens of Sinful Cove as they milled around the first free refreshment many could ever remember.

The mood was more restrained backstage where an area had been roped off for the Quality to drink mulled wine and meet the cast. Tench attracted his assistant's attention and led her forward. "May I have the honor of presenting Mrs. Katharine Brandon, sir?"

"Delighted to meet you again, ma'am." Phillip put his tumbler on the plank which served for a buffet. "That this evening is a success, none can deny. That you have made it so is beyond doubt."

She curtseyed. "On behalf of everyone I wish to thank Your Excellency. Without your example and Captain Tench's guidance our efforts would have been in vain. May this occasion be the first of many when our differences in condition are set aside and we unite to achieve harmony for the good of all."

"I'm sure it will be," Phillip replied, snapping his fingers. Bryant had been promoted to senior steward for the evening. "A drink for our charming mistress of ceremonies!"

"Aye aye. Sir."

Kitty Brandon accepted the spiced wine and freeloaded from the officers' cheese and wafers.

Phillip frowned with concentration. "That 'blow for blow' joke. Did you get it, ma'am?" But she was distracted by her own thoughts. "I said, did you get the point of that joke?"

The mistress of ceremonies looked away from the crowd. Her face was pale and drawn under its rice flour and rouge. "That was no joke, though the multitude laughed as they always will, like street urchins when a blind man falls in the gutter."

"Ma'am?"

"The richest comedy must have an undercurrent of bitter tragedy to be truly effective." She fortified herself with more wine. " 'Blow, blow, thou winter wind! Thou art not so unkind as man's ingratitude. . . .' "

"Great heavens, so that's the point?"

"Tragedy is always the point, in human affairs." Kitty Brandon curtseyed again. "Now, with Your Excellency's permission, I have certain things to arrange—"

"Of course. And good luck with the second half!"

She was going to need all the luck available as the crowd resumed its place and the bandmaster tidied his men. By accident or design, Tench the Welshman had a Sergeant Owens, a Corporal Jones, a Davis and a Llewellyn in his company, which meant that C-Company was home to a superb male quartet.

The four tenors marched onto the stage and straight into Spunge's lament from *Distress upon Distress*.

"Past twelve o' clock at night,
When ev'ry lamp was out and the drowsy watchman snor'd,
My dearest passed away,
Upon a breath of wind,
That wafted o'er rooftops wet and drear. . . ."

The second, third, fourth and fifth verses descended through starvation, ejection by the bailiffs, destitution and eventual reunion in Sweetest Heav'n Above.

The crowd demanded an encore. They were always eager to hear of anything or anyone in a more desperate condition than themselves—animals being tormented in a pit, drunken husbands kicking their wives along the street, felons dying on a scaffold.

Kitty Brandon understood. She felt wretched, too. Cribb and Levi were still nowhere to be seen.

"Thank you, gentlemen!" The mistress of ceremonies put together a plucky smile. "Your melodic melancholy prepares us for a dramatic excerpt from that notable success—*The Foundling, or, By Fortune Lost*—in which I created the part of Lady Isobel Beauchamp. Opposite me this evening I am privileged to have that epitome of a military gentleman, Captain Tench, who will interpret the role of Squire John Playfair, a neighbor who is the bearer of ill tidings for the luckless Lady Isobel. . . ."

The audience craned forward in near silence, determined not to miss a single word of the Quality's private woes as Tench climbed onto the stage, bowed to his partner and took his lines from a pocket. Mrs. Katharine Brandon had no need for prompts: she had been performing in public since the age of four, when she first sang for her supper inside a Dublin tavern and blacked the eyes of a rival entertainer.

"Isobel, is it you?"

"Yes, yes, John! I could not die without your forgiveness. Do not spurn me now! Stay but a little while longer. Say, say you can forgive my folly and I shall depart in peace. . . ."

"Isobel! Isobel! Need you ask?"

"Alas. If only I had not listened to such evil advice, how happy we could have been—"

"It is not too late! All is forgiven!"

"No, no, I must pay the price for my foolish pride."

Hunter was leaning closer to Phillip. "She's good!"

"Isn't she?" the governor agreed, also smiling. "No wonder she did so well in London. For a while."

The crowd was rapt as the melodrama reached its climax with John Playfair on one knee, clasping the dying Lady Isobel's hand. "Don't go! Say you won't!"

"I must." Kitty Brandon made as if to swoon. "I stand upon the threshold of a better, a happier world, which beckons me to a higher life! Will you not say one word of love before I obey that summons and pass beyond?"

"I do! I do!"

"Ah, I grow faint. Keep a little corner, forever in your heart, for your poor, your wretched Isobel. . . ."

"Yes! Yes!"

"Oh, but it is so hard to say farewell. Yet, we must part. Until we meet, again, in eternity. . . ."

The handsome couple got a standing ovation as she died in his arms, then revived, for six curtain calls. She straightened on the fourth and began flashing smiles left and right. Cribb was back under the lantern. He no longer wore the red *diklo*.

Kitty Brandon beamed at the fifer for whom she had whistled a simple, unforced melody earlier that afternoon. An expectant hush fell as she stretched out her arms to embrace everyone—lags, marines, officers.

> *"Cherry ripe, ripe, ripe I cry,*
> *Full and fair ones, come and buy.*
> *If, perchance, you ask me where,*
> *They do grow, I answer, there!*
> *Where my lover's lips do smile,*
> *There's the land of Cherry Isle.*
> *There cherries grow which none may buy,*
> *Till 'Cherry ripe' themselves to cry. . . ."*

The crowd went wild. She blew strings of kisses at them. Phillip smiled and nodded at Collins. Tench was smiling and nodding at Dawes. Cribb was elbowing the bloke beside him. "Louder, you sod!"

"Wha'?"

"Clap louder! I'll tell you when to stop!"

Cribb nearly sustained enough applause for an encore of the song he had last heard in Vauxhall Gardens, after his return from the war, but Kitty Brandon had already untied the bonnet to display her crowning glory braided *à la grecque*. Both hands together, prim and demure, she flirted with every man in the audience as the fifer cued her next song.

"I have a bonnet trimmed with blue,
Shoes with bows and stockings new,
Ribbons blue will tie my hair,
When I go to Dublin fair!

In my bonnet trimmed with blue,
Do you like me? Yes, you do!
And I'll wear it when I can,
Go to the fair with my young man!"

They adored her. Phillip was enraptured. Tench studied the trim ankles which tapped and twirled inches beyond the footlights. Collins also had a rather dreamy smile. Kitty Brandon paid no heed. Levi had also returned. He was under another lantern, at the rear of the audience. He wore another bright red neckerchief—

"Gentlemen all! If I may claim your indulgence for one moment!" The mistress of ceremonies was radiant. "I propose to depart from the advertised program and insert an item of my own choosing, one which I am proud to dedicate to the memory of a very gallant Irish soldier, Captain John Shea of the Second Battalion, Portsmouth Division, the Royal Corps of Marines—!"

Kellow's men howled their approval.

Her charming English accent vanished as she struck up an unaccompanied solo from Home. No longer singing. Chanting. Menacing. Rising.

"When I was a maiden fair and young
On the bonny banks of Lee,
No bird that in the greenwood sang,
Was half so blithe as me—o!

My heart ne'er beat with flying feet,
No love sang me his queen,
Till down the glen rode Sarsfield's men,
Arrayed in their jackets green—o!

King Billy stormed with shot and shell,
At the walls of Limerick,
Where my own true Padraic stood,
Upon the bridge none dared to cross,
While he swung his sabre keen—o!

> *But I weep not my true love dead!*
> *Nor pity I the foe!*
> *I'd send them all to hell again!*
> *For he fell in his jacket green—o!"*

There was a gale of yells as other exiles also remembered the last great uprising, barely a century earlier, when William the Dutchman and James the king battled for a crown at the Boyne. But only tonight's mistress of ceremonies would ever know that her mother's grandfather, the Devlin of Clonmel, had fought in Patrick Sarsfield's green-jacketed cavalry before going into French service to raise the immortal *Brigade d'Irlande*. And fall in Flanders.

"What was all that about, John?"

"I've no idea!" Hunter leaned closer. "But whatever she meant, by God it's having an effect!"

The applause thundered on and on while the woman blew bouquet after bouquet of kisses at her audience. Kitty Brandon could see a lantern bobbing nearer, in the darkness behind Levi; it was time to bring down the curtain. She advanced in triumph to the footlights for the parting ode, borrowed from Lady Teazle in *School for Scandal*.

> *"The transient hour of fashion too soon spent,*
> *Farewell the tranquil mind, farewell content!*
> *Farewell all Quality of high renown,*
> *Pride, pomp, and circumstance of glorious town.*
> *No more in vice or error to engage,*
> *Or play the fool at large on life's great stage."*

The quarter guard sergeant halted at the end of the officers' row. The folded message slip passed from Dawes to Tench to Hunter to the governor. Phillip did not have his spectacles with him and the signal was passed for Collins to read. The judge advocate general sat bolt upright. He read the note again, then urgently whispered something in Phillip's ear. The governor's fists clenched. His Excellency stood. The show was over.

61

"THE WHOLE camp's in absolute turmoil!" Collins replied, halting for a moment on the track. "Damn rumors flying about like bullets, everything from an imminent mutiny to the sighting of our relief convoy. So much for the Old Man's hopes of a revived spirit of endeavor!"

"Well, I doubt you'll find it any more tranquil over there," Tench continued, folding both hands around his sword hilt and looking back at Government House in the gray morning light. He glanced at Collins. "Have you managed to squeeze anything from Nash, yet?"

The judge advocate shook his head. "Not a damn thing. He's being very stubborn—or correct, according to one's point of view—by declining to make a formal statement regarding last night's incident, unless we arraign him in court first."

"Hm! Hardly your average 'barrack room lawyer.' "

"Hardly our average anything," Collins observed. "In matters legal Nash is on home ground. He knows the law inside out."

"Rather you than me, then," Tench said, preparing to continue back to camp.

"Meaning?"

The other captain of marines made an expressive shrug. "My dear David, the Old Man is out for blood. He set great store upon yesterday's display of official goodwill to our unwashed, unready, unwilling subjects. He told me so himself before involving me in last night's theatricals."

"But—"

"But nothing. It is your Mr. Nash's misfortune to have abused that magnanimity, and yours to now be in the position of passing judgment on a gentleman of connection." Tench tugged his cloak against the chilly wind. "You have my most sincere condolences. . . ."

"As you have mine," Collins replied, shifting his laden despatch bag under the other arm.

"What?"

The judge advocate made an equally expressive shrug. "Jimmy Campbell's troops have drawn ten rounds apiece and seized the strong points. Kellow's have surrounded the convict lines. And when you get back to the orderly room you'll be instructed to keep your troops in quarters, 'in reserve.' Because, drunk or sober, our gallant battalion commander remains very much in control of himself—and us."

"Good God."

"Good day." Collins replaced his hat, turned and continued striding up the track toward Government House. His pace only slowed when he was alone again.

Tench was right. It is one thing to routinely neck some luckless item trapped in the turnip fields; it is another matter altogether to sit in judgment on a gentleman and then to sign one's name on the transcript for other gentlemen, in due course, to pass judgment on the court president.

The judge advocate's own father had not been promoted major general merely for boldness on the battlefield and discretion in bed. Arthur Collins also had a sound grounding in tactics along the dusty corridors of Westminster.

David Collins had long ago been taught how many a promising military career could sink from sight after striking the hidden reefs of civilian life in London. And that had been during times of relative stability, not in the midst of a constitutional crisis with a mad king on the throne and an heir pledged to toss out his father's administration, bag and baggage, while a bankrupt nation teetered on the brink of war.

Collins recognized that, unless he were very careful, he could regret today's work for the rest of his life.

Jane Dundas heard the sentry's salute. She opened the door and stood aside. "Captain Collins, Your Excellency."

Phillip looked straight past her. "Well? What's he got to say for himself?"

The younger man finished taking his accustomed place. Then he set his bag on the table. "I'm afraid that Mr. Nash declines to make a statement until we—"

"He *what*? The man burgles my bedchamber and 'declines to make a statement'?" The governor crouched forward. "By God, if he were aboard a man o' war I'd damned well shackle him to the capstan until he agreed to make a statement, and then I'd yard-arm him!"

"Of course, sir," the judge advocate replied, starting to tread the dangerous and narrow path between public duty and private interest. "But, unfortunately, Admiralty Rules no longer apply—"

"Uh?"

"Because the moment I administered your oath of office, New South Wales passed under the general jurisdiction of the Crown. The laws of the territorial United Kingdom now hold sway: *lex Anglia numquam sine parliamento mutari potest. . . .*"

"Talk English!"

" 'The law of England cannot be changed except by Parliament.' It's all in the book, sir." Collins displayed his copy of *Blackstone's Commentaries* for the governor to check if he so wished.

Phillip did wish. He dragged the volume closer and flicked through its four hundred or so pages, many of which were still uncut. The legal manual had only been bought a few weeks before embarkation, once Collins could be sure that his loan to buy the law commission would be covered by his fees attorney and contingent, interpreting colonial justice during the years abroad. " *'Lex Anglia . . .* '?"

His Excellency slapped the book shut and looked back at his law officer. "So, regarding my burglar, what do you propose doing now?"

"I am about to arraign the defendant, strictly according to the rules of procedure, and we'll get right to the bottom of this business, sir." Collins felt it was safe to promise that much, at least.

"And when he's found guilty?"

"Er. Punish him, of course."

"How?"

"Strictly according to law."

"Be sure you do." Phillip shoved *Blackstone* across the table. "Meanwhile, I am going for a tour of inspection to assure myself that everything else is in hand. When I return for lunch I expect to find the proceedings ready for review and my signature."

"Of course, sir."

Collins was glad to stow his law library and march downhill, across the bridge, and up to the orderly room again. Several lags had sweetened their way through Kellow's picket line to assure the assistant storeman of their continued loyalty. They quickly excused themselves and sidled out of the hut, leaving the ge'men and the guards alone.

Nash smiled indulgently after them and turned to the judge advocate. "It is truly said that 'most friendship is feigning,' and in my experience with that class of individual one must expect nothing better." The smile became sad and withdrawn. "You know, Collins, you're such a lucky devil. . . ."

"Me? Lucky? Why?"

"Because, waiting for you at the end of every day's duty in this terrible place, is the company of equals around the mess table. It is an enviable condition." Nash hesitated. "I still have to endure another thirty months of purgatory before returning Home to my friends. The trouble is, I shall have changed. And so will they.

"Charley Fox will now be Prime Minister and First Lord of the Treasury, Dicky Sheridan will almost certainly be Cabinet Secretary, and I'd wager one hundred guineas that His Majesty—whom I formerly knew when he was just the prince of Wales—will have elevated poor old Burgoyne to Paymaster General, 'for services rendered. . . .' "

The gentleman exile tried to put the best face on these changed circumstances. "It ought to be quite amusing, catching up with the stirring events of the past few years, once we get together again. Speaking of which, is it true that you're hoping to publish your journals after we get back to London?"

"Yes. I am considering it."

Nash frowned. "Isn't there a risk that Tench will pip you to the post when Debrett brings out his book?"

"Mine will be quite different."

"That's a relief!" Nash was smiling again. He stood, stretching his cramped limbs. "Don't forget to send me the subscription list. I mean, who better than I—a minor participant in the experiences you'll be describing—to draw His Majesty's attention to what will be, I'm sure, the event of the season."

"Thank you."

"My pleasure." Nash glanced around the unlined hut of bark slabs and green poles, then back at the attendant officer. "Well, then, what's our next step?"

"The trial. I've balloted the names," Collins replied, glancing at his pocket watch. "Will an hour be sufficient to prepare a defense?"

"More than adequate. Meanwhile, may I suggest that you prepare a duplicate copy of the indictment so that I may be said to have studied it first? If not, your findings could be ruled invalid if this matter were directed to an appellate court."

62

IT WAS MIDMORNING before Collins finished discussing procedures with the defendant because, although the officer of marines was a judge, he was also an advocate with a clear duty to render legal advice impartially.

The quarter guard clicked to attention as the two gentlemen left the hut and stepped outside. Yesterday's fine spell had passed and there was low cloud draped across the tree tops of Port Jackson.

"I do hope it doesn't rain," Nash observed, pacing uphill. "One gets so bored, stuck indoors with nothing to do."

"Yes."

"Why don't we try and liven things up the way we do whenever the Prince is in town?" Nash continued in the same affable, conversational tone. "You'd never believe the difference a really well organized rout or assembly would make here, not that I'm criticizing Tench's admirable efforts yesterday evening," he hastened to add.

They had reached Government House and Collins was saved from having to make further comment. The guards were dismissed to huddle inside their capes under a nearby tree as the two gentlemen continued ahead and went indoors.

"A chair for Mr. Nash."

Jane Dundas obeyed as the judge advocate took his seat between the two pairs of officers whose names had been drawn for today's trial.

Collins busied himself with his papers for several moments, then looked at his colleagues again. "I need hardly say that this morning's work promises to be rather more interesting than the normal sort of business we have to despatch, whenever we are called upon to sit in judgment."

The other four officers nodded as their president went on. "It would, of course, be quite wrong of us to allow that judgment to be influenced in any way by the singular circumstances of this case. We must bear in mind that the law must not only be impartial—at all times, for all men— it must also be seen to be impartial so that we can subsequently answer with a clear conscience for any action we may have taken during the course of our official duties."

Nash was also nodding in agreement as Collins went on. "That understood, I must now remind you of our duties as members of this court. It must never be forgotten that our only task is to determine the guilt or innocence of the alleged offender as to the charge, or charges, upon which he has been brought before us and, if found guilty, to determine an appropriate sentence.

"The fact that such a charge or charges has or have been preferred against him should never be construed as *a priori* evidence of guilt. Remember, the determination of guilt or innocence has to be based entirely upon the weight of evidence which can only be determined after resolving all material issues of fact. And to do this we must maintain open minds, free from bias or prejudice."

The other officers exchanged whispered comments as their president opened the convening order. "Charles Foveaux Nash? It is alleged that, on the night of the fourth, instant, you did feloniously break, enter and maliciously damage sundry properties within the quarters of His Excellency the governor. How then do you plead? Guilty or not guilty?"

"Not guilty, sir."

"And yet you were apprehended within the bedchamber of Government House, were you not?"

"That is correct." Nash was quite unperturbed.

Collins glanced left and right at the other freshly shaven profiles, their threadbare collars buttoned around freshly laundered chokers, then back at the defendant. "Can you account for the apparent burglary?"

Nash stood, bowed to the court and straightened again. "With due respect, gentlemen, I must lodge my first objection. The crime of burglary is defined as the breaking and entry of another's dwelling, during nighttime, with intent to commit a felony. Now, although it is true I did enter His Excellency's bedchamber, does that of itself constitute a felonious entry . . . ?"

The officers exchanged more whispers as their clerk's pen scratched and dotted across his paper. Nash allowed the fellow a few moments to catch up, then continued to address the court in the same calm, measured phrases.

"Please bear in mind that it is the intent which is triable at law; *intentio mea imponit nomen operi meo*, or, intent is the purpose to use a particular means, motive is that which impels the action. Therefore my intent last night was not to burgle His Excellency—God forbid!—but, rather, to destroy certain documents formerly in the possession of the late Captain Shea. An act, let me hasten to add, entirely motivated by feelings of the deepest loyalty to Commodore Phillip, and to an important personage whose friendship I esteem more than life itself."

The judge advocate sat forward, hands clasped on the table in front of him. "Could you clarify that?"

"Certainly." Nash waited for the clerk to turn over a fresh page. "However, before revealing my motives, I must be assured that everyone present today will keep a confidence. A state secret." He assumed their silence was assent but, even so, he continued to hesitate. Then he straightened his shoulders, a proud, unafraid man of honor. "Yes, I deliberately burned Captain Shea's journal. I did so because he had placed, on official record where it could be read by a hostile committee of scrutiny, certain baseless allegations impugning His Royal Highness the Prince of Wales—"

"Order! Order I say!" Collins laid his gavel aside. "Proceed, Mr. Nash."

"Thank you." The defendant straightened from another bow. "I was therefore under an obligation, as a loyal subject as well as a close friend, to apply the dictum of *qui jussu judicis aliquod*—meaning that the law cannot suppose I acted from wrongful motives—because it was my bounden duty to obey the commands of he whom we may confidently suppose has recently ascended the throne of his fathers. . . ."

"Um. What's 'juicey'?"

Nash patiently spelled it out for the clerk.

Collins waited with equal patience. Such a strong, such a logical and, above all, such a legal defense, would read well in London. His own modest contribution, as court president, could be safely kept to a minimum.

The judge advocate lightly tapped his pencil on the table. "Perhaps you could be more explicit, Mr. Nash?"

"Of course. But first it must be recalled that I was transported to this place under rather unusual circumstances, having chosen to plead *nolo contendere* to the abduction of M'Lord Denbigh's niece." Nash just as lightly dropped the name and watched its impact on the more impressionable faces of the younger officers.

"The details do not concern the matter before us today," he went on, "but it did mean that I was able to travel as a gentleman ought and that Captain Mason of the *Prince* was happy to enter me as a passenger on his manifest. And so I was content to remain. However, Captain Shea persisted in pressing his attention upon me. It was very hard to maintain a proper distance, our cabins being adjacent.

"Now, I have every respect for the profession of arms. Indeed, had not the war been cut short, I would have followed it myself but, as we all know from personal experience, there are officers like yourselves and others like Shea. Not to put too fine a point upon it, he soon became a pest, though let me hasten to add I have nothing against the Irish, in their proper place, or even against honest poverty, but Shea's constant 'harping on . . . !' "

Collins restrained the laughter with a few quiet taps of his gavel.

Nash allowed the clerk to catch up. "As I was saying, Shea's cadging became a trifle tedious after the first few weeks at sea. Unwisely, as I am now the first to admit, I donated some twenty Spanish dollars for him to buy himself a few personal comforts at Teneriffe; Lord knows he had few enough. However, when we came to Rio he demanded the same consideration again for, as you must remember, he had the curse of his breed—drink. And drink, you will also recall, was cheap enough in Brazil.

"Thinking back on it, there were many nights when we could hardly sleep for his coughing and snorting while he punished another bottle." Nash shrugged helplessly. "It was quite plain to me what a few extra coins in the pocket would do to him, and enough is always enough. Besides, although I may have abducted an heiress and gone through a form of marriage to prove the sincerity of my motives, 'her chastity was her dowry.' "

Collins tapped the table again as the defendant poured himself a drink of water from the carafe.

"Thus matters stood," Nash went on, taking a sip from the glass before putting it down. "Shea became more sullen and morose and, by the time we reached the Cape, we were no longer on speaking terms. Ask anyone who traveled with us aboard the *Prince*, they'll tell you how abusive he became. And matters had not improved when we eventually arrived at our destination. If possible our relations became even more strained whenever he sent his housekeeper to wheedle and pilfer at the stores; I trapped her one morning, redhanded, brazenly helping herself to the dried fruit on his behalf. Or at his behest? Alas, we shall never know.

"But to know all is to forgive all and I forgave her, thinking I knew all," the defendant continued, warming to his speech. "Then, yesterday morning, a page—torn from Shea's journal by his housekeeper while sharing his quarters—came into my possession. It must have fallen from her pocket. At any rate it was found by an illiterate who brought it to me; I often render such small services for those unable to read. However, you can imagine my indignation, my horror, when I beheld the gross distortions of fact which my erstwhile companion had been writing about his relations with me, and mine with His Royal Highness! It was utter treason!"

Collins had to rap the table again, only harder.

Nash took another sip of water and waited for the clerk to catch up once more. "In a metaphorical sense it was 'gunpowder.' I realized that, if those libels fell into the wrong hands—especially with so many malicious rumors already in circulation—there was no telling where the damage would end. So I resolved upon a desperate, some might say foolhardy, plan. I would rid the world of those calumnies. After all, Shea was dead. Only his housekeeper, a convicted murderess, knew of their existence. If I could destroy the material evidence before she had time to set her plot in motion, I might yet avert catastrophe—"

"Plot, Mr. Nash?" Collins interrupted, starting to frown.

"Correct." The defendant had begun pacing the floor. "Gentlemen, I am uniquely placed, in the stores, to overhear the daily gossip of our underclass. They imagine I'm not listening, that I could never understand their 'flash' talk, but one soon gets the gist of it. Almost from the start of our stay here it was apparent to me, at least, that all was not well with our society. Insolence and insubordination abounded wherever I looked. Then, as matters continued to deteriorate, the air thickened with conspiracy. Indeed," Nash added as the officers exchanged quick glances, "only this morning I noted that the guards had been doubled at every strong point, so I could not have been too wide of the mark, could I?

"But to continue. I remained troubled by these puzzling, these contradictory details until it dawned upon me that their common denominator was Shea's housekeeper—a Miss Brant, or Brand, or something—who had often been seen loitering around the kitchen doorway of the very building within which we now find ourselves."

Nash snapped his fingers, spellbound by his own brilliance as an advocate. "One of Major Ross's most trusted noncommissioned officers—a Corporal Asky, whose vigilance will, I hope, soon win him speedy promotion to sergeant—had been keeping me informed as certain events matured. I realized that Shea's papers, 'improved' by a notorious forger whose identity I shall reveal in due course, were to be used to ignite the 'gunpowder' of mutiny and rebellion!"

Collins's gavel hammered the table.

"Mutiny and rebellion!" Nash's finger slashed the air. "His Excellency was to be poisoned, just as poor Jack Shea had been poisoned, by that Jew who slinks around the dispensary! Every one of you was to have his throat cut by a gang of ruffians led by the renegade soldier who used to be our scavenger! The magazine was to be broken open so that our arsonists, our murderers, our burglars, our whores, our pickpockets could arm themselves before setting off for China! For China? How absurd!" Nash laughed. "And yet, by its very absurdity, how true we know it to be. For that which you and I take for granted in the domain of knowledge remains a closed book to the illiterate rabble."

Nash paused again until order was restored.

He shook his head at sorrowful memories. "Which of us does not remember that terrible week when the very fate of the kingdom was poised upon the precipice of disaster? When the nation's capital was held to ransom by Gordon's mob? When London was pillaged by criminals indistinguishable from those out there now—!" The imperious finger aimed at the window, at the west bank of Sydney Cove, at the transported slum.

Nash steadied his voice. "I am not ashamed to confess that I felt an icy shiver when I beheld that seemingly innocuous piece of paper, so providentially placed in my hands by one who could not comprehend the importance of his action. What was I to do? Time was short. What other evidence did I have? All around me I could smell the hellish brimstone of treason. How could I prove it?" The defendant studied the rapt faces of his judges. "Put yourselves in my place. What would *you* have done . . . ?"

The five officers remained quite motionless as Nash stood tall and proud. "I resolved to act with speed and resolution. I would smash the Brandon woman's plot once and for all. Last night's theatricals, in which Shea's former housekeeper played such a prominent role, were my opportunity. It was then or never!

"Under the cover of the noise and near riot, knowing what her secret intentions were for helping Captain Tench, I broke into His Excellency's bedchamber. Yes, gentlemen, I freely confess that I broke and entered, but never were my intentions felonious. On the contrary, they were, they are, they will always be motivated—note that choice of word—motivated by sentiments of the most profound loyalty to that outstanding officer whom his late majesty, George III, was graciously pleased to place over us." Nash bowed with reverence. "I rest my case."

The two young ensigns were awestruck. Even Collins had to restrain himself from applauding as the defendant sat down. Instead the judge advocate glanced left and right again. "Well, gentlemen? That seems pretty conclusive, don't you think?"

Lieutenant James Dowd was an elderly veteran of the East and West Indies, of Bunker Hill and Lexington. He had also been John Shea's deputy in B Company. "Ought we not to hear a few prosecution witnesses? Sir."

"Oh. Of course. We must have those."

The other officers shared their president's opinion of this formality as he raised his voice. "Bring in the housekeeper!"

She took the oath.

"You are Jane Amelia Dundas, ex-*Alexander*, transported for life after being found guilty of issuing a forged bank draft?"

"I—I am, sir."

"Do you recognize the accused?"

"I do, sir."

"Tell the court where, when, and in what manner you last saw him."

"I saw him here. Last night. Sir."

"Why?" Collins demanded impatiently.

"Why did I see him, sir? Why, because he was in here," the serving woman replied with a simple smile. "I had intended going to the assembly with everyone else, but a headache, which had been troubling me, became worse and so I decided to retire to my place for the night. However, such was the noise of music and people I could not rest, and so I decided to repair one of His Excellency's shirts which needed its cuffs turned.

"Accordingly I took my taper and came across from that corner"— she pointed at the scullery—"and pushed the door to one side. There was a dark figure crouched by the stove. I screamed and must have dropped my light, for the next thing I remember is guards running to see what was happening. They had taken the man and removed the mask from his face. It was only then I knew that it was Mr. Nash, the storeman."

"Is that all?"

"Yes, sir."

The judge advocate addressed the defendant. "Do you wish to question her?"

"Not particularly."

Collins gestured her dismissal and called for the next prosecution witness.

"You are Corporal Edward Drury?"

"Sah!"

"Do you recognize the accused?"

"Sah!"

"Where, when and in what manner did you last encounter him?"

"In the quarters of 'Is Excellency, last night, sah!"

"Briefly describe the event."

Drury stood ramrod stiff as he delivered his report. "I was alerted by an alarm. I ordered the building to be surrounded while I investigated the cause of the alarm. I entered the room and saw the pris'ner by the stove lit by flames from the lid of the stove. There was a black mask on 'is face. A box of papers 'ad been forced open. Upon seeing me approach 'e dropped the poker and jumped for the window as if to escape. I ordered 'im to 'alt. That 'e did not. My men were waiting outside and took 'im. Sah!"

"Do you wish to question this man, Mr. Nash?"

"Not particularly."

Drury was the last material witness of last night's incident and Collins ordered the court to be cleared while the verdict was deliberated *in camera*.

The clerk was grateful to rest his aching fingers while the officers consulted their own notes, those which they had remembered to jot down during the proceedings.

The judge advocate put his own papers in order. There could be no question of finding Nash guilty on a capital charge, of course. But neither would it be prudent to antagonize His Excellency the governor regardless of whichever king now sat on the throne. It was time to consult Blackstone's writings and prepare to blame them for the outcome of today's legal work; there would be no repercussions, Sir William had been dead for almost eight years.

Collins opened his copy of *Commentaries on the Laws of England,* then looked at his brother judges. "I think we are all agreed that this morning has been somewhat above the average. However, before considering our verdict, I feel it my duty to insert the following points in our transcript and to remind you of the basis upon which you must each, individually, arrive at your decision, so that subsequently you can answer for it with a clear conscience."

The judge advocate watched the clerk smooth a new sheet of paper, before continuing. "In general terms there are only two kinds of evidence from which an English jury may properly find the truth as to the facts of a case. One is direct evidence, such as the testimony of an eyewitness, and the other is indirect or circumstantial evidence. That is to say, the proof of a chain of circumstances pointing to the existence, or non-existence, of any given fact."

Collins waited for the clerk to catch up with him. It was essential they implicate the late Sir William Blackstone as closely as possible. "However, as a rule, the law makes no distinction between either form of evidence but simply requires us to find the facts in accordance with the preponderance of all the evidence in a case, both direct and circumstantial. That is to say, we must remain cognizant of such evidence as, when weighed with that opposing it, would have more convincing power in the minds of any unbiased jury. And yet, although this weightier evidence is assumed to be the more convincing, it does not necessarily mean that it has to be offered by the greater number of witnesses.

"For instance, we have heard today one defense witness and two for the prosecution. If arithmetical rules applied we would now have to believe the defendant guilty, but they do not, and we must each decide if the fair preponderance of evidence favors Mr. Nash, or Drury and the Dundas woman.

"Finally, we must bear in mind the time-hallowed principle of the presumption of innocence. That is to say, the crown has to prove every element of an offense, beyond reasonable doubt, and that the defendant has no burden to prove his innocence. Unless this can be done, strictly according to law, the defendant must be presumed innocent. It is then the responsibility of the presiding judge to acquit the defendant entirely, or find him guilty of a lesser offense."

Collins waited for the clerk to turn a page and stop writing. "Very well, gentlemen. The only question to be resolved now is whether or not Mr. Nash feloniously broke and entered, as charged, or were his motives of such a nature as to reduce the crime to that of a common misdemeanor?" The judge advocate glanced at the youngest member of his court. "Bradley?"

"Not guilty? Sir."

The captain of marines nodded. "Carver?"

"Not guilty, sir."

"Mr. Knight?"

"Not guilty, sir."

"And Mr. Dowd . . . ?"

"Guilty as hell. Sir."

Collins tallied the ticks on his writing pad. "Three to one. There's no need for me to cast a vote, is there?" He glanced up, smiling for the first time that morning. "Sergeant! Call in the accused."

Nash resumed his seat with quiet dignity.

Collins flexed the slip of wood which he was using for a ruler. "Well, you'll be delighted to learn that the majority verdict of this court is that you are not guilty of the offense, as charged, but only of a misdemeanor—"

"'Objection!'" Nash bounded to his feet. "The term 'misdemeanor' connotes guilty intent! The defendant's honor demands an absolute acquittal certified by the entry *autrefois aquit!*"

"Oh."

"I shall apply to a higher court of appellate jurisdiction for an interlocutory injunction," Nash swept on, swept along by the power of words, his words. "I hereby present notice that the appellant brief will assert that the evidence, so-called, of Dundas and Drury, is inadmissible *perjuri sunt qui servatis verbis* and that, as a consequence, the preponderant weight of evidence rests with the defendant who is entitled to a summary acquittal on all points at trial!"

The advocate sat down with a satisfied bump. He had done very well for his client. He had also done well for the inexperienced judge advocate who was now saved from committing himself to a formal verdict during the term of the injunction.

Collins initialed the top sheet, followed by Lieutenants Dowd and Knight, Ensigns Carver and Bradley, then tapped the pages together and bound them with red ribbons. "Thank you, gentlemen. That will be all until we learn His Excellency's opinion."

Nash stood with the rest of the court and, still smiling, began moving toward the door.

"One moment . . . !"

He turned. "Yes?"

"I think it would be best if you confined yourself to the orderly room." Collins hesitated. "A mere formality, of course. Pending review."

63

"COME IN, David. You'd better sit down." The governor dabbed his lips and tossed the napkin aside.

The younger man was glad to drop his heavy despatch bag on this table for the third time today.

"You know, it was such a relief to get out into the fresh air while everyone was pursuing their legal duties in here," Phillip went on, tilting back in his chair while he probed a toothpick after a stringy shred of kangaroo meat. "It is not often I have the opportunity to inspect my jurisdiction without the usual bustle of our people hurrying about their business. Fortunately, Captain Kellow's sentries have presented our work force with an excuse to declare yet another holiday. I also noted that my strong points are well guarded by my marine detachment and that the gallows is still resting in the carpenter's yard where our worthy 'finisher of the law' propped it after he last completed a case. Speaking of which," the governor began sitting forward again, "I believe you had quite an interesting time with my burglar. Do you wish to discuss it with me?"

Collins did. He opened his bag and laid out the transcript, together with *Blackstone's Commentaries,* which had now been cut and interleaved with paper tabs to mark several entries. "I'm afraid Nash knows this book better than we do, sir. I've been through it, backward and forward, and he is right on every point. The crown's case stands or falls upon a correct interpretation of intent and motive, with the *onus* of proof resting upon us."

The governor nodded in time with the other man's words. "Oh dear, it never rains but it pours. And I understand you have a hung jury, if not exactly a hanging one, so that a formal verdict has yet to be recorded?"

"I'm afraid so, sir. It's that damned injunction. I've just taken Nash to task over it, but he is quite determined to draft a writ *apud acta* for his hearing in London." Collins gave a helpless shrug. "It looks like we've been landed with that wretched Ross *versus* Tench business, again."

"I must say you don't seem particularly heartbroken," Phillip observed neutrally, flicking the transcript's pages. "Neither do you seem to have cast your own vote yet, but I'm sure you'll do your duty at the appropriate moment."

"Er, yes sir."

The governor removed his spectacles and looked up. "Speaking of which, what is Ross doing at present? Surely not even he can still be sleeping off the effects of our modest repast, yesterday afternoon?"

"I—I don't know, sir."

"Neither do I, though to judge from the number of troops guarding my lieutenant governor's mansion, one would think he is taking this rumor of a mutiny very seriously indeed. Or perhaps he is merely waiting to see which way the cat jumps?" Phillip reached for the transcript again. "That would make sense, would it not? As I understand it, your Mr. Nash has been closely identified with Major Ross's interest. So, perhaps, there might be more to this business than meets the eye." He finished tapping the papers square and looked up, still smiling. "What do you think, David?"

" 'Pon my word, sir, this is getting too Oriental for me!"

"Yes, it is. You had better leave everything with me."

"Thank you, sir."

"And you had better leave *Blackstone*, as well. I may need to check a few details."

"Of course, sir."

"That will be all."

Collins stood and clicked his heels.

"Oh, one final thing. On your way back to the orderly room, stop by at the carpenter's yard. We don't want any unseemly haste if, for whatever reason, my burglar loses his appeal."

"You mean, hang him?"

"Such things do happen, you know."

"But he's a gentleman! A friend of—!" Collins checked his tongue. "Shouldn't we consider the effect on, well, the rest, if ever we did such a thing?"

"I have." Phillip breathed on a spectacle lens and gently polished it with a piece of soft leather. "Please shut the door carefully as you go out, there are quite enough creatures undermining my authority without the local insect population also conspiring to drop everything on my head."

Collins did as he was told, then quickened his step downhill toward the bridge. The governor was right, practically all work had stopped for the day and Sydney Cove was strangely tense, unusually quiet. The judge advocate crossed the stream and paused for a moment, uncertain which path to take, then turned and went directly to the orderly room.

Nash was now into his third page of legal argument. He had not enjoyed himself so much since preparing his defense during the abduction business. This present scrape with colonial law was laughably easy after succeeding against the combined forces of M'Lord Denbigh's interest in the House of Commons.

The defendant glanced up. "Hello there, Collins. and what did Sparrow Legs say when he learned that I was going *apud acta?*"

"His Excellency said that he would look into it."

"He has to, there's no option," Nash chuckled. "I shall combine it with a writ *quod voluit non dixit* so that it can only be heard by the full King's Bench of the chief justice and three puisne judges. I'm most awfully sorry to do this to you, Collins, but as you must surely have learned from that little *contretemps* between Ross and Tench, the final court of appeal is still London. . . ."

"It is?"

"Yes." Nash sat forward. "Now, ought we not to direct our attention to these alleged poisonings? Shylock the Hemlock could strike again at any moment. Perhaps you would like me to clear the ground for a writ *inquisitio post mortem* so that we can properly investigate poor Shea's untimely demise?"

"That matter is also under consideration."

"Splendid!" Nash rubbed his hands together. "I'd start with Asky, the man who first alerted me to what was going on, so that we'll have grounds to interrogate the Brandon woman's gang." He paused. "Collins? Where the hell do you think you're going—?"

The judge advocate had turned away. He stepped into the light drizzle and beckoned the orderly sergeant to follow. The redcoat listened, clicked his heels and marched off to the carpenter's yard while Collins walked down to the water's edge and stared out across the leaden waters of Sydney Cove.

The sergeant returned. "The finisher 'as been alerted, sah!"

"Carry on."

"Sah!"

Collins strode across the bridge to Government House for the fourth time in almost as many hours.

Kitty Brandon waited until he was out of sight, then spoke briefly with the sergeant who nodded and let the dispensary maid go into the hut, alone.

"I do hope you're not leaving me a keepsake in your will?"

Nash was annoyed by her interruption. "Quite the reverse! I am setting aside today's judgment before directing the law to concentrate upon you, instead."

"May I ask why?"

"You may ask but I am not compelled to answer," Nash replied, "because do you know what the trouble is with you, Brandon? You've never learned when to leave well alone. I was quite willing to make you a member of my interest, but you had to meddle in matters which did not concern you. You had to control everything to the extent that you would stoop to that childish trick last night—!"

"It sucked you in."

"Briefly. But, really, those two witnesses you primed were dreadful! You'll have to do much better than that. You must not expect to win by cheap trickery alone."

" 'Let girls in my station be as fond as they please of appearing expert, and knowing in their trusts; commend me to a mask of *silliness* and a pair of sharp eyes for my own interest under it,' " Kitty Brandon replied. "I never deceived you, Charley, you did. Had you paid heed you would have known exactly where I stood and where the mantraps were set. But you adore the sound of your own voice too much. I wouldn't be in your shoes, now, for ten thousand guineas."

"What?"

"Your oratorical brilliance at Government House was fatal. However, without an even earlier lack of judgment, you would never have had to answer a capital charge—"

"Explain yourself!"

The woman hesitated. "This is no longer England. This is a vastly different land. One where 'cove and gent' are starting off almost equally famished and despairing. Things are not as they seem. The servant who pants 'Yes, master! No, master!' does not necessarily mean what he says—"

"*What?*"

"Mr. Thorpe was always one of us."

"Don't be absurd!"

The woman shook her head. "Ben likes being a man of consequence, something he could never have been in your England. Had you troubled to listen for a while you would not have failed to pay him the respect due to His Excellency's overseer—"

"He's a clod!"

"Time will tell," the woman replied, standing aside as a sentry saluted Collins.

The judge advocate halted in the orderly room doorway. Behind him were ranked Corporal Drury and four marines, last night's guard, bayonets fixed. He removed his hat and continued inside the hut. "I'm sorry, Nash."

"Sorry? What on earth for?"

Collins laid a small piece of paper on top of the writ *apud acta*. Nash picked it up, frowning in the afternoon light. " *'Omnia mors equat.* A. Phillip.' " He scowled at the legal officer. "Is this some kind of joke? What the hell does it mean?"

" 'Death levels all.' "

"Uh?"

"In your haste to obtain an absolute acquittal you overlooked an important point of law; His Excellency is not restricted by a governor's council of officers. Like M'Lord Cornwallis, in Bengal, Mr. Phillip rules us with a captain general's commission. The man whose bed-chamber you violated last night is our chief justice, and the puisne judges, and Sir William Blackstone combined—"

"No!" Nash knocked Collins aside and leapt for the open door. Ted Drury hardly moved. He stuck out a foot. The gentleman sprawled.

Collins picked up his hat and bag and went out into the rain. "As I was saying, the governor is the final court of appeal in this colony. And, because I did not record a misdemeanor on your summons, His Excellency has chosen to use his arbitrary powers. There will be no referral to the law lords in London. You hang."

"No! No!" Nash struggled to break free again, but there was a marine gripping each arm and another couple behind him, bayonets leveled.

"Corporal?"

"Sah!"

"Close confine the prisoner pending execution of sentence."

Drury turned. "Pris'ner and escort, ri-i-ight face! Quick march!"

They padlocked Nash's leg to the log.

Scragger had an old breadbag over his shoulders to keep off the weather. There was another in his pocket to hood the condemned man. Sydney's public hangman was learning his trade. The noose was tight and dry as he brought it over to the improvised prison stockade. "Um. First I got to measure you."

"Measure me? What for?"

"If you don't drop right you won't top sweet. Like, if I don't put something on this knot it won't shut proper." Scragger looked sad. "It's terrible 'ard getting good grease these days. . . ."

Nash was entering a state of shock but he was still enough in command of himself to know when a tip was needed. He tried every pocket, several times, but they had all been picked clean during his arrest—except for Cribb's shovel receipt, tucked in a corner, which had been overlooked. "It doesn't matter," he giggled, "they won't hang me!"

"That's not what I been told," Scragger replied with a solemn shake of the head. "Still, if you want to die 'ard, it's no skin off my nose." He turned and went away to collect the second ladder.

Cribb was waiting for him at the carpenter's yard. He held out his hand. " 'Ere."

"Wha's that, Phoss?"

"Baccy, you twerp, to slip a bit of stuff on the knot."

"Ta!"

Cribb shouldered his shovel, pulled the sailcloth tighter and began walking.

Nash had begun to shiver. "Take that smirk off your face! They won't hang me!"

"You reckon?" The reinstated sexton halted and leaned on his shovel. "There any special way you'd like to be tucked up?"

"Go to hell!"

"Glad you reminded me," Cribb replied. "When you get down there you'll find Tommo waiting to 'ave a little chat. Tell 'im I'll job Dirty Dick next, when I see a clear chance. 'E'll know what I mean."

"They won't hang me!" Nash screamed, standing, moving forward, following the sexton—

He picked himself up and huddled back to the log, alone again except for the two redcoats, still pacing their beat, muskets shouldered.

Time passed.

Nash began to straighten. He flicked water from his eyes. He waved. "Over here! Come on! Hurry up, boy!"

John Ross was taking a message from the battalion commander to Kellow's detachment. Curiosity and courtesy deflected him from the strict line of duty. He marched forward and halted. "Sir?"

Nash frowned at the apprentice officer and gentleman. "Your father's enemies hope to silence me because I know too much about Shea's housekeeper and her plans. Tell him that I can prove, beyond any shadow of doubt, that a plot exists to poison every officer in the garrison. I can name the ringleaders and prove their guilt. Tell him that I have been wrongly tried and that my connections in London will greatly advantage him when he overthrows the present tyrant at Government House. Tell him that he must act swiftly, with all the power at his disposal, to stop this miscarriage of justice! Do you understand me, boy?"

"I—I think so, sir."

"Good. Here is the first piece of evidence to validate my case." Nash handed over the damp and dirty order, signed by Phillip, for six shovels: it would have been left behind in the ransacked bedchamber, after Shea's papers were safely burned.

The young aide clicked his heels and marched off to deliver his despatch to Kellow before giving a smart eyes-right to Kitty Brandon and the chaplain as he hurried back to the lieutenant governor's hut with Nash's message.

"And how is Mrs. Johnson bearing up with the prospect of bearing a child, padre?"

"Not too well, I'm afraid," he replied.

"You must take no notice." The smiling woman gave him a reassuring pat on the arm. "I doubt if she's five months gone and it'll prove as easy as popping peas from a pod."

"Do you really think so?"

But the dispensary maid had been distracted by another matter. Ross's housekeeper was sloshing closer, also barefoot, also wrapped in a Kerry shawl. Nancy Fitzgerald's left eyelid dipped as she passed by, on her way home to prepare the battalion commander's dinner.

"I'm sorry, padre," Kitty Brandon was smiling again. "What was that?"

"I said, I wonder if giving birth to an infant really is as easy as shelling peas?"

"Mr. Johnson, I'm astonished at your ignorance! Why, we ladies evidently know more than you imagine. Mary's just being difficult, silly if you prefer, kicking up such a fuss over a trifle. The most vulgar, the most flashy, the cheapest tinker girl can squat by the hedge and get the job done in five minutes. If it'll calm her nerves, tell her I said so."

"Thank you, I shall." The chaplain pulled his cloak tighter and tipped his hat to the lady before continuing, alone, toward the prison log.

He slowed. And stopped. Prayer book and communion wafers held with both hands. "I'm so awfully sorry to see you like this, Nash. I shall do everything I can, but first I must know if you are a communicating member of the Church of England?"

"They won't hang me."

Johnson spread his cloak to include the figure slumped on the log. "Charles? In God's good time all must pass through the same dark portal into a brighter awakening, whether we are rich or poor, great or small. From the moment of our quickening we are naught but motes of dust trapped in a brief ray of sunlight, from darkness coming before to darkness returning. But this does not mean that each tiny spark of Divine Grace is extinguished, even though we mortals can no longer see or share it—"

"They won't hang me."

"Charles, listen, please. There is nothing to be afraid of. We are all beholden to return home to our Lord God. It is our birthright, promised at Calvary," the chaplain went on, starting to hurry as Collins strode nearer.

"They won't hang me."

"Listen!" Johnson implored, tightening his arm around the other man's shoulders. "You stand upon the brink of eternity! Can you not see the glorious rewards of repentance which await you? God loves a noble shame! Shame is welcomed as the mark of a good nature gone astray! Shame is the first sign of the Cross which alerts the lost sinner to the true will of God—!"

"Ten minutes, padre?"

"They won't hang me."

"Yes."

The judge advocate snapped his watch shut and continued to the stores. They were closed for the day but the storeman's annex, around the back, was still open. Collins returned the sentries' salutes and went inside. Andrew Miller was taking over his assistant's bed space, also his mattress and clothes trunk.

"His Excellency's compliments, Miller. There will be a full stock-take tomorrow morning, starting with the candles. He will be present when you count them."

"Oh, Gawd."

Collins stepped into the failing light. The quarter guard's drummers were beating a general summons and Tench's company was being assembled on the parade ground in front of the gallows. Less than half the number of troops would have been sufficient to control those lags who could be bothered to leave their cooking fires on such a miserable evening.

"They won't hang me."

"Repent!" Johnson urged the condemned man, starting to weep for him. "Let the hot tears of your contrition wash away this sinful pride—!"

Ross's aide halted. "His Excellency the Lieutenant Governor of New South Wales returns the compliments of Mr. Nash. His Excellency has instructed me to remind Mr. Nash that he was never, ever again to presume to direct His Excellency in the course of his duties."

The chaplain blinked.

"They won't hang me."

"Ready, padre . . . ?"

Johnson nodded and stood up as a sergeant crouched to unlock the iron bezel around Nash's ankle.

"They won't hang me."

Scragger bustled about with his pinion cord. "There we are, sir. Nice and snug!"

Cribb was leaning on his shovel, somewhat to the side of the meager gathering. He sighed quietly. "That's a sod of a way to go."

Thorpe nodded.

Levi nodded.

Kitty Brandon frowned. "In my opinion this should have happened to him years ago."

Only it was happening to Nash now. Far from Home. In a sullen downpour. In a squalid encampment, somewhere. And someone was reading something to him. And offering him a leather mug, with rum. And something sharp was prodding him, to a ladder. With wet rungs. Leaning forward. Leading upward. Toward a common little man. With a dirty bag, in one hand. And a rope—

"I still don't reckon it's right," Cribb grunted.

"Tch! Hush now!"

The drummer struck.

The ladder twisted.

A NOTE ON THE TYPE

This book was set in an adaptation of a type designed by the first William Caslon (1692–1766), greatest of English letter founders. The Caslon face, an artistic, easily read type, has had two centuries of ever-increasing popularity in our own country—it is of interest to note that the first copies of the Declaration of Independence and the first paper currency distributed to the citizens of the newborn nation were printed in this type face.

Composed by American–Stratford Graphic Services, Brattleboro, Vermont

Printed and bound by The Haddon Craftsmen, Scranton, Pennsylvania

Typography and binding design by Dorothy Schmiderer Baker